They are about to discover that a life full of secrets comes at a very high price. . . .

TESSA KENT—Her life is filled with fame, fortune, and passion—but the stunningly beautiful actress is denied the one thing she wants most: the love of her daughter, Maggie.

MAGGIE HORVATH—She traded her birthright and a multimillion-dollar inheritance for her independence. But her rise to power at legendary auction house Scott & Scott comes with a cost of its own.

AGNES HORVATH—A fiercely overprotective stage mother, she refused to let a teenage pregnancy stand in the way of her daughter's chance for stardom.

MIMI PETERSON—She's the last person alive who knows a famous woman's shocking secret . . . one that is now in danger of being revealed.

RODDY FENSTERWALD—The revered film director discovers an ingenue who takes Hollywood—and his older, playboy friend's heart—by storm.

LUKE BLAKE—Forced to share his famous wife with a world of admirers, the billionaire lavishes her with love and priceless jewels . . . treasures that come to mean everything.

BARNEY WEBSTER—Sexy, charming, and rich, he's the most eligible bachelor to hit Manhattan—until the true love he's denied for years makes a daring move.

MADISON WEBSTER—Forced to raise another woman's child, she feels her hatred of the girl grow with each passing day. But will her jealousy cost her her own son?

POLLY GUILDENSTERN—The entrepreneurial jewelry designer's life changes forever when she's introduced to her mysterious new roommate's privileged world.

ANDY McCLOUD—Why is the ambitious and overqualified hunk working as a temp at Scott & Scott? The answer shocks the woman he loves.

LIZ SINCLAIR—Half-owner of Scott & Scott, she's thrilled when the biggest coup of her career drops into her lap. But it comes with shocking conditions.

SAM CONWAY—Every actress wants to play the lead character in the movie based on his hot bestseller. But only one will walk away with the role—and his heart.

JUDITH KRANTZ

THE JEWELS
of
TESSA KENT

BANTAM BOOKS

New York   Toronto   London   Sydney   Auckland

This edition contains the complete text
of the original hardcover edition.
NOT ONE WORD HAS BEEN OMITTED.

THE JEWELS OF TESSA KENT

A Bantam Book / published by arrangement with
Crown Publishers, Inc.

PUBLISHING HISTORY
Crown hardcover edition published November 1998
Bantam paperback edition / November 1999

All rights reserved.
Copyright © 1998 by Judith Krantz.
Cover photograph copyright © 1999 by Tony Loew.

Library of Congress Catalog Card Number: 98-12971

No part of this book may be reproduced or transmitted in any form
or by any means, electronic or mechanical, including photocopying,
recording, or by any information storage and retrieval system,
without permission in writing from the publisher.
For information address: Crown Publishers, Inc.,
201 East 50th Street, New York, New York 10022.

ISBN 0-553-56137-5

Published simultaneously in the United States and Canada

Bantam Books are published by Bantam Books, a division of Random
House, Inc. Its trademark, consisting of the words "Bantam Books"
and the portrayal of a rooster, is Registered in U.S. Patent and
Trademark Office and in other countries. Marca Registrada. Bantam
Books, 1540 Broadway, New York, New York 10036.

PRINTED IN THE UNITED STATES OF AMERICA

OPM   10   9   8   7   6   5   4   3   2   1

For Andrea Louise Van de Kamp, Chairman of Sotheby's West Coast Operations, Senior Vice President of Sotheby's, and Chairman and CEO of the Music Center of Los Angeles County.

Even if Andrea hadn't suggested I write a novel based on the auction business and given me an opportunity to do my research at Sotheby's, I would have dedicated this novel to her because she is the most vibrant, life-enhancing and utterly solid friend one could have. A multitude claim her and rejoice in her.

Great cities are defined by their great people, and no one defines Los Angeles as well as Andrea. Her vast and genuine enthusiasms, her wonderfully inclusive laugh, her extraordinary generosity and her immense charm are legend. Only Andrea could work as effectively as she does at her demanding jobs without ever losing her focus, her sense of humor—or a battle.

ACKNOWLEDGMENTS

While I researched *The Jewels of Tessa Kent,* I needed a good deal of expert advice on the auction business, on medical issues, and on certain details of the Catholic Church. I'm wholeheartedly grateful to every one of the generous people who allowed me to question them and gave me such valuable answers.

Diana Phillips, Senior Vice President Sotheby's, Director of Public Relations.

Mallory May, Assistant Vice President Press Office, Sotheby's, North America.

John D. Block, Vice Chairman Sotheby's, North America, and Director of International Jewelry, North America.

Tracy Sherman, Vice President, Jewelry Department, Sotheby's, Beverly Hills.

Carol Elkens, Assistant Vice President, Jewelry Department, Sotheby's, Beverly Hills.

Elise B. Misiorowski, G. G. Gemological Institute of America.

Dr. Melani P. Shaum, M.D.

Dr. Mark Hyman, M.D.

Dr. Norman Schulman, M.D.

Sister Karen M. Kennelly, CSJ, President, Mount St. Mary's College, Los Angeles.

Lynn Marie Blocker Krantz

Professor Patricia Byrne, Trinity College, Connecticut.

David W. Moreno, Tiffany & Co., Beverly Hills.

Prologue

Quickly, Tessa Kent stepped out of the bank and crossed the strip of New York pavement. The door of her parked limo was held open by the driver. She slid inside, grateful that she'd left a coat on the seat when she'd entered the bank much earlier in the day. It had been a morning of indecisive weather, early fall weather, but now the afternoon sun had disappeared behind clouds that promised rain before nightfall on this mid-September day in 1993.

"Where to, Miss Kent?" Ralph, the driver, asked.

"Wait right here for a while, Ralph, there's something I want to see," she answered impulsively, surprising herself, and pulled the coat over her shoulders.

All through the endless afternoon at the bank, she'd kept going by promising herself that the instant she was able to leave, she'd return as quickly as possible to her apartment at the Carlyle, take a long, lavishly perfumed bath, put on her oldest, softest, most familiar peignoir, have a great fruitwood fire—the first of the year—lit in the generous fireplace of her bedroom, and stretch out on the pile of pillows flung down on the carpet. She intended to put the past three days firmly behind her, sipping a distinctly alcoholic drink and looking straight into the flames until she was so dazzled by them that her mind would unclench and a pleasant emptiness would take over.

Yet, as soon as she entered the limo, Tessa Kent abruptly understood that it was still too soon to escape into that peaceful moment. Something was missing, a sight that would put an absolute punctuation to the process she had just completed, the witnessing of a three-day inventory of every last one of her jewels except the few she was wearing.

She needed to see her jewels actually leave the protection of the bank, Tessa realized. She needed to watch them being brought out onto the street and whisked away in three taxis and three ordinary cars by six couriers and a twelve-man armed security team that would carry tens of millions of dollars worth of jewels in the scruffy briefcases and sturdy shopping bags that had been selected to attract no attention.

If she didn't see that final scene of the drama, she'd still be able to imagine that her jewels slept in the darkness of their velvet cases, piled high in their vaults, ready for her to come and pick out those she would wear to an opening night at the theater or a black-tie party or dinner in a favorite restaurant. Something deep in Tessa's psyche demanded that she recognize, with her own eyes, the fact that her jewels no longer belonged to her, that now they were gone. Gone for good.

Since her marriage, eighteen years earlier, Tessa Kent, the most internationally adored of American movie stars, had never been seen in public unadorned by magnificent jewels. Even in a bikini she wore ropes of seashells inset with gems. Jewels, on Tessa Kent, were never out of place, no matter the year or the hour or the style of the moment. They had become part of her persona, in private as well as in public, a signature as utterly specific to her as the sound of her voice, the shape of her mouth, the color of her eyes.

Suddenly Tessa saw the first of the couriers, carrying

three shopping bags, appear at the entrance to the bank. On either side of him, seemingly busy in conversation, were two of the armed guards, clad in banker's gray. One of the taxis that had been circling the block for hours pulled up beside Tessa's limo, paused briefly as the three men got in, and then continued up Madison Avenue.

She hadn't watched the process of transfer on any of the two previous days. She hadn't felt any need to view it until today, when the last box had been entered into the inventory and sealed. Now, as she watched more couriers and guards walk out of the busy bank and disappear into their carefully choreographed transportation, she felt such a complex mixture of feelings that she couldn't sort them out: loss, excitement, relief, anticipation, disbelief, and nostalgia, all jumbled together. Dominating every emotion was hope.

"You can take me back to the hotel, please, Ralph," Tessa told the driver as soon as she realized that all of the couriers had left the bank. Traffic was heavy and the limo had barely covered two blocks when a heavy rain began to fall.

"Oh, perfect!" Tessa exclaimed. "Stop wherever you can." As her driver knew, rain was her friend. With a big black umbrella skillfully deployed, she could roam the streets of New York without being recognized. This liberty was impossible in good weather; even wearing sunglasses and a scarf over her hair seemed, perversely, to attract the most attention of all from eager autograph seekers.

Today, after spending so many hours in an air-conditioned strong room, deep underground, Tessa yearned for a hard, private, cleansing walk more than for a bath or a drink.

Blessing the foul weather, she pulled a beret down until it reached her eyebrows, kicked off her shoes, and put on the boots that lay waiting in the back of the limo. She shrugged into the light raincoat, buttoned up the collar, and burrowed into it so that it hid her chin, and then picked up the umbrella that lay under her coat.

"Let me out at the corner, Ralph. I'll walk all the way back."

As soon as the limo came to a stop, Tessa hopped out, opened her umbrella, and strode rapidly across the street in the direction of Fifth Avenue. At any time of the year she loved walking up along Central Park, particularly now, as the lights of the city grew brighter against the darkening afternoon.

She found herself at Fifth Avenue and Forty-Seventh Street and she struck out uptown at a fast pace, breathing deeply and freely. It was wonderful to know that no one could possibly care about her in this humid confusion of burdened shoppers and people leaving their offices and seeking transportation home.

Enjoying herself in a way so frequently denied her, Tessa continued up Fifth Avenue past St. Patrick's Cathedral and was three good blocks beyond it when she abruptly stopped, and changed direction. At the age of thirty-eight, she hadn't been inside a church in years. She didn't want to calculate how many it had been, but today . . . something about today . . . drew her back to the great bulk of the cathedral, drew her up the steps to the doors of the cathedral, drew her inside. She closed her umbrella. Old habit took over as she dipped her fingertips in the font of holy water, crossed herself, and genuflected before slipping into one of the pews at the back.

She would just sit here for a few seconds and then flee, back out to the delicious freedom of the busy, dripping streets, Tessa thought. Sit and bask in the vast singing hum of busy silence that had a color and a texture and a scent uniquely its own, so that if she had been set down here blindfolded she would have known instantly where she was.

Without willing it, Tessa found herself on her knees, her head bent. She was praying, she who no longer believed in prayer, praying as ardently as when she'd been a girl, but praying without words, praying purely for the sake of prayer.

The hope she had felt earlier in the afternoon returned, stronger than ever, illuminating her heart. She was safe here, Tessa thought dreamily, and the tears she had held back for many, many days splashed comfortingly down the backs of her hands.

1

Agnes Patricia Riley Horvath, whose daughter, Teresa, would become Tessa Kent, lay in bed at three in the morning. She had been awakened, as usual, by obsessive, angry thoughts about her husband, Sandor, and the way in which he dominated the upbringing of their only child, who now, in August 1967, had reached the age of twelve.

Her parents had opposed her marriage to Sandor Horvath in 1954 and they had been right, Agnes told herself. She was humiliated to the marrow of her bones as she relived her folly, lying next to Sandor in those private hours during which she was unable to keep her mind under control.

If it weren't for Sandor's stern prohibitions, Agnes reflected furiously, Teresa would be well launched on her career, a career about which there wasn't the smallest question—a destiny Agnes knew to be as fixed as the rotation of the earth.

Her daughter had been born a star—yes, a star!—by virtue of her extraordinary beauty and the unmistakable dramatic talent she'd exhibited even as a small child. That wasn't a mere mother's pride talking, that was the opinion of everyone who'd ever seen her, Agnes told herself, trembling with frustration. Teresa should be making movies, or at the very least commercials—there was no limit to her future. But no, her husband, unable to move away from his rigid, old-fashioned, European ideas of what was correct and proper for a young girl, had steadily refused to let her take the girl to New York, where she could meet the influential people who would recognize how exceptional her daughter was.

Night after night, Agnes Horvath asked herself what had possessed her, when she was a mere eighteen and far too stupid to make choices, to insist on marrying a man who was essentially foreign to the tight-knit, devout, Irish Catholic world in which she had her enviable place as the youngest of the five sparkling, black-haired, blue-eyed Riley daughters. Why had she set her heart on a refugee from Communist Hungary, a music professor of thirty-five?

Each time Agnes asked herself this question, she couldn't stop herself from treating it as if it were a newly discovered problem that might contain some newly meaningful answer. She'd recapitulate the past as seriously as if she might still uncover some forgotten fact that would suddenly change the present.

Sandor had been an amazingly handsome man, a charming and romantic stranger, who had swept the provincial fool she had been off her feet and out of what small, unsophisticated wits she had possessed. The distinguished man who spoke English with more elegance and precision than any American boy had been irresistible to her barely formed mind and impressionable heart. Savagely Agnes reminded herself that she'd also been suffering from a bad case of seeing *Gone with the Wind* too many times. Then, and still today, at forty-eight, Sandor strongly resembled Leslie Howard, but she'd been too immature to realize how quickly his fine-boned, intellectual, sensitive beauty would become infuriating when she weighed them against the rules and regulations he imposed on her.

Now she was thirty-one, her marriage was thirteen years old, and Agnes Horvath had known for at least half of it that she'd made the biggest mistake a deeply religious Catholic woman could make. No matter how great her rage against her husband, there could be no thought of divorce. But even if the mere idea of divorce had not been a sin, what training did she have to make a living for herself and Teresa if they were to find themselves on their own? Agnes Riley had been brought up to be a protected wife and a devoted mother, nothing more, and certainly nothing less, like every other woman of her generation.

Sandor earned a good salary as the head of the music department at an exclusive girls' school in Stamford, Connecticut, not far from their home on the modest edge of the rich community of Greenwich, where they lived in order to be near their daughter's school. Teresa was a day student at the Convent of the Sacred Heart, an aristocratic institution which they were both intent on her attending.

In all fairness, Agnes reminded herself, turning over in bed, she had to admit that Sandor worked hard to make his way in his new country. Her sisters had married local boys in nearby Bridgeport, where she'd grown up, mates whose status never came close to that of a professor. Some of these good Irish-American boys made considerably more money than Sandor in their blue-collar jobs, but the whole family respected her elegant, learned husband.

Each of Agnes's sisters had produced a sprawling brood of kids, ordinary, unremarkable, almost indistinguishable kids. When she took Teresa to their frequent family gatherings there was no doubt about whose child, among the dozens of cousins, was the center of attention. Teresa's singularity was a subject of family pride rather than any sniping or competition. From the time she was a tiny baby she had so fine and rare a quality that a party would have been incomplete without Teresa to marvel at. Her own sisters, Agnes knew, were in awe of the child she'd brought into their limited world. Her cousins vied for her attention, the older ones whisking her away so they could play with her as if she were some very precious kind of doll.

Teresa was the only one of the cousins who didn't attend a local parochial school. At the Convent, one of the many Sacred Heart schools in the world, she was a "Day Hop," not a boarding student. Many daughters of millionaires were her classmates, a distinction that only added to Teresa's exalted position in the Riley family.

"Your family will ruin her utterly with all that attention," Sandor had grumbled angrily after the last Riley get-together. "Teresa's becoming spoiled. She used to be such a satisfactory child, docile and obedient, but lately, I warn you, Agnes, I sense that there's something going on inside her that I worry about . . . some sort of rebellion under the surface, something I can't put my finger on. And I most definitely don't approve of that 'best friend' of hers, that Mimi Peterson. She's not a child I want Teresa associating with, she's not even a Catholic, heaven knows what ideas she's putting—"

"You're imagining things," Agnes had snapped. "Every little girl has a best friend, and the Petersons are lovely, suitable people. They may be Protestants but they have the good sense to realize that the quality of education at Sacred Heart is better than that at an ordinary school. And they truly appreciate Teresa, which is more than her own father seems to do."

"How can you say something so unfair?" he demanded, stung. "I love her too much for my own good, but, Agnes, the world's a difficult place and Teresa's not a princess, whatever you may think. She doesn't need any more fuss made about her than she already gets from you. The way you dote on her is shameless . . . it comes close to the sin of pride, if you ask me."

"Sandor!"

"Pride, Agnes, is too high an opinion of oneself."

"Do you imagine I don't know that?" she asked, outraged. She loathed his tone when he started to talk

church doctrine, as sanctimonious, stuffy and hair splitting as if he'd lived hundreds of years ago.

"Too high an opinion of one's offspring, can, like
pride, lead to the sin of presumption."

"When I need a priest's interpretation of sin, Sandor,
I know where to go for it. How dare you preach to me?"

"Agnes, but you realize that in less than a year Teresa
will be a teenager? I've seen your sisters go through
enough trouble with their own teenaged children, why
should we be different? If only . . ."

"If only we'd had more children? Don't you dare,
Sandor! I wanted them as much as you did. Are you saying it was my fault that I had those miscarriages . . . ?"

"Agnes, you can't possibly be starting this nonsense
again, please, I beg you. I was going to say that if only
it were ten years ago life would be simpler, if only there
were *standards* . . . if only people stayed the same! In
my country teenagers behaved like the school children
they are. Please stop talking about fault. The Blessed
Virgin didn't mean it to be, and we must accept that."

But he did blame her, Agnes Horvath brooded
angrily, he blamed her in his heart of hearts, but never
as much as she blamed herself, no matter how ridiculous and futile and morally wrong she knew it was to
use the word "blame" about a situation that was in the
hands of God alone.

But at least she had Teresa, and wasn't one Teresa
worth a houseful of ordinary children?

She wished her parents wouldn't fight about her,
Teresa thought in misery as she tried to go to sleep. She
couldn't hear them from her room, but she knew from
their expressions while they'd listened to her say her bed-
time prayers that another of their quarrels was hatching.

Long ago she'd stopped listening outside their door;
their basic differences never changed, and yet nothing
she did seemed to make it better for either of them. *For
years she'd tried so hard to please.* There were her
mother, her father, the nuns who taught her catechism
class on Saturday, the priests who listened to her con-

fession each Thursday, her teachers, the many Madams of the Sacred Heart, even every last one of her relatives. For a long time she had believed she could change her mother's disappointment, make her father less severe. But nothing worked. Her mother was utterly concentrated on her; her father was suspicious and disapproving, he corrected her pronunciation, refused to let her use slang. Other kids said she sounded "stuck up."

If her parents knew everything there was to know about her! They'd die if they knew, *die,* Teresa told herself, caught up in a combination of defiance, shame, guilt, and—worst of all—the dreadful fear that she had lived with for the past year, ever since she'd realized that she wasn't going to get anywhere by pleasing.

It was their own fault! As Mimi said, the atmosphere around Teresa's house was enough to make a cat fart. To Teresa her home life was maddeningly irritable, so tense that it made her want to scream and break every dish in the house and rip up her frilly bedspread and take a sharp kitchen knife to the pile of pretty pillows on her bed so all the feathers would fly out and cover the floor with a mess that couldn't be cleaned up.

There was never a time in which she could take a deep breath, feel a sense of contentment, and, most important of all, feel safe. Oh how she yearned for a safe day, a safe hour, even a safe minute, in which all pressure would dissipate and be replaced by easy, loving, unqualified approval.

Just yesterday she'd caught a glimpse of her mother sitting in a back row of the darkened school auditorium, while the rehearsals for the school play went on, sitting so far scrunched down that nobody but she would have noticed her.

"Mother," she exclaimed furiously, as soon as she got home from her last class, "you know you promised me never to do that again!"

"Teresa, Mother O'Toole said it was all right with her so long as I stayed out of sight. No one saw me, absolutely no one," Agnes defended herself vigorously.

"Except me. How do you expect me to concentrate when I know you're there, watching my every move? *You've been doing that all my life!* Ever since the first part I had in a kindergarten pageant. I hate it! It makes everything so much more difficult. I've explained that to you again and again, but you won't leave me alone!"

"I see nothing to apologize for," Agnes responded coolly. "It's excellent training for you to have to ignore me. When you start acting for a living, you'll be the center of everyone's attention, not just mine. No one acts without an audience, and at least, in my case, you know I'm biased in your direction."

Helplessly Teresa had watched her mother head toward the kitchen, with the self-righteous conviction of someone who hasn't the slightest doubt that she always acts in your own best interests.

If it weren't for Mimi she didn't know what she'd do, Teresa thought. She didn't know how she'd manage to keep on pretending to be the good little girl her father expected her to be as well as enduring the burden of being her mother's "pride and joy."

But at least she could escape the atmosphere of her home, when she went over to Mimi's to do their homework together—to Mimi's big, luxurious house that impressed her mother although she'd never admit it. She and Mimi, another only child, were sworn blood sisters, and Mrs. Peterson, lively, easygoing, and expensively dressed with blond streaks in her hair, was too busy playing bridge or golf every afternoon to give a thought about what the two little convent girls were up to.

"Teresa, sweetie, you're a good influence on Mimi," she'd say if she came in before Teresa had left for home. "She never got her homework done before you started studying together."

But Mrs. Peterson had no idea how easy the homework was when Teresa and Mimi put their heads together and attacked it. Both bright, they could polish it all off in an hour with a system of tutoring each other that divided the work in half.

And then, homework done, at least twice a week they'd "engage in an adult experience," as Mimi called it. The Petersons' bar was crammed with bottles of everything any liquor store could supply.

Teresa and Mimi, sharing Mimi's bathroom glass, would pour three jiggers full of whatever drink took their fancy, replacing what they took with water, and carry the glass up to Mimi's room. They'd lock the door and sip slowly, taking turns, giggling like maniacs as each reported the fascinating alterations they felt in themselves.

They hadn't yet used the same bottle more than once and they'd never dared make a second trip downstairs for more, just in case they couldn't handle more than one generous drink each. They were always careful to brush their teeth and use mouthwash before Mimi's mother was expected home.

The Petersons were a couple in their mid-thirties who, Mimi reported proudly, still loved a good time. On their exploration of her parents' bedroom they easily found a large collection of *Penthouse* and a smaller-sized publication called *Variations,* which contained erotic short stories and wild letters to the editor. Two drawers of Mrs. Peterson's dresser were filled with underwear that it was impossible to imagine her wearing for anything but sex. Mimi and Teresa would select several pieces at a time—tiny, lacy panties; garter belts that attached to slinky black stockings; dainty push-up bras; or transparent chiffon teddies—and carry their loot swiftly back to Mimi's room, where they'd try on everything, using old pairs of her mother's high-heeled shoes to see themselves at best advantage.

Of course, even Mimi had to admit that, although the two of them were as tall as most women, at twelve, they were still too young and too undeveloped to look right in sexy underwear. But if you squinted your eyes and lifted your nipples in cupped hands, and stuck out your ass, you could get a pretty good idea of how you'd look in a couple of years.

As for *Penthouse* and *Variations,* they pored over one issue at a time, discovering that some of the subject matter was heart-pounding and passionately fascinating. Teresa couldn't keep from thinking about all the forbidden, unutterably exciting things a man and a woman could do together—except when she was brooding on the certainty that she was going to go to Hell after she died.

It was amazing, Teresa thought grimly, that she was able to lie with such calm to the priest at confession, producing a normal series of venial sins as she tried not to breathe the stale air in the red velvet, padded phone booth of the confessional that the old church still used in spite of Vatican II. But she knew the truth. She was unquestionably guilty of at least four of what her catechism class had been taught were the seven deadly or mortal sins. She was guilty of lust, the sin of impurity, and of gluttony, the sin of drinking too much. When she and Mimi dressed up and admired themselves she was guilty of the sin of pride . . . their sessions certainly didn't conform to the "normal pride in a neat appearance" the nuns talked of.

Every single week of her life, as she left any of these three mortal sins unconfessed, by name and number of times it had happened, she was committing yet *another* mortal sin by not confessing, so her sins were not forgiven but lay on her heavily and painfully, almost too much to endure. Yet, to rid herself of them would have been worse. If she'd ever been tempted to make a full confession, she'd be kneeling in front of a pew doing penance for hours—for days!—before she could receive absolution and the sacrament of penance. Since her mother waited to drive her home from church, praying quietly in a pew not far from the confessional, any such penance would cause an inquisition.

Hell waited for her, Teresa never doubted that. Her weekly catechism class had started when she was five and a half. From that time on she spent all of every Saturday morning being indoctrinated into the rules, laws, and prayers of the church, by a different nun every year. When she'd made her First Holy Communion at eight, she'd been certain that she'd go to Heaven. Just thinking of how pure and light-filled she'd felt walking down the church aisle in her beautifully embroidered long white dress, a little bride accompanied by a little groom, could still bring tears to her eyes.

Yes, the forest of fear of Hell she lived in now was a place she'd been prepared for from the beginning of her memory. Hell, the certainty of Hell for a sinner who hadn't confessed and wasn't absolved, had been seared into her for seven years. It wasn't knowledge she could question any more than she could question the fact that she was a girl or an American.

Hell, actually going to Hell, had only started to be a reality to Teresa after she met Mimi. Before that she had been able to confess to the mortal sins of envy or sloth and anger, as well as all the minor venial sins, and feel cleansed when she left the confessional.

Now she couldn't give up her lies of omission in the confessional any more than she could possibly tell a priest that she'd spent hours looking at pictures of naked men and women and reading vivid details about people having sex in every way anyone could imagine.

As the year passed, Teresa's confirmation loomed. "Oh, what am I going to do?" she moaned to Mimi. "I have to make a full confession, a good confession, before I'm confirmed, and even if I managed to admit—you know—my mother would know I'd done something very bad."

"What if . . . what if you went to a strange church, by yourself, without your mother, and got it over with before your confirmation?" Mimi asked, inspired. "I'd go with you, we could take a taxi, no one would ever know . . . it's a perfect plan! Then you could stop sinning, except for little stuff like swearing, until you made the official pre-confirmation confession. How about that? Am I brilliant or what? I think I could make a living giving advice to bad Catholic girls like you." Mimi pinched her companionably.

"I'd still have to *intend* never to repeat my sins—

really, truly believe that I wasn't going to. Oh, God, how I wish I'd been born to your parents!"

"Me too, then we'd really be sisters. Oops, it's Listerine time, not a minute to lose. Mom'll be back in half an hour."

Using Mimi's plan, Teresa got through her confirmation with the eyes of the entire Riley clan upon her as she walked down the church aisle, a slender, angelic, dignified young girl, whose long black hair was plaited tightly and held severely away from her unsmiling, austere, heartbreakingly lovely profile under her plain illusion veil. Her features were eloquent with reverence and her green eyes, under her smooth, expressive eyelids, were filled with perfect tranquillity. She walked, restraining her usual stride, with poetry in her steps, wearing an unadorned dress, as plain and straight a gown as she'd been able to find, much to her mother's disappointment. As the day had drawn near, Teresa had been adamant in refusing to enter the catechism class's covert competition for the most elaborate, full-skirted confirmation dress.

"She's not thinking she's got a vocation?" one of Agnes's sisters murmured to her in a worried tone as she contemplated her niece, startling in the unbending line of her marvelously shaped back and in the stern simplicity with which her long neck rose from a rolled white collar. All around her were girls decorated in a garden of billowing, complicated dresses, worn with smiling, innocent pleasure. Teresa looked years older than they did, and no smile had crossed her lips.

"Never," Agnes laughed. "It's just a matter of her personal taste. Teresa's buying *Vogue* these days, with her allowance. Does that sound like a vocation to you?"

"*Vogue*? Good heavens, that's for rich women, society women. It's much too old and fancy for her. What's wrong with *Seventeen*?"

"She says it's silly. Oh, Millie, I think she's growing up too fast."

"It's always going to be too fast from now on. Trust me, Agnes, I have six of them to worry about."

2

In the early weeks of their freshman year at Sacred
Heart's high school, soon after they both turned
fourteen, Mimi and Teresa grew closer than ever, a
clique of two who never trusted others to share their
secret activities.

In the course of the past year they had worked inten-
sively on their looks. Both girls had falls of fake hair
that reached halfway to their waists, styled in a long
flip. Both of them were adept at applying mascara, eyeliner, and eye shadow in shades from dead black to
turquoise, and they owned a dozen lipsticks in colors
ranging from deep red to frosted pale pink, as well as
lipstick brushes and lip liner. They had practiced walking in the fashionable shoes they bought and kept in the
back of Mimi's closet, until they felt totally at ease in
them. They had fishnet stockings and tights in every
color and they had used their sewing instruction to
make themselves dark, micro-miniskirts which they
wore with clinging little sweaters. Their breasts had
grown large enough to fill out the bras that Mimi's
mother owned, and they bought cheap versions of them
with some of Mimi's generous allowance.

"We look like absolute whores," Teresa said one Saturday night in mid-September when she had been allowed to sleep over at Mimi's. Her voice was filled with admiration. The two girls had groomed themselves to perfection and now they were alone in the house, for Mimi's parents had gone out to what promised to be a long night at the country club.

"You're absolutely wrong. We're divine. You look like a dark, more beautiful, much more classy Jean Shrimpton, combined with Vivien Leigh at her best," Mimi said assessingly. "I could pass for Verushka if she weren't a giant."

"And the reality is that I'm still not allowed to go out on dates, not till I'm sixteen, my father says, not that anyone's ever asked me," Teresa said gloomily, flinging herself down on Mimi's bed.

"I have an idea," Mimi said, inspired.

"Spare me," Teresa sighed.

"No, listen, for heaven's sake! We're going to Mark O'Malley's party! It was meant to be, don't you see? It's tonight, we're dressed, and my parents will never know if we're back in time. Oh, Teresa, I triple dare you!"

"Absolutely not."

"Come on, it's only going to a party, not another of your dreary mortal sins."

"Correction, it's *crashing* a party, and not even you, silver-tongued one, can convince me that's the same thing as 'going' to a party."

"What's the worst thing that can happen?" Mimi demanded. "We'd be asked to leave? Oh, I don't think so, my lovely one. There's no question in my mind that when Mark O'Malley lays eyes on us he's going to be very glad that we've favored him with our presence. He'd have asked us himself if he knew we existed."

"Maybe," Teresa said with a shrug. "Sure, maybe the captain of the football team at Greenwich High would be so overwhelmed by our charm and beauty that he'd have begged two convent girls to be his guests, that's not impossible, but somehow we've escaped his eye, even though we've never missed a game he's played in. So forget about it, and stop bugging me."

"Teresa, pay attention. I'm *going* to that party and so are you. You've got a crush on Mark O'Malley that's as obvious as a big red wart on the end of your nose! You've had it for years and I'm sick of listening to you carry on about him. You're just playing hard to convince so this is going to seem like my fault when I'm actually doing you a huge favor. Do you think I don't know you well enough to understand that much, you hypocrite?" Mimi drawled. "All we have to do is put on panty hose instead of these fishnet stockings. They're too old for even the seniors' dress code. After that, it's simply a matter of projecting the right attitude. We've trained for this for years, dope!"

"Even if I agreed to this crazy idea, there's no way we could get there and back."

"Have you forgotten the uses of a taxi so quickly, my little confirmation girl?"

"You are such a pure, true-blue, honest-to-God bitch!"

"Isn't that why you love me?"

"It must be. I can't think of a single other reason."

A careful hour and a quarter after the party had started, Teresa and Mimi slipped casually into the large crowd at Mark O'Malley's house. They were more quickly absorbed than they had imagined in their most optimistic moments, blending perfectly with all the other girls. Their hem lengths, their shoes, their hair and makeup worked to add years to their true ages. Anyone who didn't recognize them would assume that they were dates from another school.

"Let's have a drink for courage," Mimi murmured.

"Darn it, Mimi, we decided we wouldn't drink so we'd keep our wits about us. Remember we have to phone for a taxi home."

"Oh, for Pete's sake, all they have is some kind of

fruit punch, and you're an experienced Wild Turkey girl. At least carry a cup so you'll have something to do with your hands." Mimi sipped in a ladylike way. "It's mostly pineapple juice, Teresa, try it at least."

"All right, but we can't just stand here, we have to mingle . . . but don't go so far away that I don't know where you are."

"I'll keep my eye on you—oh, Mark, hi! This is a great party! You invited the world."

"I guess I must have." Their host smiled down at both the girls, fully aware that he didn't know them, but who cared with girls this cute? Wrong, the blond one was cute, the dark-haired girl was flat-out gorgeous. No way he could ever have seen a girl so beautiful and let it slip his mind.

"Anyone for a dance?"

"Thanks," Mimi said quickly, "but I'm waiting for my date to get out of the john. Teresa, why don't you dance with Mark?"

"Teresa," he said. "Nice name. Come on." He took Teresa's glass of punch and put it down, grasped her firmly by her upper arm, and led her away.

"Do you talk, mystery guest? Or do we need your little friend to interpret for us?"

"I can speak for myself," Teresa said hardily, summoning all her reserves of dramatic power to get the words out. Mark O'Malley up close was far more devastating than he was from a distance at a game. He was as tall and muscular as any fully grown man, his curly dark hair as long as the school regulations would permit, his eyes bright and blue and smiling, with a man's confidence. She could feel nothing but the warmth of his hand on her arm.

"How old are you?" he asked suddenly, stopping in mid-stride.

"Eighteen, why?"

"I thought you might be older. You make the other girls look like kids."

"No, just a simple eighteen."

"But experienced?"

"What's that supposed to mean?"

"There's something about your eyes."

"Maybe I'm what they call an old soul," Teresa said, smiling slightly. This wasn't so hard, after all.

"In a young body. I've never met a sexy old soul before . . . good combination."

"Aren't we going to dance?" Teresa asked.

"Oh, I don't think we really want to, do we? It's noisy and crowded and everybody's doing his own thing and sweating up a storm. You can't talk when you dance, and somebody might try to grab you away from me. I think what we want to do is get some more punch and find a place to get to know each other . . . I know just the place."

"But Mimi . . ."

"Your friend can take care of herself, can't she?"

"If anybody can." Teresa laughed and relaxed.

"She's the one who talked you into crashing my party, isn't she?"

"Oh!"

"Don't be embarrassed, I'm glad you did. Where do you two go to school?"

"Oh, just a little private school in Stamford, you wouldn't have heard of it."

"Where'd you see me?"

"At a football game."

"Well, I'm flattered my party lured you here. Or have you broken the hearts of all the boys in Stamford already, when it's ten times the size of this place? Are you on the prowl for new victims, old soul? What's your last name, lovely mystery girl?"

"Carpenter."

"Well, Teresa Carpenter, come on upstairs with me so we can chat without interruptions from this horde of bandits. I want to find out more about you . . . I'd like to see you again, take you out on a real date."

"I don't think so," Teresa said slowly as they mounted the stairs.

"Don't think you want to see me again?"

"I don't think I want to go into a room alone with you."

"Don't 'want to' or don't think you should?"

"I don't think I should."

"I'll be good, I promise." Teresa looked up at Mark's face and saw nothing there but lively interest and a touch of amusement at what he thought were her flirtatious wiles. He didn't realize that she'd never been alone with an older boy in her life, or a boy of any age who wasn't a first cousin, she thought. Any believable eighteen-year-old girl would know how to handle the situation.

"I thought you wanted to get more punch," she temporized, as he opened a door.

"I have my own private stash. I'm the host, remember?"

"Oh—it's your bedroom!" Teresa said as she walked in. She stopped dead and looked around at the football trophies and banners on the wall.

"What did you expect?"

"I wasn't thinking. I'd better go down."

"Teresa! Sit down on that window seat and stop being silly. You act as if I'm going to attack you."

"How do I know you're not?" she asked lightly, repressing the tremor in her voice.

"I've never attacked a girl in my life. To be frank, I've never had to, never wanted to. Yeah, that's better, sit down and get comfortable. Now, did you break up with your boyfriend? Is that why you're here, to make someone jealous? Because you could, you know, you could so easily, just by looking at me the way you're looking now."

"Looking? There's nothing special about my look."

"You look . . . let's see . . . sort of as if you might take to me if you knew me better."

"You seem . . . likable enough," Teresa said, gulping her warmish drink as she tried to make herself realize that she was alone with Mark O'Malley, the boy she'd been in love with for years, an agonized, passionate first love, a hopeless love for this boy who was the hero of the entire high school, the boy who had always been the focus of her fantasies. She could never have imagined this, she realized, the two of them talking easily on a window seat in the moonlight, not if she'd lived a million years. It was too real to be a fantasy. She felt the wild beating of her pulse in her forehead and the thumping of her heart and the sweat under her arms, and she couldn't make herself stop looking at his mouth.

"Could I have some more of that?" she asked, holding out her glass. It tasted harmless, and her mouth was dry with excitement.

"Sure thing. My dad made it and then he and my mom took off for the country club. They said they'd be back by the stroke of midnight to make sure that every last rotten kid was out of the house. I'll be glad when college starts and I get out from under their eagle eyes."

"My parents are the same way. I can't wait to be on my own."

"Where did you apply?"

"Oh, the usual places."

"With a fallback, right? Somewhere you're sure you can get in?"

"Naturally," Teresa said with nonchalance. What college would be a good fallback, whatever that was?

"Which one?"

". . . uh . . . Smith."

"Very funny. Come over and sit closer. For an incredibly beautiful girl you're an awful liar. Did you know that? Or else you've got a great sense of humor. Or a genius IQ. Which is it?" He leaned toward her and kissed her lightly on the lips. "Oh, nice. Nice. Here, give me another kiss . . . wasn't that nice?"

"Oh my God . . . oh, Mark, *yes*!"

"You've got to stop crying, Teresa," Mimi hissed as soon as they reached the privacy of her bedroom, after a taxi ride during which Teresa shook with silent sobs.

"I can't. I can't, oh God, Mimi, I can't stop."

"Teresa, damn it, you terrified me! One minute you were there and then you'd disappeared and so had he. I looked everywhere for you, I didn't do anything else all evening. I don't know what I would have done if you hadn't shown up eventually. *Where the hell were you?*"

"Oh, Mimi, I can't . . . it couldn't have happened, tell me it couldn't," Teresa pleaded through her unstoppable tears.

"*What* couldn't?" Mimi whispered, cold with fright.

"I can't tell you, I can't talk about it, I can't—"

"You'd damn well better or I'm going to tell my mother that Mark O'Malley did something awful to you. Your hair's a mess, you've lost your bra, you're in shock. . . . Mom knows his mother and they'll get to the bottom of this!"

"No! You'd never—"

"The hell I wouldn't. I'm not going to end up in the middle here. What happened? Did he rape you?"

"No, no, please Mimi, stop!"

Mimi pulled Teresa's chin up with all her strength and inspected her devastated face.

"That bastard! He won't get away with this. Shit, it's all my fault, I was the one who triple dared you. I could kill myself."

"*He didn't rape me!*"

"Then you'd better tell me exactly why you're carrying on like this."

"We . . . made love. I think . . ."

"Teresa! You're nuts! You *never* made love, that's crazy. You've got it all mixed up. Tell me exactly what happened, don't leave out anything . . . no way you 'made love,' please, credit me with some intelligence."

"We started out just kissing, nicely, just kissing, you understand? Sitting in the window seat of his room. We had a couple of glasses of punch . . . two, maybe three, it must have been stronger than I thought. And then, little by little it got more . . . hot and heavy and we ended up lying on top of his bed and we were necking, you know, and then, I guess we were petting . . . heavy petting . . . he took off my dress and my bra and kissed my breasts and sucked on my nipples and then—"

"I knew he raped you!"

"No, Mimi, I *wanted* him to, I helped him do it, I took off my panties myself, I couldn't stop myself. I can't tell you the crazy way I felt, I just wanted to finally find out, and then I had to see . . . I *had* to see what it looked like in real life, not just in photos, so I let him take it out and put it on my stomach." She fell silent.

"So that's the reason you're crying like crazy? He put his cock on your stomach? What next?" Mimi demanded.

"I touched it . . . a lot . . . I couldn't stop touching it . . . he was so hard and he got even harder . . . and the harder he got, the more I wanted to touch it . . . and then . . . and then . . . he put the tip of it in."

"*He put it in!* Jesus Christ, Teresa! Didn't you put up a fight?"

"No . . . I mean I didn't tell him not to when he asked me if I was okay, if he could . . . I wanted to feel it . . . you know . . . *inside*. Just the tip of it. Mimi, just the tip. I had to know how it felt, more than anything. It was so big and I wanted it so much. I was so . . . it was like being out of my mind, nothing else existed. . . ." Teresa whispered. ". . . And then, oh God help me, then, after just a few seconds, *with only the tip in,* oh, Mimi, he came. *Inside me.* Without even moving. He just gave this shudder and made this sighing noise and he came. He didn't pull out, he didn't wait!"

"Shit! That's not rape, that's pure stupidity. What an asshole! But you're a virgin, so there's nothing to worry about. What did he say?"

"He said he was sorry and if I'd wait a little while he'd do it again, only much slower, so I'd enjoy it. Can you imagine? Again."

"He didn't know you were a virgin?"

"He never got in far enough to find out. He thought I was eighteen, he thought I'd been around. Oh, Mimi, what am I going to do?" Teresa cried out in anguish.

"Stop that crying, take a hot bath, I'll give you two of my mother's tranquilizers and a sleeping pill, and you'll go to bed and never think about it again. *It didn't happen.* It was a bad dream. Does he know how to find you?"

"I lied about my name and I said we were from Stamford."

"With any luck he'll never see you again and he'd never recognize you anyway without makeup. The whole thing is over. Over. It did not happen. Do you understand? And I don't want to hear anything about sin, you didn't know what you were doing, he got you drunk, it wasn't your fault. Do you understand that, Teresa?"

"I understand what you think, Mimi. *But I know what I did.* I didn't have to do it, but I did. I sinned. I sinned against God the Father, the Son, and the Holy Spirit. I sinned against our Heavenly Mother and there's nothing you can say that will ever change that."

3

Mimi, I think I'm pregnant." Teresa was so pale, almost blue, with panic that Mimi's heart skipped a beat. Hastily she rose and locked the door to her room.

"You're a virgin, how could you be? You're late, that's all," she said, taking Teresa's cold and shaking hands and rubbing them to bring some blood into her fingers.

"I've never been late since I got the curse a year ago, and now it's been three whole weeks since that party. I finally made myself look up sperm in the encyclopedia at school. They swim, did you have any idea that they swim incredibly fast and they can live for a few days inside the vagina?"

"But you're a virgin! It's simply impossible!"

"A hymen isn't a solid barrier—where does the blood come from when you have the curse? Your womb. Remember we read all about it in the book your mother gave you, so she wouldn't have to tell you the facts of life herself."

"Shit. Shit. SHIT! No, I won't believe it. It can't happen."

"Mimi, it can. Face it, it has happened," Teresa said through trembling lips that belied stoic words.

"You'll have a miscarriage or whatever it's called. Tonight, tomorrow, you're only just fourteen, you can't have a baby," Mimi babbled in brute fear.

"That's what I've been telling myself," Teresa said wearily. "I've been praying on my knees for hours and hours every night, praying for God to take the baby. It's His decision, He can stop a pregnancy. I've been going to the john at school between every class to see if there was any blood, I've been kidding myself that I felt a cramp. The truth is I'm pregnant and I can either tell my mother or I can kill myself, I don't know which would be worse."

"Three weeks! That's all it is. *If* it is. You don't have to do anything for months and months! Anything could happen!"

"I know. That's what I'm counting on. It's too early to have to deal with it. I waited as long as I could to tell you but I couldn't keep it to myself any longer."

"If only . . ." Mimi said, and stopped.

"What?"

"Oh, damn it, Teresa, if only you weren't such a Catholic! My mom knows a doctor, he's a perfectly good one—"

"Don't even say it, Mimi. Never, absolutely never. As bad as I am, that's the one thing I cannot do. Never. *Ever.*"

"I know," Mimi sighed deeply. She'd been sure from the beginning of this conversation that if Teresa were really pregnant, she'd never consider abortion, but she'd had to say something, just in case there was a chance that she'd see reason. My God, to ruin her future, to wreck her life over religious conviction! Mimi couldn't make herself accept it, although she understood that for Teresa there was no other way.

"What are we going to do?" Mimi asked after a long silence.

"Pray. If God decides to stop a pregnancy, that's His

decision, and not my fault, not anything I've done to cause it. I'm allowed to pray, pray and wait. There's nothing else."

"If I pray too, will it help, or do only Catholic prayers get through?"

"Pray. 'Pray without ceasing,' as Saint Paul recommended." Teresa tried to smile at her friend, but tears rolled steadily down her cheeks. "You're such a pagan, it might be good for God to hear from the likes of you."

Agnes Horvath had not been the youngest in a family of five sisters without absorbing a great stock of female lore. She had never experienced morning sickness when she was pregnant with Teresa, but when she heard, three days in a row, the smothered sounds of vomiting coming from Teresa's bathroom before her daughter finally appeared, pale and red-eyed, late for breakfast, unable to eat, and mumbling something about stomach flu going around the school, she began to suspect. When Teresa arrived home from school each day, the stomach flu miraculously cured until the next morning, her heart was speared by the truth.

But Teresa was a virgin, to her knowledge. Teresa was absolutely a good girl, to her knowledge. Teresa had never been alone with a boy, to her knowledge. Teresa, to her knowledge, had never yet been kissed.

But Teresa must be pregnant. Teresa her daughter, perfect and adored, for whose future she had lived, was a stranger to her; immoral, unclean, evil, cunning, lying, and damned to Hell Fire for Eternity.

On Friday morning Agnes lay in wait outside Teresa's bathroom. As the girl emerged, staggering and deathly pale, her mother gripped her by one arm and slapped her with all her strength across her cheek.

"How could you do this to me!" she spat, and slapped her again, on the other cheek. "How? How? You filthy slut!"

Teresa burst into tears and would have fallen to the

carpet if Agnes's clutching hand hadn't been keeping her upright.

"Oh yes, cry, that's going to make a difference, that's going to make you a decent girl again, you fool, you *criminal* little fool. Go to your room. I'll call Sacred Heart to say you're sick. Wait for me."

A minute later she returned to find Teresa huddled in an armchair, sobbing so hard that she was getting hysterical.

"Shut up! If you don't, I'll hit you until you do! Do you think you have a right to those tears? I'm the one who should be crying," Agnes panted in rage. "I'm the one you put aside because your lust was stronger than your love for your mother."

"No . . . no . . . it had nothing to do with you," Teresa wailed.

"It has *everything* to do with me. You know that lust is a mortal, deadly sin and yet you choose it, just as you chose the influence of Mimi Peterson rather than mine—she must have had a hand in this, how else could you have met a man? But who has watched over you all your life, who has given you everything she could, who managed to find the money to send you to Sacred Heart, who has believed utterly in your future, who has nourished your talent? Look at how you've repaid my love. *You are beneath contempt.* I have no words to use for the kind of girl you are. All my pride and love was folly. I never knew you."

"Mother!" Teresa cried in anguish.

"Don't call me mother. No daughter of mine could do what you've done. Who is he? No, don't tell me! I don't want to know any of the vile details, they'd make me sicker than I am. Have you confessed your sin?"

"No."

"How long did you intend to go without confessing a mortal sin? So that you could repeat it and repeat it? You disgust me! But you're caught now. We're going to see Father Brennan this minute. After you confess, we'll talk to him in his study. He'll know where to send you."

"What?"

"You don't think this is the first time this has happened, do you? There are places for evil, godless, shameful sinners like you, places to stay until the baby is born and adopted."

"But it'll be months, months! I can't just disappear. The Madams of the Sacred Heart, all the family, they'll know, and they'll guess why."

"Teresa, you've ruined my life. I've lived for you, the person I thought you were, a person who doesn't exist. But if anyone else ever knows about this *you will have killed me.* I have only one thing left, our position in my family. Can you hear what my sisters would say about you? Do you think four women, even if they are family, will stay silent forever? Are you too stupid to imagine how the stain, the gossip will spread, how your life will become a dirty joke? Pregnant at fourteen! Don't you see that no decent man will ever have anything to do with you? I'm giving you a second chance, don't you understand? Not because you deserve it. You deserve nothing but punishment, and you will be punished, Teresa, trust in that."

"But . . . why? Why are you giving me a second chance?"

"Because I can't let my daughter become a neighborhood scandal, a dirty joke. The daughter of whom I was so proud, the girl I raised, never realizing what she really was."

"I still don't see how I can vanish and then come back here without people guessing," Teresa persisted.

"It means all of us moving, as far away as possible, someplace where no one knows us. Your father will have to sacrifice his job and find work in another school. I'll tell him tonight."

"He doesn't know? Only you?"

"It's not a man's business to know until he has to," Agnes said grimly. "Go get dressed for church now, don't forget your hat. And your rosary."

*   *   *

31

"Help me to understand you clearly," Sandor Horvath said to his wife that night, after she'd told him everything. "You expect me to give up my position and find another job?"

"You have to. There's no other way. I've thought of everything and it's the only way we can hide what's happened."

"And Father Brennan will arrange to send Teresa to this place in Texas to wait for the birth and the child will be adopted by strangers? And then she'll come home and forget all about it?"

"Adopted by a good Catholic family. We can be sure of that."

"And you can be sure I refuse!"

"Sandor! You can't refuse! You can't let her go away for six or seven months and then come back here. Everybody would be counting on their fingers, everybody would know. We might as well take out an announcement."

"Agnes, this child is our grandchild. This child may be my grandson. *I will never consent to give up this child.* This is my flesh and blood."

"We can't afford to be sentimental. Teresa's future—"

"I don't give a damn about her future! I don't give a damn about your sisters! Or your sacred reputation as mother of the family beauty. What you ask goes against everything I believe in and I simply will not do it. And you can't do it without my consent."

Agnes looked at him and realized immediately that nothing she could say would move him now, unless, unless . . . he'd agree to the plan of last resort that she'd made during the four days she'd spent thinking.

"Sandor, if we moved, if you got another job, somewhere where nobody knows us, I could . . . bring up the child as . . . my own. I'm only thirty-three, it would seem perfectly natural."

"The baby would become our child, Teresa's brother?" he asked slowly.

"Or sister, but yes, our child, yours and mine."

"And how would Teresa feel about that?"

"How she feels doesn't matter. She's given up any right to be considered. Do you think that the penance Father Brennan gave her wiped away her sin?"

"Did he give her absolution, did she receive the Sacrament of Penance?"

"Yes."

"Then God has forgiven her. Can you do less? I'll start inquiries about another position tomorrow."

"Thank you, Sandor."

How typically male, Agnes thought in strangled, furious silence. Men thought it was just that easy. Confess and be absolved. Act like a loathsome, lewd, impure whore, destroy your mother's rightful joy and pride and hope, force your father to give up a position of prestige—and still be forgiven, forgiven because you've told the priest what you'd done and said hundreds of rote prayers. No, she could never accept that, not even if it went against all the teachings of the church.

Secretly thrilled by the prospect of a grandson, a grandson to continue his name and his blood, Sandor quickly discovered a teaching position in the music department of the Harvard School, a well-known private boys' school in Los Angeles. It didn't pay as much as his present job, but it answered the problem of putting distance between his family and everyone they knew, and it was available immediately.

Within weeks the Horvaths moved to a small rented house in Reseda, a ranchlike section of the San Fernando Valley that was still so rustic that the streets had no pavement. The house had the additional advantage of being surrounded by an acre of scrubby land. Agnes had made her family believe that the move was prompted by an offer so magnificent that she couldn't ask Sandor to turn it down. Only Mimi Peterson, of all the people in Greenwich, knew the truth. She and Teresa parted in tears, knowing that they'd never be allowed to be together again after this stolen moment in the locker room of the Sacred Heart gym.

"Can't you at least send me a message when the baby's born, so I'll know you're okay?" Mimi asked.

"I'll try, but don't write back, whatever you do. I'll know how you feel, I'll know you're thinking of me."

"I'll tell you one thing," Mimi sobbed, "I'm not going to have sex until I'm married."

"I'm not going to have sex ever."

"Don't be such a dope."

"Oh, Mimi. I'll never forget you."

The months in Reseda passed more slowly than Teresa would have believed possible. She couldn't go to school, nor could she walk around window shopping on any of the main streets of the nearby small towns where a decidedly pregnant teenager would turn heads.

Throughout the long winter months of her pregnancy she was a prisoner at home, with only the few uplifting paperbacks her mother grudgingly bought her, the local newspaper, and daytime television to keep her company. She was allowed to walk back and forth in those areas of the backyard that were screened from the neighbors, but otherwise there was nothing to do but wait, often alone, since her mother had bought a small, secondhand car and distracted herself by driving around the never-never land of Beverly Hills, on the other side of the Mulholland pass. She never asked Teresa to go with her on these drives and Teresa didn't dare to suggest it, although, once in the car, she wouldn't have been noticed.

Teresa's most lonely moment of each week came on Sunday morning when her parents got into her father's car and left her alone while they went to mass in the Reseda Catholic Church. She longed to be allowed to go with them, parched for the human contact and warmth of the service, aching for the consolation of communion, but of course it was impossible to show herself and arouse curiosity.

"Isn't it a sin for me to miss mass, especially on the Holy Days of Obligation?" she asked her mother, still permitting herself a crumb of hope.

"You're sick with the baby, you're allowed to miss it," her mother snapped. "You know that perfectly well. You're a hypocrite to worry about such minor sins under the circumstances."

Teresa lived for the single Friday or Saturday night each weekend when her father took her out for a drive after dark, stopping at a place that served ice cream sodas at the car. He would touch her hand gently from time to time, but, silent man that he was, he had become even more reserved. Teresa wanted desperately to throw herself into Sandor's arms and be held there and comforted, as she had been, from time to time, when she was a little girl with a little sorrow, but she felt his deep reluctance to touch her because of her swollen breasts and her swollen belly.

She sat quietly by his side, her head turned away, so he wouldn't see the tears of wishful need that filled her eyes. Her only experience with friendly touch was what she could extract from hugging herself tightly in her own arms or patting her stomach gently as she lay in bed at night and whispering to the dark room, "It's going to be all right, little baby, it's going to be all right."

Teresa tried to attract as little of Agnes's attention as possible, since her mother's rage had only deepened with the isolation and the strangeness of California. Once Teresa's morning sickness had passed, she felt her robust health return. Neither mother nor daughter mentioned the need to see a doctor until Teresa felt the child move within her.

"Oh! It just kicked me," Teresa exclaimed, with excitement and wonder.

"Isn't that nice for you." Agnes turned away, shaking her head in disgust.

"Shouldn't I go to a doctor, just to see if everything's all right?"

"You look fine to me." She was twice as beautiful as ever, Agnes thought, the lines of her features were immaculate, exquisite and composed, above her disgusting body.

"But, Mother, I've never been to a doctor. Don't you think I should? If I'm too sick to go to mass, aren't I sick enough to need a doctor?"

"Nonsense. You're sleeping well, you're eating like a horse, you're getting exercise, your ankles aren't even swollen, you say you feel fine, why do you need to see a doctor at this point? Having a baby is a perfectly natural process."

"But shouldn't I find out if the baby's all right?"

"Of course it's all right. A baby is always all right when it isn't wanted, every woman knows that, the only ones you lose are the ones you're dying to have," Agnes said with a bitter laugh. "Don't you realize that there's a good reason why you can't have medical records? A doctor would only ask questions you must never answer, starting with your age. Any doctor will remember your face and your youth. This baby is going to be born in the county hospital under my name and the less trace there is of it in connection with you, the better."

"You still have hopes for my future, or you wouldn't bother being so secretive," Teresa said, suddenly illuminated with knowledge.

"Of course I do. As far as I'm concerned, they're more important than ever. Look at all I've done to give you an intact future, to provide you with a blank slate so you can make something of yourself. Do you realize how much you have to thank me for? *Do you?*"

"Yes, Mother. I do. I always will."

The baby born on June 15, 1970, to Agnes Patricia Riley Horvath and Sandor Horvath, was a girl. One busy intern remarked to a busier nurse that the mothers were getting younger every year, but otherwise it was an unremarkable birth of a healthy baby on an unremarkable morning after an unremarkable labor.

The patient known as Agnes Horvath was discharged from the hospital two days later and returned to Reseda with her parents. No one at the county hospital gave a thought to the whereabouts of the father. The baby's birth certificate gave her name as Mary Margaret Horvath, daughter of Agnes Patricia Riley Horvath and Sandor Horvath.

A week later the baby was baptized. Sandor Horvath had made no intimates at Harvard School, but he had struck up a friendship with one of the history teachers, an unusually friendly chap named Brian Kelly, who, Sandor discovered, was both a good Catholic and a married man. Brian Kelly and his wife, Helen, were surprised but flattered to be asked to become the child's godparents, to make the act of faith in the child's name and promise that the child would renounce the devil and live according to the teachings of Christ and His Church.

"How could I not have realized you were expecting this happy event, Sandy," he said. "You're a dark horse, never telling me."

"My wife is superstitious; she asked me not to talk about it until it happened," Sandor answered. "She's had two miscarriages since Teresa."

"Mary Margaret is a splendid baby," he said, carefully touching one of the few hairs on her head. "Now it's our duty to make sure she's brought up to be a good Catholic."

"Only if the parents don't do it," Agnes laughed. "Isn't she beautiful?" She snatched the wailing baby away from Helen Kelly as quickly as she decently could. "No, darling, don't cry," she crooned, "don't cry, your mommy won't let anything bad ever happen to you. No never, my own, sweet little Maggie will never, ever have anything to cry about."

"Maggie? Is that what you're going to call her?" Teresa asked her mother in amazement. Throughout the ceremony she had stood to one side, watching quietly, wearing the best of her old Sunday dresses firmly belted around her waist, her breasts still aching dully. The worst pain of the milk that had made her breasts rock-hard and hot for three days was mercifully gone.

"It's my grandmother's name, you know that, Teresa," Agnes said impatiently, too engrossed in the baby to look up.

"I guess I missed that part of the discussion," Teresa said, feeling even more out of touch with anything to do with the baby than she had before. From the moment they had arrived home from the hospital, her mother had attended to every need, every cry, every sign of discomfort the baby had made, ordering Teresa to leave the baby alone, stay out of her way, and stop bothering her.

"Teenagers," Sandor said indulgently. "We know about their attention span, don't we Brian?"

"All too well."

4

November 15, 1971

Dearest Mimi,

I hope you still live at your old address. Even though I always write "Please forward if necessary" on the envelope, it's like putting a message into a bottle and throwing it in the ocean since you can't answer me and it's been just over two years since we came here.

Everything's changed for the better since my last letter. We've moved to Santa Monica because my mother decided that Maggie should be brought up on this side of Los Angeles. It's so pretty here and about fifteen degrees cooler than the Valley. You can easily get to the beach on the weekends, and that's the place I feel happiest. When I take a long barefoot walk right in the edge of the water, until I fall into the rhythm of the waves, I get a blissful feeling of peace and happiness. I adore the Pacific! We've rented a cute little house and my father got a promotion, so now he's head of the department again.

My big news is all about school. I'm on a full

scholarship at Marymount, where the nuns belong to the Religious Sacred Heart of Mary. It's a *really* good school with a terrific drama department. Sister Elizabeth, who's in charge, is a ball of fire, and I think she likes me.

The other girls, most of them anyway, are pretty snooty. They all seem to have known each other all of their lives, lots of them are very rich, and the big deal here is all about which girls, two years from now, will make their debut at a ball, with their dads in white tie and tails! Lots of them are all members of "old California families"—how old can a family be in such a new state, I'd like to know!—and their mothers and their grandmothers all went to Marymount too. The fact that I went to Sacred Heart gives me a little standing in spite of my lowly scholarship status. Luckily we all wear uniforms but you wouldn't believe some of the dreamy cars with chauffeurs that come to pick them up after school, while I wait for the bus.

There have been a lot of sweet-sixteen parties lately, for the in-crowd, but when I turned sixteen, I didn't say anything about it to anyone, since my mother would never have given me a party and anyway, I didn't exactly know who to ask. Did you have a party? I like to imagine that you did and that it was absolutely wonderful. And that you missed me a little.

The amazing thing about California is that when you're sixteen you can get a driving license. Lots of my classmates are driving! Can you believe it? My mother doesn't trust me enough to let me get a job after school, but I bet I could earn a secondhand car in a couple of years. I still have to come home immediately after my last class unless there's a rehearsal. And I'm not allowed to go to anyone's house to study . . . so, naturally, it's hard to make new friends. You and your big "bad influence" are never far from my parents' minds! Ah, well, I guess I can't complain. But if I can't complain to you, who can I complain to?

I'll bet you're wondering about Maggie. Well, you shouldn't worry. She's got my mother hanging over her every waking minute and lots of her sleeping minutes. My father too, when he's home. They absolutely *adore* her. There's no question in my mind that they've truly convinced themselves that she's *their very own baby*. As I wrote you last time, my mother has never let me feed her or diaper her because I was "too clumsy" and now she's decided that I'm "too busy" with my homework to even be allowed to *play* with Maggie . . . as a special treat every once in a while I get to tell her a story! I guess they think that I'll contaminate the poor little thing.

But Maggie's a very sweet, loving little girl who's growing smarter and more fun every day. Remember how we used to talk about the power of positive thinking and how we could grow big breasts if we concentrated on it hard enough? I must be using this technique on myself, without realizing it, because I feel that Maggie *truly is* my sister. Maybe I've been brainwashed because of circumstances, but the whole maternal thing—I just don't feel it, Mimi. Nothing. I guess it's just as well, because otherwise I'd be too sad to stand it.

Maggie's fat and bouncy, and whenever she falls down she laughs as if it's a big joke. She has the best-natured perpetual grin on her round face— kind of like a gap-toothed jack-o'-lantern—unless she's hungry, in which case she just falls apart and screams bloody murder. She has a mop of jet-black curls and very pink cheeks and my mother's bright blue eyes. Riley blue, right from the Old Country. She sort of looks like an old-fashioned doll, with long, blinky eyelashes, and my mother dresses her in fancy dresses she gets filthy and grows out of in a couple of months.

She calls me "Tessa" because she can't pronounce Teresa. It used to break my heart when I came home and she was still taking her nap and I had to go straight to my room to do my homework, when I knew she was going to be waking up any minute, all smiling and smelling heavenly and warm and squashy with that wonderful baby softness and divine baby stink. But that was my mother's favorite time to be alone with her, and anyway, I really needed the time to concentrate on my schoolwork. After all, I have my scholarship to keep up, which pretty much means getting all A's. Maggie is my mother's baby, that's the way it is, and one day when I'm married I'll have one of my own.

Are you finally allowed to go out on dates? And why am I asking, since I can't get an answer? Needless to say, I've never met any boys who would ask me, and if, God forbid, one did, I wouldn't be permitted to go, because we all know what THAT could lead to (as if I'd ever do THAT again! You'd think they'd finally realize that I'm not completely crazy.). Actually I'm such a boringly good girl that I almost have to make up sins to confess, like, "Father, I took the Lord's name in vain three days ago when I burned my finger on the frying pan."

Although you're supposed to feel absolved after you completely confess a sin and truly repent and have the firm purpose of never sinning again, which I did, believe you me, it hasn't worked the way it's supposed to. The Sacrament of Penance didn't make me feel *better*, yet I was absolved, in the name of the Father and of the Son and of the Holy Spirit. The Big Three. Shouldn't that be enough, Mimi? Maybe it's because my parents treat me like a highly potential sinner, but I can't get rid of the guilt. I bet you're not one tenth as screwed up as I am, but then you never were, my bad little Mimi. You enjoyed your sins!

This is all for now. If anything amazing happens, I'll write again before next year, but I have a feeling that life is just going to go on like this until I'm eighteen and go to college. Probably Mount St. Mary's, a great education but awfully close to home. More nuns. Not that I don't like nuns, but it'll be fun to have a man teacher for a change. Maybe my parents will go bananas, give up entirely on me and let me go off to wild, wicked Berkeley, where I'll become a flower child or a hippy, or is that as over as the Swinging London we used to talk about so longingly?

With all my love, a million happy, slightly belated returns on your birthday, have a wonderful year, and have a lot of fun for me, but not *too* much. Remember, THEY SWIM!

I'll never forget you.
Teresa

5

Teresa, I'll be picking you up at school tomorrow afternoon," Agnes said, opening the door and looking in on her daughter.

"Don't tell me it's time to get my teeth cleaned again," Teresa protested, peering up from her homework.

"No, as a matter of fact I'm driving you into Hollywood to an audition for teenaged girls. Paramount is doing a remake of Little Women and they're looking for young actresses. You're as ready as you've ever been, and your father's agreed at last. Be sure to wash your hair after dinner."

"No! Really? You're not kidding?" Teresa jumped up in flying excitement.

"Certainly not. Why would I be kidding?" her mother said coldly.

"But it's been years . . . you never said anything more about . . . I imagined you'd given up on that idea."

"*Give up? After all I've done for you?*" Agnes's eyes flashed in anger and a clear edge of unmistakable contempt.

"Why did you wait till the last minute to tell me?" Teresa asked, ignoring her mother's familiar look, a deeply wounding look she tried not to let herself dwell on. "I could have reread that book! It was so old-fashioned I don't think I ever got through it."

"I have no idea what part they're reading for," Agnes replied. "This isn't something you can study. In any case, I found out about it only two days ago in the *L.A. Times*—they're holding auditions all week at a casting director's office. I have a sitter for Maggie."

"Oh, Mother, Mother, thank you!"

"There's only one way you can thank me, Teresa, and that's by doing well. I have no illusions that you'll get a part in the first movie you audition for, but there's no reason why you shouldn't eventually justify the sacrifices we've had to make for your sake."

"What should I wear?" Teresa asked, trying to head off the well-worn subject of sacrifice as quickly as possible.

"There won't be time to change, and in any case you're better off wearing your uniform. It doesn't hurt to let people know you're a Marymount girl, and something classic looks better than trying too hard. Anyway, they won't care about your clothes. Just sit down and finish your homework, Teresa. Stop looking in the mirror."

"Couldn't I at least borrow your tweezers and pluck my eyebrows a little bit? They're too thick," she begged. Anything she did would be better than nothing.

"There's absolutely nothing wrong with your eyebrows. I knew I shouldn't have told you until tomorrow, but I wanted to be certain you had clean hair and it takes forever to dry."

"Yes, Mother."

As soon as Agnes closed the door, Teresa resumed her study of her face in the mirror over her bathroom sink. She was allowed to use no makeup except a small tube of colorless ChapStick, but like every other girl at school she had a stash of forbidden cosmetics, which she, unlike most of them, knew how to use, thanks to her adventures with Mimi. Stealthily, with quick but shaking hands, she applied lipstick and eyeliner and, turning her head from side to side, tried to judge the results.

She looked far too bold, she decided, to play any of the girlish Victorian parts she remembered from the book she'd read years ago. She hadn't used makeup in so long that she hadn't realized how very mature it would make her look now. Teresa scrubbed her face and considered it in its nakedness. Clear, very white skin with a faint rosy blush over her cheeks, as if she'd just come in from cold, crisp air, a blush she'd always had no matter what the weather. Her nose was straight and long enough, it seemed to her, to be in proportion with her other features; she had her father's high cheekbones and his extra width of jawbone at that special point under the ear where the jaw meets the neck; her eyes had always been a color she could never quite figure out, an odd shade of green with a hint of gray; her mouth was as wide as ever, her neck as long. Teresa flashed herself an experimental smile. No question but her teeth were her best feature, she thought. Thank God you couldn't see her gums—that would have been a misfortune, considering the size of her smile.

People had always thought she was beautiful, Teresa reflected; she'd often heard them say so, either to her face or when she wasn't supposed to be listening. Not just relatives, not just Mimi. Even Sister Elizabeth, the ancient but extraordinary English teacher and drama coach, had once cautioned her that it wasn't "enough to be beautiful" to play Joan of Arc. She honestly couldn't see what they meant, dearly as she'd like to. Her face was just the face she'd grown up with. She wished she could manage to convince herself that she was beautiful. It would make the audition so much less frightening.

If she really were beautiful, wouldn't she have made more friends at school? Wouldn't her mother have forgiven her by now? And, by sixteen, shouldn't she have stopped asking herself such utterly self-pitying and useless questions?

Peggy Brian Westbrook, the veteran casting director, and her young assistant, Fiona Bridges, opened fresh Cokes.

"How many does this make today?" Peggy inquired wearily.

"Cokes or girls?" Fiona asked. She was a twenty-six-year-old sprig of a large London family that had made its living in and around the theater for two hundred years. Fiona, ambitious in a way that belied her blond, placid, classically Anglo-Saxon, riding-to-the-hunt features, had been in Hollywood for three years, having apprenticed herself to Peggy to learn the art of casting, one of the most important parts of show business.

"Either. They all taste the same and produce the same results. Too sweet, and they make me burp."

"About five Cokes, rough estimate, fifty-six girls, fifty-six. Not one more or one less." Part of Fiona's job was to keep detailed notes for Peggy, who saved all her concentration for the actors.

"This is only day three and we don't have anyone at all who's even vaguely possible. Not a Beth, not an Amy, not a Meg and obviously not a Jo. Will too much Coke make my hair fall out?" Peggy asked plaintively.

Children, followed by teenaged girls, were her least favorite casting assignments, but this one was for her favorite director, Roddy Fensterwald. Roddy was adored by all women, especially actresses—for all the good it would ever do them. How did such an openly gay man manage to be so maddeningly seductive, she wondered, not for the first time.

"Rot your teeth first, I'd imagine, before your hair went," Fiona said cheerfully. "Ready for the next hopeful unknown?"

"Please, I'm ready for a lovely vacation on Devil's Island."

"Actually I believe Devil's Island was quite beautiful, it was the conditions that people complained about, all locked up together for the rest of their lives, with foul food," Fiona replied. "Lots of buggery too, you know. Nasty habit but it probably passed the time."

"At this point it sounds good to me . . . at least it didn't involve teenaged girls."

"Oh, my, you are leaning toward a case of burnout, Mrs. Westbrook, my dear. Perhaps I should send the next lot away till tomorrow?"

"Bitch. Don't you dare."

"If you didn't love your job you couldn't do it," Fiona said smugly. She could always revive Peggy's vital juices by threatening to send actors away. Peggy lived to see actors, to listen to actors, to smell actors. She was like an animal that lived on one sort of food exclusively: actors, good, bad, or indifferent. She had to have her daily ration of actors to survive. She was a thespiani-vore, if such an animal existed, as well as one of the most highly regarded casting directors in Hollywood.

Fiona buzzed the receptionist. "Right, please send in the next girl, Ginger."

Outside in the reception room, Teresa sat stiffly, torn between studying the pages the receptionist had passed out to her and to all the other girls in the room, and observing the other hopefuls. She was the only girl accompanied by her mother. Not only that, but there wasn't another girl who wore a school uniform, Teresa thought miserably. Her pleated gray skirt, severe starched shirt, and navy blazer, with the Marymount crest, suddenly seemed as childish as a pair of Mary Janes.

Many of the girls, as they bent over the pages, had the crisp professional demeanor that indicated that they were accustomed to auditions, and almost all of them were dressed in a version of the latest look, slim sailor pants with a bell-bottom flare, and ribbed "poor boy" clinging sweaters in colors that matched their pants. At least half of them sported the shag, Jane Fonda's hairdo that had swept America, and all of them wore makeup that enhanced their natural prettiness.

She'd never dreamed that it was possible to see so many pretty girls in one place. But, of course, they were the pick of the crop from all over the country, Teresa told herself. These were the girls who had been heading toward this casting office, or one like it, all of their lives, and although they didn't chat with each other, there was a tacit communality that bonded them clearly as they read the pages over and over. They belonged here just as clearly as she did not. How, she wondered, could her mother sit so calmly, reading the magazine she'd brought with her?

"Teresa Horvath, please," the receptionist announced, opening the door into the inner office. Agnes rose with formidable composure. "Come along, Teresa," she said, leaving her magazine on the chair.

Consigning herself to the good offices of the Sainted Mary, Mother of God, Teresa followed her, standing as straight as possible, her shoulders back, her head high.

"I'm sorry, Mrs. Horvath, but Mrs. Westbrook prefers mothers to wait outside during an audition," Ginger said with a pleasant smile.

"What!" Agnes said in the beginning of outrage.

"She doesn't make exceptions." Ginger's smile never wavered. "Go on in, Teresa." In a rush of sudden gratitude, Teresa walked past her mother and closed the door to the office behind her, hesitating once she was inside the fairly small office.

"Hello, there," Peggy said, from behind a table littered with cans of Coke and sheets of photos. "Thanks for coming. This is Fiona Bridges, my assistant. Teresa, that's right isn't it, or do you have a nickname?"

"Yes," Teresa heard herself say. "Yes I do. It's Tessa." She stood still with amazement, caught up by a powerful and unexpected sense of selfhood, as she made this claim.

"Lovely." Peggy's jaded attention was immediately jerked into life by the clear, distinct melody of Tessa's voice. "Now, Tessa, why don't you tell us something about yourself, come on over here where we can see you."

Tessa moved forward and stood in front of the table, her hands firmly clasped behind her to hide their trembling. They had such friendly smiles, these two women. What was the worst thing they could do, after all, except send her away?

"I'm sixteen," she said, "and I live in Santa Monica with my parents and Maggie, my baby sister. We moved to California more than two years ago from Greenwich, Connecticut. My mother's from a big Irish family and my father came here from Hungary back in the 1950s. Now he's head of the music department at the Harvard School. There's nothing particularly exciting about me, except that I've always wanted to act. No, that's wrong. I *have* always acted."

"Do you have any professional experience?" the casting director asked. As Tessa recounted the simple outline of her life, Peggy had felt unexpected chills racing up her arms and crisping the nape of her neck.

"I've never been in anything but a school play," Tessa answered. "This is my first real audition, unless you count the ones at school." She spoke with a simplicity that was as strong as her sudden sense of fearlessness.

"I see," Peggy said slowly. "So you wouldn't have any head shots, any eight-by-ten glossies?" Good God, a schoolgirl without an agent or experience or even pictures . . . but those chills . . . how long had it been since she'd felt chills when an unknown spoke?

"I have snapshots in the family album, but my mother didn't bring them," Tessa answered. "I didn't know I needed glossies."

"Actually you don't. It's just that some of the girls leave them behind so we'll remember what they look like."

"Just think of the girl in the dumb uniform." Tessa laughed with an utterly spontaneous sense of the ridiculous, a wonderfully affirmative sound that rang through the little room.

Peggy and Fiona looked at each other swiftly. Normally, at a first audition of an inexperienced unknown, they'd just chat, make notes, and send her on her way, after getting her phone number in case they decided to reconsider her. But neither of them would have dreamed of letting Tessa go without a reading.

"Take off your blazer and sit down, Tessa. Let your hair out of the ponytail so we can see it, and undo the top buttons of that very well-ironed blouse, so you can breathe a bit," Peggy continued, writing a note to Fiona. *That laugh! Trained voice???*

"Have you had voice lessons, Tessa?" Fiona asked.

"No, I haven't, but I've sung in the choir all my life—I'm a contralto. And my father's very insistent on proper speech. He learned his English from an Englishman at school in Budapest."

"Choir?"

"At the Convent of the Sacred Heart in Greenwich and now, at Marymount."

"So you're a very, very good little convent girl, are you?" Peggy asked on a teasing note.

"I feel like the original model, from day one," Tessa answered, shaking out the gleaming tumble of her hair and trying, without success, to make its lively waves fall neatly with her fingers. "But I can't answer for the good part," she continued thoughtfully. "It's really hard, almost impossible, to be good, because it's so surprisingly easy to commit a venial sin." She'd forgotten herself while she tried to respond as honestly as possible to these women who seemed so interested in her.

"So *all* your acting has actually been done in a Catholic school?" Peggy probed gently.

"I haven't been to any other kind of school, or to summer camp either. But the Madams at Sacred Heart put on a wide range of plays, and so do the Sisters at Marymount. Of course I've had lots of chances to play a boy, since I used to be taller than most of the other girls. I think I've stopped growing now. Last year's uniforms still fit."

"You've been given the four pages—sides—we'd like you to read. The context of the scene is that Jo March, the part you're reading, is having an argument with her older sister, Meg, who's dignified and proud and proper.

Jo is independent and tumultuous and rebellious. You don't remember the book by any chance? No? Well, it doesn't matter, we're just looking for a rough idea. Fiona will give you your cues. You read the lines that are underlined. I think you should read the scene over again first, several times, to feel a little familiar with Jo."

"Yes, please."

As Tessa bent her head over the pages, Peggy and Fiona turned their swivel chairs away from her and conferred quietly.

"Isn't she much *much* too beautiful for Jo?" Fiona whispered. "Jo isn't supposed to be a raving, tearing beauty, she's a tomboy whose 'hair is her one beauty,' remember? What a glorious kid! Those eyes! Have you ever seen a green like that? Glenda would throw a fit."

"Glenda doesn't have casting approval," Peggy hissed. "That middle-aged love goddess begged Roddy to let her play Marmee so the Academy members will take her seriously come Oscar time. If it should, by a miracle, turn out that Tessa can act, Glenda won't have to worry about anyone saying she can't be believable in a serious role as the mother of four. They'll be too busy looking at Tessa."

"Still, she's not at all the character, except for her height and her hair," Fiona fretted.

"Miss Bridges, this is Hollywood, not the BBC. Kate Hepburn played Jo in nineteen thirty-three and trust me, she was never an ugly duckling. Casting to type bores me, anyway. All the other girls have to be pretty but Jo has to knock you right off your chair, one way or another, because she's the heroine. It would be more constructive if you'd worry that Tessa can't act, that maybe she's all looks and no delivery. That's what you should really be afraid of."

"I'm as ready as I'll ever be," Tessa said.

Fiona started to recite the cues she'd memorized in the course of the past three long days. Tessa read without gulping the words, giving herself an instant to look up from the pages whenever she could, look straight at

Fiona and say the next line as if she'd learned it, as if she were living it, before having to consult the script again.

In spite of this being a first reading, Tessa's luminous intensity was immediately switched on. All the light in the room seemed to condense around her. Tessa *became* Jo March as if she'd been inhabited by an uncompromising spirit. To Fiona, the words she'd spoken so often became new and fresh with meaning as she awaited Tessa's response. Then, so suddenly that Peggy shivered in surprise, the four sides were over and the reading ended.

But I want to hear what she says next, I need to hear her, Peggy thought. That hasn't happened in ten years. Fifteen! "Thank you, Tessa," she managed to say, calmly. "That was excellent."

"Is that it?" Tessa asked in evident disappointment, withdrawing from the character slowly and dreamily. She struggled to put on her blazer, the young, arched fullness of her breasts evident for the first time against her starched white shirt as she wriggled her arms into the sleeves.

"Oh, no, I doubt that'll be it," Peggy said, blowing her nose violently. She had tears in her eyes, another thing that hadn't happened for fifteen years. That's not it, not if I know anything about this damn business, and I do. This girl is *unconditional*; it's all or nothing with her. She already knows all those essential things you can't teach. But I can't make any final decisions, all I can do is point her in the right direction.

"Ginger," she said, buzzing the secretary. "Would you please ask Mrs. Horvath to come in?"

Agnes entered, wearing a resolute smile.

"Mrs. Horvath, can you bring your daughter back tomorrow?" Peggy asked without ceremony. "I'd like to have her read for some other people. And there are some more pages I'd like her to study overnight. Oh, and be sure she wears her uniform again, if you don't mind."

"Tomorrow? Of course," Agnes said, coming forward quickly.

"But, Mother, tomorrow afternoon there's that field

hockey match with Westlake—" Tessa reminded her, unwillingly.

"Sister Elizabeth told me not to bother about it if these ladies wanted you back."

Her mother would have to confess before communion, Tessa thought with glee.

"Sister Elizabeth? Don't tell me she's still at Marymount!" Peggy Westbrook exclaimed.

"Do you know Sister Elizabeth?" Tessa asked in amazement.

"She was head of the English department and also coached the plays when I was there, a long time ago, and she wasn't young then," Peggy confessed.

"But, you never said!"

"No, I never do . . . usually. I've spent more time in that uniform than you have, Tessa."

"We just did *Saint Joan,*" Tessa offered eagerly.

"What part did you have?"

"Joan."

"And you satisfied Sister Elizabeth?"

"She said I was right for the Maid of France, that's all. She doesn't give an opinion if she can help it."

"So I remember. Thank you, Tessa. We'll see you tomorrow. And Mrs. Horvath, please leave your phone number with the receptionist."

After the door closed behind Agnes and Tessa, Peggy and Fiona sat in silence for stunned seconds, both of them struck by the sudden flat dullness of the room as soon as Tessa left it.

"What was that business about *Saint Joan* and Sister Elizabeth?" Fiona ventured, realizing that Peggy had gone somewhere she couldn't follow her.

"Sister Elizabeth never, ever put on a production of Saint Joan unless . . ."

"Unless?"

"She'd discovered someone she considered worthy of the part."

"And what's so terrific about this Sister Elizabeth, besides a long life span?"

"Fiona, she was the best director I've ever worked with. Ever. If she weren't a nun she'd be a Hollywood legend. To my knowledge she hasn't put on *Saint Joan* in twenty years. Miss Bridges, you've just been fortunate enough to witness a born actress, a schoolgirl with acting born in the bone and muscle and the fiber and the throat, the passion and the pacing, the arrogance and the humility, all there. And we were the first to hear her! You should pay me for letting you be here today!"

"I was over the moon about Tessa before she mentioned Sister Elizabeth. And you . . . you were gone from the minute she said hello in that marvelous voice. Must be the Hungarian father, I should think. Yummy Hungarians. Seriously, Peggy, did you really think she wouldn't be able to act worth a damn?"

"Consider it my form of knocking on wood. As for Sister Elizabeth, it never hurts to have a saintly and infallible second opinion when magic strikes. Send the other girls away, Fi, I'm much too excited to give them a fair reading now. I've just remembered why I chose this infernal profession."

"Righto. Want another Coke to celebrate, oh, secret convent queen?"

"You know perfectly well where I keep the Dom Pérignon, so stop being disrespectful to your betters."

"I'm just jealous of that sexy uniform."

"As well you might be. Now get out the champagne!"

6

The next afternoon, Roddy Fensterwald sat in the casting office alongside Peggy Westbrook and Fiona Bridges. Much to his irritation, Glenda Bancroft had insisted on being present. She had heard from her assistant, who had been told by the all-knowing Ginger, that he was reading an exciting unknown for Jo.

"Roddy, lover, I'm thrilled that Peggy has found someone she thinks might do for Jo," Glenda had said on the phone the previous night. "There's no way I'd play Marmee with any of the hot young girls who are already out there," Glenda continued earnestly. "They've all been spoiled by too many photos of them making the club scene. I'm dying to see a fresh face. Don't be an old meanie. I promise I'll be a fly on the wall. She won't have any idea that it's me. I'm aware that might make her freeze. I can't be good if the whole cast isn't good, you know that. After all, it is an ensemble piece."

"You worry me when you make sense, Glenda. What do you plan to do, come in drag?"

"Give me credit for more subtlety than that. I often spend the afternoon shopping at the Price Club—it's my secret vice. I've never been spotted yet. If you have to introduce me, say I'm your secretary. I'll make notes."

"Damn it, Glenda—"

"Roddy, you won't regret it. Till tomorrow, lover."

He regretted it already, Roddy Fensterwald thought. Glenda Bancroft had taken a chair and put it quietly in a corner, as far away from them as she could sit, a diabolic move that somehow made her a focus of attention. She'd made a genuine effort not to be recognizable, he had to admit, in a truly dowdy pants suit and a head scarf, so that her signature red hair was hidden. But she couldn't, in spite of not wearing makeup, hide her features, and she exuded that certain power that only a world-famous actress can possess. Bitch that he knew her to be, she hadn't bothered to turn it off, as he knew damn well she could, if she pleased.

He stood up and walked over to her. "Fly on the wall?"

"You'd walk right past me, Roddy, don't say you wouldn't."

"But this room is a little too small for star power, Glenda. Lose it, darling, or I'm giving you the boot."

"But of course," she said, losing it with a small satisfied smile. She did adore Roddy, he never disappointed her, Glenda thought, looking vaguely in the direction of her feet.

"Are we all ready now?" Peggy asked patiently.

"Yup," Roddy said.

When Tessa entered, Peggy introduced Roddy, who stood up, shook her hand, and smiled at her as if he'd never been so delighted to meet anyone in his life. She smiled back at him, thinking how much younger he looked than she'd expected. He'd directed a lot of movies she loved, but she'd never seen a photograph of him. His thick, messy hair, already lightly streaked with gray, fell carelessly to his shoulders, and he wore enormously thick glasses that were a droll contrast to his slightly monkey-like features. His skinny, tall frame was carelessly covered in jeans and a baggy old sweater that had once been either white or yellow. Roddy Fensterwald, Tessa thought, would not reassure her mother.

"I know how hard this is, Tessa," he said, "but all I really care about today is getting an idea of who you are and who you could be, under the right circumstances. This isn't about showing me how you'd act in front of a camera, or about becoming Jo March on screen, even though you'll be reading lines in the context of the scene. For the next few minutes it's not acting nearly as much as being Tessa Horvath, the one part you've been playing all your life, the one part you can't help but be perfect in, can you, no matter what you do? So consider that you've already got that A in drama."

"Thank you, Mr. Fensterwald," Tessa said, visibly relaxing.

"Call me Roddy. Everybody does."

"I'll try, but I can't promise."

"Well, as long as you don't call me 'Sister Elizabeth' we're fine."

As Peggy laughed along with the others, she thought that no other name could possibly be as appropriate, and, of course he knew it and knew they knew it.

"Did you get a chance to study the new sides, Tessa?" Peggy asked.

"Yes, I've memorized them."

"Oh, I didn't mean you to do that. You must have been up all night."

"I had it memorized before dinner. But I was up all night anyway, too excited to sleep."

"Well, don't try to do this from memory," Roddy said. "It just makes it more of a trial, and I want you to be comfortable. Would you like some water?"

"Yes, please."

Fiona poured the water while Tessa gazed nervously around the room. Why hadn't they introduced the slim woman taking notes in the corner? Was she someone important? Even sitting down she had important posture, straight, alert, commanding.

"Before we start reading," Roddy said, taking the sides from Fiona, "here's the situation." Peggy and Fiona darted their eyes at each other in surprise. Usually the director would just sit quietly during an audition, watching with every ounce of his attention and forming an opinion. Roddy was known to be a fine actor, but this was the first time he'd ever read in their office. It was Fiona's, or, in some cases, Peggy's job to read with the actor under consideration. As Roddy started to speak, both women sat as expressionlessly as if they weren't in the room.

"All right, Tessa, this is what's happened up till now. Jo, and Meg, her older sister, have been invited to an evening party, a New Year's Eve dance. They each have only one good dress to wear—they're very poor, you see, but still ladies. The problem is that Jo's dress has been scorched in the back when she stood in front of a fire, and it's been mended in a way that would show if she were to dance. She doesn't really care about things like that, but Meg is so self-conscious that she has made Jo promise to keep the back of her dress out of sight. So not only is Jo out of her element to begin with, but her style is really cramped, because there's no place she can possibly stand except up against a wall. She feels absolutely out of place and pretty soon she finds herself alone, watching other people enjoying themselves, a total wallflower. Then, to her horror, she spots a boy walking in her direction as if he were going to ask her to dance. She quickly and bashfully disappears behind some curtains.

"But lo and behold, there's another person there, Laurie Laurence, the boy who lives next door. Jo barely knows him, although they've met before when he brought her wandering cat home. He's hiding in the curtains because he's been living abroad, at school, and doesn't know American manners. As they meet, the scene begins. Start whenever you're ready."

Tessa looked around the room as she thought over what Roddy had told her. She stood up and started to speak, stammering in surprise.

"Dear me, I didn't know anyone was here!"

"Don't mind me, stay if you like," Roddy said, looking startled but laughing.

"Shan't I disturb you?"

"Not a bit. I only came here because I don't know many people and felt rather strange at first, you know."

"So did I. Don't go away please, unless you'd rather."

As the scene continued, they became more and more friendly, exchanging confidences and information about their lives, until Laurie asked Jo to dance. Jo explained why she couldn't move about in her dress.

"Though it's nicely mended, it shows, and Meg told me to keep still so no one would see it. You may laugh if you want to. It is funny, I know," Tessa said, as she spoke the last line of the pages she'd been given.

Roddy Fensterwald looked closely into her eyes, judging her ability to be surprised. He grabbed the script out of her hand and threw it, with his own, into the air and swept her into an approximation of a swinging, springing, breathless polka, with which the actual scene in the book ended. Peggy and Fiona continued to sit absolutely still, although they were both resisting the urge to cheer.

Roddy bowed to Tessa and led her ceremoniously to the office door. "Wait outside, Tessa, while we huddle, will you?"

"Thank you, Roddy! I've never had so much fun!" Tessa exclaimed. "Oh! Would you mind—could I just have a second to ask Miss Bancroft for her autograph before I leave?"

"Miss Bancroft?"

"I was wondering who she was, and then when she caught my eye, just before we started the scene, of course I knew immediately," Tessa explained, suddenly shy. "After all, there isn't another pair of eyes in the world like hers, is there?"

"Go on, get your autograph and then scoot."

Tessa collected her autograph from a subdued Glenda Bancroft and left the room as quickly as possible.

"Peggy and Fiona, could you leave us for a minute?" Roddy asked quietly.

" 'Caught her eye'!" he stormed, as soon as they had gone. "Damn it, Glenda! Caught her eye! How could you be such a thundering bitch? If there was one thing calculated to throw her off, that was it. It's unforgivable, I'll never trust you again," Roddy raged.

"Oh, for heaven's sake, lover, it was an accident. Did you expect me not to peek to see what that girl looked like? She happened to catch me just when I was looking at her, that's all. And anyway, don't carry on as if anything could stop all that tiresome inexhaustible energy. Jesus, Roddy, what a heap of ingenuous, innocent gaiety. It's just as well something got her off the ceiling and down to business. You're not actually thinking of casting her, are you?"

"That's none of your business, Glenda."

"Roddy, I want this picture to be a success even more than you do. We agreed it was an ensemble piece—that great big, enthusiastic girl would throw it entirely off balance. I'm not saying she's not beautiful, I'm not saying she can't act, I'm not even saying I don't wish I were her age, for the love of God! But she's too bloody much! She eats up all the air in the room, she's a stage actress, not a film actress, she doesn't have the right *dimensions*. She's as big a presence as . . . as Ethel Merman! She's a talent, I admit that willingly, but not for this particular picture and not until she gets some experience in acting for a camera. You know that as well as I do."

"Glenda, go home before I forget I'm a gent and hit you, will you darling?"

"What am I seeing here, Roddy, a little tiny crush on a great big tomboy? Roddy Fensterwald in love? Don't tell me that's making you lose your judgment."

"Perhaps you're right," he grinned thoughtfully. "Interesting interpretation—but why not? We're all capable of anything, under the right circumstances, I always say. So this is what love feels like! Be still my heart. No wonder people carry on the way they do. But

61

just think, if even I could go for this girl, how will every other man in America feel?"

"*Little Women* is a fucking woman's movie, Roddy. And that fucking girl's too old for me to play her fucking mother!"

"Glenda, as I said before, go home so you can have this particular fit with your agent. He gets paid enough to listen to you. But remember that your contract isn't signed yet."

"That's unworthy of you," Glenda retorted with dignity.

"I love you when you try to be grand. And, sweetie, I adore your getup. Especially the head scarf. It's a whole new you. I've always insisted you had untapped range, no matter what anyone else said. Will you send Peggy and Fiona in on your way out?"

7

Tessa woke up one summer morning in 1974 feeling defiant before her feet hit the floor. She was going to be nineteen in six weeks, but her life was three times as full of things she was obliged to do as it had been when she was still a schoolgirl at Marymount.

Today was Saturday, a day on which, by rights, she should have at least a few free hours to herself. But every single minute was scheduled. Right after breakfast she had a riding lesson, a new skill her agent insisted she needed to develop; then home to shower again and change for a talk with her business manager over lunch, a meeting her father had arranged and sternly told her not to forget. After lunch she had to go back home again to change once more for an interview set up by the producers of her new film, *Gemini Summer*. The interviewer, a French journalist from *Paris Match*, would be accompanied by a photographer who wanted to "follow her around" all afternoon. As soon as that major ordeal was over, her mother expected her home for dinner, here in Santa Monica. There was no space for *her* in her day, Tessa realized, as she brushed the hair that fell in a drifting cascade of natural waves no studio hairdresser would ever try to subdue.

Even worse, she thought, she loathed horses; she wasn't interested in "equity diversification," the subject her business manager was going to try to explain to her once again; and she was intimidated by the idea of the interview with the man from *Paris Match* and his inquisitive photographer. She'd rather have a cavity filled.

Novocain and drilling, a mere pinprick followed by an annoying noise that was over in a half hour, would be better than picking her way across a tightrope without losing her balance during three hours with a reporter–photographer combination, particularly when they'd told the PR people that they wanted to watch her "being herself." Holy Mother, she thought, wasn't it just plain crazy to expect her to be herself—whoever that was, anyway?—when *they* knew that *she* knew that the camera was capturing every move she made and the interviewer was recording every remark she made, no matter how silly?

Feeling more put upon by the minute, Tessa reminded herself that tomorrow, Sunday, when she'd finally have a few free hours after mass followed by the obligatory family lunch, all the stores in Beverly Hills would be closed.

Yet this past March, on Oscar night, when she'd won the Best Supporting Actress award for *Little Women,* Tessa had promised herself a present. She'd had to postpone buying it because of the demands on her time, and the longer she waited, the more alluring it became. She craved it, this gift from herself to herself, the Oscar present and the major nineteenth-birthday present she wouldn't be anywhere near Tiffany & Co. to buy on her actual birthday. Tessa came to a decision. She was going to play hooky. She was going to Tiffany's this morning and that was that.

She picked up the phone that had been recently installed in her bedroom and called Fiona Bridges, her just-as-recent personal assistant, and told her that she thought she might be coming down with a cold and that her riding lesson had better be canceled. She hated to lie, but she didn't want even Fiona to go with her when she bought her present. It should be a private moment, a secret delight, with nobody looking on and giving advice. She didn't need advice, Tessa assured herself. She'd know it as soon as she saw it—it would leap out at her.

Tessa carefully considered what to wear. She wanted to look like someone who had every right to expect service at Tiffany's and at the same time she didn't want to risk being recognized, something that was happening to her more and more often whenever she went out in public. Hastily she went through all the new clothes that Fiona had helped her to buy and realized that none of them would do. They had been purchased for special events and were all meant for the late afternoon or evening. Like every other California kid, her normal wear consisted of jeans, sweatshirts, T-shirts, and shorts.

Finally, in desperation, Tessa decided to wear her best green linen suit, with her best white silk shirt, both of which were strictly reserved for Sunday mass. She poked and pulled at her hair until it fell untidily around her face, concealing her features as much as possible. She decided not to put on any makeup.

The general effect, she thought, as she glanced with concern into her mirror, was that of someone with the money for good clothes, someone who was too hip to care what she looked like—a casual, old-money look she'd noticed was a favorite with the mothers of her former schoolmates in Greenwich, a look that she hoped would inspire a certain amount of respect in a jewelry salesman.

She phoned the local taxi company. As soon as she saw the cab stop at the front door, she was out in a flash, calling "Bye, Mother, have to meet Fiona," before her mother could stop her to ask why she wasn't having breakfast, what had happened to her riding lesson, and why on earth she was wearing her good suit.

"Tiffany's in Beverly Hills," Tessa told the driver, feeling a sudden surge of freedom as the cab pulled away quickly. She hadn't been this excited since the audition that had won her the part of Jo. And what if she hadn't talked Steve Miller, her business manager, into letting her open a little checking account of her own, Tessa asked herself delightedly. What if every last penny of the money she'd made were tied up in those safe investments that Steve told her would give her financial security when she was too old to work?

"I'm young, for heaven's sake, Steve," she'd told him, amazed. "I can play ingenues and leading ladies for another twenty years and I'll still only be thirty-eight. Wow, imagine, thirty-eight! That's practically middle-aged! Then, when it's time, I'll move into character parts. You'll see, Steve, I plan to get older in some wonderful way, maybe a dignified, distinguished way, like an English actress, or in a sexy, fascinating way, like a French actress. I'll play anything—mothers, maiden aunts, teachers, taxi drivers, nuns, you name it—because I intend to keep on working until I drop dead from real old age one day, waiting for my close-up."

He'd laughed at her, but eventually she'd managed to get him to fork over three thousand dollars, more money than she'd ever believed she would have in her possession. Tessa's never-used checkbook lay snugly in her handbag.

The taxi stopped in front of Tiffany & Co. at the corner of the Beverly Wilshire Hotel. She'd never been in the store—she'd hardly ever been to Beverly Hills, for that matter—yet she didn't linger to gape at the windows but entered eagerly, marching through the door as if she'd done it dozens of times before. She moved with her characteristic walk, coltish yet swinging, both youthful and immodestly alluring, slightly boyish but enduringly graceful—a walk she was never to lose.

Swiftly Tessa cruised around the store, her proud

head on her proud neck set at a critical, appraising angle, as if she weren't sure there could possibly be anything here she'd want to buy. She took in the lay of the land quickly. China and silver to the right; men's watches and cuff links at one counter; women's jeweled pins, necklaces, and earrings at another; silver picture frames, clocks, and key chains at a third. No, not what she was looking for. The salespeople all seemed to be occupied with customers, and for a minute Tessa stood still and looked around. At five feet seven inches, she was so perfectly made that she looked taller, and her disciplined posture was commanding without her realizing it. She made a vivid sight in her green suit: this tall, slim girl with a treasure of almost-black hair tumbling around her face, a face whose features were instantly translated into beauty, no matter how little of them could be seen.

"May I be of assistance?" asked a man's voice. Tessa turned to see a pleasantly smiling, reassuringly middle-aged man who had materialized behind her.

"Yes, thank you. I'm looking for . . . for a pearl necklace."

"You've certainly come to the right place," he nodded. "Let's go over to the back of the store. That's where we keep our pearls."

Tessa followed him to a long counter where, under glass, lay dozens of pearl necklaces and earrings. She noted that there were many differences in the size of the pearls and the lengths of the necklaces.

"Are these for a gift or for yourself?" the salesman asked.

"For myself," Tessa answered, the normally spontaneous tone of her voice suddenly tentative as she realized that pearl necklaces came in more varieties than she had ever imagined, although she'd been daydreaming about one for over a year.

"Well then, if you can give me some idea of what you have in mind . . . ?" He gestured at the abundance of choice. If it were up to him, he thought, he'd dip into the case and hand her as many pearls as her two hands could hold and tell her they were a gift from an admirer.

A genuine pearl necklace I can buy for three thousand dollars, including sales tax, Tessa told herself, but she heard herself say, "I really won't be able to tell you much until I try one on, will I?"

"That's absolutely right," the salesman agreed. "Each necklace is different from any other. Even two necklaces that seem identical to the naked eye will look different on your skin." On this girl's very white, extraordinarily perfect skin, he thought, any necklace was going to look exquisite. No necklace would be the best adornment of all.

"Of course," Tessa said, looking down at rows of pearls that all seemed to be the same color. Pearl color.

"I assume you're looking for a sixteen-inch necklace?"

"Probably," Tessa said guardedly.

"It's the most useful length, unless, of course, you have one already." How could she not, he asked himself? How could such a splendid creature, who so obviously came from a moneyed background, not have an entire wardrobe of pearls? Of course, she was still so young she'd probably been borrowing her mother's.

"Why do you think sixteen inches is so useful?" Tessa asked, not about to admit that she'd never measured the inexpensive string of artificial pearls she'd been given for her confirmation. Years of hard use had worn off their glossy surface in many places and shown them to be mere painted glass beads.

"You can wear a sixteen-inch strand with anything from a ball gown to a sweater," he said, trying to decide whether her amazing eyes were more green than gray. Tessa looked up at him. Far more green, he decided, a green like early spring in the forest on a day that was touched by a faint mist. "When you get to eighteen inches there's always the problem of the necklace dipping under your collar."

"Then let's go for sixteen," Tessa said, relieved to have one element isolated from the other possibilities.

"As for the millimeter . . . ?" The salesman paused tactfully. The size of the pearl determined the price.

"The millimeter," Tessa mused, not betraying the fact that she was entirely at sea. Was the millimeter the weight of the pearl or the diameter? "The millimeter, yes, naturally. Now what would you buy, if you were me?"

"For a young woman, I usually recommend eight and a half to nine millimeters, not too big a pearl, not too small, and it's always appropriate. This strand, for instance," he said, reaching into the case and pulling out a necklace whose pearls were only slightly bigger than those of the old necklace she'd worn out.

"Is that eight and a half or nine?" she asked, ignoring a definite stirring of disappointment.

"Both," he answered. "A discrepancy of one half millimeter is standard in a necklace of uniform size."

"Oh, of course, because they're natural," Tessa said hastily, realizing that pearl divers couldn't be expected to pop up out of the ocean with a bunch of pearls that were exactly the same size.

"Not natural, no." The salesman repressed even the hint of a smile. "These are all cultured pearls. You can only tell the difference if you X-ray them. There haven't been any natural pearls available since the 1930s, unless you buy them at auction, and then they're fabulously expensive."

"At auction?" Tessa said shocked. *"Secondhand pearls? I'd never do that. How would you know what you're getting?"

"Precisely. Whereas here . . ."

"They're Mikimoto," Tessa finished his sentence, remembering the name from the ads she'd seen for Mikimoto cultured pearls.

"Actually, they're not."

"No? Hmm." Tessa looked dubious to hide her confusion.

"These come from our special sources. Mikimoto is a trade name and it includes many standards of pearls, but only one standard is considered good enough for Tiffany and Company. Our experts eliminate all the others, even if you, or I, for that matter, would never be able to tell the difference."

It was her mouth, the salesman thought, that was making him ramble. It was just enough larger than the mouths of ordinary women to be utterly fascinating: sharply incised at the corners yet rising to an unusual plumpness, the deep indentation in the middle of her upper lip precisely the right distance from the ravishingly high peaks on either side. No wonder she didn't wear lipstick. It would obscure this natural gift of all the pagan gods and goddesses.

"I think the only way for you to decide," he continued, "is to sit down in our private room and try on a number of necklaces. The light is better in there."

"Fine," Tessa agreed quickly. Out of the corner of her eye she'd noticed several people looking at her with the kind of interest that she'd learned meant that she'd been recognized.

The salesman unlocked the case, extracted three identically sized necklaces, and escorted Tessa to a small room lined in gray velvet, where there were a desk, a chair, and a large round mirror on a stand. He laid the necklaces out carefully on a square of gray velvet.

"Which one would you like to start with?" he asked Tessa.

"That one," she said, pointing at random. He undid the clasp and, standing behind her, fastened the necklace around her neck.

Tessa fell silent in wonder. The necklace that had looked so similar to her old necklace was quite different as it lay on her neck, reaching just below the hollow between her collarbones. There was something softly mysterious about it, as if a light were gleaming from deep within each pearl, which made them seem slightly larger than they were. But the lapels of her suit held her shirt too close to her neck for her to get the full effect, so she shrugged her jacket off quickly and flung the silk collar of her white blouse backward, so that she could see as much as possible. Still her hair obscured many of the pearls, so Tessa fumbled in her handbag for the wide elastic band she kept there and quickly made a ponytail.

"Ahhh, that's better," the salesman approved, with what little breath remained in his lungs after watching Tessa take off her jacket. Just a girl, yes, but those breasts . . . how . . . how . . . splendid.

Still Tessa said nothing, too absorbed in the effect of the pearls to speak.

"Not exactly what you have in mind? Here, try these," the salesman said, whisking the necklace away and replacing it with another. "They have a slightly more creamy tone. The others leaned slightly toward the pinkish."

"Mmm," was all Tessa could manage.

"Not these either? Now here's a strand with a definite silvery quality," he said, replacing the second necklace with the third.

"They all look pretty much the same," Tessa commented, finding a crisp tone from somewhere, unwilling to commit herself to anything until she found out what they cost.

"I'll go and get a few more strands. You've just begun to look," the salesman offered immediately. As soon as she was alone Tessa examined the tiny white price tags that hung by a thin string from each necklace. Each one was the same price, three thousand four hundred dollars. Shocked and dismayed, she sat back, trying to decide what to say to make a graceful exit. She wished she'd never let herself get trapped in a private room. Oh, what on earth was she going to do? Especially since she'd taken up so much of the salesman's time? But before she had time to find the right words, the salesman was back with three more necklaces.

"These are between twelve and twelve and a half millimeters each. Also, they're South Sea pearls, not Japanese. With your height, the length of your neck, and the width of your shoulders, I suspected that you'd probably be happier with something larger, something more important. Now," he asked, as he closed the clasp of one of the new necklaces, "tell me if I'm right or not."

"Oh," Tessa said, fighting down a hysterical laugh, "you're right. These do more for me, there's no question about that." And they did, oh, they did! These were exactly the pearls she'd had in mind, these were her dream pearls, gleaming with a pink-white magnificence, precisely the right size, a size that made the other necklaces seem . . . dinky.

She lifted her ponytail above her head with a recklessly lovely gesture that made the salesman restrain a gasp, and turned her head from side to side, preening. "Do you have a hand mirror?" Tessa asked. In for a penny, in for a pound, she thought. "I'd like to see these from the side."

He produced a hand mirror from the desk and she looked at herself for long minutes, expressionless. "How much are they?" she asked simply. That, it had suddenly come to her, was the question any normal woman would ask.

"Fourteen thousand five hundred."

"But they're only three millimeters larger than the others. Why should they be so much more expensive?" Tessa asked, the necklace giving her the courage to sound as indifferent as a duchess who had happened to notice a sudden rise in the price of eggs.

"It's a question of time: the years and years it takes to lay down all those layers of nacre, and then, of course, to find such a perfect match, such luster."

"There's one problem."

"I know. You want earrings to go with them. That won't be a problem at all."

"It's not that. I have only three thousand dollars in my checking account and I don't have a credit card. So I'm afraid I'll have to leave these here," Tessa sighed. She should have known better than to let him put them around her neck. She'd never forget how they looked. "Perhaps they'll still be here when I come back . . . or something like them."

"But, Miss Kent, we wouldn't dream of expecting immediate payment! The manager is opening a house charge for you as we speak."

"He is?" Tessa said blankly.

"Yes, he told me who you were when I went out to get these necklaces. I have to admit I didn't know . . . I rarely get to the movies. I didn't even watch the Oscars, but please accept my congratulations."

"A house charge? *A charge account at Tiffany's?*" Tessa breathed, unable to believe his words.

"You can keep them on and wear them right out to lunch. I'll just remove the price tag for you," he said, as he quickly snipped the thread. "Now, they're yours! You've made the perfect choice, if I may say so. Perfect! Now, shall I bring you some earrings? Simple studs, perhaps?"

"I think I'd better come back later for the earrings," Tessa said, smiling freely for the first time since she'd entered Tiffany's. She knew she hadn't needed Fiona. "I'm having lunch with my business manager and I don't want him to have a heart attack." She got up, put her jacket back on, and took the band out of her hair, combing it with her fingers.

Tessa Kent walked out of the private room, wearing her first real pearls, straight into a burst of applause. Dozens of people had gathered around the door and were waiting to see her emerge.

Startled, she stopped, but almost immediately she threw her head back and began to laugh triumphantly. "Thank you," Tessa said, as she walked easily and happily through the crowd, stopping now and then to sign an autograph. "Thank you all, thank you so much."

8

‗‗‗‗‗‗‗‗‗‗‗‗‗‗‗◻‗‗‗‗‗‗‗‗‗‗‗‗‗‗‗

Agnes Horvath stood by the stove in her kitchen while the water came to a boil for tea, listening to the confusion of laughter and squeals that came from Teresa's room, where her daughter and Fiona Bridges were packing for Teresa's flight to London the next day. There she would rendezvous for costume fittings and makeup tests with David Lean and the cast of his new film, an epic set in sixteenth-century England, in which Teresa would star as the young Mary Queen of Scots. Peter O'Toole and Albert Finney would be playing her second and third husbands, and Vanessa Redgrave would play Queen Elizabeth, Mary's first cousin and nemesis. Or rather, Agnes thought with the ever-deepening affront she had learned to mask, *Tessa Kent* was packing for London. Tessa Kent the phenomenal young star, Tessa Kent, Agnes told herself with a burst of bitterness, for whom her own name was not good enough.

Teresa Horvath, that ingrate, her now recently-turned-twenty-year-old daughter, had allowed herself to be rebaptized by her agent, Aaron Zucker, an agent handpicked by Roddy Fensterwald. Zucker had the audacity to consider himself an expert on finding the perfect names for his clients, if, like Teresa, they bore a name he didn't consider a good fit with the actor's persona. "Kent," for a girl who was half-Irish, half-Hungarian? "Kent?"

Zucker and Fensterwald, Agnes thought, provoked almost beyond endurance—that unholy twosome had been entirely responsible for the film she'd seen the previous night at a cast-and-crew screening. They'd been not only responsible, but delighted with themselves. Again Fensterwald had directed Teresa—Fensterwald, that wicked, manipulative creature who had attached himself to her daughter's career. Agnes felt only vast suspicion and dislike toward him, although Teresa insisted that it was entirely normal for him to feel responsible for her success and to consider her in many ways his creation.

Gemini Summer, it was called. An occasion of mortal sin, she'd call it, this piece of filth, hand-tailored for her daughter.

In *Gemini Summer,* she'd been cast as a temptress born, a shameless, hot-blooded child-woman discovering the extent of her powers as a femme fatale. Teresa played a waitress at a summer colony for distinguished creative people, who plunged simultaneously into love affairs with two older men, a great writer, played by Robert Duvall, and a great painter, played by Robert Mitchum, leading Duvall to kill himself over her.

In her too-tight waitress uniform and the ultimately seductive shorts, T-shirts, and bikinis that wardrobe had invented for her to wear during her liberal time away from the kitchen, Teresa's lush young body had been revealed more tantalizingly than if she'd been naked. Agnes had been so deeply shocked the previous night that she'd been literally unable to speak after the film ended, and, in any case, Teresa had been too surrounded by the adulation of the audience to have listened to her. Who was interested in the reactions of a mere mother, anyway?

Her feelings were totally unimportant. The film was made, they weren't going to remake it because she thought it was as vile and tawdry and immoral a spectacle as she'd ever seen. Her position about anything had ceased to have the slightest meaning from the minute she'd taken Teresa to that first audition. From the instant Peggy Westbrook laid eyes on Teresa, Agnes had become a nonperson. She wasn't even treated with the attention due the goose that laid the golden egg, she thought, her rage festering. She was less than an inconvenience; she simply didn't exist for them any more than the straw of a bird's nest, once the bird has flown on its own.

She, Agnes Riley Horvath, who'd given up her own life to make her daughter a star—a star who owed that Oscar to her mother, not to Roddy Fensterwald, if any truth still existed—was left without any reward more tangible than her sisters' excitement, transmitted by telephone from three thousand miles away.

Her sisters hadn't even been envious of her, Agnes had realized bitterly. They'd been glowing with reflected glory, basking in it, enjoying it thoroughly, just as they thought she must be. Teresa's spectacular change of fortune had been far too overwhelming to inspire any emotions in the Riley family except astonished delight.

It wasn't fair, it wasn't fair! The thing she'd wanted so badly had happened, happened beyond her possible imagining, and all she felt was emptiness and loss. Her life was so small now, in comparison to Teresa's, so pitifully minor key. Utterly diminished, without even her dreams of the future to keep her going. Yet she was only thirty-nine.

There was no justice on the face of the earth. What was left to her now? A pious husband of fifty-six whose career had settled into an unexciting groove, and a noisy, messy five-year-old to bring up, a daughter with no touch of the star quality that Teresa had possessed from the very beginning. Maggie was just starting kindergarten and was gone much of the day, a happy, friendly, pudgy little creature who was as ordinary as a child could be. True enough, she gave Agnes no trouble, but no woman who had been the mother of Teresa Horvath could comfort herself with daydreams about Maggie's future.

Was this life, this barren life, all she'd earned from her years of planning and sacrifice? Where was justice? she cried out to herself. Surely there must be some accountability somewhere, some reward for having behaved with perfect judgment and foresight, some acknowledgment of all her sacrifice. Oh, she knew what a priest would say. He'd blather on about accepting the will of God and not looking for her reward here on earth. Sandor, too, would probably tell her to wait for Judgment Day, she thought grimly. That was the predictable way his mind worked. He'd missed his vocation, more's the pity.

True, Teresa had wanted to buy them a house and a new car and heaps of toys for Maggie as soon as she'd heard the amount that Zucker had negotiated for *Gemini Summer,* but Sandor had refused everything but the toys, and only allowed a few of them at that. He'd conferred with Teresa's business manager, Steve Miller, who also handled Fensterwald's and Zucker's money, and once he'd been satisfied that the man was highly qualified and honest, he'd informed Agnes that he had always earned enough to support his own family and he had no intention of taking a penny from his daughter. She must invest her salary sensibly, and as much of it as possible, for who knew how a career in acting might turn out in the passage of time?

Agnes added sugar to her tea and held the cup so that it warmed her cold hands. Still, the laughter came from above, shutting her out, just as she'd been shut out of everything else. When Teresa had started working on *Little Women* she'd become so busy that she might just as well have left home. She'd left school abruptly and against their wishes, but there was nothing they could do since she was over sixteen. Whatever little time she wasn't needed on the set was devoted, under Zucker's decree, to continuing her lessons in fancy new activities;

ballroom dancing, driving a car, horseback riding, and tennis.

Her own role, Agnes reflected as her tea grew cold, had long ago been reduced to running a bed and breakfast, nothing more than a necessary convenience for a daughter who grew more independent, more self-assured, and more sophisticated every day. It seemed as if a glittering scarf of Teresa's triumphs, a wide mantle of sparkling stars and silvery moons, flashed perpetually about her shoulders. This image burned into Agnes as she watched the happy girl dashing here and there on the rounds of her indisputably important life. At her parents' insistence, Teresa lived at home, but there was almost no time in her existence for her family, except the meals she ate at home.

Yet, until a few months after the release of *Little Women*, Teresa's life had possessed some element of stability. Until she won the Oscar in her first film role, the development of her career, even the time-devouring lessons, were on a level that could be comprehended.

But after the win, media madness had taken over and Teresa, unforgivably, had blossomed visibly every day yet maintained her poised excitement during every second of it, as if all the attention, flattering as she laughingly admitted it was, were only normal, only justified, *only her right*. She was consumed by the blaze of glory and the flourish of trumpets that the movie industry reserves for its newest royalty.

A Town Car and driver were at her beck and call. Fiona Bridges worked with the fashion designers whose clothes Teresa wore for her frequent appearances at premieres and award shows, chose her escorts, directed the girls who answered her mail, arranged time for journalists and photographers from all over the world, all with the advice of the publicity firm Roddy Fensterwald had recommended.

And now Teresa would be off, flying away to England with more brilliant success in sight . . . Mary Queen of Scots and Queen of the Isles, that most tenacious of Catholic queens, that passionately devout Queen . . . just the sound of the words was deeply romantic. Agnes sighed heavily, unable to bear her own dreary life.

"We're starving, Mother," Teresa said, bounding into the kitchen. "Is there anything to eat? Packing is hungry work."

"Finished already? But you'll be gone for months and months."

"All done! Fiona decided that almost all of my clothes just won't do, and anyway, I can buy whatever I need over there. I'll be in costume much of the time and she can always shop for anything I need. For big nights, designers will send me stuff."

"How convenient," Agnes said, glaring at Fiona, who didn't pay the slightest attention in her bland blondness, her impudent good humor, the efficiency that nothing blunted. It was Fiona who'd taken the place that rightfully belonged to Agnes. She was the lucky one who had all the fun and excitement of being intimately associated with a star, without carrying the burden and expectations of having to be the star herself. She, Teresa's mother, could have done anything Fiona did and done it better, Agnes thought in cold hurt.

"Mother? Food? I don't see anything interesting in the fridge, only boring old leftovers and the stuff you're making for dinner tonight—at least I guess that's what it is."

"Try calling room service," Agnes snapped and left the kitchen abruptly.

"Agnes," Sandor said that night, after Maggie had been put to bed, "What happened with you and Teresa this afternoon?"

"Nothing 'happened.' I barely saw her. You spent more time with her than I did before she and that Fiona creature went off together, who knows where?"

"She told me that you'd been upset with her because

she and Fiona invaded your domain demanding something to eat and she thought you were absolutely right, that you shouldn't be expected to cater to her when she's almost never home. She asked me to tell you that she was sorry to have been so thoughtless. She also said that when this next picture's over and she gets back to Hollywood, she's going to move out, get her own place, and become responsible for herself the way she should be at her age."

"High time," Agnes said stonily, refusing to betray her feelings of rejection.

"I didn't agree. I believe that it's only appropriate and proper for a young woman to live under her parents' roof until she gets married, and I told her so."

"So?"

"She made a case for herself. She said that first of all, legally now that she's twenty, there's nothing wrong with her living in her own home with Fiona to keep her company. But even more important was the fact that it doesn't make the slightest sense for us, in this small house, to be bothered with her constant phone calls. What's more, she needs space for bigger closets, a guest suite for Fiona, and space for a secretary to work. She wants room to entertain and a private space for business conferences. Obviously they'd both talked it all out, every detail. Finally I realized that Teresa made sense, much as I don't like it. We simply don't live in the style to accommodate the traffic and service a movie star has reason to expect. There's every reason why Teresa needs her own establishment and some sort of staff."

" 'Establishment'—I imagine that's a highfalutin word she used, or did she learn it from that degenerate, that pervert, Roddy Fensterwald?"

"Agnes! What does he have to do with her moving out? I disapprove totally of what he is, but I believe that he sincerely wants the best for Teresa—he's devoted to her—he's used all his skills to advance her career. How could she possibly have won an Oscar without his casting her and directing her?"

"Without me she'd have no career at all," Agnes said savagely. "And as for Fensterwald, who was responsible for that degrading piece of pornography we saw last night?"

"Now you know why I wouldn't allow you to take her to New York to be seen by talent agents when she was twelve, Agnes. I remember how frustrated and resentful you were then, but I knew that beauty is always exploited, even that of a twelve-year-old, and I prevented it as long as I could."

"So you approve of *Gemini Summer*?"

"Of course not! But it's out of our hands. We have to accept that, no matter how much we hate it."

"Damn you, Sandor! For a lifetime you insist that everything in our lives be as strictly Catholic as if you were the Pope's brother, and then, when you see Teresa becoming rich and famous, you suddenly turn into a philosopher! She's a sinner, Sandor, a sinner, have you forgotten? And she'll sin again once she lives in that 'establishment' she talked you into."

"I've forgiven the sin, Agnes, I've told you that before. Once the Church of Christ forgave her, once she received the Sacrament of Reconciliation, who was I not to forgive her?" Sandor asked, trying to keep his temper. "Since that time, Teresa has never been alone with a young man, as far as either of us knows. Her 'dates' are all arranged by the publicity people and she's always in a group. She's never been kissed except on the set with dozens of crew members watching. I consider her chaste, even if her film wardrobe was disgusting. But you've never forgiven, never forgotten, have you?" he said, his voice trembling with anger. "You've been clinging to your anger for years, holding and nourishing that anger in your breast, and that, Agnes, is most clearly a sin in the eyes of the Heavenly Father."

"Don't you try to tell me how to live in the eyes of God," she shouted, flooded with fury at the lofty, holier-than-thou voice in which he spoke, which always showed her so clearly that he considered her a less devout Catholic than he. "I'm the one who preserved our family's standing, I'm the one who figured out what to do about Maggie, I take care of her every day of every year. I had the vision to work and plan to give Teresa her chance, what would she be without me but another single mother with a kid to bring up . . . ?"

"Oh but you're proud, Agnes. You constantly commit the sin of presumption, you think you can save your soul without God's help. . . . Have you ever prayed to stop being angry at our daughter? Have you ever confessed that anger to a priest? Of course you haven't, because it's still with you and you can't let yourself give it up. Agnes, you're consumed by the deadly sin of envy. You envy our daughter her success. I see it on your face every day. Envy and pride, two of the deadly sins, Agnes, the mortal sins, the capital sins. Can you deny them?"

"You know nothing about me and you never have," she retorted, drawing herself up in rage and scorn. "But you, Sandor, have you looked at yourself? Where are your precious spiritual values now? Drowned in the sin of covetousness, that's where. Not for yourself but for your daughter. You've become greedy for her, willing for her to flaunt herself in any piece of trash if it pays well enough."

" 'Covetousness,' " he said slowly, shock on his fine features, "covetousness. . . . I hadn't thought, but perhaps you're right. I hadn't seen that in myself, but yes, it's not impossible . . . I'll discuss it with Father Vincent tomorrow, face-to-face in the rectory, the way we do now."

"Enjoy yourself, Sandor. Split hairs like a couple of cardinals. Perhaps Father Vincent will give you a little red biretta for your qualms of conscience. I'm going upstairs. I'll sleep in Maggie's room."

"Brian," Sandor Horvath said to his friend, Brian Kelly, Maggie's godfather. "We've come to know each other pretty well in the past few years, wouldn't you say?"

"Sure thing, Sandy. I'm only sorry that our wives haven't managed to hit it off better. When that happens it keeps couples from seeing as much of each other as I'd like."

"But at least you and I don't have that problem. I look forward to our lunches more than you realize."

"Same here, Sandy. Is there something wrong? You don't sound happy at the moment."

"Nothing wrong, just a favor I'd like to ask you, in your capacity as a godfather."

"Ask away."

"I've written a letter I'd like to have delivered thirteen years from now, if I'm not around to deliver it myself."

"Come on, quit kidding."

"I'm perfectly serious."

"Delivered to whom?"

"Maggie."

"You're not talking about a will?"

"You don't need a godfather for that, Brian."

"All right, assuming that you're not around, which isn't going to happen, what about Agnes?"

"It doesn't concern her. It's between me and Maggie. That's why you're the one person I can count on to make sure this letter gets to her, wherever she might be, when she's eighteen."

"Give it to me and forget about it, unless you change your mind. I'll keep it in my safe-deposit box until she's almost eighteen. It's not a date I'm likely to forget, is it? And if, God forbid, I'm not around myself, I'll have arranged for it to be delivered. People with as many kids as I have keep their wills in good shape . . . every year or so I disinherit another kid. Keeps them on their toes."

"You're not curious about what's in the letter?"

"Of course I am, but I know you wouldn't go to this trouble if it were something you could tell me."

"Thank you, Brian, you relieve my mind more than I can tell you."

"I'm glad to help, Sandy. We all love Maggie, you know. Whenever she comes over to play the kids can't get enough of her. What a funny little doll she is! Now, let's order and talk about something important, like my golf game."

9

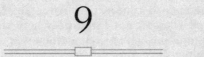

Yesterday, David Lean had told her that Mary Queen of Scots was the first woman known to have played golf, Tessa thought, trying to keep her mind occupied with that bit of trivia. Was the young queen also the first woman to have almost frozen to death in a room of the royal apartments of Edinburgh Castle while waiting for the sun to come from behind a cloud, or would Tessa Kent enjoy that distinction, she wondered? Clad in the elaborate construction of a dressing gown, fit for a nine-months-pregnant queen, with the great necklace of black pearls Mary always wore, and a mound of padding on her belly, Tessa stood motionless, framed by an imposing medieval window. Every rampart and sentinel tower of the castle was penetrated by the chill of hundreds of years of Scottish weather. The castle's dramatic height above the city exposed it to the wild wind whistling in from the sea.

Tessa, riveted to her mark by the window, from which there was a 270-foot sheer drop down basalt cliffs, told herself firmly that it was a warm afternoon in mid-June of 1566 when no woman of the period, much less a robust, hot-blooded, golfing queen, could possibly have felt the cold. Alas, she wasn't royal; she didn't golf; and her blood must have been thinned by years of exposure to the California climate, Tessa realized, despite her best attempts at time travel. After all, Macbeth had murdered Duncan not far from where she stood and what's more, she hadn't been warm, except in bed under two quilts, since the film company had arrived in Scotland.

Behind her she felt the tension of a unified crew praying for the precious rays of light to return, all conversation stilled in anticipation, every technician at the ready, the camera operator ready to roll film as soon as the director spoke. There was no question of her being replaced by her stand-in because of the potential waste of time. There were barely ten seconds left to be shot in this scene as the queen looks through the window into the distance of the Firth of Forth and speculates aloud about the importance of the sex of her anticipated child; but they needed those ten seconds to set the scene for the birth of the baby boy, James VI, who eventually became James I of England, heir to Queen Elizabeth I. Thank God, Tessa thought, for the next two days the script called for her to be in labor with James . . . that should be warmer work.

She began to shiver, slightly but uncontrollably. She didn't dare turn her head or move so much as a fingertip, for that would interrupt the continuity of the scene. She could only hope that when the sunlight reappeared, the shivering would stop as she became Mary Queen of Scots again. She should never have allowed her attention to wander during this pause in the work, it was totally unprofessional, she scolded herself. Suddenly Tessa heard the sound of quick footsteps moving toward her and, almost before she could wonder that anyone would dare to move on the set, she was engulfed in a heavy garment, deliciously warm from body heat, held around her tightly and protectively by a man's strong arms.

"What the hell do you expect from this girl, David?

Death in the line of duty?" a voice shouted as the sun appeared.

"You bloody, bloody fool!" her director screamed. "Take that thing off her and get the hell out of my set, you ass!"

"Can't," the strange voice said calmly. "There seems to be a button tangled in her wig."

"Wardrobe!" someone shouted, and Tessa felt quick, familiar fingers attempting to separate her wig from whatever was enveloping her so comfortingly. She stood as still as a mannequin until the coat was removed.

"Now look at her," the wardrobe woman cried in dispair. "The wig's all crooked and her necklace is broken! Hair, props, quickly!"

"Never mind, we've lost the light," David Lean said with immense frustration.

"Shit, I didn't realize . . ." the strange voice said.

"If I thought you had, I'd kill you with my bare hands, you crazy son of a bitch. Oh, Tessa, sorry. You can move now. Eddie, tell everyone it's a wrap for today."

Tessa turned, expecting to see the intruder being manhandled roughly off the set. Instead, he and Lean were wrapped in a laughing bear hug.

"Next time you do that, Luke, I'm throwing you headfirst through the nearest window."

"Just keeping an eye on my investment, David. You should really have somebody posted to keep out people like me," her would-be rescuer replied. "I didn't know you were shooting; there wasn't the slightest sound in here."

"You might have asked yourself why we were all standing around holding our breath, but all you saw was a lady in distress. I expect nothing less of you. Tessa, this is Luke Blake, unfortunately one of my most cherished friends. Luke, this is Tessa Kent."

"I appreciated feeling warm, even if it was only for a second," Tessa said, taking the hand he held out to her. It was the single warmest object she'd felt in three months, she thought, but she couldn't very well stand there and slip both her hands into its shelter as if it were a muff. Although she'd dearly like to, more than anything she could possibly think of. With her hand in this man's hand she felt more than warm, she felt safe, she thought in confusion—safe in a way she couldn't begin to explain, safe in a way she'd never felt before in her entire life.

Unconditional safety was not a state of being but a state of emotion, Tessa realized suddenly, an emotion stronger than any other, and until this very minute, unknown to her. A feeling of amazing discovery was rising in her chest, so powerful that she was afraid she was going to burst into tears. Such a thorough conviction . . . how was it possible? Her eyes sought Luke Blake's. Warmth was in them, too, a warmth as powerful as any force of nature, not the physical warmth of his hands but human warmth, telling her that he approved totally of everything about her and always would. His gaze had intelligence and humor, but it was the warmth that was all-important. Luke Blake must be the most likable man in the world. No wonder David Lean had forgiven him for spoiling the shot.

"Here, have my coat back," Luke Blake said. He was big and burly in his heavy ribbed wool sweater, with dark red, curly hair, cut very short; open, weathered features; a dominant nose; and a most authoritative flash in his blue eyes. He was obviously an urbane man, yet he had the look of someone who spends his life outdoors, Tessa thought, to say nothing of the unmistakably commanding set to his shoulders and his interestingly firm, imperious mouth with amused corners.

"Tessa's going right down to wardrobe," the director replied.

"Have it anyway, you don't need to freeze on the way there," Blake insisted, helping Tessa carefully into his duffel coat, giving her padded stomach a friendly pat. "Hello, James, you little rotter," he said. "Never even protested when Auntie Elizabeth cut off your mother's head, did you? Kids—always looking out for themselves."

Australian . . . why did it take me so long to realize? Tessa wondered as his slight but perceptible accent registered.

"Why, Luke, can you possibly have been reading history?" Lean asked in amusement.

"Certainly. Enough so that I know what happens to Mary after the film's over. I don't have tunnel vision, unlike you, David, I get interested in these characters. When you're finished with Mary you'll be roaring off with another script and another bunch of actors, forgetting that poor girl imprisoned by her cousin for twenty years, you can't deny that."

"You make me feel like a savage," he laughed.

"All directors are savages, couldn't be such heartless buggers if they weren't, letting Miss Kent stand there covered in goose bumps. You're a disgrace. I'm almost ashamed to know you. However, in view of the past, dinner tonight?"

"Of course."

"Good-bye, Mr. Blake," Tessa said, resisting the pull of the wardrobe mistress. Maybe he'll invite me too, she thought. "How should I get your coat back to you?"

"Don't give it a thought, I have others. Anyway, aren't you and I planning on dinner tomorrow night? We can discuss it then."

"You're staying around?" Lean asked, in surprise.

"Indefinitely. If I'm welcome."

"I warn you, one false step and I'll glue you to the floor."

"A small price to pay."

"Tell me about her, David," Luke Blake asked as they sat down to dinner, without formality or preliminary.

"You might at least ask how I am, and how the film's

going, it's your twenty-five million pounds that's paying for it, as I remember."

"Bloody details. Tell me about Tessa Kent and stop playing games, cobber," Luke said, grinning fondly at the great director.

"She's out of your class, boy."

"Who decided that?"

"Everyone. I've known you too long. You have a bad record. Forty-five years old and never married, the man who's kept half the available great ladies of the last quarter century. A famous moving target who, to my knowledge, has never come close to love as we mortals define it. You're asking about a barely twenty-year-old kid who's more innocent than any actress I've ever worked with, a girl who still lives at home. Not your kind of material, old friend, not in your wildest dreams. Not bedable, not keepable, not obtainable at any price."

"So it would seem."

"Don't even think about it," he said warningly.

"And I thought you were a pal, David."

"As a pal, I'm asking you an important question: Why make yourself miserable? There are some things in life, even in the life of Luke Blake, that not only can't happen and won't happen, but shouldn't happen, and Tessa Kent is one of them."

" 'Shouldn't'? I don't see where you get the authority—or the bloody nerve—to make that judgment."

"The age difference."

"Besides that?" he said, waving it away.

"She's a virgin."

"I have to admit that you're never wrong on that score."

"And a Catholic."

"Well, so am I as a matter of fact, lapsed thirty years ago, but still a cradle Catholic, to say nothing of having been a splendidly efficient altar boy."

"You'd never set out to seduce a twenty-year-old virgin, Luke, that's just not your style." Lean laughed.

"You're right, I'm basically a good sort of chap. What I can't stand about you, cobber, is that you know all my weaknesses, all the decent things about me I try to hide. They could hurt my captain-of-industry image."

"Not fair, is it?"

"Not at all. Where'd the whiskey get to?"

"The waiter's bringing it. How's the beer business, Luke?"

"Better than ever. Who would have thought, when my sainted great-granddad started making the stuff, that Australians would drink absolutely any amount they could get?"

"Anybody who had brains."

"Yeah, you're right. Dry, hot, thirsty work, being an Aussie. It turned out to be a lot better business move than if he'd tried to find gold the way everyone else was doing at the time." Luke laughed.

"Are you the richest man in Australia, Luke?"

"Damn close, David, but not my fault, just born into the right family. Beer was so damn good to Great-granddad, David, that the next generation was able to buy the gold and copper mines other men had discovered. Then Granddad expanded into railroads and cattle ranching and timber, leaving me old dad to move right into the oil companies and the steel mills—amazingly complicated, a fascinating business. What's more, we're still selling beer to the whole world."

"What about that guy they call Bad Dennis Brady?"

"He's probably richer than I am, but he's a loafer, not interested in making more money, spends all his time on the Riviera gambling, lets his board of directors make all the decisions. You'd never catch me doing that. I think of myself as the company's chief troubleshooter, and we have companies all over the world now."

"Don't you consider your investing in pictures gambling?"

"It's my hobby, cobber. Or call it informed risk taking. With you, the risk is so substantially reduced that it almost qualifies as another business."

"Show business is always a risk, trust me. Your hobby's still a hobby. Shall we look at the menu?"

"I'm going to be late," Tessa moaned in agitation to Fiona, who was helping her get dressed.

"So what, he should understand that you've been having a baby all day and it takes a heap of cleaning up to look good after that kind of hard labor."

"I hate being late," Tessa said, frantically trying to brush the last of the tangles out of her hair. "The hair stylist sprayed my hair until it was plastered down, and the makeup artist went overboard—she made me look as if I were being tortured to death instead of just having contractions."

"You look gorgeous now, for God's sake," Fiona said. "You've been fussing for an hour. Sit still in front of the mirror, I want to show you something important." As Tessa obediently looked at herself in the mirror, Fiona put her finger on Tessa's nose, just below her eye, and traced the shape of the bone leading to her eyebrow and her eyebrow itself. "This happens to be one of the most bewitching curves on any face in history, a space unpoetically called an eye socket that you've grown up with and take totally for granted. So stop fussing with your hair, Tessa. What man would care about your hair when you have those eye sockets? And I won't even mention your smile, you know too much about it already. What's the matter with you, anyway? Luke Blake's got to be more than twice your age, and let me tell you, the man's been around the block a time or two or ten."

"You're nothing but a common gossip, but since you grew up reading the English tabloid press, I shouldn't be surprised." Tessa stared at her eye sockets with new interest. Could Fiona possibly be right?

"Hah! Gossip my ass! If he dropped dead tonight, his

New York Times obit would start, 'Luke Blake, major Australian industrialist and world-class pussy-hound, died in Edinburgh yesterday.'"

"Fiona, why are you such a spoilsport? Can't you let me enjoy myself? I've never gotten dressed for a real date before and you know it. All I'm doing is having dinner with a man who was nice enough to try to keep me warm."

"I'm trying to warn you, in my own subtle way."

"You think he's going to try to add me to his list of conquests?"

" 'Think'? I haven't the slightest doubt of his motives. I bet he's never bought a woman dinner without the intention of getting her into bed in the back of his mind—no, make that the front of his mind. And succeeding nine point nine times out of ten."

"Fiona, have you ever gone out with a man without the possibility of sex, not necessarily that night, but maybe, just maybe, sex *sometime,* entering into the disgusting swamp of your brain?"

"Oh! Shit!"

"Aha!"

"You're right. I'm as bad as any man ever born. That is if we're not considering obvious noncandidates, like, oh, let's see, the local minister, or college professors, or my best friends' fathers, men like that."

"I wouldn't trust you with any of the categories you just mentioned, except my own father." Tessa laughed, doing up her black velvet pants and standing so that Fiona could zip her into her black velvet Regency-cut jacket, trimmed with a heavy white-lace standup collar, and cuffs that fell to her fingers.

"Come to think of it . . . yeah, college professors . . ." She hummed thoughtfully. "Of course, I never went to college, so I wouldn't know."

"Neither did I. Never even finished high school. But there were a couple of cute nuns at Marymount . . ."

"Go, meet that man, Tessa, you fool." Fiona shooed her out of their suite. "He's still waiting in the lobby.

Shall I stay up for you to come home so you can tell me all about it?"

"Goodnight, Fiona. See you tomorrow."

"Thank you for the thermal long johns and the electrically heated socks," Tessa said as she sat down to dinner in the small, perfectly appointed French restaurant with tables set at a pleasant distance from each other. "They came this morning first thing."

"Did they help?" Luke asked, barely able to speak as he looked at her face framed in white lace. She was like a portrait of a young Renaissance princess, so radiantly, luminously beautiful that you could study the painting for hours, yearning to have been alive when she existed in real time.

"Actually, I had to take them off after the first half hour. Mr. Lean's childbirth scene was messy, sweaty stuff, but the baby's going to be born tomorrow, thank goodness, and after that they'll be more useful than you can imagine."

"How does a virgin know how to play a woman having a baby?"

"Exactly how do you know I'm a virgin?"

"Oh." He fell silent and dropped his eyes in embarrassment.

"Is it common knowledge, does it show somewhere, or did you just assume it?" Tessa demanded, her eyes flashing mischief.

"David told me," he admitted.

"Out of the blue? As if virgins are as rare as unicorns and you had to be alerted when there's one in the neighborhood, like a special tourist attraction?"

"Actually he was warning me not to pursue you."

"I hope you told him to mind his own damn business."

"Something more or less like that."

"Does he also think I'm not old enough to be let out alone with such a hardened sinner as you?"

"Definitely that, at the very least. Who told you I was a hardened sinner?"

"Everybody. It's common knowledge, as famous as my deplorable virginity."

"Well, that makes us even, doesn't it? Two of a kind? Two of an opposite kind, that is." I'm babbling, he thought. I'm not making sense, except, I don't feel foolish.

"That makes us people who shouldn't even be having dinner together," Tessa said serenely.

"Is that why I feel so blazingly happy with you?"

"I don't know." She shrugged her shoulders in an eloquent gesture of lyrical, shameless ignorance. "I don't know you at all, certainly not what makes you happy. I just know you're kind and good and I feel something with you I don't feel with anybody else, not even Roddy."

" 'Roddy'?" he asked, feeling a shaft of jealously more intense than he'd experienced in forty-five years.

"Roddy Fensterwald. He directed my first two pictures."

"I know him, great guy," Luke signed in relief. "What is it you feel with me that you don't feel with Roddy?"

"Safe," she said quietly. It took all her courage, but she was determined to tell him. "Totally and completely safe. As if nothing bad can possibly happen to me, as if you'll protect me from all the frightening, hard, awful things in the world. It's crazy, it makes no sense at all, I've just met you, but in my whole life I've never felt that way before. It's like discovering that I can be a completely new person. It's as different as—as if I woke up and discovered I was six feet tall and had just won the Olympic gold medal in ski jumping. It happened to me yesterday when we shook hands. I decided I should tell you because it's too important to keep secret. I don't mean to make you feel any sense of obligation, I don't realistically expect you to take care of me for a single second, that's not what it's about in any way—but I wanted you to know."

"You don't frighten me."

"I wasn't trying to."

"You have to know that what you just said would scare the living Jesus out of most men."

"I felt you were tough enough to take it. And if I'm wrong, it's better for me to know now. I thought about it all night."

"I thought about you all night long, too."

"What sort of things?" she asked without coyness.

"About the facts that you're very young and a virgin. I discovered how amazingly important that virginity is to me, and I never knew that about myself. Your age isn't of consequence, you're definitely a grown-up and that's the essential thing—but the fact that you've never made love with a man—that's different. Altogether different. I've been with a lot of women, but there wasn't one of them who didn't have some experience. It's got to be the old altar boy in me—I have absolutely no right at all, considering the life I've led, to prize virginity so much. I'm not absolutely clear on why virginity is deeply, mysteriously meaningful, and, for me, wonderful beyond words—but it is. Enormously. Maybe it has something to do with my mother and her mother. They were both virgins when they married—naturally in those days—but my mother always told me how important it would be to her for me to marry a virgin. I discounted it, I thought she was simply being a good Catholic, but nevertheless she got to me. More than I can say."

Tell him now, Tessa thought. *Tell him now, before this conversation goes further.* But tell him what? She *was* a virgin, in every technical way, and giving birth hadn't changed that fact. The three-second episode with what's his name didn't count, couldn't possibly matter, she'd been drunk and not responsible and it wasn't remotely sex. The only kisses she'd ever experienced had been before a camera. She'd never even been allowed to go out on an unsupervised date. There was nothing to tell, except the part she'd confessed and been absolved of, and that was between her God and herself. She took a deep breath and sat back in her chair, glad to forget the ridiculous, self-defeating idea of telling him the truth.

"Is that what makes you feel happy with me, my all-too-much-discussed state of virginity?" Tessa asked with wry curiosity.

"I felt that way almost before I knew damn-all about you except that you were freezing. It started right after I put my coat around you. It's something about your eyes and your smile and your voice—if I'm not careful I'm going to sound like lyrics to a Gershwin song, minus the wit and invention."

"All those women you've had, did they make you happy?"

"Not one, not truly, or I'd have married her."

"You don't frighten me, either," Tessa said as lightly as she could, suppressing a tremor with her actress's skill. She had to change the subject or the surprising, inexplicable tears of joy that menaced her might rise to the surface. She felt atoms of happiness swirling and churning and slowly turning into a solid pillar somewhere in her chest. "What sort of things do you like to do?"

"Sail a small boat and fly a small plane," he said, thinking of priorities, "and marinate a rack of home-grown lamb in my homemade sauce, and dance a samba in Brazil and eat a Peking duck at Mr. Chow's in London and read until three a.m. and go to auctions and ski the fall line and, oh, I almost forgot, kiss pretty girls. And take care of my business. What about you?"

"Me? Not fair!" Tessa said indignantly, instantly jealous of his easily produced list of delights that included so much enviable experience that had nothing to do with her. "I haven't had time to choose what I'd like to do because I've been so busy taking the lessons Roddy and Aaron decided I should take. I can dance, but not a samba, whatever that is. I love to read, but I don't even know what a Peking duck looks like. You're overprivileged, Luke Blake. Where do you live?"

"Here and there, more or less. I have a place in Melbourne and another in Cap-Ferrat, near Monaco, but I rarely spend more than a few weeks in Australia and a few weeks in the South of France every year. That's where I go to sail and unwind. I have business all over the world, so I roam about, living in hotel suites most of the time."

"What sort of business?"

"Mining, milling, brewing, finding new ways to dig things out of the earth."

"Why can't you just leave the earth alone?" she said, provokingly.

"I often wonder. My great-grandfather started it and I'm trapped in the family business. Now too many people depend on me to even think of stopping."

"Under the circumstances, with all this rape of the planet you're hopelessly involved in, in spite of certain philosophic reservations, for which I give you very little credit, don't you think we might have something to eat?"

"Did I forget to order?" he asked in wonder.

"Not even a drink."

"Lord, I'm sorry. What will you have?"

"I'll try a Blake's, see what all the fuss is about."

"You've never had a Blake's?"

"Never had a beer, actually."

"Why the hell not? You're hurting my feelings."

"I used to experiment with real liquor when I was a kid, a day student at a convent, and I was being naughty with my friend Mimi, but then . . . we stopped . . . and I haven't had a drink since, except for sips of champagne at family weddings. I've lived at home, you see, until I left for location on this picture, and my parents never keep liquor around, so I didn't drink on dates— well they weren't date dates, just publicity things."

"Lucky David didn't know about all this. He'd have locked you in your room, and me in mine."

"Don't tell him anything! My reputation's too good as it is."

"Waiter, two Blake's, please."

"I'll try, sir," answered the waiter in the most authentically French restaurant in the aristocratic, sophisticated old city. "But I'm not sure we have that particular brand of beer." Amazing, he thought, why don't they ask for Coca-Cola while they're at it?

"Shocking. Well then, bring us a bottle of champagne. I'm sure you have Dom Pérignon. What shall we drink to, Tessa?"

"My first real grown-up date," she said with decision.

"You don't mean—you can't mean—me?"

"You. And about time, I think."

"Good God in Heaven!"

"Yes, indeed."

10

--------☐--------

The next morning Tessa was pulling on her jeans and sweaters for her early-morning wardrobe call when Fiona came in with a note and a bunch of pallid daffodils. Tessa tore open the note, read it twice, turned quickly, and hurled the daffodils into a wastepaper basket.

"He's gone!"

"What? Let me see that." Fiona grabbed the slip of paper and muttered, "Have to leave for London suddenly, hotel florist not open, hope you like daffodils, keep warm, et cetera, et cetera."

"Do you believe that?" Tessa raved.

"I still don't know how last night ended," Fiona said, reaching for a pragmatic tone.

"He brought me back to the hotel, escorted me up to the door to our suite, looked into my eyes for a very long time, as if he were memorizing them, kissed me gently on the top of my head, and abruptly left, leaving me standing there stupidly waiting—I don't know what I expected but it was definitely not that after we'd both said things . . . things that I thought meant . . . obviously I was wrong . . . meant that we liked each other very much. More than very much. Oh, Fiona, we *weren't* flirting, I was so sure of that. We were speaking from our hearts."

Tessa's eyes were full of incredulous disappointment, deception, and disbelief. She felt utterly abandoned in a way so basic that she could barely comprehend what had happened. How could she ever reconcile last night's long dinner, and the intimate, serious, revealing conversation that had lasted until late in the evening, with the note she'd just received? Until she'd read it, she'd been plunged into a pool of tremulous emotion, so new in her experience of life that she'd been up all night long, alternately examining everything she had said to Luke and Luke had said to her, reliving every detail, abandoned to her happiness, her heart so full that she'd wept for joy and laughed at herself and wept again.

"But Tessa, he doesn't say he isn't coming back," Fiona said, as briskly as she could, but still sounding only a hollow note of hope.

"When? The very next time he has business in Scotland. Between trains in five years." Tessa abandoned her attempt at brittle scorn and cried out, "What kind of man could do a thing like this? *What kind*, Fiona? Can you explain it? You've been around, you know men. Is it typical, is it something I should have expected? He 'had to leave for London'? Why didn't he even mention that detail last night when he was so busy telling me how blazingly happy—yes, those were the words he used—I made him? Can you think of a single reason, even one, that makes any sense? I know that Mr. Lean expected him to stick around for a while. He mentioned that yesterday."

"Damn, I was afraid of this," Fiona said viciously. "A bloody hit-and-run driver."

"You were so right. And you can say 'I told you so' as much as you want to—I deserve it. Oh, what a fool I was!"

"At least he didn't get the pearl of precious price."

"That's probably *why* he left, it's the only thing that I can think of to explain his running away. He has a virgin fixation. I believe that in his crazy, mixed-up mind I'm too pure, I'm *taboo,* somebody he shouldn't possibly have anything to do with. Not even a kiss on the lips. Messing with a virgin is against whatever religion he has left, he said it as flatly as that."

"Tessa darling, I'm sick that you've been so badly hurt, but Luke Blake wasn't for you and you knew it all along. Come on, admit it. My God, the guy's middle-aged and more than lived-in. You're ten thousand times too good for him, too young, too fresh, too talented, with too many wonderful things that are going to happen to you. Your life's just beginning. What did you see in him, anyway? It's just one of those location things, happens all the time. And what's this virgin fixation all about. It's utterly ridiculous!"

"He'd heard, as apparently everybody in the whole of show business has, that I'm a virgin, and he's a lapsed Catholic, thirty years lapsed, which is plenty lapsed, believe me, but it's still left him with a major complex about the marvel of virginity. Sick, that's what it is, sick! *Oh, I hate him!*"

"The bastard's not worth hating. Don't waste your energy. You're going to be late as it is and you have a long day's work. Come on, let's go. They'll feed us in wardrobe and that's what we need, both of us. Daffodils! Those grimy little things. It would have been better to have sent nothing. It's odd, but I feel *personally* insulted."

"You know what's really and truly the worst thing about all this," Tessa asked Fiona in a flood of fresh misery as they were driven up to the castle. "I can't trust my instincts ever again."

"I don't see why. You can't trust your reactions to this particular man, I agree, but instincts in general, why not?"

"I had a feeling, an overpowering feeling about him, as soon as I met him. He made me feel, don't laugh

Fiona, but he made me feel completely, wonderfully . . . *safe* . . . safe in a way that changed my whole life. That sounds impossible now, but it happened. I thought I couldn't be wrong. You can't imagine how intimately we talked. I told him so many things, things I thought, things I hoped, things I believed in. In fact, I even told him about how he made me feel in considerable detail . . . I probably should never . . ." Tessa faltered and stopped.

"If you ask me—" Fiona bit her lip in dismay and wished she'd never indicated that she had an opinion. Tessa was so young, so inexperienced, so protected, such a child in so many ways, God knows what she'd said to that hardened charmer, words that any other woman would have learned not to voice long ago.

"What? Go on, you're older and wiser, *what?*"

"You're right, you shouldn't have told him. It wasn't just the untouchable virgin thing that sent him flying away, it was the idea of responsibility. You made him responsible for your emotions, and what kind of guy can accept such a heavy trip from someone he hardly knows, no matter how he feels? He just couldn't take it. The proof is his history, not even a divorce to his credit. I hate to use that awful word 'commitment,' but I'll bet this is a man who's frightened to even have a dog, much less a woman, in his heart. Listen, Tessa, you're still in one piece, that's the important thing. Men aren't as courageous about emotions as women, remember that."

"Or as smart or as sweet," Tessa said, hugging Fiona.

"Too true, love. I just wish we didn't have those crazy moments when we forget that."

Three days later, on a Saturday afternoon, Tessa found herself alone in her suite. Fiona had just left for the orgy she'd promised herself all week, a cashmere shopping trip in the heart of cashmere country, but Tessa was too deeply plunged into depression to feel any temptation to go with her. She'd slept only fitfully and eaten almost nothing, unable to stop going over the fatal dinner in her mind. Only sheer discipline had enabled her to get out of bed each morning and go to the set. All her energy had bled away, except what she had to summon for the camera. Worried, Fiona had threatened not to leave her alone this afternoon, until Tessa had convinced her that she'd feel guilty for life if Fiona missed this opportunity.

She didn't want a single sweater or scarf that reminded her of Edinburgh, Tessa thought apathetically. She couldn't wait to leave Scotland next week after the film wrapped and she was free to return to gloriously warm Los Angeles. What she needed was a good book. She all but dragged herself over to look through the large, tempting stock of paperbacks she'd brought with her. Nothing seemed remotely readable, although she'd chosen the books carefully before leaving California. Like many actresses, Tessa had learned early the advantage of having a good book always on hand for the inevitable waiting around that takes place on even the busiest film set.

"You should learn to play solitaire," she said out loud to her reflection in the mirror. Her eyes, in the clear northern light, seemed more distinctly green than ever, although they never lost their faint overlay of gray, like the most illusive wisp of smoke through a tropical rain forest. "Eye sockets," she said mournfully, "a hell of a lot of difference they made."

The phone rang. "Mr. Blake would like to know if he may come up, Miss Kent," the concierge said.

"*No!*" Tessa slammed down the phone, her depression turned into a lightning strike of pure rage. What was he doing here? Come back to feast his eyes on a virgin, like some sort of vampire? Come up to say good-bye forever, I'm off to fly my plane around the world, come up to tell her about the delights of the latest Peking duck he'd gorged himself on in London? Or the dozen pretty girls he'd kissed? She wouldn't bother to spit on his shadow.

The phone rang again. "What is it this time?" Tessa asked furiously.

"Mr. Blake would like to know when it would be convenient for you to see him."

"Never! Never, tell him that, tell him I said never, and I mean never! And don't call me again. I've been working all week, I'm trying to rest and you keep interrupting me, don't you understand that?"

"I'm most dreadfully sorry, Miss Kent, it won't happen again. I'll put a 'Do Not Disturb' on your line."

"Do that."

She was so angry she found herself pacing the floor, unable to sit still. They say that murderers can't keep away from the scene of the crime. Come to gloat, had he, she thought bitterly? Not if she knew it!

There was a knock on the door.

"Yes?" Tessa said neutrally. It was probably the maid.

"Let me in, Tessa," Luke Blake demanded.

"*I will not.*"

"What's wrong with you? Didn't you get my note?"

"It came."

"Then why won't you let me in?"

"I don't want to see you."

"That's impossible, of course you do."

"God damn! Get away from my door or I'll have you thrown out of the hotel."

"I own this hotel."

"Is that supposed to be some sort of threat? It's as unimportant as everything else about you. I don't care if you own this whole miserable city!"

"Tessa!" he shouted, his voice severe in its demand.

She didn't answer, waiting for him to leave. Several minutes passed before she heard his footsteps retreating. In less time than seemed possible, Tessa heard the tramp of heavy footsteps and a shout of warning to stand back, then saw the door to her suite splinter under an assault from two burly firemen armed with axes.

"It's in the bedroom," Luke directed them. As they

rushed to the bedroom he looked at Tessa, open-mouthed and immobile in shock, standing in her old, quilted pink bathrobe. "I should have guessed it," he said finally. "You detest daffodils."

"Are you insane?"

"Probably. But what does that have to do with it?"

"I have nothing to say to you. Get out of here, you and those firemen."

"Chaps?"

"Yes, Mr. Blake."

"It's okay, Miss Kent managed to put it out herself. I'll have the door put right tomorrow." He tipped them and sent them off.

"Tessa, I'm utterly hopeless at writing to people, I should have called . . ."

"There was nothing to say." She tightened the sash of the bathrobe around her waist and grew taller in freezing dignity as she looked at him with biting scorn, her eyes dismissing him as the smallest and least worthy of any pitifully abject creature that has ever crawled on the face of the earth.

"But, at dinner—"

"Forget that dinner, wipe it out of your mind. I was feeling exceptionally vulnerable, I said things I didn't mean . . . I was being actressy . . . over the top, I didn't realize how far over I'd gone or how ridiculous I'd been until it was too late. Obviously you're accustomed to saying things you don't mean, you've been doing it for a long time, haven't you? I didn't understand that since I haven't met your kind of man before, fortunately for me. Once is more than enough."

"Tessa, I meant every word."

"Oh, please, Luke, that's not necessary," she said, producing a marvelously indifferent ghost of a smile. "I don't need your empty reassurance, although why you feel the need to repeat your performance is beyond me. Does this amuse you in some twisted manner? I'm tired, and I'd like you to leave at once."

"God, I'm a fool! You couldn't have known, no wonder you're acting like an avenging angel."

"Known what?"

"I went to London to get something for you, something important I'd known existed for years, but the man I thought had it said he'd just sold it, so I had to go to New York and it turned out I had the wrong information so I had to go to Geneva. I got there in the nick of time, Sotheby's was selling it at auction the next day, so I had to stay overnight. . . . Anyway . . . here it is."

He took a small blue leather box from his pocket and tried to give it to her.

"I don't want anything from you," Tessa said, recoiling.

"I keep getting it wrong." Luke hit himself on the forehead in frustration. "I've never done this before; I don't have any practice. Could I start over?"

"I asked you to leave," Tessa repeated, with no hint of thaw in the glacial hardness of her voice.

"Tessa, hear me out," Luke demanded, standing foursquare in the middle of the room. "Before we even had dinner I knew that you and I were going to get married. I'd given up hoping that I'd ever find a woman I could love, and then, you—*you, Tessa, you happened to me*. One word from you and from that second on there was never the slightest doubt about it in my mind. I knew, spot on. My God, that sounds as if I think this is all about me and what I want, but it isn't. It's about you, too. So I decided it had to be something special, your engagement ring I mean. That's what's in the box."

"You've spent three days chasing after an engagement ring for somebody you've never even asked to marry you? Is this some kind of playboy's bad joke?" Tessa asked, so armored against him that she was unable to recognize the sound of truth in his words.

"Don't you want to marry me?" Luke asked, surprise in his voice for the first time.

"Marry you? How would I know something as important as that after one dinner?" Tessa responded, with the first possibility of belief. She had fought against hope from the moment she'd received his letter; refusing to let hope enter her mind was the only way she knew to deal with her deception.

"It was much more than dinner," Luke said relentlessly. "You said you loved me and I said I loved you."

"Never!" she shouted, outraged again. "The word 'love' never passed my lips, or yours."

"Tessa, it was the subtext of our entire conversation, of every word we said to each other," he insisted.

"No, it was not!"

"Then listen to the simple text, Tessa. I love you, you're the only woman I've ever loved, and I insist that you marry me," Luke informed her, more commanding than ever, his eyes dominating her eyes, refusing to let her get away from him, continuing to defy her attempts to build a safe emotional barrier between them.

"So, you 'insist' do you? That's irresistibly romantic," she said as scornfully as she could. She must not hope.

"Answer me," he demanded.

"I don't have to," Tessa answered, holding on to her grievance as if it were a bastion that would keep her safe from the future.

"Ah, I knew, damn it, I *knew* I should have called, but I was running from one airport to another and I'm sorry you don't like daffodils—"

"I *adore* daffodils!"

"Don't you love me?" Luke asked. "Can you look at me honestly and say that you don't?"

"I don't know how I feel," Tessa answered, maintaining her dignity. She could refuse to hope, but she couldn't look at him and say she didn't love him.

"Will you marry me, Tessa?" he asked, unsmiling.

She looked thoughtful, considering the situation. Did a proposal of marriage constitute a basis for hope, or would she make a fool of herself again?

"Tessa, Tessa, please say you will." He was finally reduced to pleading, something he didn't know how to do. "You're driving me mad and I know you're enjoying yourself, damn it. Don't say you're not, because I won't believe you. All I want is a yes. I don't deserve it, but love has nothing to do with merit."

Tessa turned away, to hide the fact that her eyes had filled with tears of joy. Pushed to the wall, she acknowledged that she'd never been able to truly get over the hope that he'd return, not even for a second, not in her lowest minutes. She finally admitted to herself that all her life had been spent wandering around the wrong galaxy, looking, although she hadn't known it, for this one particular man, this one particular destiny, and no other. It took her seconds of intense concentration to be able to speak clearly, but she wanted her words to be uncompromising.

"I love you totally, and I wanted to marry you the minute you took my hand."

"Thank God," he said with inutterable relief, stepping forward, gathering her in his arms and kissing her lips over and over until she couldn't bear the burden of such confusing, unfamiliar rapture for another second. She pushed him away long enough to whisper, "Where's that ring that's so special that you made me suicidal over it for three days?"

"It must be here someplace." He groped around on the floor until he found the box he'd dropped. Luke turned on a lamp against the twilight that was creeping into the room and opened the lid.

Tessa looked at it mutely, as if a piece of a star had materialized in the room. It was a perfect heart-shaped stone, cut in facets, as big, she thought, as a huge chunk of hard candy—and it was green, a marvelously soft green, the most mysterious, elusive color she'd ever seen.

"It's the color of your eyes in a certain light," Luke told her as she stared at it, still speechless. "It's a green diamond, the rarest of natural colors after red, and red was wrong. Except for the 'Dresden Green,' this is the biggest green diamond in the world. What's more, it's a chameleon."

" 'Chameleon'?"

"It changes color. It's the only diamond that does so. It turns yellow in the dark. I thought that would be convenient for finding you in the middle of the night. I knew I had to have it for you, instead of some obvious blue-white rock."

"It's shockingly beautiful," Tessa said, daring to lean a little closer to the ring.

"It's all right for a beginning, but just barely. Will you put it on, Tessa, darling?"

"It will change my life," Tessa said, with a faint, odd feeling of reluctance. The ring, in spite of the soft fire of its color, was as triumphant, as regal as a queen's tiara. Was she ready to wear it, to carry it off? It had implications she couldn't begin to understand, but she knew they were buried in the extraordinary stone.

"Any engagement ring I give you will change your life, even if it's just a cigar band."

"True," she replied, gathering the courage to extend her hand. The ring fit her finger perfectly. It sat there like a tame butterfly from a magic planet far away. Suddenly Tessa exploded in giggles.

"What's so funny?"

"Fiona! Fiona . . . she said I was ten thousand times too good for you, and I agreed . . . now how am I going to explain this?"

"Tell her she's absolutely spot on, but I bribed you."

"Luke, tell me," Tessa asked, hiding her laughter in his strong neck. "Do you really own this hotel?"

"Not likely. It belongs to one of Bad Dennis Brady's companies. I just said I was him when I called the firemen so they'd come more quickly. People can't tell one Aussie from another, you'll find out. Anyway, there might have been a fire, you could have been burning my note."

"I threw it away. Don't ever write me again," she commanded, "unless you learn to express yourself properly."

"I'm never going to be far enough away from you to need to write."

11

Holy shit, Tessa, you can't do it!" Aaron Zucker screamed, holding the phone as close to his mouth as possible—as if Tessa would be convinced by the sheer volume of his conviction.

"Give me one good reason." Tessa laughed. "By the way, you're invited, too, so get your plane tickets right away, it's only ten days away."

"One good reason, holy shit, I'll give you twenty. This is madness! You have offers for the leads in the three best scripts I've seen in years, you're the hottest new star in decades since *Gemini Summer* was released, you'd be throwing away opportunities right and left that I'd give my left nut for, you're too young, you've never left home before, you don't know this man, in fact you don't know diddly about men in general or, even worse, in particular—don't try to tell me you do because I've followed every move you've made since Roddy cast you in *Little Women*. You're making a life decision without my guidance—"

"Aha, I thought that was it," Tessa chortled, delighted with herself. "I'm getting married without my agent's approval, that's your real problem, Aaron. Your feelings are hurt. When I called Roddy, he said the same thing, almost word for word, if you substitute 'fucking stupid' for 'holy shit.' "

"I'll bet your parents don't approve either," Aaron shouted.

"I haven't told them yet. Isn't it any satisfaction to you to know that I called you and Roddy with my news first?"

"Why haven't you called them?" he asked suspiciously. "I bet it's because you're sure they won't approve either."

"I'm sure they'll be happy for me, so I wanted to get the two of you fussbudgets over with first."

"And what's the big rush? Not only don't you know the guy—why do you have to get married ten days from now? It's obviously not a shotgun wedding. I just don't get it."

"We won't have time for a honeymoon if we don't—Luke has to be back in Australia in three weeks. But most of all we don't want it to turn into a circus, we want to keep it as private as possible. No publicity, Aaron, that's the most important thing, and you must help me on that. I'm counting on you."

"What did you say this guy Luke's last name was again?" Aaron asked in a more normal volume, hearing in Tessa's voice her determination to do this insane thing no matter what he thought about it.

"Blake."

"Like the beer?"

"He is the beer."

"You're marrying a brewer?" he asked incredulously.

"His great-grandfather was the brewer. Luke's basically in mining and other stuff too complicated to explain."

"He's THAT Luke Blake? Holy shit! How? Where? When? What a story!"

"So now you're impressed? So now it's all right with you, now you're excited for me? Aaron, I'm ashamed of you."

"Isn't Luke Blake, Tessa, come on, *Luke Blake*, a little . . . mature . . . for you?"

"Nope. We're perfect for each other. Our ages don't matter one little bit."

"Okay, whatever you say, but Tessa, what about your career?"

"I'll still make movies, but only one a year."

"WHAT? Tessa, you can't mean it! One a year . . . why not just retire, turn into a little housewife and get it over with?"

"Now, now, Aaron, don't exaggerate. Luke and I have discussed the whole thing thoroughly. Outside of one film a year, I'll be with him and when I'm working, he'll stay wherever I am."

"Where will you be based?" Aaron moaned.

"I have no idea. Luke's a rover, he goes where the problems are, we'll be gypsies together, with a place in Cap-Ferrat and one in Melbourne, for whenever we both have some time off."

"One picture a year," Aaron said, regaining a little composure. "So you'd count on three months shooting, four maximum, plus pre- and postproduction. Well," he sighed deeply, "it might not be everything that it could have been, considering how fast you've become a star, but one film a year, if it's the right one, will be enough to keep your career on a steady track."

"You're feeling better already, aren't you, Aaron? But no scripts, no matter how good, that need a day more than three months shooting time—I don't want to hear a word about four—or anything but the shortest time for hair and wardrobe beforehand, Aaron. Do you get that? Only send me stuff with a predictable normal amount of looping, no location shoots, no period scripts, no water, no kids, no animals, no Scotland. You'll have to be very picky or I won't consider it."

"Picky is my middle name."

"Holy Shit is your middle name. When are you getting your plane tickets?"

"Today, today! But why are you getting married in Monaco? Is your intended a tax refugee?"

"It seems that . . . well, he flew down there for the day to get some stuff he needed out of the bank and he dropped in on these good friends who live there so he could tell them he was engaged, and they want to give the wedding, absolutely insisted on it as a matter of fact, and since Monaco is central enough for everybody to get to—"

"Are they anybody I'd know?"

"Princess Grace and Prince Rainier."

"Holy . . . cow."

Agnes put down the vacuum cleaner and picked up the phone.

"Mother, oh, Mother, I'm so glad I got you. I didn't know if you'd be home." Tessa's voice didn't reveal her fluttering heart. She knew that there would never be a good way or a good time to break her news to her mother, but she'd nerved herself to make the call before the news leaked out as it was bound to do, try as they might to keep it private. She'd used Roddy and Aaron to rehearse, to warm up, to get used to saying the words, but hearing her mother's "hello" had been enough to make her feel like a mistrusted child again.

"And just where did you think I'd be, Teresa?" Agnes was as dry as if Tessa were calling from around the corner. Long distance worked no wonders on her.

"Shopping, marketing, picking up the laundry, out with Maggie . . ." Stop vamping, Tessa told herself sternly. "It's not important, I'm delighted that I reached you right away because . . . well, you'll probably never believe it, I can hardly believe it myself, but I'm engaged . . . engaged to get married." The telephone air was empty. "Did you hear me, Mother? I said I was going to get married."

"The last time you called home, not long ago at all, you said you and Fiona had been each other's dates for the whole picture, that you hadn't had any other social life. How could you possibly be getting married?"

Agnes's voice was calm and as close as she came to indulgent. Obviously this was another example of Tessa's impulsive, overnight-movie-star nonsense. Would she ever grow up?

"Look, Mother, I simply hadn't met him the last time I called. I admit it is sudden, but he . . . Luke . . . is so incredibly wonderful, and I'm so happy. I'm so certain about this, there's not the slightest doubt in my mind . . . oh, you'll love him when you meet him."

She'll probably hate and disapprove of him, Tessa thought. Just the way she hates and disapproves of Roddy and Aaron and Fiona and anyone else important in my life, only ten thousand times more.

"Teresa, for heaven's sake, stop carrying on. You realize, don't you, that you haven't made any sense up till now? Can you tell me exactly who this miraculous stranger is, this man you've decided to marry after knowing him for no time at all?"

"His name's Luke Blake, he's an Australian, a close friend of Mr. Lean's, Mr. Lean says he's an absolutely wonderful guy and—"

"I wasn't asking for David Lean's testimony or opinion, Teresa," Agnes cut in. "And how does your director happen to know about it before I do?"

"I wouldn't have told him until I'd told you but Luke was so excited that he beat me to the punch, oh, Mother—"

"I assume this Luke person isn't Catholic, Teresa?"

Finally, Tessa thought, finally the one question I can answer in a way that will please her without qualification.

"Luke was born and bred a Catholic. He was even an altar boy. We're going to have a religious ceremony in a cathedral. That should satisfy you, Mother, after all the worry I've been to you."

"It's a relief, I'll say that much." Agnes paused. It was some relief to know that there would be—presumably—one less occasion for sin in Teresa's life, but there were major drawbacks that the girl naturally hadn't thought about, bad Catholic that she was.

"I suppose you realize that rushing into an impulse marriage with another Catholic is much worse than if he weren't Catholic?" Agnes said severely. "You don't know this man, you're merely infatuated with him. If it's a mistake, and at your age it must be, you'll be in a terrible situation. If you get a divorce you could only remarry outside the church and in that case you could no longer receive Holy Communion. A Catholic marriage can only be ended by the death of one of the spouses, Teresa."

"Mother! My God! How can you think that way, why do you say these things? You'd turn the best wine into the most sour vinegar if you could. You sound like some gloomy old priest, not a mother! I can't imagine ever wanting a divorce from Luke."

She'd known it would be bad, Tessa thought, but this was worse than she'd expected as she had tried to prepare herself for what her mother would say.

"Of course you haven't thought about divorce. No girl ever can be realistic when she imagines she's in love." She was an expert on that particular error, Agnes thought bitterly, but it wasn't something she would ever tell her daughter, and even if she did, Teresa wouldn't pay attention to her. "How old is your young man, Teresa?"

"Older than I am, but he's never been married, in fact he's never even been truly in love before—"

"I asked you how old he was, Teresa."

"Forty-five."

"Have you gone stark raving mad?" Agnes shrieked.

"I know exactly how it sounds, I don't expect you to understand until you've met him, but I promise you that his age doesn't matter. We're meant for each other."

"A man twenty-five years older than you are? A man you admit you barely know? He's a middle-aged man! 'Meant for each other'—in what possible way,

Teresa? Everything you tell me makes this worse and worse. Can't you hear yourself? Can't you see how wrong it is? At least consult that agent of yours, consult Roddy Fensterwald, get some opinions from other people—"

"I'm in love," Tessa said, barely managing to keep her voice under control, "and I'm going to get married. You don't have to accept it or like it or approve of it because there's not a damn thing you or anyone else can do about it." Tessa was finally angry. She refused to be defensive about Luke with a woman as small-minded and unromantic as her mother.

"I hope you're going to wait until you know him a great deal better, that's my final word on the subject."

"The ceremony is in ten days. I hope you and Father and Maggie will come. I'm planning on having Maggie as my flower girl. I'll get a bunch of dresses ready so there will be something perfect for her to wear," Tessa announced with the composure that came of knowing that whatever she said would make no difference to her mother now.

"Teresa, I warn you, this is the mistake of your life, and you won't be able to count on me to get you out of it this time. Of course, I assume he doesn't know about your past, you're not that big a fool. He'll never learn it from me, if you're worried on that score."

I wondered if she was going to bring it up, Tessa thought. I shouldn't have wondered, I should have known. Her voice grew lilting and easy as she changed the subject without a pause.

"We're getting married in Monaco, Mother. Luke has a place near there. We've decided on a Low Mass in St. Nicolas's Cathedral. Luke is sending planes for you and Father and Maggie and the whole Riley family, all the aunts and uncles and every single last one of my cousins who's guaranteed to be toilet trained. You'll all be staying as his guests at the Hôtel de Paris. The other guests are all Luke's top executives and their wives plus his stepbrother Tyler and Tyler's wife and kids. Luke doesn't have much family. We're trying desperately to keep this engagement secret, so it doesn't turn into a circus."

"I see." Agnes paused and allowed a silence to develop. "Yes, I understand it now, Teresa. You're marrying a man with money."

"Not a man with money," Tessa said deliberately. "Luke is an enormously rich man, Mother, although he doesn't talk about it. He just does things that indicate that spending amazing amounts of money isn't a problem for him." Tessa spoke smoothly, twisting her engagement ring so she could close her hand on the diamond. She still smarted from Agnes's unnecessary reminder of the dire trouble she'd been in at fourteen. Did her mother think she could ever forget?

"I see."

"Why do you keep on saying that you 'see'? You can't think I'm marrying him for his money, can you? If you don't know me better than that, you don't know me at all."

"There's no reason on earth why you would, it's not as if you don't earn lots of money yourself. But money you have to work for, and pay your agent a commission on and then pay half of it out in taxes—that's not the same kind of money as money you marry, is it? I'm sure even a well-paid girl like you would realize that."

"Mother, when you meet Luke, you'll understand everything," Tessa said, as patiently as she could. It wasn't worth getting angry with her mother about a subject so ridiculous. "You'll know immediately that it's not about money, you'll see that the difference in our ages doesn't mean anything. You can't make judgments about us now, it isn't right."

"Why do you care about my judgment? You're going to do this no matter what I think, or what anyone thinks. It's the way you've always been, Teresa, wild, stubborn, headstrong, and a fool about the consequences."

"I suppose I must have been hoping that you could

be happy that I'm happy, even if you don't approve. Is that really too much to ask?"

"I can't lie to you, Teresa, I think this is utter folly. Unthinkable folly."

"So be it. I'll send you all the details as soon as I can—what to wear, when you'll be picked up, how long you'll be gone—so Father can explain to the school that he'll be away for a few days. Good-bye, Mother. Tell Father and Maggie for me, will you? With the time difference I won't be able to make the call myself. . . . Oh, by the way, Princess Grace is giving the wedding reception, lunch at the palace after the ceremony."

"Good-bye, Teresa."

Agnes put down the phone and walked slowly into the kitchen, where she drank two glasses of water. She walked back into the living room, unplugged the vacuum cleaner, and, without pausing, threw the heavy machine into the fireplace with such force that she could hear its insides shatter.

Marketing, picking up the laundry, that's what Teresa had imagined her doing when she called, she said to herself, panting in fury. A drudge, that's what she was to her daughter, that's what she was to the world.

She stalked around the living room, not looking for anything else to break, because she didn't want Sandor to know how she'd acted, but unable to sit down and consider the news. All she could see in her mind was a kaleidoscope of jagged fragments of imagined scenes: Teresa in the arms of someone who looked like Cary Grant; Teresa covered in a coat of white mink with a train that dragged on the ground; Teresa covered with pounds of diamonds, with a private jet and her own Rolls-Royce and the most beautiful clothes ever designed; Teresa with houses all over the world and in each one of them, among the large staff, some unknown, pathetic, dried-up little woman, whose job it was to vacuum the floors. Teresa laughing as she moved farther and farther away into the otherworldly stratosphere of people who were all famous and rich and beautiful; Teresa adored, heedless, not even noticing that she was standing and moving in a spotlight that never turned off.

Finally, exhausted, Agnes flopped down into a chair. She'd lived for people to appreciate her daughter, she told herself. She'd fought with Sandor so that Teresa could be exposed to the opportunities for fame and fortune. Why did she hate it now, so much that it was almost literally unbearable, so much that she wanted to scream and scratch her skin until it bled and pull out her hair?

It was not envy, no matter what Sandor thought. Who had ever heard of a mother who envied a daughter? Outlandish! If she honestly thought she was committing a mortal sin, she'd go to confession and get absolution, but she knew it couldn't be envy. That would be too unnatural to be true. She didn't want to marry some man she'd just met, no matter how rich; she didn't want to be a movie star, she didn't want to win an Oscar—how could the way she felt be something the church called envy?

Oh, how she wished that she'd married an ordinary man and never left Bridgeport, an ordinary man who would have given her a pack of ordinary kids who would have all been under her maternal rule, living in an ordinary house in which she would be the queen. In a home like that, creatures like her daughter would be so alien to her way of life that she'd either be too busy to read about them or she could idolize them in a casual void the way people had idolized Grace Kelly when she got married. Oh, yes! The woman she envied was the simple woman she had not been since the day she met Sandor Horvath. She envied Agnes, the prettiest, youngest Riley sister. You couldn't be accused of envying your own younger self, could you? That couldn't possibly be a mortal sin, especially when your younger self didn't want anything special except what all the other girls she knew had expected and received.

Agnes fell into a reverie from which she was aroused by one name. Grace Kelly. *Princess Grace* was giving her daughter's wedding reception! Princess Grace, who represented the ultimate dream of every Irish Catholic girl, Princess Grace who was living that dream every day. That was it, that was the envy she'd known it was impossible for her to feel toward her own flesh and blood. If she envied anyone it must be Princess Grace, and that kind of envy was too silly to even mention to a priest. It would be as ridiculous as telling him you had sinned in the moment or two you spent scrutinizing a beautiful model on the cover of a magazine.

As she composed herself, more and more of the details Teresa had given her in the last minutes of their phone conversation returned to Agnes. Private planes; the Hôtel de Paris, which must be the best hotel in Monaco or Monte Carlo or whatever they called it exactly; a wedding luncheon in the palace—she'd be at the bride's table with Princess Grace and Prince Rainier. The mother of the bride was always the most important person at a wedding besides the bride and groom themselves. And her sisters knew nothing yet!

Oh, this would destroy them, this would cap everything, this would put them away for life, they'd never recover, she thought, suddenly full of energy. Her sisters had been thrilled when Teresa won the Oscar for *Little Women,* but that was nothing, nothing compared to this!

Who could remember who'd won last year's Oscar for Best Supporting Actress? Nobody. Who could forget that your sister's daughter had been given a wedding by Princess Grace? Nobody. It would be the high point in the lives of the entire Riley family, the story that would be told over and over until everyone who had been there was long gone.

Agnes was poised to pick up the phone to call her eldest sister when she suddenly remembered Teresa saying she wanted Maggie to be her flower girl. Oh, no, Teresa, she thought, you're never getting married in church before a priest with your illegitimate daughter walking before you, strewing flower petals, with no one in the world to suspect. No, my girl, sinner that you are, that's not going to happen while I'm alive to prevent it. You're not getting away with that the way you got away with everything else. That would be a sin indeed, a sin in the eyes of the Holy Mother herself. She didn't have to consult a priest about something so self-evident. Yet, what could she do to stop it?

Hastily Agnes ran over various scenarios. She knew Sandor would agree with her about this; he'd think Teresa's brazen plan even more a defiance of the sacredness of the Sacrament of Marriage than she did. She'd tell Maggie that it was a grown-up party and children weren't invited. She'd get somebody trustworthy to take care of Maggie for the few days that they'd be away. Perhaps Helen Kelly. After all, she was Maggie's godmother. Whether she liked Helen or Helen liked her was unimportant. Helen would be fine to deal with Maggie for a short time. And she'd tell Teresa that Maggie had developed a high fever and something that the doctor suspected might be German measles the day before the flight. There was nothing more terrifying to any group of women, if even one of them was possibly pregnant, than German measles.

There was nothing she could do to prevent Teresa from marrying a man she barely knew in a religious ceremony in front of her entire family with Princess Grace gloriously, unbelievably, conferring her unspoken blessing on the whole hasty, misbegotten procedure. But Teresa wasn't going to be allowed to have absolutely everything she wanted. Someone would be missing, someone whose absence would be noted. Maggie wasn't going to be part of this . . . this . . . sacrilege.

12

"Promise me it's over," Tessa demanded faintly, out of her haze of exhaustion as she and Luke drove up the Moyenne Corniche on their way to Luke's farmhouse just below the high-perched town of Èze-Village, where they were going to spend their honeymoon. "Promise me we never have to do *that* again."

Luke glanced at her profile. Tessa's splendid head was thrown back on the leather seat. Her eyes were closed, and the faint mauve shadows that he could glimpse on the tender skin under her lower lashes were infinitely touching. Her lips, so ardently, alluringly prominent, were parted slightly in fatigue. Only Tessa's flashing waves of hair, liberated from their elaborate wedding updo and taken by the wind, still seemed to possess any spirit. In the light of the approaching sunset, he thought he could see an occasional red glint in the darkness of its strands.

"Not unless you insist on repeating our vows on our tenth anniversary," he answered her tenderly. "In which case I'd have to agree. Of course I'd try to talk you out of it. I'll say 'paparazzi' over and over again until you've changed your mind."

"You'd just have to say it once," Tessa sighed, thinking of the outrageous mobs of photographers and journalists who had only been held in check by Monaco's formidable police force. "We should have eloped, Princess Grace or no Princess Grace. I've learned my lesson. Never let anyone give you a wedding no matter how generous she is. No, make that, especially if she's generous. I couldn't have taken one more minute of being a bride. Is a person supposed to enjoy her own wedding?"

"Oh, I shouldn't think so, darling, I've never heard of anyone who did."

"Then why did we do it?"

"It's a rite of passage or something."

Or something, Tessa silently agreed. Something she should have had the imagination and good sense to have avoided. And most of it was her fault. The wedding itself, this morning, had been a dreamlike blaze of white: clustered garlands of white flowers spilling down from large baskets suspended under dozens of splendid crystal chandeliers, high banks of white flowers and tall white candles at the altar. Her progress down the center aisle of the vast stone cathedral had seemed like a promenade in a garden, a slow, proud promenade toward her beloved. Oh, the wedding was a dream and the only details she could remember about it were the times she'd peeked at Luke's face as he knelt on his prie-dieu during the ceremony and the joyful strength of his voice when he answered that he took Teresa for his lawful wife, according to the rite of their Holy Mother the Church.

If she hadn't had the idea of inviting all her family, every last aunt, uncle, and cousin, maybe the three days preceding the wedding might have been delightful. Maybe they could have been just a question of being responsive to everybody, of thanking people over and over again for their good wishes, unconcerned about what they were really thinking or feeling—since brides only had to be suitably bridal to fulfill their role. But no, she'd been greedy, she'd wanted them all to witness her happiness, and that's where she'd gone so very wrong.

It had never occurred to her that her relatives would feel utterly out of place from the minute they arrived in the Principality of Monaco. Her concept of family gatherings were those of a child or a teenager, memories of a relaxed clan of giggling, gossipy, warm-hearted women and beer-drinking, joking men, all good-natured and feeling at home in their skins. But during the entire time in Monaco they'd been on their best behavior, as stiff as if they'd been stuffed, wretchedly self-conscious in their obviously new clothes, afraid to make any kind of gaffe, and solemn and careful of speech in a manner more suitable to a funeral than to a wedding.

They'd all but turned to stone in the presence of the prince and princess at the rehearsal dinner Luke had given at the International Sporting Club; they'd danced so sedately at the wedding luncheon in the palace itself that it was hard to remember them pulling up the rugs at home and showing off their prowess. They hadn't even dared to have one glass too many of the champagne. She and Luke and even Princess Grace had worked hard to jolly them up, but it was her own small Hollywood contingent and Luke's executives and their wives, almost all of them Australian and not burdened with awestruck preoccupation with the icon of Grace Kelly, who managed to rescue the rehearsal dinner and wedding reception and provide some suitable note of joie de vivre.

And even the wedding lunch wasn't the worst of it, Tessa reflected, too frazzled to open her eyes and look at one of the world's most thrilling views of the Mediterranean as Luke drove skillfully up the steep, twisting mountain road to Èze. The single worst thing of all was the way her aunts had treated her mother. It had started when her parents had arrived without Maggie, on a different plane than the one that had brought the rest of the family. Maybe if little Maggie, sick at home, had been there, too, her humanity would have made her aunts realize that their sister Agnes had not been transformed into the Queen Mother.

Much of Tessa's time had been spent at the Hôtel de Paris with her mother and her aunts, and it had grown more and more painful to watch the . . . reverence, there was no other word . . . with which her mother's sisters surrounded her. Her mother had been elevated beyond any sisterly relationship.

Agnes Horvath had become the closest thing to a Grace Kelly that the Riley family possessed, and oh, how her mother had rubbed it in. She'd taken every chance to glorify herself, to position herself on a different level from the others, to indicate in a dozen ways, both verbally and with her dignified body language, that she was, quite simply, better than they were. More successful, more sophisticated, and infinitely more blessed, not by God, but by her own hand, her own will, her own vision. She had somehow, over the years, caused this entire event to take place, she was responsible for this grandness-beyond-anyone's-dreams. She, Agnes Horvath, was the center of the wedding as far as her sisters were concerned.

She wouldn't have begrudged her mother a second of her glory, Tessa thought, if she hadn't known how she really felt. Luke, in the unenviable position of a man who was marrying a much younger bride, had made a special effort with her parents, and she could see her father taking his measure and judging her choice a wise one, in the same dry, suspicious way he had finally approved of her agent and her business manager. Her mother had not so much warmed up to Luke as she had cooled down from the anger of their phone conversation. He was different from what she had expected, so unpretentious, so charming and friendly, so attentive to her, that Agnes had finally whispered to Tessa, "Well, I must say I can see why you made this foolish, hasty decision." Those words were as close to a blessing as she was likely to ever receive from her mother, Tessa realized.

As for her cousins, the very same cousins she used to have so much fun with, they hadn't managed to feel any comfort with her, Tessa realized. It wasn't as if they treated her as someone who was better than they were, it was as if she had become so *different* from anybody they could possibly have a conversation with that there was absolutely no common ground, no way to be human together.

And all their little children! The ones she'd so grandly insisted on including—was that the way kids acted now? Constant squabbles, whining, teasing, talking back to their parents, showing no signs of manners?

There had been too many occasions when she'd been ashamed of her family, Tessa admitted to herself, ashamed of having been ashamed.

She'd always been the petted baby of the family, but now her cousins and their spouses and their children looked at her with eyes big with wonder and awe and too much admiration to be comfortable for them and certainly for her.

Is that what winning an Oscar did to you, she wondered? Did it happen in the families of everybody who'd won? Or was it because of Princess Grace giving the wedding? Or was it her engagement ring, which none of the women would try on, no matter how much she tried to get them to? Was it the visible difference between the Teresa they'd known when she was fourteen, before she'd moved to California, and the way she looked now, six years later, Tessa Kent grown up, after all, and the product of the constant polishing process that is professionally imposed on any working actress?

Families, she thought, families. They remained the same in your mind, but you yourself weren't allowed to change more than some predetermined amount or you didn't belong to them anymore. They cast you out once you'd left their unspoken but clearly defined frame of reference, once you'd gone too far up or too far down.

Yet, on the other land, Tessa reflected, Tyler and Madison Webster had taken her in with ease and pleasure, delighted to see Luke so happy. Luke's stepbrother and his wife, a handsome young couple from Essex County in the New Jersey hunt country, had been the only guests at the wedding who'd been perfectly natural with everybody, from her father to Prince Rainier, from a shy wife of one of Luke's executives to the youngest of her badly behaved second cousins. They had the kind of bred-in-the-bone manners that were unobtrusively the same for one and all.

Of all the guests who'd known her before she'd started making films, Mimi alone had remained herself, as devilish and free-spirited as ever, totally unaffected by Agnes's darting looks of incredulous disgust at her presence. Fiona, heaven-sent Fiona, was bossily preoccupied with the amazing number of details that accompanied the wedding dress and her own maid-of-honor dress (which she and Tessa had purchased at Harrods' Wedding Salon on a flying trip to London), as well as everything else Fiona had, in obvious delight, deemed necessary for her trousseau. Mimi, unimpressed by Fiona's earnestness, waltzed around in Tessa's suite wearing nothing but the green diamond, lace bikini underpants, and high heels. She was as irrepressible as ever, relating scandalous gossip about the post-school adventures of their classmates at Sacred Heart, detailing the pros and cons of her long train of boyfriends at college, demanding that Luke provide her with an Aussie exactly like him, ordering improbable things at improbable hours from room service just to prove that it could be done—only Mimi, and Tessa's small group of Hollywood guests, had the fun that she'd wanted them all to have.

Oh well, her intentions had been good, Tessa told herself. She felt the solid wedge of tension between her shoulders begin to disappear as the wedding memories stopped occupying her mind. She could feel the light of the late-afternoon sun grow dimmer on her eyelids. Maybe . . . maybe, she'd just take a little nap until Luke stopped the car . . . they should be there soon . . .

Tessa woke up slowly, with the feeling she normally associated with a particularly good night's sleep. Oh, she thought, without opening her eyes, why weren't naps more appreciated? A nap was the only form of sleep that didn't have any concept of duty attached to it. A nap wasn't something you "needed" or "shouldn't miss" or "had to have" to perform the following day. It was a divine treat, a brief blessing, in which you had no dreams but only a deep, luscious blankness that wiped away whatever had been bothering you before you fell into it. Churchill took naps, she remembered, every day. Would she become like him if she followed his example, or would she have to add brandy and the cigars to the mix? She must ask Luke, he knew things like that. Luke!

She sat up abruptly. She was still wearing the dress she'd put on after the reception, and there was a warm quilt covering her, but she seemed to have been napping right in the middle of a large bed in a room she'd never seen before. Luke must have carried her in from the car. There were heavy beams overhead and arched windows were cut into the thick stone walls. Tessa hurried over to the nearest window and looked out. A long field of still unharvested lavender, its spiky, concentric clusters planted in strict rows; olive trees; cypress trees; vines that crept around the outside of the window—nothing unexpected for a farmhouse in Provence. Not if you ignored the color of the light . . . light the clear color of dawn, not of sunset.

I must have slept at least thirteen hours, maybe more, Tessa thought, wrapping the quilt around her shoulders, and my God I need to pee more than I need to find my bridegroom.

Fortunately the first door she opened was that of a perfectly appointed bathroom. After her urgent quest had been satisfied, Tessa discovered that her cosmetics bag had been placed, unopened, by the side of the sink. She hastily splashed her face with water, brushed her teeth, took off her crushed dress, and decided to take a quick shower since there was no sight or sound of Luke in the bedroom.

Once she had had her shower, she realized that traces of makeup were still on her face. She removed it expertly, brushed her hair until it fairly stood up and saluted, and, looking in the mirror, pronounced herself ready to meet the day. Now, all she needed was something to wear and a husband, in that order. She searched the closets for her suitcases without success. Wrapped in a large bath towel big enough to fasten into a sarong, Tessa opened the other door in the room and almost fell over Luke. He lay there, fully clothed, like the faithful bodyguard of some paranoid empress, sleeping on a runner in the corridor, huddled in a nest of pillows and covered by another quilt.

She knelt by his side and scratched the back of his hand gently. He slept on. She kissed his earlobe lingeringly. Nothing. She pulled gently and then less gently on various short tufts of his hair. His breathing didn't even change. Tessa sat back on her heels and contemplated the sleeping man. He might as well be in a coma. She didn't want to shock him awake, but on the other hand she didn't want him to keep on sleeping now that she was up. Who knew when he'd fallen asleep? He could have been up half the night keeping watch over her before he'd mysteriously chosen to settle on the floor. But if she allowed him to keep on sleeping now, they'd be out of sync; one of them would always be sleeping when the other was awake, and that was no way to begin a marriage. Anyway, she was chilly in the morning air.

With determination Tessa removed her towel and crept under the quilt stark naked. At first it was enough just to be warm again. A man who could be counted on for body heat, was Luke Blake, she thought, lightheaded at being naked next to a sleeping man. Surely he'd feel that she was there and wake up . . . wouldn't a person know when someone had joined him under his quilt? Some bodyguard he'd make . . . a troop of rape-minded Cossacks could have stepped over him in the night, and it had been, officially, her wedding night, at that.

Tessa indignantly unbuttoned Luke's shirt. At least he'd taken off his tie in the car, so she didn't have to deal with that. She put her head next to his chest and puffed all over it, thinking to wake him with her breath. Luke slept on. Tessa reflected. She could poke him in the ribs, she could tickle him under his arms—but she didn't know if he was ticklish. She could shake him, but he was too big to shake. Or she could unbuckle his belt. Yes, that would be the next logical thing to do, now that she had his shirt open. It would give her a wider field of operation. She unbuckled his belt easily and unzipped his fly easily, considering that she'd never done either of those things before except on a pair of her own jeans. Luke rolled his head away from her, but otherwise there was no change in his sleep. Tessa followed the line of hair on his chest down past his waistline, pulling firmly on it at every step. Wouldn't you think that if somebody pulled your stomach hair, you'd wake up? She certainly would, but there was no hair on her stomach.

Eventually her exploring fingers found a thicker growth of wiry hair and Tessa stopped abruptly. You couldn't, you simply couldn't pull a man's pubic hair. That must come under the heading of things not done. Particularly with a man whose penis you'd never seen. But, on the other hand, an unseen penis was not in the same category as pubic hair. It was a definite invitation. An irresistible invitation, which came under the heading of things you could investigate if you were so inclined. Squirming until she could reach lower, Tessa took Luke's penis in her hand and cuddled it, without moving. It felt . . . friendly, she thought, not at all frightening, like a soft, warm, agreeable, oddly shaped little animal, a sort of household pet. A pet with potential, a pet more responsive than its owner, since he continued to sleep while his penis showed signs of acknowledging her touch. Fascinated, she continued to hold it as it grew larger and longer and harder, losing its pet qualities by the second, although it still, to her way of thinking, remained definitely friendly. Soon it was so big that the only way she could take its measure was to move her hand up and down its length. It had all sort of interesting parts and subdivisions to it, she thought, breathlessly. It would reward further exploration.

"Hey! What the hell!"

So that was the secret of waking him up.

"You were sleeping," she said accusingly, not letting go, in case he thought this was a particularly vivid dream.

"Stop that!"

"Aren't you supposed to like it?"

"I do, but let go!"

Reluctantly, Tessa abandoned her discovery and raised her head to a level with Luke's. "Good morning," she said demurely.

He snorted with laughter at her tone. "What convent did they teach you that in?"

"I was merely following my natural instincts."

"Oh, darling," he said, covering her face with kisses, "I hate to repress your instincts, but not on this floor."

"What are you doing out here, anyway?"

"I brought you in from the car and put you in the middle of the bed because I was afraid that if you woke up on the side of a mattress in a strange bed you'd fall off, trying to find out where you were. Then, when you didn't wake up for hours, I didn't want to move you, because obviously you needed the sleep. I thought about going to sleep on the rug next to the bed, but I was afraid you'd wake up in the middle on the night and fall over me in the dark. So this seemed like the best place to wait, where you'd find me when you woke."

"Why didn't you leave a little light on in the bedroom so I'd see you on the rug?"

"Oh."

"You weren't thinking straight," she said, forgivingly.

"I've never been in this situation before. In fact, no woman has ever been in this house or on that bed before."

"But I thought you'd had a place in Cap-Ferrat for years?"

"I do, that's where I keep my boat. I bought this when I came down here after we got engaged—a place just for us. My God, you're naked!"

"I wondered when you'd notice."

Luke scooped her up, quilt and all, and carried her back into the bedroom and deposited her gently on the bed.

"Will you wait here, without going anywhere else, just stay put, absolutely put, while I brush my teeth and take a quick shower?" he demanded.

"May I breathe?" Now that Luke was properly awake and in charge, she found herself taking refuge in a sort of silliness that wasn't natural to her.

"From time to time."

Tessa waited for him, confused beyond measure, overcome with curiosity, anticipation, and anxiety. Her mind refused to function as she looked at the beams of the bedroom ceiling without seeing them. A short interval passed, a blank time of waiting, almost without breathing. When Luke returned he peeled off his towel, and rolled under the quilt next to her. Tessa was overcome with a sudden attack of acute shyness. She pulled away from him and hid as much of herself as she could under the quilt. One of her eyes looked out from under her hair.

"Darling, Tessa, darling, you're breaking my heart. Don't look at me that way," he pleaded. "We don't have to do anything at all, there are no rules about this, we can get up and have breakfast and go exploring, we can spend a week doing nothing at all if you let me kiss you from time to time."

"No."

"No, you won't let me kiss you?"

"No, I don't want to get up and have breakfast."

"What do you want to do?"

"I don't know. You're supposed to know."

"Normally I would. But you're a . . ."

"I know, I know, don't remind me, just do whatever you'd normally do if you were in bed with some woman."

"You're not 'some woman,' you're my wife, the love of my life."

"Then make something up."

"First I'll investigate the only part of you I can see," he said, smiling at her childishness. He drew closer to her and traced her eyebrow with his lips. When she didn't pull farther away, he kissed her with tiny, soft kisses along the curve of her bone from her eyebrow to her nose.

"Fiona said that was my best feature," Tessa mumbled.

"I can't tell yet," Luke murmured. "You could have a better one hidden away somewhere." Gently he turned her head so that he could kiss her lips. Mutely, Tessa returned his kisses, but Luke could tell, from the tension he sensed in the trembling pressure of her mouth, that she was filled with apprehension. Of course she is, he thought, what could be more natural? He modulated his passion to her timidity, keeping his kisses utterly undemanding, reining in any sign of his desire. For long minutes they lost themselves in a chain of soft, almost tentative kisses, while his fingers were plunged into her hair, caressing her skull with calm, reassuring movements. Some time after he felt her lips grow more confident, Luke allowed his mouth to stray from her mouth to her ear, holding her bundled up from her collarbone downward. He kissed her ear, leaving no fraction of its lobe untouched, and then he kissed her down the long, firm curve of her neck; and when he reached her shoulder he kissed her along the fragile skin at the base of her neck. Each time he reached her collarbone, his mouth retraced its journey down from her ear, never venturing lower and never breaking its rhythm.

Tessa's breathing grew faster with each voyage of his lips from her ear to her collarbone, until, suddenly, she flung back the blanket and revealed her high breasts, their small pink nipples as erect as if he'd been sucking on them without mercy. "Put your mouth on them," she panted, "and leave my ear alone, you're driving me crazy!"

"That's more or less the idea," Luke mumbled, as he bent his head toward the points of flesh whose delicacy had grown so bold. Tessa reached her arms out blindly for him, but Luke drew the lower part of his body out of her reach so that she couldn't again tantalize his rearing penis. She needed so much more to make her ready, he thought, so much long and careful preparation, yet she could have no idea of what her touch did to him. They lay facing each other while he cupped each of her breasts in his hands so that he could move quickly from one nipple to another, using his tongue, his teeth, his lips, firmly holding back the full force of his passion, entirely focused on giving her delight throughout every cell of her exquisite nipples that grew more engorged by the second. Tessa squirmed under the quilt that covered her from her waist down, trying to push it off, but Luke's superior strength prevented her, even as he held her breasts captive to his sweetly plundering mouth. She pushed herself forward, trying to get as much of each breast into his mouth as possible, and when he switched from one to another, the instant during which he was unattached to her seemed unendurable. "Come on, come on!" she implored him through clenched teeth. Oh no, he thought, you won't make me rush you, you can't make me take you before you're so excited that it won't hurt.

Suddenly, with a lightning change of pace for which he was unprepared, Tessa gathered up all her strength, freed herself of the quilt, and in one swift movement raised herself up off the bed, pushed Luke over on his back, threw one leg over him, and straddled him. Stunned, he felt her grasp his penis and pull it back from his belly so that it stood at a right angle to his body.

"No!" he cried, but Tessa was already arched above him, her expression rapt and isolated in an absolute purposefulness. Her eyes were tightly closed as she guided his penis directly between her parted thighs. She circled the head of his penis in her fingers and lowered herself until he was just inside her flesh. "Oh," she said to herself, "oh . . . yes . . ."

"Darling . . ."

"No, don't move, don't say anything, I have to do it myself," she commanded. He lay absolutely still, disciplining himself with all the authority of his maturity, fascinated by her intent caprice, as a fraction of an inch at a time she pressed down onto him with her taut, quivering body. Both of them barely breathed, her lips were pressed firmly together, there was no sound in the room as moment by moment, at a pace determined by Tessa, she resolutely impaled herself on him. It seemed to Luke that she was as ruthless with the pain she must be feeling as she was ruthless in her insistence on his passivity. She looked like a stranger, with the fierceness of an Amazon branding her brow, her teeth pressed into her lower lip. From time to time she paused briefly, all her senses utterly focused on the point where his flesh met hers, and then she pushed on. Time stopped until finally Tessa gave a deep breath and Luke became aware that he was enclosed, up to his hilt, in her warmth. He looked up at her face, close to him now, her lips finally parted, her eyelids fluttering, an expression of relief recreating her face, familiar again.

Only then did he dare to fold her in his arms and, making certain that he didn't move too quickly, gather her closely to him and turn her over, so that he was above her. He stayed motionless, watching her face as a smile came to her lips, a complex inward smile of accomplishment, pride, and astonishment.

"Look at me," he whispered, but she kept her eyes closed, her smile suddenly teasing. "Look at me, my darling," he insisted, and she opened her eyes and saw his, bright with tears. "Did I hurt you?" he asked.

"Only a little, because I could control it—it's all right now—why are you crying?"

"Because you're my virgin bride and it's more beautiful than anything I could ever have imagined."

"But I'm not a virgin anymore."

He drew back slowly, until his penis left the cave of her body, and then, with infinite care, he pushed it in again as far as it would go, filling her completely. "No," he said, "now you're not a virgin anymore."

13

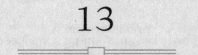

I never knew people could be domestic for four whole days in a row," Luke said, as he and Tessa cleaned up the kitchen after the lunch they'd walked into the village to buy: a newly baked baguette, sweet butter, fresh ham sliced from the bone, and five kinds of cheese. "Would you like to go out for dinner tonight? We're invited to a party on board a yacht tonight, it's only a half-hour drive down to the harbor."

"So love in a farmhouse has already made you itch for social life," she sighed mockingly, hanging up the apron that Madame Boulet, who owned the neighboring farm, used each evening when she brought over the dinner she'd cooked in her own house.

"It's not social life, it's the sheer brutish macho satisfaction of showing you off to a roomful of people, knowing that every man there feels desperate envy of me. I'm basically a disgusting swine, just a step more evolved than a caveman about some things, and you might as well know it now. No, don't laugh, I'm serious, Tessa. I'm going to be profoundly jealous and utterly possessive and I'm going to flaunt you all over this little planet. Thank God you're much too young to want children. By the time you're—oh, maybe thirty—I suppose I'll be able to face sharing you with them. I've never felt the slightest need to reproduce, although I guess you will."

"Why didn't you mention any of this sooner?"

"I didn't truly know it sooner . . . well, perhaps I had intimations, but I'd never thought about it for five consecutive seconds until we got married. Would you have married me if you'd known the kind of man I am?"

"I would have married you if . . . if . . . I can't think of anything that would have kept me from marrying you except a wife and six kids."

And even that, Tessa thought, even that wouldn't have been enough to stop her from doing everything in her power to be with him. Her all-important new sense of safety had grown steadily more solid and established during the past four days they'd been together, long, unsurpassingly perfect days, consuming days of promise and fulfillment, brimming with a heavenly green-gold light that had changed her forever. Whatever combination of cells once made up her brain and heart had mutated into a new soul, someone she'd never known, a soul who dwelt at the heart of a secure fortress of safety and had no fear of adoration.

Tessa had reached a point at which it was emotionally and physically painful to be farther away from Luke than the next room, and then it was only possible to endure this separation for a few minutes at a time. She begrudged the time he spent in the shower and shaving, the way he quickly scanned *Le Figaro* when they went into the village, the minutes he disappeared to bring in wood for the fire they made at night as soon as the sun set. She couldn't settle in a chair or on a sofa without her eyes straying to his blunt, powerful fingers and becoming intensely aware that the quivering, tender flesh between her legs was growing avid again. She couldn't fall asleep, no matter how he'd satisfied her, until he'd drifted off and she could lie in his arms, remembering each honey-and-fire-filled hour of the safe, safe day. Even as she felt their breathing merge, she could barely allow herself to drift into his dreams and waste these exquisite minutes.

"Yes," Tessa agreed, forcing the light words, "by all means, let's go to the party. What should I wear?"

"A little black dress."

"But I don't have one with me. How about a little white dress?"

"Is it plain?"

"Plain how?"

"Unadorned, not embroidered or whatever, just plain white."

"Is this some new fetish of yours? Another terrible thing I wasn't warned about? A plain white wardrobe?"

"Just not decorated," he growled.

"It's as plain as plain can be," she assured him.

"You'll understand it all at the proper time," he said, coming to stand behind her, his arms crossed in front of her so that each of her breasts was lightly enclosed in his warm hands. He buried his face in her hair as Tessa bent her head in swift, docile delight. They stood without the slightest movement, barely breathing, as Luke's penis rose, under his trousers, and grew, jerking slightly and swelling upward against the small of her back.

"In the kitchen?" she gasped, her heart beating so heavily that she thought he must be able to hear it.

"Bedroom," he groaned. "Understand now why I didn't want to make the bed?"

"I knew why. I didn't think you'd make me wait this long."

All afternoon they lay in bed, making love, dozing, and making love again, sometimes as playful as animals in a zoo, sometimes deeply earnest, caught by the voluptuous gravity of a whirlwind of passion that Luke, for all his experience, had never known before.

Tessa, discovering an untapped well of sensuality that only her dreams had ever revealed, let herself go freely into her deepest fantasies, sometimes disarmingly submissive, pliant and willing, urging him, in deliciously wanton, indecent words she'd never used before, to fuck her quickly, to fuck her good and hard, to give it to her as if she were a whore, to treat himself to a quickie. Sometimes she was as dominant as he, insisting on her right to make him submit every inch of skin on his body to her, to lick him slowly behind his knees, under his arms, inside his elbows, on the arches of his feet and the balls of his heels, to tantalize the head of his cock without any fairness, touching him with nothing but her tongue, holding him off ferociously, listening with delight to his pleading, and finally, when she could stand it no longer, grasping his penis and plunging it hungrily and still awkwardly into her body, while he reveled in her candid lust. More often they strove to match their separate passions and more and more frequently they discovered that their rhythms blended together and that the miracle of two separate human beings becoming one was achieved.

"I never expected you to be so . . . inventive," he told her. "Or have I fallen into that old cliché about wild convent girls?"

"I surprise myself," she admitted. "Mimi and I used to read sexy stories when we were fourteen—I almost memorized them—and I imagine I must have been waiting for the right opportunity to present itself ever since."

"Thank God it was me."

As the sun began to set, sated for the moment, they prepared themselves for their evening out. Tessa was glad that Fiona had insisted on her buying the far-too-expensive strapless white dress they'd seen in the Couture Boutique at Harrods. Although it had a matching chiffon stole with a wide, hemstitched border, it looked like nothing on the hanger, yet when she put it on, its finely pleated, Grecian shape, cleverly draped, outlined her body to below her hips, eloquently justifying its Dior label. When she whirled in front of the mirror the short skirt, unpleated, swished around her thighs and kissed her knees. When she leaned forward, she could see that the bodice of the dress began no more than a hairline above the top of her nipples.

Tessa put on white silk sandals and the string of pearls she'd bought at Tiffany's in Beverly Hills just before her nineteenth birthday. She'd spent another fifteen hundred dollars for matching pearl studs, telling herself that they not only would commemorate the film but were also the only ornaments a woman could wear at any time of the day or night and be certain that she was suitably decked out. Even her mother had approved of the purchase, saying dryly that she supposed that Tessa was looking forward to occasions on which she wouldn't feel "good enough" in artificial pearls. She'd worn them with her wedding gown and they'd been exactly right, Tessa thought, as she fastened them around her neck.

With a final twirl in front of the mirror, flourishing her engagement ring at an imaginary audience, Tessa picked up her wrap and presented herself to Luke, who stood in the living room of the farmhouse, clad in the unaccustomed formality of a white linen suit, a blue shirt, and a yellow tie.

"That's your plain white dress," he inquired, " 'as plain as plain can be'?"

"You said a yacht," she reproached him, "and anyway, show me where it's not plain, just show me one bit of decoration."

"It's perfect," he assured her, "but pearls don't do it justice, they're too proper."

"I'm afraid you don't appreciate understated elegance."

"Close your eyes."

"Why?"

"Promise to keep them closed, no matter what?"

"Why?"

"Because I said so."

"All right."

Tessa stood with her eyes tightly closed as she felt him unclasp her pearls and take off her earrings. What now, she wondered, shivering, as she felt him fumble at the back of her neck and heard a slight click as a heavy necklace was settled around her neck. Suddenly the lobes of each ear were embraced by a weight of cool metal. "Yes," Luke said, "absolutely spot on." He took her shoulders and guided her steps until she stood in front of her bathroom mirror. "You can look now."

"Good God!" From a necklace of five huge, pear-shaped emeralds, brilliantly graduated in size and mounted in thick crusts of diamonds, hung a pendant fashioned from a single giant pear-shaped emerald, an emerald almost the length of her little finger. It lay on her breastbone, rimmed in its own diamond setting, a fathomless drop of the very essence of green. The earrings were great round emeralds, of a color perfectly matched to the necklace, set in large diamond domes.

"You're mad, insane, out of your mind . . ."

"I knew you'd say something like that, darling. They're your wedding present, but I didn't want to give them to you until you were ready for them. They're utterly inappropriate for a girl."

"But I am a girl."

"No, you're a woman now, Tessa. Get used to it . . . it isn't going to go away."

"But I'd never . . ." Tessa turned this way and that, falling into a reverie as the fabulous emeralds exerted their spell. "They're so alive—I always thought emeralds were a hard green with a sort of blue flash."

"Most of them are now. But these are very, very old ones, the aristocrat of emeralds, they have a special radiance that seems to make them reflect the sun. Experts use the expression 'honey-like' for their color."

" 'Old' emeralds, what a strange word to use," she said dreamily, moving her shoulders so that they caught the light in an explosion of sparks.

"They were mined in the fifteen hundreds, in Colombia, but officially they're called 'Indian emeralds' because the Indian moguls bought up all the finest stones. The pendant comes off so you can use it as a clip. It once belonged to Alphonso XIII when he was king of Spain."

"You really are a collector, aren't you? You missed your calling, you should have been an auctioneer," she said, fending off the magnificence of the stones by mocking him. "Tell me, oh professor, what does the pendant weigh?"

"Almost fifty carats, give or take . . . actually forty-eight point nine five, since you ask, which incidentally isn't considered the most elegant way to receive a gift from the heart."

"And where am I going to wear an almost-fifty-carat emerald clip?" Tessa demanded, undaunted by his words.

"Wherever you like, on a belt, on a lapel, on a flannel nightshirt, even on your bikini—it sure do make a nice touch o' color."

"I couldn't begin to!"

"Then don't, just put them on for me. Here, do you want me to help you take them off? I don't want you to feel uncomfortable."

"Damn you!" She stepped quickly out of his reach. "Don't you dare touch them."

"I always say it's astonishing how quickly a woman can get comfy with emeralds. It takes a lot longer for rubies. Some women never can make their peace with rubies."

"You took advantage of me, and now you're making fun!"

"Be a brave girl, pretend you're married to a man whose ego can only be subdued when you wear some of the finest emeralds Harry Winston has sold in his career, or so he assured me, and I promise I won't even smile sideways at you. Think you could do that? You're an actress, you should be able to forget what you have on. And frankly, if I were you, I'd be a lot more self-conscious about letting my nipples show when I raise my arms."

"They do not!"

"Wanna bet?"

Tessa raised her arms to adjust the thick chain of semicircular diamond links that held the emeralds around her neck. Her breasts rose inches out of the top of her dress. "Oh," she breathed in disbelief, "no!"

"You won't be able to dance in that dress," Luke said regretfully.

"Wanna bet?"

"What would your mother say?"

"She's just had three days in Paris, maybe she's a changed woman. Maybe my father took her to the Lido or the Folies-Bergère. They're supposed to have flown back this morning. I'll make it a point to call her sometime this week and ask her if I need to confess a sin of immodesty that can't possibly be my fault."

"It wouldn't have been your fault if I hadn't warned you, but now that you know, if you dance in that dress it's certainly a sin of immodesty, a major sin."

"Stop splitting hairs. You've already ruined my character with emeralds and it hardly took a minute. Oh, Luke, should I be such an easy mark? I didn't know I loved jewels until you gave me the ring. And now these . . . is there something wrong about feeling so . . . thrilled? So absolutely smitten with excitement and delight?"

"Are you asking me as your spiritual advisor?"

"There's no one else around to consult."

"You're not kidding, are you darling? Underneath you really mean it, you really feel that there has to be something wrong with enjoying them, don't you?"

"Maybe," she said sheepishly. "Jewels must be the most purely materialistic enjoyment there is."

"Feeling guilty about something that isn't wrong is a waste of time. For more than four hundred years these stones have made women happy. Today it's your turn. Now listen to me, I won't—I will not allow it! It's unreasonable. You're not taking anything away from anybody. I bloody well want to feel free to give you jewels and I don't want to be deprived of that pleasure. But, if you're really disturbed by it, I'll stop. It's your decision, but couldn't you try, at least, to get used to it? For my sake?"

"I guess so," Tessa said after a pause for reflection. "But there is something that would make it easier."

"Just ask."

"I feel so disoriented, light-headed, kind of wispy. It must be the shock. My arms feel much too bare, as if I might float away. Shouldn't I be weighted down so that I feel as if my feet are touching the floor? I think what I need is a few, not too many, but still rather . . . heavy, yes heavy, even massive . . . bracelets?"

They were still sleeping the next morning when Luke woke to a repeated knock on the front door. Cursing under his breath, he recognized the voice of Len Jones, his second-in-command, whom he'd left in charge of the business. No one else in his empire knew where he was, a state of affairs that had taken many days to arrange. Len had been instructed not to disturb him for any reason at all.

Sliding quickly out of bed, he left Tessa tucked under the quilt as he pulled on his robe and went to answer the door.

"Luke, I'm sorry, but I had to let you know—"

"Bloody hell, Len, whatever it is, couldn't it have waited?"

"I'm terribly sorry, but no, it couldn't have. It's Tessa's parents. It's bad news, Luke, the worst. They were in a taxi on their way home from the airport . . . their taxi was sideswiped by one of those damn big tanker trucks. The driver and Tessa's father were killed instantly, her mother's still alive but she can't last long . . . the people who are taking care of Tessa's sister called me at the number you sent them . . ."

"Damn, damn, damn! Look, go back to the office in Monte and arrange for my plane to be ready to leave from Nice in three hours. No, two and a half. I'll get Tessa ready."

"Do you want me to send a car to drive you?"

"Not necessary. You'd better come along to L.A. too. I'll be busy arranging the funeral—funerals—so I'll need you. There's a list of wedding guests on my desk. Contact Tessa's aunts and tell them what's happened. Alert them to be ready to fly out to the coast, we'll make the arrangements after we find out how Agnes is. And call Fiona and Mimi, Tessa will want them there. Take care of the press—as few details as possible. What else? Tessa's agent and Roddy Fensterwald, call them. Ask them to keep it out of the news as long as possible. Take two large suites for us at the Beverly Hills Hotel, no, make that the Bel-Air, it's harder for photographers to get into. Thanks, Len. Sorry to put all this on you, but Tessa's my priority. I'll see you at the plane."

Slowly Luke walked back to the bedroom of the farmhouse. He sat on the side of the bed for a few minutes, unable to wake Tessa to the news. Everyone's parents die, he thought, but not with such brutal suddenness, not at the end of their daughter's wedding festivities. He prayed that Tessa's deep sense of guilt, a guilt that he could understand in the context of a very Catholic upbringing, didn't make her blame herself for having brought them to Europe. If only they'd returned with the others in the planes he'd chartered. If only her father hadn't insisted at a look at the Paris he'd loved long ago. Luke lifted a strand of her heavy hair and rubbed it lightly between his fingers. Suddenly he understood why the Victorians wore brooches containing curls from the hair of their lost loved ones. He worshiped her, he admitted helplessly. He would give almost anything to spare her this, but not a day more of their life together than was necessary.

With the tip of a cautious finger, he caressed the back of her hand, hoping, at least, to wake her into a moment of brief happiness before he had to tell her the news. "Tessa," he whispered, "Tessa, Tessa darling, wake up. Wake up, my little sweetheart . . ."

"Can she speak?" Tessa asked the nurse as she approached the door of her mother's room in the intensive-care unit of St. John's Hospital. She'd insisted on Luke's remaining in the waiting room, knowing that her mother wouldn't want him to see her broken and dying.

"She's said your name, from time to time, but that's all."

"Can you leave me alone with her?"

"Of course. Ring when you need me."

Tessa pushed the door open and forced herself to approach the bed. Terror and pity brought her to her knees the instant she looked down at Agnes. Only a few strands of her mother's hair, dark, curly, and still incongruously alive, identified her as the handsome woman she had been. Tessa was too deeply shocked to cry. Quickly she struggled up from the floor and sat in the chair by the hospital bed. It wouldn't help her mother to see her kneeling as if by a grave.

"Mother, it's Teresa. I'm here, Mother."

Agnes's eyelids, under the cast on her forehead, remained closed, but her lips moved slightly.

"Mother, can you hear me? It's Teresa."

"Teresa," Agnes said in a dry whisper, "I'm dying."

"No, Mother, no you're not, you'll get better . . ." Tessa's voice trailed off at the expression of faint scorn with which her mother received her attempt at comfort.

"Listen, Teresa . . . important, don't tell husband about Maggie . . . never . . . never . . . promise me . . . important . . . my pride . . . my life work . . . don't ruin . . . worked so hard . . ."

"Mother, don't worry, for God's sake don't worry, I won't tell anyone anything, but don't worry about Maggie. Luke will take care of everything, everyone. Maggie's safe, I'm safe. Mother, I love you."

"Proud of you . . . good girl . . . don't spoil your life . . . I always loved you best . . . always . . ."

"Mother. Mother!" Tessa searched her mother's face. The spark of life had suddenly but unquestionably blown out. She knelt and prayed at length for her mother's soul. She looked up at the bed and saw that she could just reach the fingertips on her mother's right hand where they protruded from the cast, the nails still bearing the discreet shade of soft pink she'd chosen for the wedding. Tessa clasped Agnes's fingertips in one hand, closed her eyes, and held them tenderly.

"Always loved her best," her mother's last words . . . why did they surprise her, Tessa asked herself in desolation. Hadn't her mother put her first for as long as she could remember? Believed in her, fought for her, planned for her? Used all her power to keep her from the consequences of her mistake? And how had Tessa repaid her mother? She'd been angry when she'd crept into school rehearsals, she'd deceived and mocked her with Mimi, she'd replaced her with Fiona, she'd taken her devotion for granted or scorned it as meddling—this woman who'd had such a tiny measure of love in her life.

Suddenly Tessa remembered how her mother had been barred from her first audition and how nastily superior she'd felt, entering that fateful room alone. Even that pleasure, a pleasure that would have meant so much to her mother, a pleasure she'd thoroughly earned, had been denied her. Painful tears, tears of shame, filled Tessa's eyes as she took the meager measure of her mother's life. Agnes had been a hard mother to love, she had a knack for saying the wrong thing in the wrong way, she'd never forgiven Tessa for getting into trouble when she was a teenager, yet nothing could change the fact that for years she'd been the chief joy of her mother's life. Her mother had been as good a mother as she'd known how to be, as she'd been able to be, Tessa realized, sobbing for the young, hopeful Agnes Riley, who'd believed she was making a romantic marriage—sobbing for herself and the understanding she'd reached too late.

Behind her she heard the steps of the nurse returning. Tessa rose to her feet.

"Oh, Miss Kent, she's gone. I'm so very sorry. Was she able to recognize you before . . . ?" the nurse asked, unable to repress her curiosity.

"Yes. She was . . . herself . . . until the end . . . herself, more than ever herself."

14

I s she—?" Luke asked as Tessa walked slowly into the waiting room.

"She's gone. She recognized my voice, she said a few words, but then she . . . I watched her die . . . one second she was alive and the next she just . . . wasn't . . . she was only thirty-eight . . . oh, Luke, I wish I'd been a better daughter, but it's too late, too late now, too late forever."

"Oh my darling, my Tessa, don't say things like that," Luke urged, pressing her tightly against his shoulder. "If you could have realized how proud she was of you, her eyes lit up when she looked at you, you made her happy. Nothing can make this accident worse than it is except thinking like that."

Luke patted Tessa's back as if she were a child who had fallen and hurt herself, but she made herself draw away from him, knowing that if she broke down again, she'd never gather up the courage to leave the circle of his comfort. In time she'd have to absorb the loss of her parents, but now she had an immediate duty, a responsibility that couldn't wait.

"Luke, I have to tell Maggie. The Kellys promised

not to say a word until they heard from me. We should go there right now. Maggie is worried because her parents are late."

"Do you think she has that precise a sense of time?"

"She'd made a little calendar before they left and crossed off each day. Mother told me that in Monte Carlo. Now Maggie knows that all the days have passed and they still haven't come back. Oh, Lord in heaven, how—no, *what* am I going to tell her?"

"The truth, what else is there?"

"A five-year-old child? This was the first time they'd ever left her, they were her whole life . . ."

"There's no way to get around it, darling. Maggie will never see them again, you'll have to explain it clearly."

"But how? Mommy and Daddy went to a wedding and then to Paris and then straight on to heaven? How could a little girl understand that?"

"You have to tell her about the accident."

"I know."

"I'd tell her for you, if I possibly could, but she's never laid eyes on me."

"Oh, Luke, Luke, there are some things even you can't protect me from," Tessa said. "What you can do is deal with the hospital administrator and call Father Vincent at their church—it's St. Charles of the Holy Savior in Santa Monica—and start making the . . . arrangements, while I go and talk to Maggie. I think it would confuse her to meet you for the first time at this moment. I won't be alone—Mimi's still waiting downstairs in the car. You were an angel to know that I'd need her and to get her here so quickly. Then we'll all come back to the hotel with Maggie. Fiona should be there by then."

"Your aunts are waiting to hear, I can take care of that too."

"Oh, would you, darling? They know you and I'm not sure when I can get to a phone."

"Right. Just tell me something before you leave, is Maggie . . . just how emotional and sensitive is she?"

I'm not sure, Tessa thought, I don't truly know her that well.

"I refuse to believe this," Mimi said as they sat side by side in the limo, the window raised between them and the driver. "A bride and an orphan in six days. No wonder you look so . . . I can't find any word but 'blank.'"

"I'm not letting myself feel any more emotion than I can help, not until I've told Maggie. At least my mother and I managed to say we loved each other before she died. We did, you know, in a strange and difficult way, I realize that now, Mimi, when it's too late. Naturally that's always the case, isn't it? Funny, I was always convinced that my father loved me. In his own severe, upright, old-fashioned way, I could tell somehow that he cared for me but he just couldn't talk about it, not really ever. But with a father, my father anyway, you don't expect much . . . you get so you don't mind. The only thing that helps is that they knew they didn't have to worry about me anymore . . . especially my mother . . ."

"Was she able to say anything else?" Mimi asked hesitantly.

"Oh yes, she managed to make herself very plain. With her last words. She was an amazing woman, Mimi. So strong."

"What does that mean . . . or shouldn't I even ask? I have no idea how I'm supposed to behave now."

"You're supposed to be Mimi and nothing but Mimi and you're the only person in the world who can ask that question and get an answer. She told me never to tell Luke about Maggie, never to tell *anyone* about Maggie, never to, I guess she meant 'destroy,' or something like that, her pride, her life's work, never to ruin— she only said 'ruin' but obviously she meant the entire story, the whole edifice she'd built up with her family, her sisters, the way she simply made everything happen, even starting me in my career. She kept herself alive to tell me that, I'm sure of it."

"But—"

"What?"

"Well, I mean, you weren't *planning* to tell for God's sake, were you?"

"I don't know what to do, Mimi, I just don't know what's the right thing to do. After all, she . . . Maggie . . . is my daughter."

Tessa began to weep again, not merely tears over the loss of her parents, but tears of utter confusion. Her mother's dying words resonated in her ears no less strongly than Luke's when he'd told her, over and over, how deeply important it was to him that she was a virgin. And she'd tacitly confirmed that lie each time he'd said it. Over and over. There had been exactly one perfect chance, one ideal moment to tell him about Maggie, on their first evening together, and she'd rejected the opportunity instantly, with every bit of intuition and instinct and reason she possessed. If she made herself tell him the truth now, he'd never believe in her again, never trust her again. She would have made him into a fool. She'd allowed, no, she'd encouraged him to believe she was a virgin. He'd know her to be a deliberate, constant, confirmed liar, and perhaps his love would die. Or if not die, certainly change. Consciously or not, she'd used her technical virginity every minute she was with him. It *illuminated* their love. But Maggie had a mother of her own, even if that person was on her way to tell her that her mother and father had gone to heaven.

"Tessa! Stop it right now!" Mimi handed her a wad of Kleenex. "You don't have time to cry! Now listen to me. Maggie has only known one mother in her life, not two. You're her big sister, the one she's damn lucky to have, the sister who can make sure that she spends the rest of her life being happy and taken care of. If you're thinking of some damn stupid moment of truth, some need to bring up the past, stamp on it!"

Tessa blew her nose and listened to Mimi, whose admonishments had so often shown her the way—

although, she reminded herself, not necessarily the right way.

"Remember your mother's last words, Tessa. You simply can't go against them! The truth Maggie knows is that her parents and your parents are the same people and they're dead. What on earth would you have to gain by stepping forward and claiming Maggie now? What a media orgy that would be if it ever got out, and how wouldn't it? Give me a break! 'The Secret of Tessa Kent's Bastard Child!' Please! She's yours anyway, no one can take her away from you, you're her next of kin."

"I know."

"Then where's the problem? You must have a major self-destructive streak if you ever *dream* of telling him. Shape up, girl! You're thinking crazy. Luke doesn't know and doesn't ever need to know, your mother would die all over again if you told anybody . . . or she'd come back and kill you herself . . . and as far as I'm concerned, it was a virgin birth and I can swear to that."

"Don't remind me. Oh Lord have mercy on me, we're here."

"I don't see why a little girl should go to a funeral," Mimi said. "It's bad enough without seeing the whole thing."

Tessa, Luke, Mimi, and Fiona were having a room-service lunch while Maggie took her nap in the bedroom next to the sitting room. She hadn't burst into tears when Tessa had told her. She'd sighed deeply, asked one question, and then silently, stoically, and solemnly thrust her thumb into her mouth and sat passively in Tessa's arms, refusing to snuggle or talk or ask any more questions. Later she'd refused anything more than a glass of milk at lunch, although they'd all taken turns at trying to tempt her to eat. Tessa wondered how much Maggie had been able to take in of the facts she'd been told. She had no idea how a five-year-old thought about death, she realized, trying to remember details of her forgotten catechism classes. Even though Maggie hadn't started them yet, she'd been going to Sunday mass for years; she'd certainly absorbed the basics.

"I don't agree," Tessa said to Mimi. "I think there needs to be a feeling of finality, a visual punctuation mark, a ceremony she can watch and talk about with us and remember afterward, so that Maggie understands that her parents haven't merely disappeared for a while. When I told her about the accident she asked, 'Like on the five-o'clock news?' Those were the only words she uttered. She didn't even ask what was going to happen to her now—that's an enormous amount of denial. I don't know what to do except let her see the funeral."

"I think you're right," Luke agreed. "We can make the mass as easy as possible for her, but I don't think she should go to the cemetery and see the caskets lowered into the ground. That's too much reality. I remember my grandfather's funeral, and the burial part scared me for years. I still have nightmares about it."

"That's where I could come in," Fiona volunteered. "The mass is scheduled for late morning. After it's over I'll have lunch with Maggie here and then we'll watch television or play or she can take a nap, whatever she wants to do, until you get back from the cemetery."

"I've talked to Father Vincent," Luke continued, "and we've agreed that the closed caskets will be placed at the altar of St. Charles of the Holy Savior before anyone comes in. He tells me that in any case a Requiem Mass is short. I've left instructions that somebody should take the black ribbons off the flowers people send . . . silly, I suppose, but it seems less ominous for a little girl. There'll be the organ music, of course, and I've asked for as large a choir as possible—I hope she'll be more interested in that than in the mass. Tessa and I won't take communion at the end because it would mean leaving her with people she doesn't know."

"You've thought of everything," Fiona said, "except for the wake."

"Wrong, the wake was easy. One phone call to the manager. It'll be right here, at the Bel-Air. Thank God for wakes," Luke said, taking Tessa's hand. "People will come straight here from the cemetery. By that time, if I remember correctly, they're all starving and dying for a drink, not necessarily in that order."

"Amen," said Mimi. "Will we see all the wedding guests again?"

"Except for my cousins and their kids," Tessa said. "However, lots of the people I've worked with will probably come, and Luke's employees who live nearby, Maggie's godparents of course, and my parents' other friends, my father's pupils, his fellow teachers—Lord knows who'll show up."

"Tyler is on his way from New York," Luke added. "He'll be here in time for the funeral."

Tessa raised her eyebrows in surprise. She wouldn't have expected Tyler Webster, that elegant gent who had talked horses to her in Monaco, to come all this way for the funeral of people he'd just met and barely knew. Still, Luke was Tyler's stepbrother even if they rarely saw each other. It was thoughtful of him, but then he'd seemed to be a particularly sweet man.

Had they turned into angels already, Maggie wondered, listening to the sound of the grown-ups' voices in the next room, as she lay curled into as tight a ball as possible, clutching her favorite doll, one of the armload of toys the blond lady named Mimi had hastily gathered up to bring with her, along with some of her clothes. How long did it take to get out of Purgatory? In church, they never said the number of hours or days or weeks, but she knew that when Tessa said her mommy and daddy were in Heaven, Tessa didn't understand about Purgatory. Nobody ever told you anything about what Purgatory looked like. The priests talked about Hell and

Heaven, but Purgatory was a big nothing. A big fat nothing.

Anyway, they'd be in Heaven soon, she was sure of that, because if you were good that's where you went when you died even if you had to go to Purgatory first. Died. That was the right word. Her best friend, Susan, said that people "passed away," but it said in the Bible that Jesus died on the cross, not that he'd passed away on the cross. They'd have big white wings and wear long white dresses like her mother's nightgowns and sit at the foot of God. When the angels flew around in heaven, did they ever have accidents, did they ever bump into each other, could they ever die again like in a taxi accident? The priests on Sunday said that Heaven was a place of perfect happiness that lasted forever, but how could her parents be happy when she was all alone down here? How could they be happy when they missed her? They'd said they'd miss her when they went away for the wedding but they'd promised her that they'd be back in a week, and now Tessa said they weren't coming back, not ever, because of the taxi accident. So they'd miss her unless she went to heaven too, but she didn't want to die, not even to sit at the foot of God and fly around on wings and be happy forever.

It was all mixed up, Maggie thought, tears rolling down her face, and nobody, not even the grown-ups, not even the priests, could explain it right, or maybe they really did know but they kept it a secret from little kids and that wasn't fair. She wished Susan was with her so they could talk about it, even if Susan said "passed away" and not "died."

15

The wake had been in full swing for several hours when Mimi took Tessa aside. "Do you think you could split for a few minutes?" Mimi whispered in her ear. "I've got to get some fresh air."

Out of the corner of her eye Tessa saw Patsy, her least favorite aunt, bearing down on her. Hastily she turned, put her arm around Mimi's waist, and headed for the doorway.

"What a brilliant idea," Tessa breathed in relief. "I shouldn't stay away long, but this wake is getting to me. And I'm afraid to have a drink because I have to remember so many names."

They walked down the stone pathways of the Hotel Bel-Air, inhaling the rich scents of the flowering bushes and fragrant annuals that were planted in thick borders everywhere, until they came to a quiet courtyard with a central fountain and a wooden bench.

"Wow, your family can really drink up a storm," Mimi said in amazement.

"You're one to talk."

"Maggie seemed to be having a better time than I would have expected."

"That's one of the things about wakes, people pay a lot of attention to kids so they get distracted and forget why they're there for a while."

"She was so composed at the funeral it scared me," Mimi said.

"I know, I noticed the same thing. More denial? Oh, Mimi, would you believe that I can't even think straight about my parents, all I can think about is what to do with Maggie?"

"I can't tell you what the answer to that is, but I do know the one thing you can't do, not ever, and that's raise her, you and Luke."

"But that's the natural—"

"It would be, if she were your sister, no matter how complicated it got, but in the circumstances, no, Tessa, just plain no. Find another way."

"Why, Mimi, why? I could carry it off, I'm an actress, he'd never guess . . ."

"Maybe not, but I'm thinking of you, living each day fooling him and fooling her and trying to fool yourself, what is quaintly known as 'living a lie.' You wouldn't make it, Tessa, not for long."

"You can't know that!"

"I've been your friend forever, remember? You and your crazy sense of guilt and sin. Teresa Horvath, the last of the big-time sinners, do you think I've forgotten, or that you've basically changed? Sooner or later, as Maggie grows up and gives you the usual problems kids give, the big sister facade would disappear and the maternal instinct to tell her what to do would take over. You'd crack, Tessa! You couldn't avoid making a slip, or you'd give up and just confess the truth, but before that happened, you'd be a wreck. Always nervous, always watching yourself trying not to act too motherly, always keeping an eye on Luke's reaction to the two of you together, always afraid of doing too much for Maggie, or worse, not enough."

"You've always loved to tell me what to do!" Tessa protested.

"You wouldn't be the woman Luke married anymore," Mimi continued, paying no attention, "and he wouldn't understand why, and of course he'd blame Maggie. My God, Tessa, you had exactly four days together before this happened. You're a couple of barely newlyweds with a lot of adjustments to make like everybody else—you hardly know each other when it gets down to that, to say nothing of the major age difference, which I've been too polite to mention till now. Luke's a guy who can have anything he wants, and children haven't been high on his list. Don't tell me *that's* an accident. Or is there something I don't know?"

"He's never wanted children," Tessa admitted miserably. "He said, maybe in ten years . . . I'll only be thirty . . ."

"Well then! You simply *cannot* take on the burden and responsibility of a five-year-old child on top of everything else, not when there are four aunts, each one of whom made a point of telling you that she wanted Maggie to come and live with her, each one of whom has plenty of child-rearing experience."

"My mother was the youngest of them all. The aunts are in their forties, some even in their fifties, and their kids are mostly grown up."

"So what? Do you imagine that at twenty you'll be better and smarter about bringing up a kid?"

"They're not her mother," Tessa said stubbornly, seeing Maggie's set, plump, big-eyed face, the long, dark braids she tugged at, the valiant way she walked, never dragging her feet no matter how new the situation.

"Her mother died, come on! She's already accepted that. You're her sister, who visits her whenever you can and brings her wonderful presents and ends up being the person who understands her best, the person she can really talk to and confide in, the person whose advice she follows—you're her fairy godmother, instead of the person who tells her to finish her homework and eat her peas. You get to spoil her to your heart's delight!"

"Oh, Mimi, you should have your own advice column. 'Ask Mimi, the All-Wise One,' circulation one hundred million. You're so quick to jump at a decision for someone else, imagining that they think the way you think. Hasn't it occurred to you that I *know* I'm not Maggie's sister, that I *know* I'm her mother, that I *know* I have a duty toward her? *Don't you understand that I love Maggie?* I was never allowed to mother her the way I yearned to, but there was never a minute when I didn't love her. I gave birth to her, for the love of God, I carried her for nine months, all the good reasons in the world can't change those facts. Oh, Mimi, I'm in agony. No matter what I do, I'm going to be wrong, there's no way out of this, no honorable way."

"Will you think about what I said?"

"Naturally, but I can't let you make up my mind for me."

"God forbid."

Tessa wondered angrily why she was still awake. After the last guest had left, after Maggie and blessed Fiona, without whose help she'd be utterly lost, had settled down in the neighboring suite, she'd planned to go to bed no matter how early in the evening it was, and sleep as long as she possibly could. Jet lag, her parents' funeral, followed by an Irish wake—the longest, saddest day of her life—surely all that would put her into a state of immediate and necessary unconsciousness. But after trying to let go and relax for a half hour, thinking about Maggie each minute, she gave up and went to find Luke, who was reading in the sitting room next to the bedroom.

"What are you doing here, sweetheart? You look like Ophelia on a bad day," he said, plunking her down in his lap and kissing her neck under the tangle of hair she'd been too tired to bother brushing.

"Can't sleep. I still have jet lag on top of everything else. Look, that damn old sun hasn't even set yet. I wonder what time it is back in Èze."

"Almost dawn."

"I feel as if I've left some hugely important piece of my soul there."

"We'll go back, darling, I promise, we'll go hundreds of times."

"But when? And anyway, it'll never be the same."

"Nothing is ever exactly the same, but we'll be there together."

"How long could we have stayed if . . . ?"

"I'd been able to carve out ten days after our wedding. Counting from the day I met you, I haven't attended to business, and normally I never take more than a week or two off, maximum. After Èze we have to spend a week in Melbourne; there's a major board meeting that's been planned for months. Then, we fly to Houston for a few days and go up to Anchorage to take a look at . . ."

"So even if we hadn't had to come back here, we'd have had only another few days in Èze anyway?"

"Four more, but I could be wrong by a day."

"So it wouldn't make sense to go back there now and then have to turn around and leave for Australia when we're halfway to Australia already?" Tessa asked in a forlorn, willfully blind attempt to roll back events and recapture her honeymoon.

"Is that what was keeping you up? Impossible confusions of time changes, the International Dateline, and travel schedules running through your head?"

"Everything is keeping me up," she said, bursting into tears, pressing herself tightly into the shelter formed by Luke's lap and chest and arms and letting herself go completely, weeping as loudly and unselfconsciously as a child locked away in a closet, wailing and moaning in a raw wordless lament that went on and on. Luke did nothing to stop her, gripping her as tightly as he could without hurting her. High time, he thought, high time.

After a long while, with a final descent into a diminishing series of sniffs and whimpers, Tessa started to dab at her eyes with the hem of her nightgown. "I need a bath towel," she said in a choked voice, "but I feel better."

"I'll get you a wet washcloth and a face towel," Luke said.

"No, don't go away, not for a second, don't let go of me yet," she pleaded.

"I won't," Luke said, picking her up, carrying her into the bathroom, grabbing a couple of towels and a box of Kleenex, and returning with her to the chair. "There, everything you could possibly want. How about a drink? Or vanilla ice cream with chocolate sauce?"

"Just a kiss. And another kiss. God, I love you. What a honeymoon you've had. Aren't you glad you didn't get married before?"

"I'm glad I didn't get married to anyone else."

"Even now?"

"Especially now. Tessa, I know I told you that I didn't want to share you with kids for ten years, but darling, that was before and this is entirely different, and what I said shouldn't count anymore." He set his lips sternly. "We'll bring up Maggie."

"Oh, Luke, you just said we have to go to Melbourne, Texas, and Alaska and that's only in the next few weeks."

"Darling, we'll hire the best nanny in the world to travel with us. Kids are flexible, Maggie'll have fun seeing so many new things, and then when she's old enough for school, we'll get her a tutor too, several tutors if necessary, and by the time she's, oh, eight or nine, whenever little girls usually go away to boarding school, we'll send her off, so she could make friends of her own age. There are some marvelous schools in Switzerland or England, even in Australia, wherever she'd be happiest, and she could be with us on vacations."

"But Luke, Maggie's in kindergarten now, she's already had two years of preschool, and next year she starts first grade. Children need to be 'socialized' from practically day one, not three or four years from now."

"They do?" Luke looked blank. "Socialized?"

"I honestly didn't remember either, until you started making those sweet, impossible, mixed-up plans. I'd forgotten what it was like when I was little, all those happy hours throwing sand into the other kids' eyes, playing games, making friends. Look, all of my mother's sisters want Maggie to go and live with them."

"How do you feel about that?"

"I think that the most important thing is for her to be brought up in a family with kids roughly her age, so she has a normal family life. Each of my aunts assured me that Maggie would be treated like a little princess, and I know only too well what they meant."

"What, exactly?"

"She'd become a fabulous, glamorous orphan, someone to concentrate on completely now that most of their own children are grown and out of the house. She's the little sister of a movie star, protected by a man, her brother-in-law no less, who has more money than they can begin to imagine, a man who naturally would want Maggie—and, by extension, themselves—to have the best of everything. A new house, a new car, and all expenses paid for them. For Maggie, private schools, riding lessons, ballet lessons, beautiful clothes—"

"Well, of course she should have all those things," Luke said indignantly.

"It would make Maggie the *power* in the house, the center of everything, overwhelmed by attention and spoiling, and she'd understand the dynamics quickly enough. It would be the worst thing possible for her. And any aunt we decided to send Maggie to would queen it over the others, just the way my poor mother acted with her sisters at the wedding. You missed seeing that, but I didn't. It was ghastly."

"But there's no other answer," Luke said, shaking his head.

"I can't say I liked my cousins at the wedding, but at least some of them are the right age, with young families. I think that while you're in Australia I should take a trip back East, take Maggie with me, and get to know them better, spend time with each of their families. There's got to be one family Maggie could fit into happily."

"Hmm," Luke murmured. "Let's talk this over in the morning. I promise you we'll find a solution. It's too complicated to settle tonight, and anyway, you look so exhausted. I bet if you went to bed and I held your hand, you'd be asleep in minutes."

"I'll try," Tessa agreed, yawning.

"What an accommodating girl you are."

As Luke watched Tessa fall into a profound sleep, he thought about her cousins, a bunch of unfriendly, impolite, classless oafs, in his opinion, with a mob of ill-mannered, unappealing kids. Perhaps they'd been totally intimidated by the whole occasion, perhaps they were the salt of the earth in their own homes, but he didn't mind admitting to himself that snobbish or not, he had no intention of letting his wife's sister be brought up with yobs. There was, thank God, another solution.

Very early the next morning, Luke got up quietly, leaving Tessa still deeply asleep. He called his stepbrother, Tyler Webster, who was due to fly home in a few hours, woke him, and asked him to meet him in a half hour in the dining room.

"Good of you to have dressed so quickly, Tyler."

"Least I could do, Luke."

"No, Tyler, it's only the beginning."

"Huh?"

"Tyler, there's something very, very important you can do for me."

"Just ask," Tyler replied, with his sweet and thoughtful smile.

"It's something that won't go unrecognized, in fact, something that will be most highly rewarded, even by your standards."

"Luke, come on guy, you already do more than enough."

"I'm aware of that," Luke said, concentrating on spreading marmalade carefully on a piece of toast.

The Webster family lived entirely on Luke's largesse. Charming Tyler combined fatal bad judgment with a talent for laziness. He had never been able to keep a job for more than two months. Luke's father had thrown him out of the family business in less time than that, afraid of what promises his bumbling, incompetent stepson might make on no authority but his own desire to please. However, because Dan Blake loved his American second wife, Tyler's mother, he had made Tyler a generous allowance, so generous that Tyler was able to concentrate on his one serious passion. Riding horses beautifully was the only occupation for which Tyler was fit, and horses were the only thing he cared deeply about.

After his father's death, Luke had continued the allowance, and when an unresisting Tyler had been married by Madison Grant, a plain Jane of a good family, a clever girl who saw Tyler clearly and knew that he was her best chance at a good life, Luke had increased the allowance and bought them a handsome stud farm near Madison's family's home, in the New Jersey hunt country. There Tyler could live as one in that line of old-fashioned country gentlemen whose gene pool he had too liberally inherited. Luke paid for everything, from the children's schools to Madison's beautiful clothes and the parties she gave so well. The Websters' neighbors, horse people like themselves, assumed that they had a large private income and Tyler's mettle and judgment were never tested. The stud itself, even under a qualified manager, just about broke even, but in years when it lost money, Luke made up the difference without flinching.

"Luke, what's up? You look so serious."

"I want you and Madison to bring up Maggie, Tessa's sister."

"What!"

"There's no one else who'll do. Maggie's aunts are too old and her cousins aren't suitable. She's a dear little girl and she needs to be in a good, stable, loving family environment. Tessa and I aren't going to be leading that kind of life—there's a worldwide business to run and there's Tessa's career; we'll rarely be in one place for long. How old are your children now?"

"Uh . . . wait a minute . . . right, Allison's eight, Candice's ten, and Barney's, gosh, four and a half."

"Spot on. Does Barney have a nanny? Excellent, he can share her with Maggie. As I remember you have a guest suite, right? Good. Plenty of room for Maggie. What I'd appreciate your doing, right now as a matter of fact, is calling Madison and telling her to pack herself and the kids up and fly out here today. They can take the company's New York plane; they'll gain three hours, so they can be here before dinner."

"Today!"

"The sooner Tessa knows that Maggie's going to be happy in her new home, the better for everybody."

"Oh, sure, I can understand that. Gosh, I wonder what Madison's going to say."

"She'll understand, Tyler. You won't even have to explain when she knows how important it is to me. *Essential,* as a matter of fact. Waiter, could you bring a phone to the table please?"

Madison Webster and her three children walked over the bridge in front of the entrance to the Hotel Bel-Air, as unrumpled as if they'd just driven over from Beverly Hills. Maggie stood shyly, but holding her ground, as the introductions were made.

"Well, well, so this is Maggie! What a dear little girl you are," Madison said, bending down to kiss her cheek. "I'm so glad to meet you."

"Thank you," Maggie mumbled.

"Barney, why don't you shake hands with Maggie," Tyler suggested nervously.

"How old are you?" Barney demanded, looking Maggie in the eye.

"Five."

"You're older than I am but I'm taller than you. Much taller," he announced with satisfaction, a big, warm, friendly grin splitting his freckled face. He took her hand in his and squeezed it tightly, pumping it up and down. "Wanna play?"

"Play what?"

"Just play, Maggie. Come on, I'll show you. I know lots of good games, fun games, maybe we'll build a tree house, you'll like that." Barney didn't bother to say hello to his uncle Luke or his new aunt. Without letting go of Maggie's hand, Barney tugged the little girl away into the gardens, both of them soon breaking into a run. Maggie's laugh rang out as they rounded a corner and vanished from sight.

"Me Tarzan, you Jane," Tessa said, smiling for the first time in days.

16

Before Maggie Horvath came to live with them, Madison Webster had formed for herself a number of complicated rules of domestic economy. All of her singularly expensive, marvelously simple clothes were bought at Bergdorf's, but she took care of them beautifully and wore them forever; she'd never indulged in redecoration of their large country house, but instead cultivated the shabby English look. If a piece of furniture was on the verge of becoming too shamefully worn, she replaced its fabric with the same pattern, remaining consistent to the style already established.

She bought no jewels at all, contenting herself with those few simple pieces Tyler had inherited from his mother; she used a third-rate caterer for her parties, making all the most important dishes herself, for she had taken several Cordon-Bleu courses and could cook beautifully, although none of her friends knew it. She learned to care for indoor plants so she never had to pay for fresh flowers except for entertaining. She could still use her grandmother's invisibly darned, heavy lace table linen for parties as well as the heavy, old-fashioned silver she'd inherited directly when her grandmother died, along with a number of dark, impressive family portraits, which she'd hung carefully in places of honor.

She made sure that her station wagon and Tyler's Jaguar were regularly serviced and then washed daily by one of the stable boys, so they could keep their cars until they became classics. Her sheets and towels were bought at white sales, all of her daughters' clothes were bought on sale, she used drugstore makeup and supermarket generic brands of soap, toilet paper, paper towels, and canned goods. One of the maids was delegated to clip coupons, and Madison did all the shopping herself, never trusting her cook to find bargains. She kept two fridges, one for the help's cheap food, one for the family's. All four of her dogs came from the pound.

However, she spared no expense on certain details. She made it a point to have at least one more waiter than necessary whenever she entertained so that her parties ran with smooth perfection; her cellar was so excellently stocked that Tyler passed for a wine collector; she went for a trim every three weeks to the best hairdresser in New York; she never bought an item of leather that wasn't from Hermès; her cocktail napkins and guest towels came from Frette; a chipped Waterford glass was promptly replaced with another; and her daughters both attended the hideously expensive Elm Country Day School, while Barney was destined for Phillips Andover.

This combination of invisible thrift and conspicuous luxuries was not imposed on Madison by the limitations of the allowance Luke made to Tyler. She could have spent far more money than she did and still stayed well within its yearly amount.

Luke didn't know, and Tyler didn't notice, that Madison steadily saved healthy amounts each year, investing them in a deeply conservative, no-load mutual fund with a steady performance record. Her personal dreaded rainy day would only come if Luke died. Without him, the Webster family would have no income at all. Not a bean. Unlike her grandmother, her parents could leave her nothing, and Tyler . . . well, Tyler was a gentleman, not a businessman, to put it as gently as possible.

Maggie's arrival four years earlier had been a guarantee that as long as the little girl lived with the Websters, they could count on receiving far more money from Luke, or his estate, than they had before—a guarantee made in writing by the chief partner in the law firm Luke employed in Manhattan.

Why couldn't she like Maggie, Madison asked herself in irritation. Why couldn't she feel even a flicker of genuine warmth for the nine-year-old who had made it possible for her to invest so much more than ever before? Maggie's presence in their house had, from the day she arrived, ensured a minimum of thirteen years of respite from any rainy day, since she would certainly live with them until she was eighteen. Even when she went off to college, Madison told herself, Luke would unquestionably agree that she'd need a home to come back to for school vacations, no matter how often she was able to visit her sister.

It simply wasn't possible that she could be so stupid as to still resent the imperious, high-handed, arrogant way in which Luke had taken it for granted that she would welcome a strange child into her home. He hadn't even had the courtesy to ask her to do it as a favor to him . . . yet she could never forget that oversight, try as she had. To be perfectly honest, his presumption *had,* in the most cold-blooded way, rubbed their noses in their indebtedness to him. It was not as if there had ever been any question that they owed him everything . . . but could they be blamed for not liking to be reminded of it? It made her feel so . . . *powerless,* so deeply humiliated, Madison told herself, as she had done far too many times in the past four years, ever since Maggie had been dumped on their doorstep.

True, Luke had never asked them to do anything for him before. Perhaps those early years of scrupulously hands-off treatment had dimmed her understanding of the ignominious position her husband was in, a position which, in moments of gloom, made her feel exactly like the wife of a worthless remittance man.

But even now, every time she laid eyes on Maggie, she was reminded of how much she owed Luke, or was it how much she owed Maggie? One thing came down to the other, if you considered it with any precision—which, thank you, she would prefer not to have to do, although she couldn't help being obsessed by it. God knows, Tyler never gave their position a thought. But then Tyler didn't consider anything with precision, and she'd always known it, so why should she resent being made conscious all over again of the deliberate bargain she'd made? She had, sensibly, preferred marrying an incompetent fool to remaining single. What woman wouldn't?

But there was no getting away from it: when Maggie called her "Aunt Madison" she rejected the term in her mind. When Maggie came to live with them, they had decided it was the least confusing form of address for a child of five who was—too ridiculously for words—Tyler's stepbrother's wife's sister. Or, to make it more confusing, her own brother-in-law's sister-in-law. But she wasn't Maggie's aunt, damn it, and Tyler wasn't her uncle. They weren't the slightest relation to Maggie. Maggie didn't come from their kind of background, she didn't come from a family heritage you could respect, and nothing could change that. Under normal circumstances she would never have taken Maggie into her home to live, and she knew her neighbors had raised many an eyebrow when she'd tried to explain the tragic circumstances that had, so suddenly, made Maggie a part of their family.

She'd put the best possible face on it, but she knew that many members of the bridge club, the hunt club, and the tennis club wondered why Maggie occupied the guest suite, when her own daughters shared a room. What would they say if they knew that she'd never dared to severely reprove Maggie, although the girl drove her crazy with her inability to keep her blouse tucked into her skirt or her pants, to say nothing of the way she managed to get spots on clean clothes within minutes of putting them on. She was such an unfeminine thing, always dashing around with Barney as if she were another little boy, her unruly hair looking as if it had never been brushed, her face as if it had never been washed. None of the exquisite, and totally inappropriate, party dresses or fine sweater sets that she brought back from her visits to her sister had ever survived more than a few weeks of Maggie's treatment, but then they were entirely unsuitable for a child in any case, and infuriating when she had to imagine what they'd cost. The money that was lavished on that child! It was unseemly, in her opinion, utterly unseemly.

You could always tell when Maggie was in the house: the sound of her bold laugh, entirely too loud and too frequent, the sound of her feet—couldn't that child ever walk instead of running up and down stairs?—and then her boisterous entrance into any room, with the expectation of a hungry puppy, bursting with observations and questions. She seemed to need attention and, worse, long for affection that Madison didn't, couldn't possibly be expected to feel and would have to be a skillful actress to produce. Really, it was too much! Affection on demand! Maggie took up more air than any nine-year-old should be allowed to do. Didn't she have any decent sense of self-consciousness? Couldn't she learn to be less visible? Maggie acted as if she owned the place, Madison thought bitterly, and although the child couldn't possibly realize it, in an indirect way, she did, for every acre of their handsome property belonged to Luke, and Luke and Tessa had no heirs other than Maggie.

Madison sighed, thinking of her own daughters: Candice, the exceptionally pretty one, who was now fourteen, and Allison, who might or might not become the extraordinarily beautiful one, but was now, at twelve, merely promising. What satisfactory children they were! Neat, polite, modest, ladylike girls with perfect manners, who hung up their clothes, polished their riding boots, kept their bedroom and bathroom tidy, and got their homework in on time without her prompting. If only some of their breeding had rubbed off on Maggie!

But, one had to admit, breeding didn't "rub off," it was innate. Tyler came, as she did, from a long line of what she could only term "American aristocrats," every last one of them Protestant, every last one of them proper, every last one of them quietly, admirably at ease in his social environment. Well, all she could say was that whatever momentarily fortunate mix of Irish and Hungarian genes had produced the ravishing Tessa hadn't been in operation when Maggie was conceived. Everything about her high coloring, with skin so white, and cheeks so red, with her thick thatch of black curls and the fierce blueness of her eyes, screamed "Black Irish."

Not that she had anything against the Irish, goodness knows, she wasn't a snob, Madison assured herself, but there simply didn't happen to be any living in the neighborhood. Nor enrolled at Elm Country Day, where Maggie was the only child who had to be driven to confession every Thursday and catechism class every Saturday—a thirty-mile trip each way, with nothing for her to do but sit in the station wagon and read while she waited for the damn things to be over. And yet somehow she didn't dare direct any of the staff to take over those trips. It was much . . . safer . . . for Maggie to report to Tessa that Aunt Madison took her. Thank the good, reasonable Episcopalian Lord that she had the excuse of going to her own church on Sunday, so that she could send Maggie off to mass with the cook.

And what an unsuitable to-do last year, when Maggie made her First Holy Communion! First she'd been endlessly involved in finding a perfect dress. They'd actually had to go all the way into Manhattan to find a decent selection. The only saving grace was that the church was so far away that her friends hadn't been aware of the ceremony. They all knew Maggie was Catholic, of course, but some details were best left to the imagination, such as, good grief, a child of eight outlandishly decked out in a long white dress, a miniature bride drinking the blood and eating the body of Christ.

Shaking her head at the thought, Madison decided to shut herself in her bedroom with the *Wall Street Journal*. It had such a calming effect on her nerves.

"Maggie, do you really have to get up on that pony?" Barney begged, as he watched from the rail of the riding ring. "You know you're not supposed to ride her without a grown-up around."

"I've got to keep practicing," she said, stubbornly, "or she'll never get used to me." Maggie gave her new pony lump after lump of sugar in the forlorn hope that they might ensure good behavior.

Her mount, Fairy, was a Welsh pony, a recent ninth-birthday present from Luke, the equivalent of a valuable thoroughbred horse. Unfortunately, Fairy was smarter, Barney knew, than she should be, an overbred, neurotic, cocky, smug animal with a well-developed mean streak. Maggie should be riding some old school horse that had held ten thousand kids and wouldn't mind what she did to it, but Luke hadn't known, and no one had wanted to tell him.

"Maggie, you stink on a horse, why won't you admit it? There's nothing to be ashamed about."

"Yeah, well tell that to everybody around here. If you can't ride, you might just as well be dead."

"You could at least wait till tomorrow, when your instructor'll be here."

"He bugs me, all those do's and don'ts, it just makes it harder."

"But the do's and don'ts are what help you control the horse."

"You're such a know-it-all, Barney, rules, rules, rules."

"I'm just trying to keep you from breaking your arm again, like you did last year. You know how upset your sister got."

"That wasn't my fault. The horse was spooked by a bird on the trail, and around here a broken arm is no big deal. How can Tessa understand that? I'm riding Fairy, Barney. If you don't want to watch, go back to the house."

Muttering prayers to the Holy Mother and the Infant Jesus under her breath, Maggie led the pony over to the rail, stopped her, and scrambled into the saddle. She settled herself, adjusting the reins perfectly, and gave Fairy a gentle nudge to get her started. The animal walked sedately around the ring. So far, so good, Maggie thought, but riding wasn't about walking around in circles. She gave her mount the signal for a trot and was delighted and surprised to find Fairy responding.

Her real problem, one she had thought about long and hard, was that she was petrified of horses. Every horse she'd ever seen, except newborn foals, looked menacing to her. She hated their rolling eyes, their slobbering lips, their nightmarish nostrils. This fear was something that was absolutely impossible to confess, when everyone in the Webster house, every girl at school, and everyone she'd met since she arrived in Essex County lived to ride.

It was easier to ride badly, but show courage, than to say she didn't want to ride. If she did, everybody would understand her secret. Fear, Maggie knew, would be recognized instantly as the only possible reason anyone could have for not riding, and she'd rather die on a horse than let anyone know she was afraid of one.

"Lookin' good," Barney called encouragingly. Once he'd seen that Maggie's pony was trotting, he'd mounted his own horse, a sturdy, trustworthy little mare, and was following her around the ring.

He'd never seen such a bad seat on anybody, he thought miserably. She just didn't get it. She had bad hands, she couldn't make a horse do what she wanted by using the reins, and the last thing in the world Maggie would ever do was give Fairy a good kick and let the animal know who was in charge. She was too tender-hearted, she said. Bullshit! She was plain chicken, although he'd never tell her he knew, and she was too stubborn to admit it, even to him, her best friend.

Barney watched carefully as Maggie somehow urged the pony into a canter. This was where she usually got into trouble. A cantering Fairy could become a galloping Fairy all too quickly, and Maggie and a galloping horse spelled disaster. He watched closely as she tensed up, pinching the pony with her knees in an effort at control that was doomed to fail since using her knees meant that she couldn't hold on firmly with her calves. Her legs flopped around, her upper body became rigid as she became conscious of her legs, and soon she was jerking the pony in the mouth, trying to get it to stop. Annoyed, Fairy broke into a gallop. White-faced but silent, Maggie hung on, pulling harder and harder on the reins.

Barney easily kicked his mare into a gallop and pulled up alongside, grabbing the reins and gradually slowing the pony down to a snippy little trot.

"Thanks," Maggie said, biting her lip.

"It's nothing. Fairy has a mean temper."

"You know that's not why," she said, panting.

"You could do better on my horse, I know you could."

"I don't think so." Even Fairy was better than getting on a horse she didn't know, Maggie decided.

"You won't even try. Come on, let's stop now."

"No," she insisted, setting her face in a ferocious grimace. "I'm going to get Fairy to canter properly if I have to stay here all night."

Oh, no, Barney thought, there went his baseball practice.

17

Four years earlier, when Tessa had agreed with Luke that Maggie would be happier living with the Websters than with any of her Riley cousins, she had accompanied Maggie to New Jersey while Luke had gone off to his board meeting in Melbourne.

For a week Tessa had lived at the Websters' house, sharing the guest suite with Maggie. She'd come to the conclusion that Maggie was making a reasonably quick adjustment to the new circumstances and would soon feel as much at home as she could anywhere else, considering that the only home she'd ever known had been swept away from under her feet in a flash of incomprehensible loss.

The instant devotion of Barney, a pint-size, gallant cavalier who was fascinated by Maggie and never let her feel alone, had touched Tessa's heart. There was an excellent kindergarten in the neighborhood, and in a year, when Maggie was six, she'd be ready to start first grade at Elm Country Day. Candice and Allison were pleasant, kind children and, of course, Madison and Tyler both had been so welcoming, so full of assurances that one more child around the dinner table would be a joy to them, that Tessa had felt comfortable about joining Luke in Houston. When she had said good-bye to Maggie, she had finally managed to incorporate into her heart as well as her brain all the reasons why this separation was not just the best but the only possible good solution to a situation that had no absolutely perfect solution.

During Maggie's first year with the Websters, Tessa made as many flying visits as she could manage, whenever she was close enough to the East Coast and free from marital or film obligations for several days, but soon she realized that these visits were fundamentally unsatisfactory. They disrupted Maggie's adaptation to her new life, they obliged the Webster family to surround an unexpected guest with gracious attention when she was sure that it couldn't suit them to do so, and she wasn't able to be alone with Maggie in the way she had imagined. Having Maggie visit her, on the other hand, had none of these disadvantages, and from that time on, from 1976, the little girl went to visit her sister when it could be arranged during school vacations or on holidays.

Although Luke tried as hard as he could to take a real interest in Maggie, he never could connect with her on any true emotional level. Tessa soon realized that the visits were more joyful for her and Maggie when they could be alone together, unhampered by a powerful, demanding male presence whose entrance into the house immediately, as if in obedience to a law of nature, switched her focus of attention away from Maggie, do what she could to prevent it.

During these private, precious days together, days that depended on Luke's being away in some far part of the globe where he'd be too busy to need his wife's company, on Tessa's not being in the middle of making a movie, or on Maggie's being able to get out of school— days that were possible to arrange at the very most only several times a year—Maggie was able to bask in her sister's full attention. Whatever city they were in, Tessa arranged her days around Maggie, listening to her stories of the Webster household, sympathizing with the limitations of Candice and Allison—"all they think of is how they look"—joining in fond abuse of Barney—"he never leaves me alone, it's like having a dog, but a nice, friendly old dog"—and fascinated by the details of Madison's thrift—"we'll have a big rib roast for dinner but everyone in the kitchen only gets a stew made from the cheapest meat, isn't that mean? Of course she thinks I don't know, but the cook's my friend and she tells me lots of stuff on the way to mass."

Tessa had a collection of dolls and toys she kept for Maggie to play with, but the little girl lost interest in them as soon as she discovered the joys of "dressing-up." "Dressing-up" was divided into two distinct and very different segments.

The first involved Maggie rigging herself out in bits and pieces she found in a trunk crammed full of fabulous odds and ends that Tessa accumulated by becoming friendly with the wardrobe head on every picture she made. They let Tessa scrounge around and walk off with samples of forgotten, packed-away leftovers of decades of movie making: spangled satin dancing dresses from the 1930s; fur pieces; feather boas; pleated velvet capes; rain slickers; embroidered vests; animal costumes and masks; a score of hats, feathered, veiled, or garlanded with flowers; sequined high-heeled shoes—all manner of gorgeous and fantastic stuff they no longer had use for. All of it found a home in the special trunk that Tessa had had flown across continents when one of Maggie's infrequent visits was anticipated.

Tessa would leave Maggie alone to create a costume on her own and then, when Maggie appeared to startle her with one of her ever-changing inventions, Tessa would create a story to go with the costume, a story in which Maggie was always the heroine.

The other part of "dressing-up" was a far more solemn affair, for it involved Tessa's jewelry. During the four years of their marriage, Luke had discovered or invented all sorts of occasions that served as reason to give Tessa jewels: the first and last day of filming on the one picture she made each year; her birthday; St. Patrick's Day; Valentine's Day; the anniversary of the day they met, of their engagement, of their wedding; the anniversary of the founding of Melbourne; the National Day of Monte Carlo; the auctions of "Magnificent" jewelry at Sotheby's each spring and fall. Failing an occasion, he'd come home with something he'd seen and couldn't resist.

Tessa invariably traveled with a large and ever-changing selection of her jewelry. Luke liked to see her wearing jewels at all times, no matter how casual the occasion. Tessa had huge, unfaceted cabochon sapphires, almost as simple as deep blue glass pebbles, in invisible platinum settings, to wear with jeans and denim shirts. She had baskets full of amusing fantasy jewels designed by Verdura and David Webb in combinations of turquoise, coral, and enameled gold, to wear with her country cottons and she slept in a fabled string of Imperial jade, of an intense green, because Luke superstitiously believed it warded off sickness. But for all her serious clothes, the clothes she wore when she entertained Luke's business associates or met with Hollywood people, or went shopping for the large and varied wardrobe she needed for her complicated life, Tessa had a vast choice of extraordinarily important jewels. She was never tempted, in spite of her age, to play with the "young Hollywood" sloppy look. Tessa was a great international star and she dressed like one. Her jewels were her signature.

When Maggie visited her, often the two of them would spend an entire afternoon in her dressing room, as Tessa showed Maggie some of her jewels, modeling them first and then decking Maggie out in them and letting her observe herself in the mirrors to her heart's content. Tessa turned this special version of "dress-up" into a combination of magic and education.

She had discovered a book called *The Power of Gemstones,* which covered "healing powers, mythical

stones, superstitions, talismans, and mystical proper-
ties" of every kind of jewel, and she studied the background of each piece she intended to show Maggie.

"Here's something special," she said on one occasion
when Maggie was eight or nine, clasping a necklace
around her neck. "Can you guess what they are?"

"They look like round gray-black beads," Maggie
answered. "But I can see green lights and purple lights
in them, so they're not really black at all. And they
reflect all the lights in the room, almost like mirrors.
And, of course, they're shaped like pearls, really big
ones."

"They are pearls, black pearls."

"Does an oyster make them too?"

"A special oyster, called 'pinctada margaritifera,'
which I think is almost a name like Maggie, don't you,
the pink Maggie oyster?"

"Sort of," Maggie said, trying not to smile.

"Those oysters mostly grow in the waters of French
Polynesia, which is here, on this map."

"Will we ever go there?"

"Someday maybe, why not?"

"Are they always this big?"

"Nope, they usually don't get this size," Tessa said,
thinking of the rarity of the necklace, in which the
smallest of the graduated pearls was two millimeters
larger than the largest black pearl normally found and
the central pearl, at nineteen millimeters, was one of the
largest ever offered for sale.

"Are all black pearls this color?" Maggie asked.

"They come in about seventy different shades of
black, which makes it very hard to match them," Tessa
said casually of the necklace that had cost Luke three-
quarters of a million dollars at a Sotheby's auction two
months earlier. "Do you remember what I told you
about how to take care of pearls?"

"Don't keep them in a very warm place because
pearls are two percent water and they'll dry out and
crack; wear them a lot to keep them glowing and happy;

clean them to get rid of sweat by stirring them lightly in potato flour, whatever that is; have them restrung every six months; and, oh, never, ever put them on your neck if you have perfume there, or any kind of lotion, because that can spoil their color. And of course, don't spray your hair when you have your pearls on, because that's the dumbest, it'll ruin their luster for sure . . ."

"Anything else?"

"Hmmm—oh, I remember, don't roll them up when you put them away. Use the case they came in."

"You get an A plus in pearl care," Tessa said with a hug. "Do you know why people used to think the pearl was sacred to the goddess Diana?"

"Nope," Maggie answered, tipping her head back to look adoringly at Tessa.

"Way back, when people worshiped gods and goddesses, Diana was the deity of the woods and of young girls, and pearls were considered to be the sign of innocence, peace, and purity. Pearls were Diana's emblem, and girls, pure, innocent virgins, wore them to put themselves under her protection."

"Oh." Maggie frowned, considering the idea. "So little girls got pearl necklaces?"

"Probably earrings more than necklaces. But the odd thing is that just as long ago, thousands and thousands of years ago, pearls were also connected to the moon and the goddess Venus, and Venus and the moon are connected to lovers, so if a woman wanted a man to fall in love with her, she'd buy a powder made of ground pearls and get him to drink it in a glass of wine. They called that a love potion."

"Did it work?" Maggie asked, fascinated.

"I don't know. Maybe yes, maybe no. Personally I think it takes more than that or everybody'd be doing it and a cute man might find himself in love with a dozen women at once, with a terrible hangover. Doctors used to put powdered pearls in medicines to cure heart problems, and ground-up pearls—not the beautiful ones they could sell, but the ugly ones, about ten percent of what the oysters make—were used for ladies' face powder a few hundred years ago. Even today there are cosmetics, creams and powders, that contain powdered pearls and . . ."

"And?"

"Some Chinese used to think that when dragons are fighting each other in the sky, pearls and rain fall to the earth. I find that a little hard to believe."

"It could be true. How do you know for sure there aren't dragons in the sky? There are angels, so there might be dragons."

"In China anyway," Tessa agreed, taking off the pearls and fastening them around Maggie's neck. "How do you like them?"

"Hmm." Maggie inspected herself closely and then from a distance, revolving in front of a full-length mirror. "I'm not sure. Don't you have earrings to go with them?"

"You drive a hard bargain."

"I know you have earrings," Maggie crowed gleefully. "You have to have, or what else would go with them? And you have to wear earrings, you can't just walk around with naked earlobes, you've told me that a hundred times."

"You should work for a jeweler, on commission."

"Oh, come on, show them to me."

Tessa opened another drawer in her jewel case and drew out a pair of pendant earclips, the tops made from enormous round black pearls set in marquise-shaped diamonds, from which hung splendid black pearl drops, capped by round diamonds. The earrings, which had been sold at the same auction as the necklace, matched its color perfectly. Carefully, she clipped the heavy jewels to Maggie's small ears.

"That's better," Maggie said. "But you know what? I like your white pearls and your pink pearls better. These are beautiful, but they're sort of, well, they're not exactly my idea of pearls."

"You just lost your job in the jewelry business, but I agree with you."

"So that means you're going to show me something else I've never seen before."

"Does it?"

"It seems only fair."

"How can I refuse when you start in on what's fair and what's not fair?"

"Ha!" Maggie beamed. She always counted on Tessa's sense of justice, and she was always honest about what she thought of the jewelry her sister showed her. When she had told Tessa that the flawless "Ashoka" diamond ring Luke had bought from Harry Winston was too long for Tessa's finger, Tessa hadn't protested, although she adored the elongated shape of the forty-carat, exceptionally transparent and limpid diamond that had originally come from the fabled Goloconda mines of India, and her finger was long enough for her to carry it perfectly. No, Maggie liked what she liked and she never made a judgment without providing a reason, even if she was wrong.

"And wouldn't it be fair if I had a pearl necklace?" Maggie continued with hope. "After all I'm a pure, young, innocent virgin like you were when you went to Tiffany's and bought yourself that little necklace that I love best of all."

"No, that wouldn't be fair. I don't worship the goddess Diana and neither do you," Tessa said with a laugh. "But someday, of course, you will when you're old enough to wear jewelry, as a present from the goddess Venus."

"Promise?"

"Promise."

In the fall of 1979, when Maggie was nine, she began her fourth year at Elm Country Day. However, in the past years, she had never felt truly accepted there. None of the other girls had names like Horvath; none of the other girls was Catholic; none of the other girls lived with families that weren't really their families; and most of the other girls had mothers and fathers who knew each other and got together for dinner parties and hunt balls and bridge games and golf and that sort of stuff. Candice and Allison, or the "gang of two" as Maggie now thought of them, who were both still at school, ignored her as if they'd never laid eyes on her before, although they were polite enough in their goody-goody way, whenever they were under Aunt Madison's eye.

Why, she wondered, bitterly hurt but utterly unable to ask them, why did they treat her one way at home and another way at school? Were they ashamed of her for some reason, or did they hate her because she lived with them? They never even invited her into their room or came into her room—it was as if they occupied different houses except for the dinner table. Other girls with older sisters in the school could at least count on getting their hair pulled in recognition when they passed each other in the halls—she'd settle for that, rather than the blank stares she received, even on the staircase at home when there was no grown-up around.

One day, passing through the locker room on her way to gym, Maggie overheard Sally Bradford, one of her classmates, tell a newcomer to the class that Maggie Horvath was "a mystery girl."

"What does that mean, Sally?" Maggie asked, stopping and confronting the two girls.

"Nobody knows where you come from or who you really are," blandly dainty Sally Bradford answered her, without a sign of embarrassment.

"I come from California," Maggie said fiercely. "But I live here now."

"Sure, sure, but who are you really? You're no relation at all to the Websters, she's not your aunt and he's not your uncle, that's what I heard my mother say and my mother knows all about those things. You're some kind of mysterious orphan without any real family. Did they take you in out of kindness? Or pity?"

"I do so have my own family, I have a real sister. She's Tessa Kent," Maggie burst out. She'd never told anybody that before because she knew they wouldn't believe her. "And Tessa Kent is so related to the Websters. Her husband, Luke Blake, is Uncle Tyler's brother, I mean his stepbrother, so I'm related too."

"Yeah, and I'm my own grandma. Tessa Kent! The movie star? Do you expect us to believe that? Tessa Kent's sister! Why are you telling such a lie, Maggie Horvath, Horvath, Horvath, and what kind of name is Horvath, Horvath, Horvath anyway?"

"It's a Hungarian name and it's as good as Bradford, you bitch!"

"You called me a bitch! Naturally, you don't have any breeding, do you? I'm going to tell the teacher."

"Go on, tell her, I don't give a rat's ass, I don't give a flying fuck, you double triple bitch!" Maggie retorted in a rage.

"Oh, are you in big trouble now, Maggie Horvath, Horvath, Horvath!"

Several days later, when Tessa made her weekly phone call to Maggie, Madison asked for a word with her.

"Would you excuse me, Maggie, while I talk to your sister?"

"Excuse you?"

"I mean I'd like to talk to her privately."

"Oh, all right. I'm going upstairs anyway," Maggie said, and fled to her room. "Rat's ass" wasn't such a terrible thing to say, she told herself, Roddy said it all the time, and certainly "bitch" was really bad, but Sally deserved it. Yet the teacher had never said a word to her, not even about "flying fuck," which was so absolutely terrible she still couldn't believe she'd said it, so why was Aunt Madison going to tell on her?

"Tessa, I hate to bother you when Maggie is doing so well at school, but Miss Anderson, her homeroom teacher, called me and said that there'd been a spot of trouble between Maggie and another girl."

"Trouble? What's going on, Madison?"

"It seems that Maggie got into an argument with little Sally Bradford, and she told her that you're her sister, which Sally didn't believe, so Maggie swore at Sally. It all rather escalated, although no blows were exchanged. Anyway, Miss Anderson said that Maggie's getting a reputation as a liar, it's spreading around the school."

"Oh, no."

"I'm afraid so. You know how kids are, and with your names being different and everything, well, apparently Maggie was called a mystery orphan without any family, or something equally absurd."

"I can imagine. What little wretches," Tessa said grimly. "I'm coming to visit the school next week. I'd come sooner but I have to work every day until Wednesday when they shoot the fight scene. I'll leave right after I'm finished on Tuesday, spend the night at the Carlyle, drive out to school in the afternoon and then fly back in plenty of time to show up on the set Friday. Please tell that headmistress, Miss Dodd, isn't that her name, that I'll be there after lunch and ask her to give Maggie time off from class to accompany me on my inspection tour. In fact, I think it would be a good idea if I spoke at an assembly to the whole school. I'll talk about, let's see, yes, the truth behind the Hollywood myth, that sounds about right. But I'd like my visit to be a surprise, so would you ask Miss Dodd not to announce it? Could you arrange all the details, please, Madison?"

"Of course, I'll call the headmistress right away."

"And Madison, I'm going to have to give serious thought about sending Maggie to a good boarding school if she isn't happy at Elm Country Day."

"Oh, good grief no, Tessa, this is just one of those little things that could happen in any school," Madison said, disguising her terror. The last thing she wanted was to have Maggie snatched away from her house. Tyler would be furious, Luke would . . . she had no idea what Luke would do, and that frightened her more than anything else.

"Miss Dodd tells me that Maggie's exceptionally

bright and she's very popular there, it's only that they find it hard to believe that you two are sisters."

"I'll take care of that. Do you happen to know what Maggie said when she swore at Sally?"

"Well . . . she did use the 'F' word."

"She must have been severely provoked, I've never heard her use it . . . but of course, hanging around Luke . . . these crude Australians, and Roddy, these crude Hollywood types . . ." Tessa began to shake with soundless laughter. Good show, Maggie, she thought, you have to defend yourself from the Sally Bradfords of this world.

Tessa was glad that it was a crisp fall day when she visited Elm Country Day. Indian summer would not have suited the ultimately glamorous impression she intended to make. She put on a breathtakingly well tailored Givenchy suit in melting shades of beige tweed, adorned with a sumptuous collar and wide, notched lapels of the darkest Russian sable. The cuffs of the jacket were five inches deep in more sable, and she wore a tiny sable beret, perched on the side of her beautifully done hair. Shades of Anna Karenina, Tessa thought as she put on her perfect dark brown alligator pumps and added the extraordinary, triple-strand necklace of perfectly matched natural pearls over her cream silk blouse. Normally she would only wear them in the daytime for a meeting with Lew Wasserman. But no diamonds in the daytime, she reminded herself, choosing the simplest of the three pairs of pearl earrings that had taken months to match to the two-million-dollar necklace Luke had recently given her for her twenty-fourth birthday.

She applied her makeup perfectly, so that it could be seen from the last row of the assembly room. Understatement would not be the watchword today. She was as well groomed and marvelously dressed as she'd ever been in her life, she thought, giving herself a final inspection. The rest would take care of itself.

To drive out to Elm Country Day, Tessa had hired an enormous dark green Rolls and a smartly uniformed driver from a New York rental agency, the sort of equipage she normally would go out of her way to avoid, a touch of pure Hollywood that would leave girls' mouths gaping.

As Tessa arrived at the school and was assisted out of the car by her driver, a group of preteenagers were clattering out of the front entrance. As a group they stopped dead and stared.

"Good afternoon," Tessa said to one of them. "Could you tell me where Miss Dodd's office is, please? I've come to visit the school."

"But you're Tessa Kent!"

"Well . . . yes, I am, but actually I'm Maggie Horvath's sister."

"Oh, my goodness!" The girl's hand flew to her mouth.

"Doesn't she even acknowledge me?" Tessa asked, raising her eyebrows in amused surprise.

"No . . . yes . . . a little while ago."

"Ashamed of her sister, is she, the little devil?"

"No. Of course not, oh, my goodness."

"Miss Dodd's office?" Tessa reminded her gently.

"I'll show you the way. Oh, I'm dreaming, I'm dreaming!"

"Thank you, that's very kind of you."

Tessa chatted calmly with the thrilled, flustered girl until she reached her destination.

"Ah, Miss Dodd," Tessa said, shaking hands and responding to the headmistress's greeting, "I know I should have come to visit sooner but one thing and another has kept me away, and Madison Webster has always spoken so highly of you that I felt sure Maggie would love it here."

"Oh, she does. And we love her," responded the lean, gray-haired woman who looked as if she must have won a title at Wimbleton many years earlier. She was used to dealing with the high-powered local socialite mothers, but the vision of Tessa made her gasp. She'd never believed real people could look like this.

"I'm delighted to hear that. I hope you were able to excuse Maggie from her classes this afternoon so she can show me around. And were you able to arrange an assembly?"

"Indeed yes, at four o'clock. Oh, here's Maggie now."

Maggie jumped into Tessa's arms with a shout of joy and held on tightly.

"Oh, I'm so glad to see you," Maggie whispered, almost in tears at an apparition she'd never expected to appear in Miss Dodd's office. "You look like a real movie star."

"That's the general idea, darling," Tessa said into Maggie's ear, giving her a kiss and smoothing her hair. "Now, if Miss Dodd doesn't mind, why don't you take me to your classroom and introduce me to your classmates?"

"They're all in the lab now, we're doing experiments."

"Then let's go there, I want to see everything, but first, your friends. You show me the way," Tessa said, taking Maggie's slightly grubby hand and swinging it playfully.

In the lab all experiments came to a halt as Maggie led Tessa around the room. Maggie watched, entranced and grinning widely, as one by one her classmates mumbled their awed hellos and Tessa easily found something different to say to each one of them.

"Oh, so you're Sally Bradford," Tessa said, taking the dainty, blond girl's hand. Her voice carried to every corner of the room although she wasn't speaking loudly. "How interesting to meet you. I understand from my sister, Maggie, that your mother's an expert in genealogy?"

"Well, she sort of likes to know who's who, if that's what you mean," Sally muttered, turning red.

"That's exactly what I mean," Tessa said with her

most charming smile. "Would you give her a message from me, Sally, to add to her hobby? It's a bit complicated but I'm sure you can remember it. My husband is a man named Luke Blake. His stepbrother is Tyler Webster, Candice and Allison Webster's father. My little sister, Maggie, is, naturally, my husband's sister-in-law, but since she's so young, she calls Mr. Webster 'uncle' and Mrs. Webster 'aunt,' out of courtesy. They're not blood relations, but they are part of Maggie's family, and she lives with them because our parents, the Horvaths, were both killed in an automobile accident four years ago. Maggie and I were left orphans. I'd already changed my name to Kent when I made my first movie, but my name is really Teresa Horvath, not Tessa Kent. Now, does that clear things up? Can you repeat it?"

"Ah, ah . . . Maggie's your sister."

"And?"

"Your husband is Mr. Blake and he's also the half-brother of Mr. Webster . . ."

"No, Sally, the stepbrother of Mr. Webster. My husband's father married Mr. Webster's mother after his first wife died."

"Oh."

"It is complicated, isn't it?"

"Yes."

"And hard to understand, much less be expert about, especially when you have the facts all wrong. But do remember to give your mother my message and add that I send her my best regards for taking such an interest in Maggie's family. Good-bye Sally," Tessa said, turning away. Suddenly she stopped and stooped to look the girl in the eye. "I hope I've cleared up the 'mystery.' "

Looking at the floor, Sally nodded her head.

"Good," Tessa said crisply, going on to greet the next girl.

18

W hat a bloody bore, this Yank institution, these Oscars, this lumbering, pretentious, blatantly commercial sideshow that had managed to make itself a source of mindless, gaping worldwide attention, Luke Blake thought, as he roamed angrily around the living room of his suite at the Hotel Bel-Air in Los Angeles. The television set was tuned in to the 1982 Oscars, although the sound was off and had been off since the beginning of the telecast.

Hours earlier, in the middle of the afternoon, Tessa, dressed and ready to present the Best Picture award, had stepped into her limo, escorted by Roddy Fensterwald.

Luke had accompanied her himself the previous year, because then she'd been up for her second Best Actress award, facing a field of rivals that included Marsha Mason, Susan Sarandon, Diane Keaton, and Jessica Lange. Of course he'd been at her side to hold her hand. He wouldn't have considered letting her sit there in the audience, waiting for the results throughout the endless evening, without him, but tonight Tessa wasn't nominated for anything and her function was purely ceremonial. She'd be planted backstage for hours, gossiping with the other presenters, she'd told him, in her most persuasive tones, and there was simply no reason for him to endure hours of tedium—she knew how bored he got—just for her brief moment in the spotlight. "You'll be so much more comfortable at home, darling, watching me on television, and the view will be better anyway."

She'd been an utterly improbable vision when she'd left the hotel in the brilliant spring sunshine, wearing a strapless lilac satin ball gown, with a wide sash bound tightly around her waist above a multitude of petticoats that caused the enormous skirt to move as lightly as a swaying bell. It was the first time she'd worn the latest present he'd given her, the entire Fabergé parure he'd assembled of imperial Russian jewels: the great web of a necklace that had belonged to a grand duchess, the splendid pendant earrings, the eight bracelets, and the hair ornaments like giant snowflakes. The jewels, inspired by eighteenth-century design, were made with infinite delicacy. Their deep garlands, elaborate swags, and extravagantly complicated bows made Tessa sparkle with every movement of her head, as if she'd been sprinkled with frost and ice, as if she were a princess who'd just taken two steps through fast-falling snow in order to enter a ballroom and dance all night.

She'd turned to him, her face bright, untroubled. "Don't even bother to turn the television on until after nine, darling," she'd reminded him as she kissed him good-bye. "There's no possibility that the show will run less than four hours, and I'll be on last."

Did she guess, he asked himself, did she have the faintest idea of the shameful, grotesque torments of jealousy that afflicted him when he had to share her with her work? Was that why she'd spared herself his presence tonight, so that she'd be free to enjoy herself with her peers, free to bask in the roar of the crowds as she made her arrival outside the Dorothy Chandler Pavilion?

For the past few months they'd been in Los Angeles, abandoning the ranch they'd bought in Texas, while Tessa made her annual film, this year a romantic comedy with Dustin Hoffman. Was it possible that Tessa suspected the humiliating extent to which he was held captive in a piercing grid of jealous anxiety, from the moment she left in the morning until she returned from the studio at night? He had always exercised all his will to keep it from her, Luke told himself, and there was no reason to believe he'd been unsuccessful.

As he trod a restless path from the window to the television set and back again, he examined his behavior with Tessa for the ten thousandth time and came to the invariable conclusion that during their marriage he had managed to keep the toxic fumes of his jealousy from escaping into the air of real life. But what if Tessa was even more sensitive than he believed she was? Could she know what he was feeling, no matter how he covered it up?

Christ almighty, he wanted *all* of her, he wanted to possess her entirely, every atom of her being. Every one of her smiles should be reserved for him, she should not be allowed to look into anyone else's eyes. The thought of Tessa spending the day surrounded by her coworkers, meeting new people, perhaps becoming interested in them, somehow involved with them on a personal level, was just this side of intolerable. Didn't she know that her voice, merely asking a question or making a request, was as romantic as a valentine?

Old friends were almost as much of a threat, old friends with whom she remembered a life that didn't include him. It wasn't merely obvious temptation that his ungovernable imagination invented and then gorged upon uncontrollably. He was jealous of every laugh she had with Roddy or Fiona, of every phone call from her agent. Yes, he was even jealous of her phone time with Aaron . . . who knew when Aaron might find a role she couldn't resist accepting, a role that would cause her to break her self-imposed limit on work?

Yet he believed that he'd kept his hideous jealousy from her, a jealousy that revolted him as if it had been a running sore on his body. Luke reflected that he'd at least retained enough sanity to be sure—almost to be sure—that it was unjustified. He'd managed to hide his feelings while she made the film that had won her the Oscar the previous year, a brilliantly written movie called *The Winter of Doctor Star*, in which Tessa had been cast as an intern in cardiology who falls in love with a gravely ill patient played by Robert Redford. He'd concealed the wild insanity that overtook him whenever he thought of her kissing Redford. He didn't give a shit how many technicians would be around them, how the director would be as much a part of the kiss as Redford's lips, how it was all in a day's work. No, fuck it, no! A kiss was a kiss and no one could kiss Tessa without wanting her. He'd lived through Redford, he'd live through Hoffman, he told himself, although the damn man had a devilish charm, a wicked humor, a special quality of nervy, wound-up sexuality that had nothing to do with his looks.

Since winning for *Doctor Star*, Tessa had refused dozens of scripts before deciding to work with Hoffman, in spite of the fact that Aaron Zucker, that persistent bastard, simply couldn't resist phoning her wherever they found themselves in the world and pointing out that she was in the red-hot middle of her career and that it was madness not to work more often. Her agent never managed to accept her decision to make only one film a year, Luke thought in repressed fury, as he listened to Tessa's account of her conversation. "He said, and I quote, 'now is the time to sink my teeth into the whole fucking industry, chew it up, and swallow it for breakfast.' I think poor Aaron should leave metaphor alone, don't you, darling?"

"Well," Luke remembered saying carefully, "from his point of view he probably thinks that there should be a statute of limitations on what you promised me when we got married."

"Oh, he's never been able to accept the fact that I was utterly serious about my decision," Tessa said indulgently, and Luke had been happy to let the discussion drop.

Earlier today, he and Roddy had had time to chat while Tessa dressed and had her hair arranged. The man was no fool, Luke thought, although he certainly gave himself full marks for Tessa's career.

"Tessa was *inevitable*," Roddy had said, "I realized it the minute I saw her. Her personality and the public's taste were going to march hand in hand, she was the girl they were going to adore even though they didn't know it yet, and the smartest thing she's done has been to limit her work and choose to play such widely differing roles. See, Luke, a 'Tessa Kent' type has never developed, a 'Tessa Kent' role has never been created. She has no imitators, she's one of a kind. She was born with a physical presence no one else had ever possessed in the history of the screen, but it wasn't that alone, it was never just about beauty, but about a unique personality. She'll last, Luke, last as long as she wants to. Our girl rejects repetition and so she eludes rejection, even after almost eleven years at the top. She's like Katharine Hepburn, a star who has no fade-out factor."

" 'Fade-out'? She's only twenty-six, for God's sake," Luke had objected in spite of himself, in spite of the fact that if she lost favor with the public and returned to a totally private existence with him, he'd ask nothing more of life.

"Luke, you're not in the business, but remember that Tessa won her first Best Actress award when she was only twenty-two. I dote on that picture . . . *Ivy League* . . . I still think it's my best. Tessa playing the little grad student, and big old Clint, you tell me who ever expected him to be so convincing as a happily married professor, helpless to do anything while she slowly invaded his life, terrorizing him, seeming to be perfectly normal while she was going quietly and murderously insane? I play that picture once a month at home and

I've never tired of it. She was brilliant, Luke, brilliant, but you know that as well as I do. Any other actress might have been tempted to do another film in which she showed again how fascinatingly evil she can be, but not Tessa. All she thought about was flying off with you to your love nest in Èze as soon as she'd fulfilled her media commitments."

"She adores the farmhouse," Luke had responded stiffly.

"Shit, Luke, she *adores* you. Where other actresses put their ambition, their psychological needs for fame, pure narcissism, or any of the other motivations for what they insist on calling their 'art,' Tessa puts you. You're one hell of a lucky guy, Luke, as I'm sure you know."

"I don't deserve her, Roddy," he'd managed to grin.

"Amen! No one's good enough for Tessa," he'd agreed.

Luke sat down in front of the television, glancing at his watch and back to the screen. There was that quick audience shot, there was Roddy, sitting far up front with Maggie beside him in the seat that Tessa had wangled for her. Maggie, he mused, poor Maggie, she probably couldn't see well over the head of the man in front of her, but no one had ever been as excited as she had been at this treat.

He didn't know how Tessa had managed to get her school to let her off for the trip, but tomorrow they'd put her back on the plane to the East Coast, all one hundred sixty-five pounds of her, if not more. How could a girl almost thirteen years old so thoroughly embody absolutely everything that was meant by the "awkward age," he wondered, and still come out of the same gene pool that had produced Tessa? Maggie wore braces, both upper and lower, and suffered from a constant plague of pimples. Her ridiculously abundant hair was either frizzy, curly, or limp, depending on the day; and, worst of all, she hadn't stopped growing. She was taller every time he saw her, with breasts that already looked like those of a grown woman.

He tried not to look at her any more than he had to, Luke thought, because she was so wretchedly self-conscious, but he had to admit that when she was around, he was jealous of the time Tessa spent with her . . . her own sister! But when Maggie visited, there was just that much less time for him, that much less of Tessa's undivided concentration. Could that be the reason Tessa usually managed to shoehorn Maggie's visits into the short periods when he was making a lightning business trip to an uncomfortable place? No, Luke thought, shaking his head, there was no possibility that she could suspect that a sisterly relationship could cause him real suffering, because if she knew that unthinkable truth, she'd know everything else as well.

Tyler's regular letter, reporting on Maggie, as he'd been instructed to do, always told him how satisfactory Maggie's presence was in the family, but in the same letter he'd usually let something slip that made Luke doubt if the Maggie he saw could fit so easily into the outstandingly handsome group of Websters. His niece Allison was sixteen now, and, according to her proud father, she had turned into an out-and-out raving beauty, while Candice, who was about to finish her last year of school, was a vision of utter prettiness, less beautiful than Allison, but more approachable. Apparently coming-out parties weren't the victim of the 1960s that he'd thought they were, since Tyler reported that Madison was engrossed in preparations for Candice's debut.

Tyler's letters seemed to reassure Tessa, yet she always let Maggie know that if she wasn't happy at the Websters' she could go away to boarding school. Ever since that incident when she'd had to fly to the Elm School to defend Maggie against the little snobs there, Tessa had worried about Maggie's school experience, but Maggie consistently refused to entertain the idea. "No," she'd say, or write, "I don't want to have to start out all over again at a strange school. I'm too shy, Tessa, and anyway I've finally made a few really good friends now and everybody else here knows I'm not a liar or a mystery without a family. Don't worry about me."

Well, he didn't worry about her, Luke assured himself. He'd made the right decision back when Maggie might have been sent off to one of Tessa's aunts, and he'd never regretted it. If she didn't feel comfortable with the Websters, she'd never hinted at such feelings, although frankly something about Madison gave him the creeps.

Impatiently—it was not yet near the time he could expect to see Tessa—Luke flung himself back in his chair and closed his eyes and drifted into a reverie. Strange, how Tessa never truly stopped protesting at the jewels he gave her so often, never understood how entirely necessary it was for him. She still thought in terms of generosity and extravagance, not guessing at the deep, secret pleasure that compelled him to *mark* her as his property. Yes, he thought with voluptuous pleasure, every new jewel *branded her* once again as belonging exclusively to him, every gem she wore was a proof that Luke Blake, and only Luke Blake, of all the men in the world, had the right to possess her.

She had so many now. Jewels without end. Often there were nights when he'd whisper to her to take off all her clothes and lie down on their bed. She knew exactly what he wanted, lying there with her eyes tightly closed, her legs pressed together, her arms at her side, while he slowly covered her from her neck to her feet with the contents of her jewel cases. He'd make himself leave her breasts exposed, and the maddening dark triangle at the base of her belly. He'd watch her face as she struggled to remain perfectly passive, never knowing when he would finish laying the jewels, one by one, in a mosaic over her skin, forcing himself to take his time, to prolong the delight until it was painful for him.

The only way Tessa could be certain that he'd finally exhausted the contents of the cases was that moment when, probing as delicately as if his tongue were a feather, he'd flick at the tips of her pubic hair. Just the tips, the wispy, silken tips. Yes, that was the signal that the game had begun, and what a royal game it was. Tessa had to keep her eyes closed and remain motionless and mute, a goddess bound by chains of gems, a goddess who allowed him to make whatever use of her pleased him that night. He'd have been thinking about it all day, trying to decide if he wanted to make her come with only his mouth, stopping often, oh, so often, to feast on her expression, to watch her bite her lips to keep back the slightest sound, too proud to change her aloof expression, to utter the words that might urge him on. Or else he'd choose to torture her more intensely, using his lips and his teeth on her nipples, pausing as often as he could endure, until her breasts were engorged and her nipples stood straight up. Only then was he willing to insert his fingers into her body, teasing them in and dragging them out with such a hesitant, brushing, glancing, deliberately indirect touch that he missed her clitoris far more often than he found it. He would refuse to satisfy her, holding back until finally she was unable to endure the torment any longer and, sweeping all the jewels to the floor, she would grasp him and press him into her, wordlessly, savagely. On other nights he used no refinements, but used her directly, suddenly, brutally, with no warning, treating her as his prisoner, a prisoner whose own pleasure was unimportant, meaningless. But always, after he came, and he would come with deliberate quickness, so that she had no chance to become aroused, he would make it up to her with his hands and his mouth and his cock. He never, never let her go until she was satisfied.

Which way would he take her tonight, Luke asked himself, when she came home from the Oscars? Which way would make her forget most thoroughly that any other world existed except the one they inhabited together?

19

The day after her birthday in August 1985, Tessa stopped taking the Pill. Luke had said he'd be ready for fatherhood, or at least ready to contemplate it, by the time she was thirty, and thirty she was.

She decided not to tell him of her decision. Normally Tessa told Luke everything important, but she didn't want making love to become a self-conscious act, with conception in the back of their minds. And, she admitted to herself, what if he were to suggest postponing having a baby for one more year, and then another?

Tessa understood Luke Blake's nature far better than he realized. Yes, he was as intensely, jealously possessive of her as any man could be, and she gloried in his possessiveness. Yes, he was thoroughly, hopelessly selfish about how she spent every second of her time when she wasn't actually working on a movie, and she gloried in his selfishness. Yes, he wanted all of her attention when he wasn't working, and she gave herself to him gladly in an undivided way. She had no time and no need to cultivate friendships with other women; her only adult relationships outside of Luke were with people connected to her career.

Tessa knew that in the deepest sense she conspired to join Luke in their tight, exclusive relationship, one that some, perhaps most, women might find stifling. But to her it was essential, for with Luke she continued to live in the heart of that sense of safety she was still consciously aware of needing every day of her life, an emotional safety that no amount of her own success could ever guarantee. She'd never been able to take her safety for granted, she'd never forgotten the years before he'd come into her life and transformed it with just the touch of his hand.

But now she wanted a baby. Desperately. She'd waited without showing her impatience, she'd kept her part of the bargain—well, perhaps it hadn't been a bargain but just a statement Luke had made—but now was her time to get what she wanted. No, what she needed.

Seven months passed and Tessa still hadn't conceived. She began to grow concerned that the problem might lie with Luke. God knows, she had living proof that she could get pregnant. Perhaps Luke's childlessness at forty-five, when she'd met him, hadn't been through faultless contraception but because he couldn't father a child. Nevertheless she bided her time. She wasn't fourteen now, and everyone knew that it was more difficult to get pregnant when you were older, and, of course, in one of nature's little ironies, always more difficult to get pregnant when you wanted to than when you didn't.

In April 1986, Tessa missed her period. Still she said nothing to Luke, waiting to be sure. Every day she expected to experience the morning sickness she remembered, the horrible bouts of vomiting that had finally alerted her mother to her pregnancy. Had they started in the first month or the second? She couldn't recall such details now; so much of that entire period of her life had almost completely vanished from her mind, leaving only a merciful blankness that demanded that she not probe too deeply.

To Tessa's relief, Luke's business travel had slackened somewhat in recent years, as he found more and more good men to work for him in different parts of the world. That spring they were able to spend a long, quiet time at Èze, a time she contrived to make as inactive as possible, pleading fatigue after the completion of her latest film. For the next three weeks she cocooned herself as much as possible, ambling up the road to the village from time to time but otherwise sitting contentedly on the terrace outside of the farmhouse. She spent hours reading or merely daydreaming, as she gazed at the signs of new leaves on the grapevines, watched the circles of lavender grow taller by the day, listened to the gentle wind in the cypress and olive trees, and basked like a cat in the sun of the Midi.

All of France, Tessa knew from the newspapers, was in its usual state of turmoil, but in the countryside of Èze the peace was total, unless you deliberately went into a café in the village and listened to the retired residents grumble ritually over their card games. Yet even that grumbling fell into a predictable rhythm, Tessa thought, reveling in this respite from their world of travel, acquisition, and moviemaking, the familiar routines of her life with Luke about which the only predictable element was that they were ever-changing.

How would they live when they had a baby? Tessa wondered. She found it impossible to decide, with all the world open to them. All she was certain of was that their existence would be very different from the life they had led up till now. She would give up work for years, if not forever. Luke would simply have to travel much, much less. They would stop their nomadic existence and finally establish a true home somewhere—perhaps the Texas ranch, perhaps Melbourne, perhaps the villa from which they sailed at Cap-Ferrat, perhaps someplace entirely different. They might even buy a house in California, where they'd always stayed at a hotel during her bouts of filmmaking. Why not Santa Barbara, one of the most beautiful places on earth? But did it have good schools? Ah, all she really knew was that they would settle down, she promised herself, or it wouldn't be fair to the baby. And, of course, she thought as she drifted off into a nap, of course the baby would be born in the United States . . .

"Now, about this matter of your breasts," Luke said several nights later, as he pushed the straps of her nightgown down and weighed them in his hands.

"What about them?"

"They're fuller than they've ever been, and warmer, like two just-baked loaves of bread. Heavenly bread. And your nipples are getting slightly bigger and just a touch darker."

"Goodness! The things you notice, honestly, you have your nerve . . ." she protested feebly.

"Darling, when did you plan to tell me?"

"When I was . . . sure."

"What would it take to make you sure?"

"Another few days, maybe a week. . . ."

"And if I said I was sure, would that do it?"

"If you said you were happy, that would make me positively sure," she said in a small voice.

" 'Happy'? That isn't a big enough word for how I feel. God, Tessa, I love you so much . . . how long do I have to wait for our baby?"

"Seven months, or a little less." She laughed for joy. "I'm not really certain."

"Aren't you a little behind schedule?"

"Huh?"

"I thought we'd agreed at thirty. I've been waiting for nearly a year, and doing my bit to help, as you might have noticed."

"You remembered!"

"I never forget a promise."

"So you won't mind sharing me?"

"I'm only human—from time to time, I probably will. But I've had you to myself for more than ten years, the best years of your life some people might say, certainly the best of mine."

"What if the best years are ahead?"

"But they are, darling," Luke assured her, trying not to remember that he'd just past his fifty-sixth birthday and she was still only thirty. Thirty, my God, he'd been a kid at thirty. Nothing but a kid. "You know I almost never agree with what people say."

Tessa stood outside the cheese shop on the shopping street of Èze-Village. Normally she loved to go in and pick out each of the five cheeses they always bought, four of which they requested, the fifth a surprise, chosen with glee by the proprietor herself. The French, whatever the government's policies, would never run out of new varieties of cheese, but today the thought of the pungent interior of the shop was suddenly repulsive and she'd told Luke to go in by himself.

"We don't need cheese that much," he assured her. "It can wait."

"No, don't be silly, darling. I'd rather stay outside, but that doesn't mean you have to deprive yourself. I'm fine, honestly," she'd responded, all but pushing him into the always-crowded store.

But was she fine, Tessa asked herself? She still hadn't had a minute of morning sickness, but the feeling of well-being she'd enjoyed only a week earlier had departed, leaving her nervous and jumpy, instead of deliciously languid. It was impossible to know whether she had been pregnant for two months or several weeks longer, but now, as she waited, she resolved to drive down to Monte Carlo this very afternoon and see a gynecologist.

She'd probably waited this long because she hated French doctors, with their offices in their homes, furnished like living rooms, and their casual way of telling a woman patient to remove all her clothes before an examination, without providing a screen or a robe, for the sake of decent modesty. It was exactly like doing a striptease. There was never a nurse present, yet she'd never met a Frenchwoman who thought it was at all odd. They even bought especially beautiful lingerie expressly for visits to the doctor. She'd bring her own cotton robe, Tessa decided grimly, and wear it back to front.

What was taking Luke so long, she wondered? Suddenly the gentle sun seemed far too hot, the light breeze far too strong, the quiet street much too noisy. Was it the first sign of a mistral? Most likely. And that would account for her nerves. She took a step forward to rap impatiently on the window of the cheese shop and almost stumbled, grasping the trunk of a chestnut tree. As Tessa stood holding on to the tree, she felt a severe cramp beginning in her abdomen. She pressed herself tightly against the tree, trying to stop the pain, to crush it before it could grow, but it mounted rapidly upward, gaining in intensity. Unable to remain upright, she bent over, doubled up, still grasping the tree, and saw in horror that blood was dripping from the bottom of her slacks, pooling darkly between her sneakers and dripping onto the cobblestones of the street. Jesus, she prayed, Jesus, no, no, but by the time Luke had gathered her up and carried her to the car, driving down to Monte Carlo as quickly as possible on the dangerously twisting road, she understood that she was having a miscarriage. She didn't need a French doctor's opinion to tell her why the bleeding, the terrible bleeding, hadn't stopped.

Maggie reread the postcard from Tessa she'd received several weeks earlier, before adding it to the cache of cards she'd kept in a special drawer in her desk ever since she came to live with the Websters. There must be dozens of them, she thought, dozens of postcards from all over the world that had arrived in the course of the past eleven years, and although she was sixteen and grown up, the contents of the postcards she received didn't seem very different from those she'd been sent when she was six or seven.

"Luke and I are in South America or the Arctic Circle or on the planet Jupiter," Maggie thought, "Luke's working hard"—when didn't he?—"and I'm keeping him company and entertaining the people he does business with"—when didn't she? Or else they'd be sent from Hollywood or a film location, with news of the progress of one movie or another. Boring, boring postcards. Just enough to "keep in touch," never enough to really know what Tessa was thinking or feeling.

Maggie had written long letters to Tessa month after month in the past few years, but she'd never sent them. Busy Tessa, always traveling, always the wife, always the movie star, wouldn't want to be bothered with the absurd problems of a silly adolescent, she thought, when she reread her letters. Better to pour it out on paper and then tear it up than make her sister feel guilty for even a minute because she was going through one petty, unimportant misery after another.

Now, from the point of view of sixteen, she was glad she'd kept it all to herself, because all that tortured self-pity about the way she looked had turned out to be wasted. Somehow, almost overnight, in some miracle of growth and change, she'd turned out to be passable, even fairly attractive, if she did say so herself, Maggie thought, closing the postcard drawer firmly and returning to the endlessly fascinating subject of her new assets.

She had grown and grown and then stopped, at a not-too-tall, not-too-terrible five feet, eight inches. Her skin had cleared up, without a pimple to be seen anywhere on its surface; her braces had finally come off, leaving perfect teeth—Madison, she had to admit, knew a lot about orthodontists—and even her hair had decided to behave decently. She'd overheard Madison describing her coloring as "Black Irish," but if that was an insult she didn't understand it, Maggie decided, admiring the as-good-as-blusher-pink and white of her cheeks, the snappy blackness of her hair, and the blue, blueness of her eyes. Hello, gorgeous!

She would do! Yes, indeed. As for her breasts, the ones she'd hated so much when she was so fat, now that she was, if not skinny, marvelously voluptuous, her breasts were just absolutely the greatest! She had the biggest, sexiest breasts in the sophomore class at Elm, everyone on the field hockey team had agreed about that. Even though she got straight A's, everyone at school agreed that sexy tits were the best thing that could happen to a girl in this lifetime, Maggie thought dotingly, as she pushed them high and kissed them to see how they'd feel to some man, if some man ever came her way. She'd never even had a date, not a real one.

She couldn't manage to reach her nipples with the tip of her tongue, try as she would, but kissing the soft skin of her breasts soon felt so good she had to stop. The house was bursting with strangers busy with the arrangements for Candice's wedding, and she couldn't be sure that some flower person or caterer's assistant wouldn't come bumbling in by accident and see what she was doing. Thank heaven for the haven of her bathroom, Maggie thought, locking the door behind her and stretching out on the thick rug. She was so excited that, as she had to do several times every day, she quickly rubbed her fingers over her panties, coming to a swift and blissful orgasm.

Better, much better. Maggie panted in relief. The worst was when there was no place to do it, that drove her wild. But between certain stalls in the johns at school, where she could do it standing up, between classes, and her bathroom here, she usually managed. The bonus was that she wasn't afraid of horses anymore, now that she got so aroused riding. Could it be that those animals could tell how their motion made her feel and that was why they behaved for her now? Was she having sex with a saddle? Or had she finally absorbed all those lessons she'd been forced to take? No matter, there were plenty of hidden places off the bridle path, in the woods, and the horses never noticed what she'd stopped to do.

She wished she'd learned all about this heavenly delight sooner. Her childhood would have been one hell of a lot happier, Maggie thought, smiling at her flushed cheeks in the mirror above the sink, admiring the way the natural pearl necklace of great quality that Tessa had sent her for her sixteenth birthday hung between the sumptuous globes of her certifiably fabulous tits.

Thank heaven she'd lost her faith when she was fourteen. Imagine having to confess this! Father, I've engaged in impure deeds. What kind of impure deeds? Sins against Holy Purity. What kind of sins? Touching myself, Father. How often have you desecrated your Temple of the Holy Ghost? Twenty-five times since my last confession. And how long ago was that? One week, Father.

The poor man would certainly think she was going straight to Hell. Losing her faith was the best thing that had happened to her, even though she'd felt awful about it for almost a month, especially when she'd had to tell Madison she didn't want to go to mass anymore. Madison had been surprisingly decent about that, Maggie remembered, in fact quite understanding. In fact, now that she came to think about it, positively relieved. Well, it must have been inconvenient to have a little papist cluttering up her house.

Poor old Madison. When she'd mentioned the desirability of her joining the Junior League as soon as possible, Maggie had said she'd rather join the Communist Party. When Madison had hinted that it wasn't too early to start planning Maggie's coming-out party, she'd replied that she'd rather drop acid. It was easy to handle Madison, now that she knew how. Madison was afraid of her. She didn't know why, but she was sure she was right. Madison had never felt the slightest drop of warmth toward her, and, do what she could, that hurt her as much as it always had, but she'd lived with the coldness and lack of interest so long that it had become part of the climate of her life, Maggie told herself. And, thank God, it was still her secret.

20

During the next year, Tessa had another miscarriage in the middle of her third month. Her doctors, the best in Los Angeles, insisted that they could find no reason for this inability to maintain a pregnancy. Two miscarriages in a row were absolutely not a sign that she would never have a child, they assured the Blakes. Tessa was only thirty-one and although, strictly speaking, she was not at the peak of fertility, she was well within her prime. Luke was as vigorous as a man half his age. After six months had passed, they advised them to "try" again.

Holy Mother, how she loathed that word "try," Tessa thought. Each time Luke made love to her, she imagined that half the superb medical community of Cedars–Sinai Hospital was in bed with them, a jovial, largely Harvard- and UCLA-educated cheering section, exhorting them to "try, try again!"

At least that wouldn't be the case for the next six months, during which the doctors had prescribed a holiday from even thinking about conception, ordering her to give her womb a rest and putting her back on the Pill. Stress, tension, and anxiety, they emphasized, were to be avoided. Oh, sure, Tessa thought, turn off your mind, little lady, there's nothing to it. Doctors!

Luke was fifty-seven now. On his birthday Tessa saw a man who had barely changed since the day she'd first laid eyes on him. Yes, there was gray in his thick, dark red hair, but only at the temples. His features, those powerful, weathered features she had loved at first sight, were certainly more deeply lined around his mouth and eyes, but otherwise he was indestructible. *Indestructible*. Only his gaze, when he looked at her, betrayed, in certain unguarded moments, his sorrow at her two miscarriages, a sorrow deeper for her than for himself, for she was the one who had to go through the physical ordeal, while he could only suffer quietly, and with a measure of guilt. What if she'd tried to have a child sooner? What if he hadn't wanted her to himself for so long? He asked himself those questions so often that he had to banish them from his mind. You can't rewrite history, Luke told himself, and in any case, she'd agreed to wait, she'd wanted to wait as much as he did.

Before Tessa's second miscarriage, they'd bought the family home she'd daydreamed about in Èze, choosing Los Angeles rather than Santa Barbara because there Tessa could be closer to her work. Luke no longer asked that she make only one film a year, since he understood that work was her best therapy now, in this difficult period, and he cut down deeply on his own travel to be with her during the six or seven months she spent making two films in 1986 and early 1987.

They settled in Beverly Hills, high up in the winding roads north of Sunset, in a historic Wallace Neff house of old whitewashed brick, timbered in the style of a manor in Normandy, and covered with flowering purple trumpet vines. Four acres of land descended from terraced gardens down to a swimming pool and finally to a tennis court, which neither of them used. From the upper level of their gardens they couldn't see another rooftop, so thick was the lush landscaping that surrounded their invisible, unheard neighbors. It was as peaceful here as at Èze, Luke said, and even the vegetation was uncannily similar, as long as you didn't venture into the local equivalent of a village, where an Armani boutique held down one end of Rodeo Drive and Chanel and Fred Hayman the other.

Now both Tessa and Luke found themselves much more a part of the Hollywood scene. They no longer had the excuse of constant travel to keep them from the dinner parties, the charity benefits, the private screenings, and the galas that were such an important part of the local social life for nine months a year, barely stopping during the summer months when most of the same people moved to their Malibu beach houses and entertained each other more casually.

It suited them both, at this particular time, to welcome distraction, to accept a number of invitations; and, to Luke's quiet pleasure, it gave Tessa many more chances to wear her most important jewels. Even now, at the peak of the lavish 1980s, when great jewelry was being worn by many women, Tessa's vast collection of jewels was indisputably of the highest quality, the most extravagant, and the most original ever owned by any woman in one of the richest communities on earth.

"What shall I wear with this tonight, darling?" Tessa asked, turning around to show him the white silk linen dinner suit she'd chosen for an intimate dinner party in a private room at Le Dôme, where Fiona was celebrating the completion of her first production. She waited for Luke's answer, looking puzzled at the daunting number of possibilities available to her, since everything went with white. "Don't you think, maybe rubies?"

"Yes, absolutely," Luke said, smiling at her from the armless slipper chair in her dressing room, where he liked to sit and watch her finish dressing.

"But which rubies?" she responded, vanishing into her closet where her built-in wall safe was open. "I don't want to overdress, even if everyone else does these days, but somehow tonight all my rubies seem a bit over the top. Don't you think so, Luke?" She raised her voice slightly, so he could hear her from inside her vast closet.

"Remember, darling, I know you said I'd never cozy up to them but that's only because they're simply not cozy in and of themselves—but it doesn't mean I don't love them. Luke, come on in here and help me choose . . . no, never mind, I'll bring out the trays and let you see everything," Tessa said, as she emerged from the closet laden with six black velvet trays of jewels.

Tessa screamed and dropped the trays. Luke was slumped sideways and forward, his left arm hanging to the floor, his head and shoulders following the line of his dangling arm.

Tessa ran to him, using all her strength to push his upper body back into the chair. His head flopped forward, his chin rested on his breastbone.

"Luke! Luke!" she begged, "what's the matter? Open your eyes, for God's sake, is it your heart?" He didn't move, didn't open his eyes, didn't speak.

In a panic that gave her superhuman strength, Tessa managed to pull the phone table toward her and dial 9-1-1 while still propping Luke up in the chair. He had fainted, she thought, she mustn't let him fall. Tessa managed to give the emergency operator the address of the house and the fact that Luke had passed out before dropping the phone and attempting to take Luke's pulse. As soon as she reached for his wrist he started to fall forward toward her. She abandoned the attempt, wrestling with his weight to keep him in the chair.

Now Tessa tried to listen to his heart, putting her ear to his chest. She couldn't feel a heartbeat in the heart whose exact location she knew as well as that of her own—but his jacket was in the way, that was all. She couldn't find his heart because he was so heavy, so heavy, such a mass of firm muscle. Above all she mustn't let him fall.

Tessa was still holding Luke steady in the chair and imploring him to speak to her, when two paramedics burst into the room. She stood back only when they laid him down on the floor. One of the paramedics checked Luke's pupils and took his blood pressure while the other checked his pulse and quickly reached for the defibrillator paddles. "We're going to shock his chest," he explained to Tessa rapidly.

"He's never had a heart problem," she cried, incredulously watching the bizarre activity that had suddenly erupted in the fortress of her home. "His heart is perfect, what's wrong, what's wrong with him?"

"I don't know, ma'am," one of them answered. He had no intention of telling her that the paddles showed only a flat, straight line that indicated no electrical heart activity. That duty was for the doctors, thank God.

"How could you not know?" she shouted. "Do something, for the love of God, do *something*."

"Yes, ma'am, we're doing everything possible," he told her, reassuringly.

The paramedics exchanged a look. The man's pupils were fixed and dilated, there was no pulse, no blood pressure, he was asystolic, but they were trained to go on the basis that there was always hope. They shocked his chest, put an airway down his throat, and put an I.V. into his arm to try and push medication into him.

"Call the hospital," one of the paramedics told the other. Suddenly three firemen entered the room, responding to the initial call Tessa had made that indicated that a healthy man was down. One of them was bringing an oxygen tank, the others helping to strap Luke onto a stretcher. The paramedic on the phone said quietly, making sure that Tessa didn't hear him, "We're coming in, yes, asystole, fast as we can."

The paramedics, the firemen carrying the stretcher, and Tessa, grabbing her purse, all ran down the stairs to the ambulance that waited in front of the door, ignoring the servants who had finally materialized by the front door.

Tessa climbed into the ambulance and tried to gather Luke in her arms even though he was strapped to the stretcher. Neither of the paramedics tried to stop her.

"We're getting him to the hospital as quickly as possible," one of them said. He would not tell this poor woman, whose contorted features were so familiar and yet unplaceable, that her husband was dead. Stone cold dead. He'd known it the minute he'd looked in his eyes. It had been pointless to try the techniques they used for heart-attack victims. It must have been an aneurysm, he thought. Nothing else could kill as quickly. Nothing else ended a healthy life like a bolt of lightning unless you put a loaded gun in your mouth and pulled the trigger.

Maggie and all the Websters, even Candice and her husband, flew out to Los Angeles as soon as possible after Fiona had called to tell them that Luke was dead.

Madison, Tyler, and Maggie dropped the others at the Beverly Hills Hotel and went directly to Tessa's. There they found Fiona, Aaron Zucker, and Roddy Fensterwald already gathered.

"Where's Tessa?" Maggie asked as soon as she saw the little group huddled around a coffee table in the living room.

"In her bedroom. She won't come out," Fiona said, "and she won't let anybody in."

"Do you mean nobody's seen her since it happened?"

"Just me," Fiona answered. "She gave the hospital my name last night and I went to pick her up and bring her home right away—there was nothing she could do at the hospital—but when we got here, she ran upstairs to the bedroom and locked the door. She won't answer the house intercom and she hasn't rung for anything to eat. I listened at her door but I couldn't hear a thing, not a sound, and no matter what I said, she wouldn't answer, not even to tell me to go away."

"I think we should break the door down," Roddy said. "This can't go on."

"Fiona," Maggie asked, "what was she like when you went to the hospital?"

"In shock. Total. She wouldn't talk to me, she wasn't

crying, she was barely breathing. I don't know if she even realized who was driving the car home. I must have been the only person she could think of to call because she knew I was at Le Dôme."

"What did the doctors tell you, exactly, Fiona?" Maggie said, still trying to comprehend what had happened.

"He had something called a cerebral aneurysm," Fiona answered wearily. She'd already explained this to Roddy and Aaron. "Some people are born with the possibility of it happening. You can die from it at any time, or live to a ripe old age, it just depends. It's like a bubble or a bunch of berries on a vine in a blood vessel that comes out of the neck and goes around it, something called the Circle of Willis. If it pouches out, you have an aneurysm, and you die instantly. The pathologists at the hospital did the autopsy and called me this morning. There's no way to know if you have it or if you don't, and no point in knowing either."

"Oh," Maggie said in a small voice. "So Tessa still doesn't know why Luke died."

"I agree with Roddy," Aaron said. "We've got to do something, we just can't sit around here while she's going through this all by herself. Can't we take the door off its hinges?"

"Let me try to get her to open it first," Maggie said. "I'm the only one here who's family."

"You're right," Fiona agreed. "Do you want me to come with you?"

"Oh, yes, please, Fiona. I need someone to show me the way, this is the first time I've been here."

As they walked up the staircase Fiona, who hadn't seen Maggie in several years, was amazed by the steadiness of her step and her all-but-visible resolution. She's not a kid anymore, Fiona thought, but how old can she be? Surely no more than seventeen?

"I don't know how she'll live without him."

"No," Maggie said, "neither do I."

At Tessa's door, Maggie knocked. When she

received no answer she spoke through the door, raising her voice so that it was impossible that it wouldn't be heard.

"Tessa, it's Maggie. I'm here, Tessa, I'm here for you. Please let me in. You can't stay in there all by yourself, you need to be with somebody. I'm your sister, Tessa, I love Luke too. I've loved him almost since I can remember. He held my hand at our parents' funeral, remember that day, Tessa? You on one side and him on the other? I still think of that. He never let me be by myself, he never let me be frightened. I knew he'd take care of me, even though I was only five. Luke wouldn't want you to be alone now. You know he'd want you to be with your sister. Please let me in."

"Maggie? Are you alone?"

"Fiona's here with me, but she'll go away if you want."

The door opened and Tessa stood there, still wearing the white suit she'd had on the night before, tearless, composed, with blank eyes as dead as fossils in her white face.

"Maggie," she said, without any inflection, without any sign of surprise at Maggie's presence. "Maggie, have you heard about Luke."

"Yes, Tessa, that's why I'm here. May we come in?"

"Something happened to Luke, Maggie, something I don't understand."

"I know, Tessa. Please let us come in. We both really need a cup of tea and something to eat." Maggie and Fiona both entered the room, stepping carefully over the dozens of ruby necklaces and bracelets and earrings that lay scattered all over the floor where Tessa had dropped the trays.

"A cup of tea," she echoed.

"Yes. And something to eat."

"Oh, I'm sorry, I forgot. What time is it. I'll call down. Where did you come from, Maggie," Tessa said in her mechanical voice from which all emotion, even curiosity, had bled away.

"From home, Tessa. Tyler and Madison are downstairs, and Aaron and Roddy."

"So many people," Tessa remarked, slowly. "And Fiona, you too. Do they all know that something's happened to Luke."

"Yes, Tessa, they know. They came to be with you."

"What can they do for me?" For the first time there was a question in her voice.

"Just be with you. We love you, Tessa," Fiona said.

"Be with me? Do you think that will help?" Tessa asked blankly.

"A little, Tessa. It's better than being alone."

"Oh no, Fiona, it's the same thing, it's the same thing as being alone."

Only after the Requiem Mass was Tessa finally able to begin to accept the fact of Luke's death. For five days, despite Maggie and Fiona's entreaties, she shut herself up in her room once more, went to ground like a small animal whose legs had been gnawed off, and mourned for Luke, unable to stop weeping, sleeping only hours at a time, waking hideously to a nightmare that never ceased, eating only when her body insisted. Luke, her one and only love, was gone, her safety was gone, there was nothing left to live for, but no way to die. She was condemned to life and condemned to danger. Eventually Tessa's mind began to work again, as the useless jets of wrenching sobs, in which she'd forget everything but Luke, slowly turned to a dull perception of reality.

She must learn to live without Luke, she understood, since she was still alive. If she could only act as if she had strength, perhaps she would eventually find some measure of true strength, Tessa told herself, with all the courage she could fake. Searching in the only direction she knew, she took the first step to stitch up the tattered rags into which her heart had been ripped. She phoned her agent and asked him to come to the house.

"I need a job, Aaron. Within a week."

"Tessa, Tessa, what kind of crazy idea is that?"

"I have to have it, Aaron, a location shoot, as far away as possible, as difficult as possible, something that will keep me from thinking or feeling for as many hours of the day as possible."

"Wouldn't it be better to—"

"What?" she interrupted him, "sit here and mourn? I could spend the rest of my life doing that, Aaron, and never have the slightest reason to stop. I'm afraid of that . . . oh, it would be so easy, Aaron, you have no idea, so horribly easy . . . tempting . . . oh, so tempting. It terrifies me when I think how *almost right* that would feel to me." Tessa rose with determination. "The alternative is to go back to work. I know that's what Luke would have wanted me to do. And if I don't, how can I keep on living? Work is the only thing I know how to do now."

"But what about Maggie? She wants to come and live with you. She can do her senior year here. She truly yearns to do that Tessa, she hopes so much that you're going to let her, she'll be such a comfort to you."

"Oh, Aaron, Aaron, Maggie is such a darling, but she has no idea how bad an idea that would be for her. She may be ready to sacrifice an all-important year of school, but I'm not ready to let her do that. It's a year in which she'll become everything she's been working toward, in a place where she's finally conquered and triumphed and become a leader. How could I let her do that? How, Aaron? Only the most selfish woman in the world could allow it. She deserves her senior year at school, she needs it, you know it and I know it."

"I'm not as convinced as you are."

"All I can hope to be, Aaron, for a long, long time, is a woman who is using her work to survive. No one can 'be a comfort' to me. The only sort of comfort I can imagine is in making movies back to back, using the one part of me that I know still exists, still functions. I'm going to be on the move, and your job is to make sure of that. Maggie's place is in school. Do you seriously imagine I could drag a seventeen-year-old girl around from one location shoot to another, *for companionship*? You know how unfair that would be to her. Aaron, I'm ashamed of you for not understanding that! She's helped me beyond measure, she was there when I needed her, but now it's time for her to go back to her own life."

"No reason her life can't be with you," Aaron persisted. "No reason why she can't take a year off. Tessa, she's the only family you have."

"Aaron, no, no, and no," Tessa said, cutting short the conversation. Now that the first numbness had worn off, she saw clearly what was right for Maggie. She was free now to tell Maggie the truth, to claim her daughter, to claim the only child she'd ever have, but that revelation would bind Maggie more strongly to what she imagined, so wrongly, so sweetly, was her mission of comfort. She felt a strong urge, Tessa admitted to herself, to allow herself to take Maggie's youth and courage and lean on it, to possess, at last, a child of her own, to hold her close, to let Maggie be strong for her. *To cling.* But it was wrong, clearly wrong. She must wait to tell Maggie until she felt less needy, less vulnerable. She must wait until she had done the long work of mourning that remained to her, until she stopped being this stranger, this wounded, grieving, empty shadow of herself, with only a craft left to keep her going.

"I'm sending Maggie back home tomorrow," Tessa said, summoning up all the resolution at her command. "I'll call Madison and arrange it. She's been away too long as it is."

"I'll tell her," Aaron said sadly. "She's going to feel she's abandoning you."

Tessa continued as if he hadn't spoken. "Now you, Aaron, you have no more than a week to get me that job, and if nobody has what you consider to be a decent location script ready to cast, don't worry, take anything, anything at all. I don't care about quality. One week, Aaron, and I'll be packed and ready to go up the

Amazon or anywhere else that's far enough away. You know you can do it. Don't bother to argue with me again, because I don't care what anyone thinks, not even you, Aaron. If I don't get going, soon, I'll never work again. Luke . . . Luke wouldn't have wanted me to let go of life, no matter what happened to him. Remember Aaron, remember how proud he was of me . . . ?"

21

S he wouldn't have to stand it much longer, Madison Webster told herself, sitting at the desk in her bedroom, as she listened to Maggie clatter down the stairs, off to one of the countless events that marked the end of her last year in high school. That—that *peasant*—would be out of the house soon, although it could never be soon enough as far as she was concerned. She didn't need to provide a home for Maggie any longer, not for another second, yet for the sake of appearances she obviously couldn't throw her out until her graduation, Madison thought, as she bent over her accounts.

Her own private investments in the past thirteen years, solid and substantial as they had become in the amazing market of the 80s, remained intact. She'd had the instinct to sell everything and cash in several months before the stock market crash of 1987. However, her own impressive funds, built up through thousands of domestic economies, seemed minor compared to the twenty million dollars Luke had left Tyler in his will. Although the settlement of Luke's complicated estate was not yet final, there was no question that they were far richer than she had ever dreamed they'd be, yet she still hadn't changed any of her frugal ways.

Aside from what Luke had left them, he'd arranged the affairs of his company in exceptionally good order, leaving ten million dollars each to his six top men, dependent on their pledging to remain in the employ of the company for the next ten years, and he'd passed on his position as chief to Len Jones, who had been his second-in-command for so long. He'd left seventy million dollars to various charities, and everything else, the bulk of his estate, had been left to Tessa, except for another twenty million he'd left Maggie, to be kept in a trust until she was thirty-five, with Tessa named as one trustee and his tax attorney the other.

If Luke had enough to leave a hundred seventy million dollars to others, Madison wondered, biting the inside of her lips, what must Tessa be worth? She couldn't begin to imagine. Certainly, if she were Tessa, she'd never be able to bring herself to spend it, she told herself comfortingly and honestly. How odd and yes, how pleasant, how deeply reassuring it was to know that she'd become so accustomed to a certain way of life that she'd never want to make drastic changes no matter how much money she might have.

In fact, for some reason she didn't explore, Madison felt more devout about protecting her secret funds than ever. That was real money. It made her feel richer than the twenty-million-dollar bequest, which, after all, had been left to her husband, not to her.

Well, she thought, old money had always been conservative. Her family hadn't had true old money for two generations, although they'd had the wit to make it look as if they had it but were too secure to spend it. A great deal of well-polished, ugly old silver, heavy in the hand; unfashionable, darkly varnished mahogany; her great-grandmother's worn oriental rugs; lots of dogs—she'd grown up surrounded by all that, and as long as her horse was decent and her riding gear well cared for, the money had been assumed to be there, by her friends, the only people who mattered.

Ah, but there was one thing she promised herself to spend money on openhandedly, her private celebration when Luke's estate was settled. She was going to redecorate Maggie's rooms, erase every trace of her. Once that big, gaudy girl with her vulgarly large breasts was out of the house, once she'd been shipped off to college, the guest suite would become her own office from which she'd manage the estate, since Tyler had neither the ability for nor the interest in such practical matters. He could be trusted to buy a few promising stallions if their manager approved the prices, but Madison had her own ideas about making the stud farm profitable, plans she'd never been able to put into action in the past.

As for Maggie, clearly it was Luke's intention that she now be in Tessa's charge. Obviously he'd intended that Maggie make her home with Tessa, once she was of an age to go to college and no longer needed the steadiness of living in a family. Let Tessa cope with her sister for a change! Let Tessa try to get her to wear a bra!

Anyway, chances were Maggie would spend most of her holidays with classmates just as she'd encouraged Barney to do. That boy hadn't been home for almost a year, what with a summer at a friend's ranch in Nevada and Christmas and Thanksgiving in Boston and Philadelphia. He was such a popular boy that his disappointing marks didn't matter. The main thing was that he was making exactly the kind of friends she'd hoped he'd make when they'd decided to send him to Andover, when he was twelve, more than five years earlier.

Tyler thought that the reason for Luke's bequest was gratitude for their sacrifice in taking Maggie into their own family. He was probably right but, the good Lord knows, she'd more than earned it. In all justice, he should have left them more than he'd left Maggie. Tyler was his stepbrother, Maggie merely his wife's sister. But justice wasn't Luke's strong point, as it was hers. Wasn't she planning to give that girl a combination eighteenth birthday and graduation party, which, considering that Luke would never know about her generosity, she could perfectly well have skipped?

Even though it was soon going to be too dark to ride, Maggie wandered down to the stables and perched on the post-and-rail fence surrounding the empty practice ring. It was almost twilight on this soft spring Friday evening, a week before graduation. All the horses had been turned out to the fields, the six stable hands had gone home to their own lives, and she had the place to herself. She was surprised to feel a piercing nostalgia as she gazed at the scene of so many childhood hours of fear and humiliation. Yet heaven knew, she didn't feel anything but anticipation at the prospect of going away to college, leaving a home that had never been a true home under the cold care of shit-for-brains Tyler and snake-blood Madison, who had never once greeted her with a trace of warmth or even cared enough about her to criticize, so she'd know what she was doing wrong.

There was no question in her mind now that Madison truly disliked her and always had, for all these years. She had grown used to the hurt of it, grown to accept it. Only the physical buffers of Candice and Allison, both now married, had kept Madison from openly revealing her unexpressed, but unrelenting and most mysteriously unexplained, hostility, which seemed to have grown more open since Luke died.

No, her nostalgia was certainly not for her years in this house where she was, at best, tolerated, though unwanted; where Elizabeth, the cook, was the closest thing she had to a mother figure; where, after thirteen years, she still felt like an intrusive, unattractive, inferior stranger, as if she were some kind of charity case they'd been forced to take in, although that didn't make sense no matter how she tried to figure it out.

Her sense of loss was centered entirely on the time she'd spent with Barney, her faithful old protector, Barney who had forgotten her, disappearing into a world of grand new buddies and frantically social preppy vacations. She'd never had a chance to surprise him with how well she could ride. They hadn't even had a chance for one of their private talks in years, because when Barney did come home, just long enough to get his shirts washed and pressed, he'd been too occupied with his parents and the impressively connected friends he brought with him, to do more than say a quick hello to her.

Damn Barney to hell, anyway! He was only seventeen and a half and she was about to be eighteen in a week, a grown woman feeling sorry for herself because she'd been ignored by a boy, a mere adolescent, who, unlike a female, wouldn't really mature for years.

She was at the top of her class academically, Maggie told herself fiercely, she was popular with all the other girls, she was editor of the school paper and president of the debating team, she was highly computer literate, she'd been accepted by Smith and Vassar and the University of Michigan—and you'd better bet she was going to Michigan, where there were guaranteed to be men, genuine grown-up men, thick on the ground. Elm Country Day hadn't any male presence except on the faculty. Once Maggie had made it clear that she wasn't going to have a coming-out party, Madison hadn't introduced her to any of her friends' sons, not that she wanted to meet them, so her feeble experience of guys was limited to the geeky brothers of her classmates, not one of whom turned her on as much as her favorite horse.

Once she got to Michigan, after a decent week's wait, she was going to head straight to the student health department and ask to be fitted for a diaphragm, so that she'd be ready for whatever happened, Maggie promised herself. She didn't want to go on the Pill, she'd read too many articles about contraception to start the Pill at eighteen, with at least thirty fertile years ahead of her, but a diaphragm was safe.

She knew she'd meet the right guy during freshman year. It was impossible for anyone as ripe, as eager for experience as she was, not to find a guy, and it didn't matter if the guy was a mistake, as he was almost certain to be. She wanted to fall in and out of love as many times as was possible for a sane person. Four years of serial love affairs, Maggie promised herself with a wide smile, wasn't that the underlying purpose of higher education? She'd have to keep her grades up enough to stay in college, but fundamentally she was going to major in passion.

And when she graduated she was going to go to New York City and get some kind of wonderful job and have another five years of love affairs before she even thought of getting married. Almost more than anything else, she wanted, needed, a family of her own, because it had been so hard to grow up without one, but when she did marry, Maggie thought ferociously, she wanted to stay home and really be with her kids, the way she could still remember her mother being with her, although the memories were dim and fragmented. She was almost sick with a wild ambition to do and feel everything! She wanted it all, everything!

She'd been stuck in boring, limited horse country for most of her life. If ever a woman needed to be liberated it was she. There was a vast, marvelous world out there that she was going to bite into and chew up, piece by delicious piece, Maggie promised herself. She was going to be a raving success, she knew it in her bones. She felt as determined, as sharp, as purposeful and powerful as a shining sword. She took a deep breath, reveling in her sense of all the exciting, unknown adventures that were going to happen to her. She was ready for the world and all its surprises, oh, more than ready!

"Hey," said a quiet voice behind her.

Maggie almost fell off the fence in surprise, prevented by a pair of muscular arms grasped around her waist.

"Don't say anything, it's me, Barney," he whispered urgently in her ear, and lifted her easily off the fence so that she stood directly in front of him.

"What are you doing here! You're not supposed to get out of school till next week. What's going on? Why are you whispering?"

"I've been expelled."

"Shit! Why?"

"Pot party, I made the buy and they caught me on the way to my room where the other guys were waiting."

"Oh, Barney, you asshole! You *moron*, you've fucked up your life. Jesus! What happened to the others?"

"They said they didn't know what I was up to, a surprise to them."

"Nice guys."

"Why should they risk admitting anything when they didn't have any weed on them? I'd have done the same. So I'm out, one year short of graduating."

"How'd you get here?"

"On my bike. I have a secondhand Harley I fixed up so it's better than new, kept it in a garage in town. Bikes are my thing, my real thing, I'm so good with bikes you wouldn't believe it."

"Wow, *Easy Rider* all over again," she drawled.

"You got it, I'm reinventing the genre," he grinned. "Somebody's got to."

"And what are Ma and Pa Webster going to say?"

"That's the part where it could get nasty. Let's go in the tack room and figure out a lie."

"Barney, you're delusional. The school'll notify them. You'd have it easier escaping from Alcatraz."

"I've already escaped from Alcatraz, I took off as soon as I was kicked out, didn't pack, just got my bike and headed home."

"Alcatraz? I thought you liked school."

"Nope, not really. I'm academically deeply lacking, but mechanically brilliant. I tried to be a real preppy but my heart wasn't in it. I made a lot of friends, but they're busy planning to turn into their fathers, and that isn't for me. I want to work with my hands, run a bike shop—it's my dream—only problem is I don't dare tell my folks, they'll never allow it. A blue-collar son! They'll make me get a college degree from any tenth-rate place that would have me, even if they have to bribe one."

He opened the door to the tack room, turned on the light, and closed it behind them.

"Whew! Safe at last. I figured I might find you still trying to learn how to stay on a horse, so I came down here first, left my bike behind the barn."

"I can damn well stay on any horse in the Essex Hunt."

"Yeah?"

"Yeah."

They faced off opposite each other, unable to stop smiling in sheer joy at the sight of each other. She'd never been so glad to see anyone in her life, Maggie thought. Time seemed to stretch and sway, as subtle as a spider web, time all but stopped while they searched each other's faces, suddenly speechless. Barney had shot up, he was well over six feet tall. His streaky blond hair, tangled by his long ride, flopped over his forehead; his face was tanned; his pleasant, lively boy's face had turned into that of an almost-man, strong but still changing into what it would eventually become. His impudent grin and his freckles were the only fleeting reminder of the boy she'd known since she was five.

"Bet you can't," he said. "Bet I still have to save your ass."

"What'll you bet?" Maggie challenged him.

"A kiss."

"What kind of bet is that? If I can't ride I kiss you, if

I can ride you kiss me? Heads you win, tails I lose? No thanks."

"Okay, no bet. I believe you. Do you know what a sexy, lovely girl you've turned into?"

"Of course."

"Well I didn't." He put his hands on either side of her face and bent down and kissed her full on the lips, a long, lusty, sweet, sweaty kiss that detonated like a depth bomb in her belly. Her eyes opened wide in astonishment as she kissed him back wholeheartedly, voraciously. The tack room whirled around her; bridles and saddles, hunt caps, rows of polished boots, dozens of photos of horses—everything blurred and she staggered with dizziness. Only Barney's arms kept her upright.

"You liked that," he said, stunned by her response.

"I did. I'd like more. Over here, on the sofa."

"Maggie, we're not related or anything, are we?"

"Not even kissing cousins. We're just old friends."

"Oh, God," he groaned, "you're so gorgeous, so grown-up, where have I been?"

"Too busy to notice me."

"I must have been fucking stupid."

"You are. Shut up." She reached up for him with her open, impetuous, curious, innocent lips, groaning with hungry haste and need, adoring the touch of his searching tongue. She quivered with delight as he explored her mouth, lacing her fingers in his hair to bring him closer, kissing him all over his face, smelling his unfamiliar, delicious, rough skin. She rapidly pushed and pulled him around so that she could kiss his neck and his ears and his forehead, returning always to his open mouth and his hot, eager, shamelessly seeking tongue. Oh, Barney was a man, a man and a stranger and she had never known, never understood. She loved him, Maggie thought dimly, loved him as she would love a man.

"I've got to feel your breasts," he muttered into her lips. Maggie instantly ripped the buttons of her blouse open and exposed her breasts to his hands and his mouth, catching her breath in bliss as she felt his touch, so warm, so firm, so focused, so utterly different from when she played with them herself that a new world opened up to her. She lay under him, pushing upward, as he greedily sucked her nipples and madly rubbed her mound, under her jeans, with a penis that felt like a club. In a minute they both came, fully dressed, Maggie gasping, Barney with a muffled scream.

Too shaken to say anything, too surprised to move, they lay one on top of the other, holding each other tightly. After a minute Maggie, crushed, eased herself out from under Barney's body and lay next to him, hugging him close. He was limp from the unexpected power of his orgasm, she was weak with a pleasure greater than she'd ever known.

"And we didn't even *do* anything," Barney finally said in wonder.

"We didn't?"

"Not really."

"I never have," she admitted. "Have you?"

"Yeah, not much though. You're so . . . fast."

"Is that good?"

"Damn right. Oh, Maggie, I've got to do it again."

"I do too."

"Touch me this time, touch me, please, I've always loved you, Maggie."

"I know."

"Can you take off your jeans? I want to touch you too."

"Okay, but that's all, just touching."

"I promise."

In seconds both of them were naked, kissing and nipping at each other, looking at all their secret places, exploring each other's bodies almost roughly, trying to hold back from the only thing they really wanted, until, as mad with curiosity as with need, they both had to give in and explore each other frantically between their legs, fingers wet and ruthless. Soon, much too soon, they were both racked by profound, piercing, slowly widening and exploding orgasms that neither of them would forget for the rest of their lives.

Maggie returned to her room by a back staircase while Barney settled down to sleep in the tack room. She'd managed to make herself look almost normal in case she met anyone on the way, but no one saw her as she shakily made her way home and closed her door behind her. She sniffed herself. She'd never smelled the aftermath of sex on herself before, but she knew instantly that the first thing to do was to take a shower. The pungent odor was all over her, on her hands, on her jeans, even her hair reeked wonderfully of Barney and his sticky juices. If there hadn't been the chance of someone knocking at the door to find out why she wasn't at dinner, she would have liked to have wallowed in the marvelous smells of the two of them as long as possible, but she had no choice.

After her shower Maggie put on clean pajamas and got into bed so that she could say to a curious maid that she didn't feel well enough to eat. She turned off her lights, lay back on her pillow, and finally let herself think about what had just happened to her.

Barney, Barney, was all she could think at first, still dazzled by a trembling buzz that made her nerves zing with shudders from head to toe when she thought about the look of his cock, the unexpectedly smooth skin of his cock rising from the silky nest of his blond pubic hair, the blue veins on his cock, the thickness of his cock, the way it became, literally, the center of the universe as it grew imperious, demanding, irresistible. He had a power she'd never known existed. If he had asked her, she might not have been able to stop him from putting his cock in her. She longed for it so intensely right now that she was forced to give herself to another orgasm, before she was calm enough to think about anything else.

Barney was seventeen and a half years old, Maggie

told herself when she had regained her breath and found herself finally able to consider the situation calmly. A man-boy, half-grown, who had the terrifying power to make her do crazy things because of that thick cock that dangled so heavily between his legs when he stood up to put on his jeans.

No. The word came from within her, a warning, a summons, an enjoinment from deep within her spirit. If she met him again in the tack room there was no possibility of not giving in to him. By tomorrow he would have managed to jaunt out on his bike and buy condoms, she was certain of it, and somehow he'd talk her into thinking that was safe enough, because she wanted him so much. *No!*

She was scared witless, Maggie realized with the utmost seriousness, by the thought of how helpless she would become if she lay in his arms again, kissed him, smelled him. She'd never be able to stop with just grinding and petting and the kind of touching they'd done tonight. Barney, darling, beautiful Barney, no! She knew ten times more about sex now than she had a few hours ago, she knew that his stiff cock—that cock she'd always want—was quite enough to make her take leave of her senses. *And she wasn't going to do it.*

She must not. She dared not. There were too many reasons against it, she told herself sternly. They could not allow themselves to venture any deeper into a sexual obsession with each other. As little as Maggie knew, she realized enough to sense that they were on the very verge of obsession.

They were not kissing cousins, not related by a drop of blood, this almost-grown-up Barney was as fascinating as if he were a stranger and she could too easily imagine the insane risks they'd be willing to take, if they ever really started. They'd do anything to be together and one of those times they'd be discovered and utterly disgraced. By Madison and Tyler. *No, never!*

She was on her way to college, he'd been thrown out of prep school and didn't want to go back. She was on her way to many years of adventure, he had no ambitions beyond his dream of a bike shop, Maggie told herself, forcing herself to be coldly realistic. Both of them had their lives ahead of them but they didn't want the same things. Sex wouldn't be enough, their still-childish love wouldn't be enough. The real world would crush them. They were simply too young. Kids, both of them.

What had happened to all her sense of adventure and her eagerness to get out and stir the world up around her? she asked herself. The answer came clearly. Nothing had happened. She still intended to have it all. Barney's appearance here tonight had changed nothing fundamental. The timing was all wrong. She couldn't change her own dreams for Barney, sweet, loving, heavenly, glorious Barney, even if she would never forget him. It was over. It had to be over. There was no choice. Never again.

It was, Maggie thought as the tears streamed down her cheeks, her first one-night stand.

The next day, at lunch, Maggie found herself alone at the table.

"Where are my aunt and uncle?" she asked Elizabeth as soon as she could find her alone.

"They left to fly up to Barney's school, that's what I heard them say at breakfast. There's some sort of big trouble, but I don't know what it is."

"You haven't seen . . . anyone else around?"

"You know more about it than I do, I'll bet."

"What makes you say that?" Maggie asked innocently.

"Because I found Barney hanging around here when I came downstairs this morning and I had to give him half the food in the kitchen before he'd go away."

"Barney? What's he doing here?"

"That's what I thought you'd know."

"I haven't got a clue."

Maggie wandered down to the stables, dawdling

along the path. Barney couldn't be in the barn or the tack room or the stable hands would have seen him.

"Jesus, I thought you'd never show up," he said, stepping out from behind a grove of trees. "Come here, come here darling Maggie, I've been up all night thinking about you."

"No, Barney," she said, standing in the middle of the path. "It was the most wonderful, exciting thing that's ever happened to me. It was bliss, Barney, but I can't, not again, I can't even kiss you."

The amazing hurt on his face went through her heart, but she faced him firmly.

"Nothing will ever work out for us, and I love you too much to dare to love you more."

"That's crap! Pure crap!"

"Maybe, to you, but not to me."

"Come here and explain what you mean."

"No. I'm going back to the house. I just came to tell you. And there's something else. I know that they've gone to make a fuss and get Andover to take you back, and maybe they'll manage it, but I think you should do what you're good at, what you want to do. Go to New York and work with bikes, and get what you really want. Make your own life, don't let them force you into anything. You're different from them."

"You came down here to give me career advice?" he asked incredulously.

"Yep, I did. Do you need any money?"

"Christ!"

"Well, do you?"

"No, I have enough."

"Will you let me know where you are in New York?"

"Will you come to visit me?"

"I don't know, maybe someday, but first I have to go to college, Barney, I have to grow up and so do you."

"Oh, God, I hate it when you're right."

"So you know too."

"Yeah. We're too fucking young. Now. We won't always be, Maggie, don't forget that. Don't forget me. I loved you from day one. I love you now, I'm going to love you *always*. You're *my* girl Maggie. I'd better split. I'll let you know where I am. Give me just one kiss."

"I'll owe it to you. One kiss and we'll be back where we started yesterday. Good luck, darling, darling Barney. Good luck, have a good trip, and darling, good-bye."

22

"Maggie, come on in the kitchen as soon as you get a chance, I have something to ask you," Elizabeth the cook whispered with an air of secrecy, the day before Maggie's Saturday-night birthday party. Madison reluctantly had realized that it was her duty to celebrate the occasion, considering the size of the legacy Luke had left Tyler, although why he'd felt it necessary to leave Maggie an equal amount she'd never understand.

During the past week, since Barney's expulsion from school, Maggie had barely seen the Websters, both of whom were beside themselves with anger at their son and the need to find him and somehow place him, willy-nilly, in another school so that he could get into college next year. If they hadn't turned the plans for Maggie's birthday party entirely over to Elizabeth, they would probably have forgotten about it, Maggie thought, but the cook, who'd been through the older girls' debuts and weddings, was perfectly capable of managing a dinner party for Maggie's graduating class of twenty-three girls without any instructions from Madison. What special treat had Elizabeth dreamed up? Maggie wondered, as she made her way into the large kitchen.

"You're not going to show me my birthday cake in advance, are you?" she said, grabbing Elizabeth around the waist and planting a kiss on each of her cheeks. "Isn't that supposed to be bad luck, like seeing the bride's dress before the ceremony?"

"Maggie, come in the pantry," Elizabeth said with unaccustomed seriousness. "I don't know what to do about this." She handed Maggie a letter addressed to her. "Here, read it."

Maggie opened the envelope and scanned the single page. It was a short note from Barney, asking the cook to give Maggie, and only Maggie, his address in New York. He was fine, he said, but he didn't want his parents to know where he was until he had a job and could support himself, because nothing would make him go back to school.

"What should I do?" Elizabeth asked. "Should I show this to Mrs. Webster?"

"Give it to me," Maggie said. "They're worried sick about him. They have to know he's okay."

Relieved, Elizabeth turned over the paper to Maggie and went back to her preparations. Maggie memorized the address, tore the letter into bits, and put it in the trash. She promised herself to go into town that afternoon and empty her sizable bank account so she could send Barney money to live on until he could pay her back. She knew he couldn't have much, and she'd saved most of her allowance.

Maggie waited impatiently until Madison and Tyler returned for lunch.

"Barney called while you were out," Maggie said, as soon as they arrived. "He wanted you to know that he was perfectly fine but he said he wasn't going back to school and you shouldn't worry, he's looking for a job."

"Shouldn't worry?" Madison screamed furiously. "Shouldn't worry, after what he's put us through!" She sounded relieved but doubly furious. "Where was he?"

"I asked but he wouldn't tell me, I'm sorry."

"God, what I would give to get my hands on that rotten kid," Tyler raved. "Who the hell does he think he is, how could he treat us this way, what kind of future does he think he has? A job—who would employ him? He must be lying around smoking marijuana with a bunch of dropouts just as bad as he is. When I think—all we've done for him—he could be anywhere!"

"He sounded together," Maggie ventured, "not drugged at all."

"As if you could tell over the phone," Madison scoffed. "Why on earth didn't you get more out of him? I'll bet you didn't try. How can we find him? How dare he hide from us?"

"I did try," Maggie protested, "but he's doing his thing."

"Oh, that phrase! It makes me sick. Well, obviously there's nothing to do till he runs out of money and turns up on the doorstep. He'll be forced to come back, if I know Barney. Oh, and Maggie, speaking of turning up, I left too early to tell you, but Tessa is coming to the party tomorrow. It's supposed to be a surprise but with all I have on my mind I simply can't be bothered trying to remember." Damn Tessa's movie-star conceits and damn Maggie, she thought, for not having pried Barney's whereabouts out of him; they'd always been thick as thieves.

"Tessa's coming?" Maggie cried, stunned with joy.

"She's taking the Concorde over from London, arriving at the Carlyle tomorrow morning, driving out here for the party, spending the night at the hotel, and returning Sunday."

"Oh, I don't believe it!" Maggie rejoiced, flooded with happiness. Months ago she'd given up all hope of seeing Tessa on her birthday.

As she had planned, as soon as possible after Luke's death almost a year ago Tessa had replaced Michelle Pfeiffer, a flu victim, at the last minute on a major movie set in a small Greek village. The role had kept her working for four months. Then, with only a week for hurried costume fittings, she'd made a Merchant–Ivory film that had finished filming in the English countryside, and she was now in the early days of a Jaffe/Lansing production also due to be made in and around Paris and London.

Tessa had sold the house in Beverly Hills, the ranch in Texas, and the villa at Cap-Ferrat. "Heart-Broken Star Will Never Revisit Scenes of Past Happiness," the story in *People* had said, and, Maggie reflected, they had it right.

Tessa seemed to have jettisoned all her baggage except for her jewels. The rare photographs of her in the past year had been taken when she went out for an evening surrounded by a band of coworkers, once in a small Greek seaside café, twice in unknown British pubs. Inappropriate though they were for such places, Tessa had been covered with gems, blazing as if for a ball among her casually dressed friends. She must need, Maggie realized sadly, to wrap herself at all times in the protective armor Luke had given her.

Tessa had sent her brief postcards in the past year, but none of them said when she might be coming back to the United States. Maggie, in her concern, had been inspired to phone Aaron Zucker to find out Tessa's plans for the future.

"I'm playing it by ear, sweetie," he said, lamenting. "I mail her every script that I think has a part worthy of her in it, and let her pick and choose, because I can't read her mind. I'm more like a postman than an agent. The scripts keep flooding in but she doesn't want my advice on anything. She's got nothing on her mind, as far as I can figure out, except keeping so busy she can't think. Well, I guess it's one way of mourning, but I keep wondering if she's ever going to give herself enough time to feel."

"I guess that's the last thing she wants to do," Maggie replied.

"But can you live life like that?"

"I don't know, Aaron. I don't know Tessa well enough to say."

"How can you feel like that, Maggie? You've known her all your life. She's your sister."

"There's knowing and knowing. I've spent so little time with her, even when you add it all up, and mostly I was a kid. Each visit was an incredible treat, a thrill, an adventure—not everyday life where you get to know what makes people tick. And you don't talk frankly about yourself to someone so much younger, as I am, even if she is your sister. You, and Roddy and Fiona, you all know Tessa much better than I do. For me she's an adored, impossibly glamorous stranger from another planet who drops in or sends for me every once in a while, lets me wear her jewels and tells me nothing serious. We've never had a grown-up relationship."

"Tell me about movie stars, Maggie, tell me something new. But now you're old enough to get to know her," Aaron said consolingly. "Think of it that way."

"Only if she stops rushing from one shoot to another."

"Good point, kiddo. The minute I know what she's going to do next, I'll let you know."

Maggie had hung up, after talking to Aaron, feeling farther away from Tessa than she had for years, when at least she could dream about their next flying visit.

"Tessa's going to a lot of trouble for just one party," Madison said sourly, annoyed at Maggie's expression of radiant expectation.

How like Tessa, she thought, to dump her sister on other people three hundred and sixty-four days a year, and then show up once a year and get all the credit for having made an enormous effort.

"Oh, Madison, she *is*, she is!" Maggie gulped and ran out of the room in a hurry because she was about to burst into happy tears. Tessa was coming! Coming to see her!

Two days earlier, Tessa had found herself free from pre-production chores, with a whole day stretching in front of her. London was at its best, spreading its humming vastness out beneath a sky of a singular transparency. It held not the promise of perfection but perfection itself. It was that one particular spring day that came but once a year, when every window box had reached its perfection of spring bloom; when every ancient tree in every ancient park celebrated itself with a burst of perfect new leaves, when the most conservative of Englishmen left his umbrella at home and the most conservative of Englishwomen bought herself two new hats.

Tessa stretched out in a canvas chair in St. James's Park and contemplated the passage of three tiny white clouds that punctuated the exquisite pastel of the sky framed in a circle of treetops. She could live here, she thought idly, if every day were like this one. She could buy a house in London if she hadn't spent last winter here, grimly accepting what any Californian would think of as a twilight zone, with lamps lit well before four in the afternoon. But it might be amusing to have a small place, just a mews house, with a little garden, only for the spring and fall, so that she wouldn't always have to live in hotels. . . . With a great start of surprise Tessa realized that she was making a plan. It was the first time since Luke had died that she'd thought of the future. Galvanized, she jumped up from her chair and started walking rapidly through the park, oblivious to anything but her thoughts.

If she could make any plan, even a tentative one based on the weather, she must be well along in the mourning process, Tessa told herself. Mourning Luke had been like having an invisible wound that left no outward trace. She could only judge its healing by the way her mind worked. She had reached this point by living one day after the other, hanging on, enduring. Every morning she willed herself to get out of bed and go to work, never thinking of her future. So . . . time had passed, enough time apparently, although she would never have known it if she hadn't imagined owning a mews house. If she were well enough to consider real estate, Tessa thought with a leap of joy, she could allow herself to be with Maggie without clinging to her and dragging her down into her grief. And oh, how right she'd been to leave Maggie in school to graduate. The past year she'd been hell to be with, she was aware of that, but since she had always arrived at the set on time, line perfect and ready to work as hard as necessary, no one she loved had been injured by the gloom of her moods.

Maggie would be eighteen on Saturday, Tessa reflected, hurrying back to the hotel. Eighteen, her child would be eighteen! The concierge could, had to get her tickets on the Concorde so that she could tell Maggie the truth without any further delay. Maggie could spend the summer with her in London before going back to start college. They'd have months in which to begin to learn how to be mother and daughter . . . if . . . Maggie would accept her after she'd told her everything that had happened.

Tessa broke into a run. There was so much to do, so much to plan. So much to hope for.

The morning of her birthday Maggie had awakened early, feeling very important. She'd had dreams of strange rapture, like dancing on clouds of gilded meringue, that vanished as soon as she'd awakened, but they'd left her feeling light, graced, and poised.

After her shower she put on her pearls and posed naked in front of her full-length bathroom mirror, admiring her rosy, abundant, sexy adult self from all possible angles. Then, for a mad minute, she capered about in honor of the kid she was leaving behind, wiggling her ass at herself in mockery. As she dressed, Maggie realized to the full how major an occasion today was going to be in her life.

Eighteen is a milestone, she thought, a stepping stone to the future, a sign of adulthood that no one can dismiss. The magic day had come at last, and, to make everything perfect, Tessa would be arriving in New York well before noon. She knew that the Concorde left London very early in the morning and Tessa had once told her that people who made the three-hour flight often ate two breakfasts, one early, in flight, and one late, in New York. What if she took the bus into the city and met Tessa at the hotel? Elizabeth would drive her to Essex to catch the bus, and she'd have time alone with her sister before the party.

Turning the idea over in her mind, with mounting excitement, she rushed down to the kitchen for breakfast, the first one to arrive.

"Well, here's your annual birthday card," Elizabeth said with a smile. "Your godparents in California never forget, do they? Not at Christmas and never on your birthday, or Easter, for all the years you've been here. This one looks almost like a letter. Maybe they're sending you some good advice; that's what godparents are supposed to do, you know, even if you are half a pagan."

Maggie ripped the envelope open and found that it wasn't a card, but a letter from Brian Kelly enclosing a sealed letter addressed to her. To escape Elizabeth's kindly but prying eyes, she took the two letters into the deserted dining room to read.

My very dear God-daughter, Maggie,

   As you know, your father, Sandor Horvath, or Sandy, as I called him, was one of my closest friends and I treasure the honor he did in making me your godfather, even though you haven't been around much for Helen and me to spoil, worse luck. When you were five years old, your father gave me this letter to deliver to you on your eighteenth birthday in case he was no longer on earth to do it himself. I've often wondered if he felt a premonition, poor dear man. I've kept it in my safe-deposit box for thirteen years, ever since your parents tragically passed on. The post office tells me that this should reach you well in time for your birthday, since I live too far away to bring it to you in person.

Dear Maggie, have a wonderful day and remember that both of us send you all our very best wishes and many happy returns of the day. The next time you come to California, we'd be so happy if you could find the time to visit us. You must be a very grown-up young lady by now.

With our fondest love,
Brian and Helen

Wonderingly, reverently, Maggie turned over the enclosed letter. The envelope, yellowing at the edges, was heavily sealed and addressed to Miss Mary Margaret Horvath in handwriting she'd never seen before, elaborate and beautifully formed handwriting, unlike anyone's she knew.

Mary Margaret, she thought, Mary Margaret, my father thought of me by my full name. How strange that I never knew that, that I've always been Maggie. If he had lived, maybe he would have called me Mary Margaret and that would have changed me in some way.

She held the letter, turning it over and over, and realized that she was postponing the moment of opening it. A letter from her father, written thirteen years ago, was too important to open here, she thought. She hastily took both letters to her room, where there was no chance of Madison or Tyler walking in.

Maggie put Sandor Horvath's letter carefully on her desk and slowly, being very careful not to tear it, slit the envelope open with the old wooden letter opener Barney had once whittled for her at summer camp. The letter paper was stiff and so heavily creased that it was hard to smooth out, but the elegant handwriting was as easy to read as calligraphy.

Beloved Mary Margaret,
I pray that you will never receive this letter. I

am fifty-four years old and, given a merciful God, should be alive to be with you thirteen years from now, on your birthday. But there is no way of knowing the future and I am determined that you should be told the truth about your birth when you have reached the age of reason and, I hope, compassion. If it is within my power, I will tell you the following facts myself when you turn eighteen, but if I am no longer of this world, someone must tell you, and there is no one I trust but myself.

I believe deeply in my God and in the Church of Christ. You have been sinned against by a great lie, a lie told to you by me, by Agnes Horvath, my wife, and by Teresa Horvath, my daughter. I believe that this lie has caused you real harm, which thus constitutes a mortal sin. The only thing a good Catholic can do to try to make restitution for a mortal sin is to confess it and receive absolution. My daughter, Teresa Horvath, has confessed but a small part of this sin and has received the Sacrament of Reconciliation.

However, my wife has not confessed the greater part of the sin, for which she is responsible and for which I am equally responsible. On the contrary, she continues with the sin of presumption, of pride, to believe that she can save her soul without the help of Almighty God. We both continue to break the eighth commandment, "Thou shalt not bear false witness against thy neighbor," i.e., to tell a harmful lie. A harmful lie is a mortal sin in the eyes of the church. We have, I know, certainly lost sanctifying grace and our chance of eternal life.

I have discussed this grievous capital sin with my confessor, Father Vincent, and since you are only five years old, we have agreed that the only way I can make restitution to you for this sin is to confess it to you when you are old enough to understand it. He cannot give me the Sacrament of Reconciliation unless we stop the lie in which we live, which is not now possible since it would have grave consequences for our daughter, Teresa.

Mary Margaret, your sister, Teresa, is your mother. She gave birth to you when she was still but fourteen years old. We do not know who your father was. Your grandmother, Agnes, and I decided to bring you up as our own child. This was done for several, all-too-human reasons. First of all, we wanted to spare Teresa the great disgrace of bearing an illegitimate child. In the second place, your grandmother wished to keep all knowledge of this disgrace from her family, and I, for my part, wanted another child. For that reason we came to California to live, where everybody we know believes you to be our child, not our grandchild.

Your mother, now twenty years old and known to the public as Tessa Kent, is about to leave our home and go to Scotland to make a motion picture. At the age of sixteen, when you were only two, she became a film star. I do not know when she intends to tell you the truth about your birth, but I pray every night that it will soon become possible for her. On that day I will destroy this letter. Until that day, all three of us, your mother, Teresa, and the two of us, Agnes and Sandor Horvath, your loving grandparents, are mired in this lie, which deprives you of knowledge of your true mother.

You are a good, sweet, well-behaved child, Mary Margaret, and you have given me great joy, but I have never felt that I had a right to that joy with the knowledge I possess. I have always blessed you, and will always bless you, every day of my life. Forgive me if you can.

Your grandfather,
Sandor Horvath

As she read the letter, Maggie had instinctively risen from her desk chair and retreated to the bathroom, where she could lock herself in. She reread it twice more and then once again, seeking time to absorb the shock. At the first reading she had grasped it as clearly as a single headline, but she hadn't allowed herself to know it. During the next two readings, she'd willed herself to pick her way among the complications of the story, as if they might change its message, but after the final reading she had to allow the contents of the letter, and all it meant, to pour, pounding and irrefutable, into her open, unprotected consciousness.

Long before the final reading, Maggie's emotions had galloped ahead of her mental process and assumed a vile, jagged, threatening shape that filled her chest and abdomen and pushed inward on all her vital organs, making it almost impossible to breathe. There was a growing constriction in her throat, a tightening and an ache in the length of her neck, especially under her chin, as if she were wearing a cruel leash.

She was overcome by an intense desire to hide, to disappear from a world that contained this story of betrayal and secrets and lies, all directed at her since she had been born. She felt crushed, flayed, utterly incapable of sustaining a personal identity, stripped, mocked. She was a nothing crawling on the face of the world. A cipher, unwanted, unwanted, unwanted. She was without rights, without a place of her own, a fraud, a mistake everyone could lie to, manipulate, put down or take up at will, a sin to be confessed, a throwaway toy, a disgrace, a thing to be hidden but never acknowledged. A thing, a thing, not a person.

For a long time Maggie knelt on the carpet, sitting on her heels, the letter scattered by her side, bowed over so that she could rest her head on the floor and protect it with her hands, gathered into the smallest space she could take up, too beaten down for the relief of tears, a solid wad of pain. Gradually her mind slowed and all but stopped working for a timeless period, a self-protective period in which she knew, in her slow-moving, almost dreamy consciousness, that her life had changed forever. She existed in the moment, with no past or future, enduring the darkness and the shame, panting, unable to draw a normal breath, content to stay in the darkness, content to be motionless, nonexistent.

Slowly, gradually, from a place she didn't know she possessed, thoughts gathered, strength returned. She was Maggie Horvath, and Maggie Horvath was a person. No matter how unwanted she'd been, no one could take that away from her. Maggie Horvath existed, the five-year-old to whom that letter had been written had become Maggie Horvath, a grown-up woman, not poor little Mary Margaret. The web of the letter dropped away and Maggie was left with one piece of certainty: *She existed and Tessa was her mother.*

Maggie got up off the floor and looked at herself in the mirror. She looked like the same person who had awakened to such happiness this morning, yet now she was reeling with pure rage. She could smell it. It escaped from her pores into the air. The shape of pain inside her had condensed into an anger she could barely contain. Her eyes were bright with it, her cheeks flaming with it, her heart beat with the power of it.

She dressed for Manhattan in minutes. She packed a small suitcase, grabbed her handbag, and walked downstairs, pausing only to pick up the keys to Madison's car from the hall table. She heard the sounds of lunch being served as she left the house. She hadn't taken the test for her driving license yet, but she'd known how to drive expertly for years, and within an hour and a half she'd parked in an uptown garage near the Carlyle, her mind concentrated entirely on the route and on avoiding the attention of the police. She left her suitcase in the car, walked briskly to the hotel, and had herself announced at the reception desk.

"Please go up, Miss Horvath," the clerk said, after he'd called upstairs. "Miss Kent is in suite nine hundred."

"Thank you."

As she got out of the elevator Maggie saw Tessa standing in the hallway at the door to her suite, arms open in welcome, her words tumbling out, her smile filled with excitement and hesitation and uncharacteristic apprehension.

"Maggie! Darling Maggie! Madison must have told you . . . I . . . I wanted it to be a surprise. I have so much to tell you . . . but I hardly recognize you, you've changed, you're so very much more grown up than a year ago. Oh, give me a kiss, my Maggie."

"I don't think so," Maggie said, walking past Tessa into the sitting room.

"You're not too old to give me a kiss, are you?" she said, bewildered.

"You're much too old, Tessa."

"*What?*" The smile was still on Tessa's face.

"You're thirty-two. Isn't that too old to lie to your daughter?"

They faced each other mutely. Maggie's expression a fierce, frozen challenge as she searched Tessa's face, watching the smile fade and the eyes fill with the beginning of comprehension.

"I came on purpose to tell you . . . I couldn't before because—"

"*Liar.*"

"No, truly . . ."

"Lie! I'll never believe anything you tell me, ever, ever, ever!"

"Oh, God! I can't blame you, but Maggie, please, *please* lis—"

"Don't you wonder how I know?"

Tessa was shocked into silence, unable to keep from turning her face away from Maggie's look of flaming accusation.

"I had a letter from a dead man this morning. Sandor Horvath. Not my father, not the father I watched being buried—*your father, Tessa*. He didn't trust anyone to tell me the truth—he knew you pretty

254

well, didn't he?—so he wrote me thirteen years ago and left the letter with my godfather to send. My first birthday present."

"You can't understand," Tessa said, sinking down onto a sofa. "I don't expect you to understand yet, but I was only fourteen. Fourteen. You should try, at least, to understand that, you've been fourteen, you know what it would have meant."

"Of course I understand. He explained it all. Any fourteen-year-old girl would understand. It was perfectly normal. If you hadn't been Catholic you might have aborted me. Why didn't you give me up for adoption?"

"My father wouldn't—" Maggie put her hand to her mouth in horror.

"He told me, he wanted another child. Otherwise you would have, wouldn't you?"

"Probably. That's what my mother wanted."

"And you, what did you want to do with your child?"

"I don't know, I don't remember. I just wanted it not to have happened. How could I have taken care of you? I was only fourteen. I did what they told me. I had to obey them to survive, that's all I remember. And you weren't Maggie, you were just a baby."

"I don't blame you for any of that," Maggie said in a level tone.

"Oh, Maggie . . ." Tessa turned to her with a look of hope beginning to flare in her lovely eyes.

"I blame you for everything else. I blame you for what you did to a little five-year-old child who hadn't harmed you, who believed everything you did was wonderful. I blame you for sending me to live with those cold terrible people when you married Luke. I've seen the wedding pictures a hundred times . . . I wasn't even invited to the wedding. I was only five, it wasn't too late to become my mother once you were married. *You could have kept me with you, I had no parents, you could have claimed me.* But you abandoned me forever when you married Luke. How could you have been heartless enough to do that to a child, your *own* child? I blame you for sending me away for thirteen years to the Websters, people who never had a drop of love for me, people who weren't my family, who treated me like an intruder. Except for Barney, the cook is my only friend in that house."

"Maggie—"

"How much did you pay them to keep me? It must have been a fortune to keep Madison halfway civil, no matter how miserly she is. But you would have paid anything, wouldn't you, to keep from having to take care of me yourself? You can't deny it, you don't even try. You were too busy being a star, too busy being married to a rich man, too busy jaunting around the world, too busy living for Luke, too busy being the famous Tessa Kent. There was simply no room in your wonderful, brilliant life for a child, was there? You and Luke didn't even want one of your own. I grew up without love, except the little bit you spared me when Luke was away and you allowed me to visit, allowed me to play with your jewels. Your jewels around my neck instead of your arms. Stories of how to clean pearls instead of stories about my grandparents, my family, my place in the world. I grew up with no one but you and the crumbs you gave me. My grandmother had relatives, and one of them might have loved me, who knows? I'm not that unlovable, although that's the way I felt, so ashamed that no one loved me but afraid to tell you because I thought you'd be disappointed in me."

"You should have said something!"

"I should have said something?"

"I thought you were happy with the Websters."

"Even if I had been, they're nothing to me. You're my mother. *My mother!* How could you leave me with them? How could you pretend to be my sister? How could you spend so little time with me?"

"Luke didn't know," Tessa whispered. "He never knew."

"What's that supposed to mean? What does that have to do with anything? Luke's been dead for a year. Even if I believed you never told him, and I don't believe it for a second, once he died you could have told me."

"I couldn't then," Tessa cried. "It wouldn't have been fair to you."

"This is where I came in, Tessa," Maggie said, taking off her pearls and putting them on a table. "I don't want to see you again, ever. I don't want anything from you, ever. I don't want the money Luke left me, nothing will make me take it. Tell Madison I took her car and I'll send her the claim check for it. And tell her to cancel the party, I won't be going back there."

She turned and walked toward the door as quickly as possible. It swung shut behind her as Tessa, immobile, was unable to try to follow her.

"I came here to tell her," she told herself in a small voice, hugging herself and rocking back and forth. "I came here to tell her, but I couldn't before, could I? *Could I?*"

23

A few minutes later Maggie found herself sitting on a bench in Central Park, so drained by the revelations and emotions of the morning that she couldn't imagine how she'd ever get up again. Her brain was as empty as an eggshell from which the yolk and white had been suctioned out.

Only the sight of a soft-pretzel vendor aroused her to action. After three pretzels and two orange drinks had restored her blood sugar level, she found the strength to take a ball that a little boy put in her lap and toss it for him to retrieve and gleefully give back to her for another go. She could have spent the afternoon absorbed in this game, but when his nanny dragged him, protesting, from his new friend, Maggie's mind began to work, reluctantly but efficiently.

The past was entirely past: over, finished, dead. College was out, because that would mean having her bills paid by Tessa, and any future relationship with Tessa was unthinkable. Even as she thought of Tessa, she felt absolutely nothing, no sense of loss, not even a flicker of anger, just an empty blankness devoid of pain. She was somehow insulated from emotion, Maggie realized. Her heart had withdrawn from her body and only clear facts were left.

The future was hers to invent. Her assets? The money, the eight hundred dollars she had planned to lend Barney, was still safe in her purse. She had a suitcase back in the car filled with whatever she'd packed this morning, she was dressed in her best light spring suit, and her shoes were beautifully polished. She had Barney's address. All in all she was in a relatively rich position from which to begin a new life. She needed a job and a place to live.

Resolutely Maggie returned to the garage to get her suitcase, gratefully used their restroom, and took a taxi to Barney's address, a brownstone converted into single rooms on a street between Columbus and Amsterdam Avenues on the Upper West Side. The street showed no sign of the gentrification that was taking place in the neighborhood. No tempting little shops, no cafés or enticing ethnic restaurants, no polished brass door-knobs, no pretty curtains hanging in the windows, Maggie noted. Some of the houses didn't have panes in the windows, much less window boxes.

Barney's name was scrawled next to one of the buttons on the downstairs panel, but when he didn't answer she sat on the second step of the short flight of outside stairs and waited for him. She welcomed this opportunity to decide what to tell him. Not a word about Tessa, she concluded instantly. The story, with its all-but-gothic complications and recitals of a grandfather's mortal sins—a grandfather she barely remembered—could only be explained in its entirety or it didn't make sense. It had nothing to do with Barney or her new life.

Madison and Tyler. They were reason enough, Maggie thought, watching, in an increasingly dreamlike state, the lively action of the crowded, noisy, dirty, and almost certainly dangerous street. Eventually, as she clasped her handbag tightly in one arm and threw the other around her suitcase, her lids closed over her weary eyes.

"Maggie!" Barney scooped her up and held her tight. "Oh, my Maggie, I thought I'd never see you again! How could you abandon me like that? Oh, sweetheart—"

"Barney! Wait, please *wait*. Shut up and listen to me and try to understand. You've got the wrong idea, I know how it looks, but I haven't come to be with you. I've run away. I'm never going back, I'm on my own now. If Elizabeth hadn't given me your address I'd have gone to a hotel."

"Run away? It's your birthday, you can't run away on your birthday," he blurted, totally confused.

"It's as good a day as any other."

"Maggie, for Pete's sake, what's going on?"

"I've had it up to here with your folks. I know you probably love them, but I had to get out. Your mother and I have always had problems with each other and when I realized I was eighteen and legally free, I got out. I gave them your message, by the way. Your dad's plenty pissed, your mother said you'd be back when you ran out of money."

"The hell I will!"

"I didn't argue with her," Maggie grinned. "For a change."

"Come upstairs, birthday girl, we can't talk here," Barney said, taking her suitcase and leading the way up two flights of stairs to the room he'd rented.

"It's not a palace, but it's home sweet home," he said proudly, opening the door on a back room with one curtainless window looking out on a dusty tree. The walls were already all but concealed with bike posters, he had a futon on the floor partly covered by a threadbare rug, and a table held the essentials for living: a tape deck, a hot plate, and a can of insect spray. A tiny, ancient refrigerator hummed in the corner, and the sink on the wall had room for a soap dish and a toothbrush. A mirror hung above it. The room, even the window, looked clean if nothing else.

"There's a closet, and a john down the hall. I can

cook and do my dishes, and my neighbor has a shower he'll rent out for a quarter for five minutes," Barney said proudly. "As they say in France, I have le tout confort."

"No princess phone?"

"There's a drugstore around the corner. So what do you think?"

"It's perfect. I had no idea you were so neat. It's you, Barney. The real you. Where's your bike?"

"Safe in the shop. I got a job at a big Harley repair place, entry level but plenty of room to rise to the top. I already know more than most of the guys there but I'm playing it cool, not letting them know yet."

"Wise," Maggie said, reclining as sedately as possible on the improvised couch. "Are you liking it?"

"I love every second. And I'm a reformed character."

"You? In one week?"

"Yeah, me. Joined the Y, lifting weights, no beer, no pot, early to bed, saving half my salary, no time to waste goofing off, and I figured out how to cook hamburger and scramble eggs. I can also open a can of tuna fish. Even got mayo. Want something to eat, my beautiful birthday girl?"

"I'm starving."

"Listen, you take a nap, you're half asleep already, and I'll go get something for an early dinner. We'll celebrate being free. I'll get Twinkies, too, and birthday candles."

"No, Barney, I have to get a place to live first," Maggie said regretfully, gazing at him. He looked a year older than he had last week. And ten years more adorable. If only she could kiss him . . . she sat up quickly.

"Hell, you could stay here for just one night," he said indignantly. "I wouldn't jump you."

"You wouldn't?"

"Not 'jump'. . . exactly. Maybe . . . more like a suggestion . . . a birthday commemoration? You're only eighteen once."

"Nope, no can do," she said briskly, making herself stand. "Do you think there are any rooms to rent in this building?"

"It's full up. This was the last room, a lucky break. But at the drugstore there's a bulletin board for the whole neighborhood, people selling stuff, looking for soul mates, lost cats, even legit roommates. We could go look."

"Forward, comrade. Do they make sodas in this drugstore?"

"Maybe they did, forty years ago."

"Find anything yet?" Barney asked. He'd managed to get Maggie an ice cream cone and a Coke while she investigated the bulletin board.

"Lots of local color and one possible roommate. Listen to this. 'Wanted, to share part of rent: female, open-minded, unshockable, immaculate, quiet, NON-SMOKER, no pets, no tattoos, no body piercing, no post-Beatles music. Private room and bath. P. Guildenstern.' And it gives a phone number."

"Sounds like a weirdo. 'Immaculate *and* unshock-able'—and what does 'no tattoos' mean?"

"It sort of sounds like me. I'm going to call her. What have I got to lose?"

"How do you know it's a woman?"

"I don't yet," Maggie laughed, dialing the number on the wall phone.

"Hello," said a deep, gruff voice.

"P. Guildenstern?"

"Herself," the voice said, in its normal feminine tone.

"I saw your notice. My name is Maggie Horvath. No tattoos, unshockable, nonsmoker. Is the room still available?"

"That depends."

"On what?"

"On whether I think you seem like a suitable person."

"I'm immaculate too."

"That's always a subjective judgment. Come on over and let me see for myself. It's three blocks up, the house on the corner of Amsterdam, top floor. I have a German shepherd, trained to attack if you make a false move."

"I'm harmless. All right if I bring my cousin to check you out?"

"Man or woman?"

"Man."

"No, leave him one flight down. I'll leave the door open so you can scream if you think it's necessary." P. Guildenstern's voice trembled slightly.

"I'll be right over." Maggie put down the phone. "She's ten times more scared of me than I am of her, Barney. I bet she doesn't even have a tabby cat." She finished her cone, looked at herself in the mirror of her compact, wiped a speck of chocolate ice cream off her lip, applied a little powder, and smoothed her hair. "Do I look nice and clean?"

"Distinctly nice, definitely clean," Barney agreed, using all the verbal restraint at his command.

Breathless from the climb to the top of the six-story building, Maggie knocked at the bright blue door on which was tacked a tiny card engraved with the word "Miniatures."

The door opened on a stout chain and P. Guildenstern looked up at her with wide gray eyes attempting a fierce stare. Maggie looked down at a dainty woman of perhaps five feet one inch, whose mass of curly red-blond hair was tied back from her neck with a black velvet ribbon. She had a charmingly delicate face with a small, piquant, pointed nose and Victorian rosebud lips. A German shepherd almost as tall as she stood at attention by her side, on a short leash.

"Good afternoon, Miss Guildenstern," Maggie said gravely.

"Good afternoon," she answered tentatively.

"I'm Maggie Horvath, I just called."

"Oh, good. I couldn't be sure. Sometimes strangers ring . . ." she said vaguely, while she inspected Maggie rapidly and keenly from head to toe. "Is your cousin downstairs?"

"Barney, give a yell," Maggie called.

"I'm down here," Barney called up from the fifth-floor landing.

"Tell him to stay there."

"It's okay, Barney, just stay put."

"My name is Polly," P. Guildenstern said, unlocking the door but keeping the dog on the leash. "Please come in."

"Oh, how wonderful." Maggie stood stock still, astonished by the large skylight that let a flood of late-afternoon sunshine into what was clearly a studio. "You're an artist."

"I paint miniature portraits."

"I didn't know anyone still did that."

"They rarely do, since the camera was invented," Polly said with a trace of wistfulness, "but there's still some specialized call for them. It's not steady work but it's what I do best."

"What do you paint on?"

"I use vellum, or what passes for vellum laid on card—what does this have to do with the room?"

"Nothing, I was just interested," Maggie explained, peering across the studio at a work table topped by a fascinatingly time-worn, good-size box with many drawers and a top that had been raised to form an easel.

"You may take a look at the room now."

"Does that mean you think I look like a suitable person?" Maggie was suddenly conscious of being in the presence of an utterly benign personality who, nevertheless, possessed a sharply functioning and critical mind.

"Fairly suitable," Polly Guildenstern said with a considering sniff, walking down a hallway and unlocking a door. "It's stuffy," she apologized, throwing open both of two barred windows, "but of course I keep these locked when there's no one here. You can't be too careful."

Maggie looked around. A canopied four-poster bed, hung with rather tattered pale blue and white damask, dominated the room. The walls were covered with an old floral paper in dim but still-gay yellows on white. There was pattern upon pattern everywhere, a garden of embroidered and painted flowers composed by worn but unmistakably elegant floral fabrics, some satin, others taffeta and silk. They were draped over two French armchairs, made three skirts of different lengths on a round table, and were used freely as draperies at the windows. A patched floral rug covered the floor. Nothing matched, everything had mellowed into shades of faded pastel, and everything melted together. It was like stepping through time, into an illustration from an old book of fairy tales.

"Oh, it's heaven!" she gasped.

"I collect old textiles," Polly said demurely. "I keep them away from the light, but here I used the ones that were faded beyond hope."

"It's a dream, it's like a museum, but I'd be afraid to use the bed," Maggie cried yearningly. "What if I tore something, or spilled something by accident? I'd never forgive myself."

"Everything can be and has been patched a dozen times over," Polly murmured reassuringly. "There's nothing of real worth here, though they do look lovely all together, don't they? There's a closet and a small but complete bathroom. Would you like to look at it?"

"Oh, yes, but what's the point? There's no place to cook."

"So it would seem. But nothing is quite what it seems, don't you find?" Polly asked, drawing back a four-panel screen painted with vines and revealing a compact little kitchen.

Picking up a nest of plastic measuring spoons, Maggie burst into tears. She couldn't stop sobbing once she'd started, and, not daring to sit down in one of the chairs, she sat on the floor and cried her heart out.

"Not the spoons?" Polly asked after a while, giving her a box of Kleenex.

"No," Maggie gulped, and dissolved into fresh tears.

Polly sat on the bed and let Maggie recover herself slowly, apparently not embarrassed by this large stranger's emotion.

"I'm sorry," Maggie finally was able to say. "I've had a tough day and it all hit me at once. And it's my birthday, on top of everything. I'm eighteen."

"I'm twenty-six, and you need a cup of tea."

"Oh, yes, please."

"Is two hundred dollars a month all right?"

"Am I suitable?"

"Absolutely. But first we have to talk."

"We do?"

"I'm afraid so. Come back to the studio and I'll make tea."

Maggie sat quietly, after repairing her makeup, while Polly boiled water and measured tea leaves into a pot.

P. Guildenstern, she observed, wore a white cotton dress she must have bought in a vintage clothing store, for it wasn't of this century. She covered it with a pinafore, from a time long ago when people wore pinafores, made of a sprigged material that she was certain must be called dimity, although she wasn't sure what dimity was. White ballet slippers and a locket around her neck completed the outfit. Passing strange, Maggie thought, but strangely suitable.

"You see," Polly said, passing the sugar in a silver bowl, "I'm a lesbian."

"Huh?"

"I know, I know, that wasn't the first thought that came to mind when you met me. But I am, devoutly so. It's only fair to let you know."

"I don't care, one way or another," Maggie told her truthfully, trying not to look too surprised.

"Still, you might reasonably wonder if I were attracted to you. That's why I put 'no tattoos or body piercing' on the notice. I only like my own gender when they *are* tattooed and pierced. Not that it has to be evident at first glance. I have a weakness for black leather and boots . . . on others. As I said, nothing is quite what it seems. You're a very pleasant-looking girl but simply not my type—I'd never rent to my type."

"That sounds . . . sensible."

"I learned that the hard way. She broke my heart."

"Did it mend?"

"Oh, yes, many times," Polly giggled deliciously. "I have all the virtues except fidelity."

"Oh, my God, Barney! He's still waiting! I'd forgotten him."

"I take that to mean your cousin is the faithful type?"

"Madly faithful."

"Well, let's offer him a cup of tea, in that case. Go tell him to come up." Polly called her dog. "Stay, Toto," she ordered him.

"Toto!" Maggie whirled around.

"Don't dare laugh."

"Barney," Maggie called, "you can come up now."

"About time," he growled, mounting the stairs two at a time.

"Polly, this is Barney Webster. Barney, this is Polly Guildenstern and this . . . this is Toto."

"Fucking unreal!" Barney said, taking in the scene in bewilderment.

"Barney!" Maggie reproved him.

"That's all right, you should hear what most people say," Polly laughed. "Barney, would you like a cup of tea?"

"Yes, ma'am." He looked around the studio, shaking his head in continued wonder. "This place is great! Have you been here long?"

"About five years."

"So, have you two worked things out?"

"Yes, we've covered the necessary ground," Polly said with her lilting giggle. "I believe you wanted to check me out."

"It's not important," Barney said hastily. "You look

"very . . . ladylike . . . I mean, proper and nice, very nice. And pretty, of course, I mean, you know that."

"Thank you," Polly replied, including him in the blessing of her sunny disposition. "In what way are you two cousins? I love hearing about family trees."

"Well . . ." Barney hesitated. "It's sort of complicated. My dad's stepbrother was married to Maggie's sister, before he died."

"Hmm . . . then you're not really cousins?"

"But we were brought up together," Maggie said hastily, as she felt the blood rise to her cheeks. "When we were little, that is."

Polly's keen glance traveled from Barney to Maggie and immediately comprehended the essentials of their relationship. She smiled gently to herself. Very sweet, she thought, and harmless. Straight people were so simple to figure out. And she did enjoy watching them, it was like being around two adorable, decidedly naughty children, trying hard to look innocent.

"Barney, Polly's an artist," Maggie said hastily, following the speed and import of Polly's sweeping appraisal. "She paints miniature portraits on vellum."

"No kidding?"

"Would you like to see some of my work?" Polly asked them.

"We certainly would," Maggie said eagerly. She'd been dying of curiosity, but was too polite to ask.

"People commission them, sometimes of themselves to give as presents so people will remember them, sometimes they have them made of their friends," Polly explained as they moved toward her worktable. "The largest portrait can be shown on a small easel and the smallest you can put in a locket. The medium is watercolor, and the brushes are made from animal hairs—in the sixteenth century they used hairs from the tails of squirrels. Now this one is meant to go on a night table—it's exactly two and a half inches square, and this little oval is destined to be worn around someone's neck."

Maggie and Barney bent in wonder over the exquisitely detailed, ravishingly painted, hyper-realistic miniatures, the oval no more than an inch and a quarter in length.

"I've never seen anything like them," Maggie said, choosing her words carefully. "Your work is extraordinary and amazingly beautiful, truly beautiful, Polly."

"Thank you—it's something of a lost art. Some museums have collections and occasionally they turn up at auction, but I don't know anyone else who's doing this now."

"Wow," Barney muttered. The oval miniature was of a heavy-leather, short-haired, glorious biker chick, every tattoo rendered in perfect detail, every stud on her jacket as definitive as a jewel. The square miniature showed the most magnificent pair of naked breasts he'd ever imagined. No shoulders, no torso, just full, exquisitely shaped breasts and nipples, bathed in a radiant light, the gradations of flesh tones breathtaking. "They're really . . . something else."

"They are indeed," Polly agreed solemnly. He was blushing violently. Good, she'd thought those breasts were rather a tour de force.

"Someday I'll show you some of my favorites, the ones I kept for myself," she promised him, lowering her lids so he wouldn't see the mischief in her eyes.

"Great! Say, Maggie, should I go and get your bag now? Then we can go out for dinner."

"Would you? Wonderful."

Barney retreated quickly down the stairs. The two women looked at each other, rocking with silent laughter.

"Men," Polly said at last.

"Men," Maggie agreed. "They scare so easily."

24

Maggie, xerox all these papers, file them, give the originals to Miss Hendricks, bring me two boxes of large paper clips and three packages of little Post-its, get rid of that stale bagel, empty the coffee machine and refill it, then report on the double to Mr. Rexford in Coins. He has some work for you that has to be done immediately."

"Yes, sir." Maggie hastened to the Xerox machine, anxious to get these tasks for Mr. Jamison of Animation Art out of the way so that she could go downstairs to Coins, whose immediate neighbors were the departments of Tribal Art, Arms and Armor, and Collectibles. Collectibles was her personal favorite of the fifty-nine different departments at the venerable auction house of Scott & Scott and one into which she never failed to cast an eye, no matter how rushed she was, since she was always rushed.

In her three months working as a temp, Maggie had never had a job she had found as interesting, confusing, and overwhelming as this one. She'd probably never understand the maze of complication that constituted a great auction house, she realized, and during the past two weeks, since she'd arrived, she'd been happy just to be able to observe its mysteries while she zoomed around carrying out her errands.

Collectibles charmed her because it was sometimes possible to see, through a half-closed door, the resident expert, Miss Radish, inspecting the great varieties of objects people brought in to Scott & Scott to find out if they could be sold at auction, objects that so far had included dolls, stuffed animals, corkscrews, croquet sets, farmers' tools, sports equipment, and antique toys. Almost anything that could be collected apparently became valuable over time, Maggie reflected, amazed as she was on a daily basis by the function of a major international auction house.

Did the person who had once bought a Mickey Mouse watch for less than a dollar ever imagine that one day a roomful of people would be anxious to bid against each other until one of them proudly acquired it for several thousand dollars? she wondered.

Scott & Scott seemed to her to be a combination of the attic of an eccentric, fanatic, obsessive, wildly materialistic great-great-grandmother who traveled all over the world and lived only to acquire everything she saw, and the most expensive and glamorous garage sale in the world. Of the departments, Art and Jewelry were the most profitable financially, as far as she could figure out, but her typing, filing, and general dogsbody jobs hadn't yet taken her into their quarters in the upper stories of the large building the company owned that occupied an entire block at 84th Street and Second Avenue. As for the hallowed auction rooms themselves, she hadn't had a glimpse.

The Monday after she'd moved into her room in Polly Guildenstern's apartment, Maggie had looked in the Yellow Pages under employment agencies and made an appointment with the largest one that listed temporary help. With her computer skills and her absolute willingness to do anything, no matter how lowly, she'd hoped she'd find no trouble getting jobs, and she'd been right.

There had been a long series of jobs, one more boring and repetitive than the next, none of which had needed her help for more than a few days. Now, at Scott & Scott, she felt a sense of opportunity, a possibility that she might have fallen into a job that could last for a while, because it was obvious that the auction house operated with as small a permanent staff as possible.

Paperwork was piled up on everyone's desk and often on the floor around the desk, and sometimes stacked up against the walls as well. Scott & Scott, although considerably smaller than Sotheby's or Christie's, was a global auction house with thirty-nine offices in twenty countries. It held several hundred auctions a year, and only a larger and more computer-savvy staff could have managed to keep up with the workload, Maggie noticed as she raced around, hailed by dozens of harried people who needed her help *immediately*. She liked S & S and the people who worked there, and now that fall was nearly here she felt like building herself a nest in the shelter of a job with some familiarity, even if it was on the bottom of the office food chain, where only the cleaning staff was lower than a temp.

Still, a temp is only a temp until people know your name, she told herself, and the constant calls of "Maggie, I need you over here" gave her a feeling of identity that helped to combat the adjustment she was slowly making to living on her own and being completely responsible for herself.

It helped enormously that she wasn't living in some dreary furnished room; it helped that Polly, bless her, so often invited her to share the savory stews she cooked so well, keeping her from feeling utterly alone.

It helped to know that Barney was nearby if she needed him, but she couldn't seek his company in the familiar framework of their former palship, because the discovery of their mutual passion had blocked them from being alone together, and Maggie knew that privacy would, sooner or later, lead to consummation, and that way lay certain disaster. Either they'd deepen their feelings and get into a really major mess, or they'd end up disillusioned with each other, their long friendship destroyed. Barney was like a wonderfully warm fur coat that had to be kept in cold storage, winter or no winter.

She took comfort where she could find it, however. It helped, even more than she'd hoped, that she had acquired the outward persona of a New Yorker. She'd strolled along Madison Avenue for several Saturday afternoons in her excellent but totally unexciting suit, taking mental notes. She soon realized that if she dressed in black from head to toe she could blend into the local look at any level. More afternoons patiently, relentlessly chasing bargains in the bazaars of the Lower East Side had yielded two black miniskirts, one wool, the other leather; black sweaters; an ankle-length black wool coat; a wide black belt; tall, black, low-heeled boots; and opaque black panty hose, all for less than a hundred dollars. For another ten dollars Maggie had bought herself long, vivid mufflers in bitter orange, sulfur yellow, and screaming green and parted reluctantly with twenty dollars for a pair of small, sterling silver hoop earrings that went with everything and could be polished with toothpaste.

Too much hair, she'd decided, looking at herself in the mirror, not New York hair, and she'd taken herself off to a cheap drop-in barber shop and had it cut so definitively, defiantly short that it looked deliberately futuristic and violently chic. Maggie's only makeup was black mascara and bright red lipstick, both discount drugstore close-outs, her only beauty aid Pond's Cold Cream. When she had finished putting herself together, the aggressive flag of a knotted muffler flying behind her as she dodged traffic, Maggie became a very primer of a New York career girl, the crackling blue of her eyes and the vivid pink and white of her complexion so enhanced by their crisp black frame that she looked like a piece of walking pop art.

Still and all, she was lonely, Maggie admitted to herself. She was as truly lonely as the lyrics of the most heartbroken country-western singer. She did not, could not, would not, even allow herself to think about Tessa. That was a closed subject, not subject to speculation, further hurt feelings, or fruitless fury, and in any case, what had Tessa ever been to her but a few postcards and an occasional visit to an unreal world? She was better off without her. No, Maggie decided, the reason for her loneliness must be that she regretted, more than she wanted to realize, the plans she had made for college.

Being a temp, even at a world-famous auction house, was a far cry from being a freshman at a great university, but what the hell, you could stretch a mile and consider it an education in itself, at least an education in objects, she thought as she went to the sink to wash out the coffee machine. To her irritation she saw that there was a very tall man blocking the sink, standing still, in contemplation of the faucets. He wore an ancient tweed jacket and baggy gray flannel trousers.

Maggie planted herself behind him, tapping her nails on her empty coffeemaker, hoping that the noise would alert him to the fact that the sink was not a place for meditation. He had, she saw, dismantled another coffeemaker and spread its pieces over all the available surface.

"Missing something?" she finally asked, as he showed no sign of doing anything but stare helplessly.

"Yes, as a matter of fact, I'm missing any notion of what to do with this damn thing."

"I'll do it," she said impatiently. "Couldn't you find a temp and ask her? Men aren't expected to know how to make coffee in this office, it's not a feminist-oriented workplace."

"I'm a floater, I'm not supposed to bother a temp," he answered, turning gratefully and peering down at her through his glasses. He knew immediately that he'd give a lot to take a bite—not metaphorically speaking—out of this particular girl. She was as appetizing, as fresh, as tasty-looking as a nectarine at its moment of perfect ripeness.

274

"A 'floater'?" Maggie asked, bending over the sink. "You mean there's something lower than a temp?"

"A temp, they told me, has to have real skills; a floater . . . floats, drifts, levitates . . . to wherever there's assistance needed, selling catalogs, moving stuff, cleaning stuff, making coffee, God knows what else, but silently, without making the slightest wave or creating undesirable noise."

He nattered on deliberately, his object to engage her attention for as long as possible. "My brief, as I understand it, is to act swiftly, silently, helpfully, unquestioningly, above all, *floatingly*. . . . I'd be more, a great deal more specific but this is my first day here."

"So you didn't go to college either?"

"I have a master's in Fine Arts from Harvard, a degree from Business School, also Harvard, and a year studying at the V and A in London," he admitted ruefully.

Stunned, Maggie looked up at this overeducated moron.

"The V and A?" she asked curiously, as she took inventory of the tall young man with a lot of fine red-brown hair that badly needed cutting, big hazel eyes that were really interested in her for some reason, a two-day growth of reddish beard that needed shaving, a long but handsome nose, horn-rimmed glasses that were mended with what looked like a small Band-Aid, and a large, well-shaped mouth. All in all, a sort of hairy, academic hunk.

"The Victoria and Albert Museum. They have a program that's almost a necessity for people like me. . . ."

"People like you?"

"Ceramic and porcelain people."

"You sound fragile," she laughed, giving him the reassembled, refilled coffeemaker. "You must be a glass person too."

"Oh, good Lord no, another department entirely, not my neck of the woods, although not outside of my ken, if you see what I mean, and obviously you must, with your skills. Glass and paperweights go together, like Art Nouveau and Art Deco, or Books and Manuscripts."

"But still," Maggie said stubbornly, "if you were coming to an auction to buy plates, mightn't you also need glasses, or pick them up on impulse?"

"Absolutely, but thinking like a department store is not encouraged by Scott and Scott," he informed her with a smile.

"Not when you're a lowly temp," she said, tossing her head, forgetting that she now had untossable hair, "or an even more lowly floater. My name's Maggie Horvath."

"I'm Andy McCloud," he said, offering her a large, warm hand.

"Andy!" A secretary scurried up behind them. "For Pete's sake, will you bring that damn coffee! A whole meeting on Musical Instruments just walked into my boss's office."

"Got to go. If I take you to dinner will you show me how to make coffee?"

"Dinner?" Maggie asked, surprised at this abrupt invitation from a stranger.

"Tonight, meet you after work." He dashed off, almost dropping the full coffeemaker in his hurry.

She had a date, Maggie thought excitedly. Her first real date! Andy McCloud, wordy, messy, incompetent, and surprisingly attractive floater, had asked her for dinner, and they'd have to go to a restaurant because of all the things she didn't know about him, the least likely was that he knew how to cook. On the other hand, coffeepot or not, he was a fast worker. But it stood to reason that a ceramic and porcelain person was probably gay. Still, it would be wonderful to make a new friend.

Hamilton Angus McDevitt Scott and his sister, Elizabeth Stewart Scott Sinclair, as well as a younger sister who didn't work in the business, owned Scott & Scott, an auction house that had been run by the Scott family since its founding in 1810. Hamilton and Liz shared offices in the penthouse suite of the relatively new building on the plot of land their great-grandfather had bought before the turn of the century, so far uptown that it was considered to be in the wilderness.

Scott & Scott had moved with the times. Although they had preserved as much as possible of the paneling and atmosphere of the actual auction rooms, their offices were established in a building that had been rebuilt on the old site in the late 1930s. The two of them were, as always, alone for their biweekly discussion of the state of their eight-hundred-million-dollar-a-year business, ritualistically drinking tea from a set of particularly fine Chinese Export porcelain that Elizabeth had picked up at Sotheby's shortly after her marriage to John Sinclair forty years earlier.

"Damn that freak Andy Warhol and damn his freaking cookie jars," Hamilton Scott said furiously as he put more sugar in his tea. "Cookie jars! Can you believe it?" His handsome, ruddy face quivered in outrage.

"We sell cookie jars in Collectibles all the time, as you well know. H, you'd give your left nut for the Warhol auction, cursing isn't going to change anything," his sister said with maddening calm. She possessed her older brother's handsome features in a charming womanly version and had the most elegant head of silver hair in Manhattan. There were envious women who said she must spend all her profits from S & S on clothes and jewelry, but they were very far from understanding the extent of the commissions on sales the business brought in.

"I find your language increasingly vulgar as you totter lingeringly, indecently reluctantly, on the verge of your golden years," he replied.

"And as your golden years mount up, I find your patience regrettably diminished," she replied, smiling at him with profound affection.

The ownership of a huge business was a source of constant rage for her poor brother, Liz Sinclair thought.

Instead of being reasonably content with the one-third of the profits he possessed, H had never managed to get over the competition he was destined never to win with Sotheby's and Christie's. And yet those two giant auction houses, which dominated the world, doing over a billion dollars a year each, were publicly traded companies owned by their stockholders, while she and H, who owned what was arguably the third largest auction house in the world, had nobody to account to but themselves and their sister Minnie at the end of their fiscal year in April.

H, a former world-class polo player and yachtsman, had deep connections with the serious rich and aristocratic all over the world, many of whom preferred to do business with S & S rather than with the larger companies, particularly since H was one of the star auctioneers of all time. Minnie had married a major multimillionaire, whose extensive family had collected old and new masters for generations. The couple lived for art and served on the boards of many of the important museums of the country, giving S & S entry into the art world when the time came for other collectors to buy or sell.

Liz herself was involved in a dozen of the pet charities of the very rich and social, further enlarging that vital pool of intimate personal connections that every auction house cherishes and cultivates while it waits for death, divorce, and disaster to bring about the need for the sale of property. Liz was responsible for most of the personnel decisions made at S & S. She had a sure but delicate human touch her brother lacked.

"I've got to go light a fire under the heads of the American, English, and European furniture departments," Hamilton grumbled. "They haven't been aggressive enough in actively seeking consignments. As usual. You, Liz?"

"I'm off to lunch with Bitsy Furness. She's determined to sell the huge place in Locust Valley now that Eddie's run off with that girl from his office, and I hope we can get the contents of the whole house. Bitsy has truly fabulous things, museum quality, and of course he'll have to give her practically everything before she agrees to a divorce. Nobody knows about her decision yet and she's anxious to get the matter settled without shopping around and spreading the news."

"Good hunting, old thing. I wish we had more department heads like you. It seems to me that all they do is sit and wait until things drop into their laps."

"But H, they didn't go to school with at least half the Bitsys of this world."

"Worse luck."

"Well, here's the choice. We can go back to my place and you can show me how to make coffee over drinks, or we can have drinks and dinner first, and then have the coffee lesson," Andy McCloud said, after he and Maggie met at the employees' entrance to S & S.

"If I didn't know that you really can't make coffee, I'd say that was the best way of getting a girl up to your place that I've ever heard of."

"I suppose a girl like you has good reason to be suspicious of every man she meets."

"And what kind of a girl is that?"

"A sophisticated New Yorker who gets hit on—I believe that's the correct phrase, is it not, or is it dated?—by every man who sees her."

"How perceptive of you. You've described me perfectly," Maggie beamed at him.

"Which shall it be?"

"Drinks and dinner first. You see, I never actually promised to teach you how to make coffee. I only sounded surprised that you wanted to have dinner."

"So you did," he said, remembering their exchange. "I've been presuming on your good nature."

"Without knowing a thing about me except that I had to get you away from that sink so I could use it."

"But you see, you don't look like a person who would refuse to impart vital, job-related knowledge.

You look essentially good and kind, as well as frighteningly luscious," he said, tucking her arm under his in a masterful way and rapidly walking in the direction of Third Avenue.

"There's a little bar right down the street where they don't use a jigger when they pour. I think the jigger is the most unfriendly device ever invented. It's the very personification of the deliberate withholding of pleasure, don't you agree? And why withhold pleasure when life is so short? Did you ever see a bartender use a jigger in a movie? People would walk out in protest and ask for their money back."

"Never," Maggie agreed breathlessly. Andy McCloud had an immense stride, and he was so tall that she seemed to be flying alongside him, absorbing his energy. She'd never been inside a New York bar or any other bar for that matter. Would they refuse to serve her a drink because she didn't look old enough? Oh, the humiliation!

"Here we are," Andy said, whisking her inside a dim cave of a place that was almost full. "They don't have a television set here, so you don't get those crazed fans who have to watch the game."

"Which game?"

"It never seems to matter, does it? There's always a game, no matter what the season. This is an old-time place, no innovations, no happy hour, just a jukebox that doesn't work. Now, what are you drinking?"

"Dry sherry, please." Madison always drank that, Maggie thought. It must be proper. She pulled her arms out of her coat and placed it beside her in the booth. The lack of bright lights in the bar didn't prevent every man within sight from observing her with close attention. Maggie in her unadorned black sweater, Andy thought, was almost unbearably juicy, a girl with big breasts who didn't flaunt them, and wasn't coy about them, just let them stand at attention and speak eloquently for themselves.

"Joe, the lady will have Tío Pepe and I'll have

Absolut on the rocks. Maggie," he said invitingly, "this is the kind of place in which people tell each other the high points of their lives, so I'll let you go first."

"I have no intention of telling an almost perfect stranger my life story. I'd have to know you much better," Maggie said, trying for a tone of composed, worldly aloofness. Damn! Why hadn't she thought of something to make up about herself when she'd had half the day to do it, instead of stealing precious minutes between jobs in anticipation and speculation and primping in front of the ladies'-room mirror?

"Quite right of you. Reveal nothing until you know to whom you're speaking. So, about me. You already know my education and what I do. Born and bred right here on the East Side of Manhattan, the usual two parents, one older sibling, female, several cousins, all female, usual youthful traumas, dancing school et cetera, two engagements, five unhappy romances, currently completely unattached."

Maggie giggled. "You used more words describing your job as a floater than you did in telling me your life story."

"I was stalling for time, trying to figure out how to ask you for dinner without seeming too abrupt, but I couldn't quite figure out how to do it."

"You managed quite well. Now, what about those two engagements?"

"Broken by mutual consent."

"Why?"

"General immaturity."

"On whose part?"

"Everyone's, no harm, no foul."

"Ah, I see." She sipped her sherry carefully. "And all those romances?"

"I tend to fall for the wrong girl, the neurotic, essentially unobtainable girl, the girl who falls for the obvious wrong guy instead of really loving me. I'm the Episcopalian Woody Allen, but without his talent."

"That's one of the saddest things I've ever heard,"

she said, trying to sound sympathetic. Either he was a gifted liar or he wasn't gay. Her fingers itched to take off his glasses and get a better look at his golden-brown eyes. Did he have long lashes? . . . Impossible to tell. She wondered if his hair felt as soft as it looked and if his beard felt as scruffy as it looked.

"Well, I'm still young," Andy said. "There's time to find the right girl. I'm just twenty-seven."

"Twenty-seven and only a floater!" She sounded as scandalized as she was.

"You have to start somewhere."

"What do you want to be when you finally grow up?"

"An expert, of course."

"In ceramics and porcelain?"

"That would be the basic idea," Andy McCloud replied, repressing a smile, thinking of his many intense years of specialized education. Maggie had great natural dignity, but he'd bet she wasn't much more than twenty-one, and she certainly was unschooled in the great universe of precious and rare objects. Very few men in the world could hope to be experts in the vast fields of both ceramics and porcelain, but he was deeply ambitious.

"A business executive can always be replaced," he informed her, "but an expert can count on being needed all his life, into his dotage, and, alas, often beyond. Now, may I hear a little about you, Miss Horvath, or do you have more questions?"

"Parents dead," Maggie answered promptly. "No siblings, brought up by distant connections, no money for higher education, no engagements, currently unattached." She copied his telegraphic style; it was ideal for leaving out things she didn't intend to talk about.

"Elementary school?" he probed, finding her unnecessarily mysterious. From her account she could be an alien. Yet everything about her, her body language, her accent, her gestures, her attitudes, her entire being, revealed a girl of a class he recognized, the class he belonged to.

"Just a little country school." She smiled nostalgically, as if she'd studied in a one-room schoolhouse in rural Nebraska.

"And how long have you been a temp?"

"Oh, quite a while." Maggie's tone indicated a long, interesting and varied career, something a soldier of fortune might look back on with pride.

"What did you do before that?" he asked, determined to get some concrete detail out of this girl who was growing more maddening and more alluring by the minute.

"I was a journalist, but I didn't think I had a future in it." Considering that it was a high school paper, that was certainly true, Maggie thought.

"What about love affairs?"

"None of your business," she answered. Barney didn't count as a romance, he was her oldest friend, an impossible partner in lust and confusion, but there was nothing at all romantic between them, not as she defined romance. Eighteen and only fond memories, certainly not romantic ones, of a few favorite horses. Was that all she had to show for her life? "Is the inquisition over?" she asked.

"My God, I have been giving you the third degree, haven't I? It was rude of me, I apologize, but you're so—how about another sherry? Or are you starving?"

"Oddly enough, no," Maggie said, coming to a decision. "What I'd really enjoy, what I'd most like to have right now is . . . is . . . a cup of coffee."

"Joe, check please, right away."

They took a taxi to a building in the upper sixties off Madison Avenue. Could Andy possibly still live at home with his parents? Maggie wondered as they strode quickly through the handsomely appointed lobby to the elevator.

"It's rent stabilized," he told her, reading her thoughts as he unlocked the door. Inside she just had time to gain an impression of wood paneling and walls of bookcases before he turned her around and took her in his arms.

"May I?" Andy McCloud asked, bending his head to try and look into her eyes.

"Only if you take off those glasses," Maggie answered, doing it for him as she spoke, trembling with eagerness. "I remembered what you said about withholding pleasure. Life's too short and dinner takes too long."

"Oh, Maggie, are you real?"

"Try me," she whispered, reaching up and twining her arms around his neck so that she could easily reach his lips. Yes, she thought, as he kissed her over and over again, as firm on his feet as a tree, oh, yes. She half-closed her eyes as she let him lead her into another room and sit her down on the edge of a bed. She pulled off her boots and her panty hose, and lay back of her own accord, squeezing her eyes tightly shut. Who would have guessed that he had such demanding lips? she wondered. Who would have expected him to be lying naked next to her so quickly? Who would have imagined that he could strip off her clothes so adroitly, a man who couldn't even assemble a coffeemaker?

"Maggie, aren't you ever going to look at me?"

"No, not yet."

"Why not?"

"Because I want to be surprised," she whispered, pulling his head down to her breasts. The contrast between the silky hair she twisted between her fingers and the rogue scrape of his beard as he concentrated all his attention on her breasts with a controlled but unmistakably violent hunger, a hunger that announced that he was in no hurry to satisfy it, told her that she had to do with a man, not a boy.

His mouth was deliberate and crafty, brushing her nipples only long enough to promise further attention, while he knelt on either side of her body and raptly marveled at the whiteness of her breasts and the perfection of their form. Each time he imprinted his hard mouth on them he left a mark that receded slowly, so that soon both her breasts wore a rare and rosy flush, while her nipples, all but untouched, filled and stood erect in circles of deepest pink, their tender surfaces stretched upward in a way that begged for the easement of his tongue.

Too soon, he thought, too soon. She had run the show so far, but now the power was in his hands and he chose to grasp her hips even more tightly between his knees and let his mouth drift, slow kiss by slow kiss, away from her breasts and down the fragrant skin of her torso, almost at random, ignoring her attempts to stretch upward toward his mouth. She wanted to be surprised, she'd said, and he vowed to himself to do his best.

Now that Andy's head was too far away for her to grasp his hair, Maggie stretched out her arms and caressed his shoulders, reveling in the solid forms of his tense muscles and the vigorous tufts of hair under his arms. Her mouth was dry with desire, her lips open with an unuttered plea, when suddenly she felt him elude her touch as he moved downward on the bed, holding her thighs apart with his elbows, his hands stern and commanding as he opened her wide, parting her dark pubic curls far enough to bury his tongue between her legs.

She held back a scream, panting, almost holding her breath. She'd read about this, dreamed of this, but the reality and the dream had nothing in common. The warm roughness of his artfully pointed tongue meeting the delicate concavities of her body was far wilder and more arousing than anything her imagination could have created. She listened with all of her senses as his lips and teeth joined his tongue, fastening themselves on the distended, hard, secret arrow only her own fingers, and Barney once, had ever touched. Maggie was utterly silent. Only the muffled sound of his sucking existed until, soon, with a shriek, she came with a series of acute, frenzied spasms that arched her body high off the bed.

Not until she lay almost quietly, but still quivering, did he push himself into her with exquisite carnal precision, seeking his own sure pleasure without hurry. Abruptly he stopped, startled at the resistance he met. "Maggie? Maggie?" He pulled away.

"Yes," she sighed, smiling to herself.

"Jesus, Maggie! You're a virgin!"

"I told you . . . none of your business . . ." she breathed languidly.

"But . . ."

"Please," she murmured, sliding down on the bed, tilting her pelvis upward, urging him back toward her, and rubbing one finger shamelessly on the base of his spine, "don't stop now, I couldn't bear it."

"Do you think I could?" As gently as possible but relentless with severely awakened and unrelieved need, Andy took her entirely, and afterward, as if in penance for his ignorance, he attended to her neglected nipples with all his skill until she was maddened by fresh desire, ready for him to take her again.

25

Polly Guildenstern's own life offered such possibilities for gossip and intrigue that she had little curiosity left over for her star boarder's comings and goings. However, she couldn't fail to notice that over the family holidays of 1988, Thanksgiving and Christmas, there was apparently no place on earth where Maggie Horvath was expected, nor did she ever mention any normal, conventional regret at not being able to join her family for one reason or another. Maggie, looking not at all depressed, spent the long weekends sleeping late, puttering in her tiny kitchen, reading a pile of books, going alone to movies, and devouring with gratitude the leftovers Polly brought back from the big Thanksgiving and Christmas dinners to which she'd been invited.

Was she an orphan? Polly wondered. She knew Maggie had a lover or possibly several lovers, because there were many nights when she didn't return to the apartment. Now wouldn't he, or one of them, as the case might be, invite her for a holiday dinner? Polly wondered. And what had happened to cousin Barney? If, as Maggie had said, they'd been brought up together, what had happened to that family? It was all most mysterious and worrying, for someone of Polly's warm nature.

There was a deep essential aloneness to Maggie that made Polly feel irrationally guilty, almost maternal, but it was against her principles to delve into anyone's personal background unless invited to do so. All she could do was triple her casual dinner invitations, so that Maggie would know that there was one place in the world where a plate was always set for her whenever a pot was simmering on the stove.

Gradually, throughout the winter of 1988 and the early weeks of 1989, Polly and Maggie became excellent friends. Maggie was still working as a temp at S & S and she fascinated Polly with the growing body of knowledge she was accumulating about the workings of an auction house. Eventually Maggie told her about Andy McCloud, but from what she heard, Polly shrewdly deduced that Andy was as close-mouthed about his parents as Maggie was about hers. The only solid detail Maggie could give her about his background was that his older sister was a ballerina in an English ballet company. How warm and important was their relationship, she wondered, if they chose not to talk to each other about their families? Wasn't that one of the classic ways in which lovers became friends?

Polly kept her own counsel, however, even when the registered letters began arriving for Maggie. The overweight postman who normally left her mail downstairs in her mailbox complained bitterly each time he had to climb the stairs and get Polly to sign for the letters that began to arrive for Mary Margaret Horvath on a weekly basis in January 1989. As Polly placed each one on the floor in front of Maggie's door, she noticed that they all came from the same place, a law firm named Butler, O'Neill and Jones. As she checked her own mail she couldn't avoid seeing the same registered letters in her box, unopened, with "return to sender" written in block letters across them. Was Maggie being sued, she wondered? It wasn't anything she could ask about, it would make it seem as if she were spying on her, but Polly's curiosity was aroused.

One early afternoon her buzzer sounded and a pleasant woman's voice announced that a Miss Robinson of Butler, O'Neill and Jones would like to see Miss Mary Margaret Horvath.

"She's at work," Polly answered.

"Oh, no! I've been ordered not to dare come back to the office if I can't see her in person. Absolutely all I need is her signature. And it's snowing worse than ever. I have to wait for her until she gets back, even if I freeze in a snowbank. Unless—could you possibly tell me where she works? I could try to find her there."

Polly weighed the question. She didn't intend to tell a stranger where to find Maggie, but she couldn't let a person with such a charming voice stand outside in one of the worst storms of the winter.

"Why don't you come up? Perhaps I can help."

"Oh, thank you!"

Polly Guildenstern, you're just agog, you know you're just dying to find out what's going on, she scolded herself severely, as she put the kettle on to boil, her adorably pointed nose was fairly quivering with inquisitiveness, her very hair ribbon alert with unasked questions.

Attractive, young Jane Robinson left her wet boots outside on the landing, and after she'd removed her heavy coat and made friends with Toto, she thawed out, gulping the restorative tea with pleasure. "It's my first job," she explained to Polly. "I'm just out of law school and if I don't bring back a signature to Mr. Butler, he'll probably fire me . . . and it's such a prize job too, they're a major Wall Street firm. Oh dear, oh dear, what shall I do? Miss Horvath has sent back the document unopened three weeks in a row, so they sent me. This tea is saving my life, I don't know how to thank you."

"Here, have a cookie, I made them myself."

"Oh, bless you! I didn't have a chance to grab lunch

today. Mr. Butler threw an absolute tantrum when he saw the returned letter, and practically chased me out into the storm. Oh, chocolate chip, my favorite! Could I . . . possibly have another?"

"Oh, eat them all, you're doing me a favor, I made too many. And call me Polly."

"You're an angel! What a heavenly studio! And you look just like Alice in Wonderland. I wish I'd had artistic talent, but no, not a drop, so my destiny was law school and Mr. Butler. Oh, Polly, terrible, mean Mr. Butler! This document may be my downfall, and then it'll be difficult to get another job with such a good firm."

"Document?"

"As far as I can tell, it's a major document. They have to have Miss Horvath's signature before they can settle the estate, that's the gossip around the office, but the partners are in a terrible state about the delay. It couldn't be more important to them, the deceased was their biggest client."

"Why didn't one of them come in person if it's so vital?" "Estate," Polly thought, and a "deceased"; how lucky she'd taken a chance and invited Jane Robinson up.

"Oh no, Polly," Jane said, shocked. "They're all too important to run around chasing signatures. That's for underlings like me."

"And of course they don't care about my fat old postman who has to walk up all these flights," Polly said indignantly, "or about my being disturbed having to sign for all the letters."

"Things like that simply wouldn't occur to Mr. Butler. Poor Mrs. Butler. Imagine the life she leads! Well, I'd better not interrupt your work any longer. I wonder, if I leave this letter with you, could you possibly just give it *physically* to Miss Horvath and tell her that she *shouldn't* send it back without opening it and signing it? Then I can explain that she was at work but you agreed to hand deliver it. Mr. Butler might accept the fact that I did my best, even though I don't come back with the signature."

"I guess I can, Jane, although it sounds a little like serving a subpoena. But what if she refuses? What if she won't even take the letter?"

"Well, I guess the next step would be, oh, dear, I could be wrong but I think Mr. Butler will track her down at work. *Himself.* And that would be unpleasant for her, and hard to explain—he's not an inconspicuous man. And he wouldn't be discreet. Or quiet."

"How would he know where to find her?"

"Oh, he'd use another private detective, of course. He'd have to."

" 'Another'?"

"How do you think they knew where to send the documents? Miss Horvath had simply disappeared, or so I heard around the watercooler."

Polly was speechless. Maggie had disappeared from somewhere? A private detective had been snooping around and found out that Maggie was living in her spare room?

"Goodness gracious," she breathed when she finally found her voice.

"Or, as my grandmother would say, a pretty kettle of fish."

Polly and Jane looked at each other wide-eyed. This was as close as either of them had come to such a situation and neither of them tried to hide the fact that they were enjoying the drama of it.

"Jane," Polly finally said, breaking their long, speculative silence, "there's no possibility that Maggie will get home for at least four hours, assuming that she comes back at all tonight. Often she doesn't. Aren't you roasting in all that leather you're wearing?"

"Actually I am feeling a bit overheated. And it's so cozy in here. I feel so relaxed, you've been so kind to me, Polly. The mere thought of trying to get back to the office empty-handed in this storm . . ."

"Why don't you make yourself comfortable for a while longer? Why rush to disappoint Mr. Butler?"

"Well . . . perhaps . . . it's not as though I could hope

to get a taxi in this weather, and the buses are so jammed they don't even stop."

"If you take your jacket and pants off," Polly said casually, "I'll bring you a blanket so you can stretch out on the sofa and take a nap. Naps are great when it's snowing."

"Or, consider this alternative, Polly. I could take your clothes off, very, very slowly, one adorable, dainty, tiny little piece at a time. And skip the nap."

Polly purred, her intuition validated. "I'd prefer that. Then I can see the rest of the interesting tattoo that's just peeking out of your cuff."

"I'd been wondering . . . if maybe you might . . . and hoping you would."

The next evening, when Maggie finally struggled home, trekking cross-town on foot from S & S, after spending the previous night with Andy, Polly looked up, took off the strong magnifying glasses she wore while painting, and said, "Join me for dinner? I'm baking a mustard chicken with winter squash."

"You've saved my life, I'm wiped out, completely exhausted. This filthy weather! It took hours to get home. I've got to have a hot bath and then I'll be right in. Oh, you are heaven-sent, Polly!"

Polly carved the chicken and poured Maggie three glasses of wine while the tired girl ate hungrily, the two friends enjoying the meal in companionable, rarely broken silence.

"Now that you're fed," Polly said, after Maggie had eaten two slices of her apple pie, "I have a duty to perform. I didn't want to ruin your appetite by giving it to you before dinner."

"Huh?"

"It's this registered letter," she said, thrusting it into Maggie's hand. "It arrived here yesterday. The person who brought it said that it was absolutely necessary for you to open it and sign it, and somehow or other I got talked into promising to give it to you. I'm sorry about that, but seriously, whatever it is, Maggie, you can't expect our postman to keep on walking up six flights, he'll have a heart attack and it'll be on your conscience."

"Shit!" Maggie glared at the envelope.

"Heavens! What can be so terrible? And how do you know when you haven't even opened it?" Polly asked, her curiosity more inflamed than ever by the sight of Maggie's furious face.

"I know who these lawyers are and I know what it's about. Damn it to hell, how'd they find me? I thought if I printed 'return to sender' on the envelopes they wouldn't know I lived here."

"A private detective found out where you were living, and what's more, if you don't sign it, some monster of a big-shot lawyer is going to come to your office to make you sign it."

"What! What!" Maggie burst into tears of rage. "Who told you that?"

"I did a little detective work myself on the messenger. I don't like people meddling with you, Maggie."

"Oh," Maggie wept, her angry tears redoubled, "why can't she leave me alone? I told her I didn't want the money, that I wouldn't touch it, isn't that enough? She put a detective on me, she knows where I am, maybe she has me followed everywhere . . . oh, God, Polly, I don't know what to do."

"What money?"

"A bequest . . . a will."

"Well what's so terrible about that?"

Maggie looked at Polly through her tears and saw the sensible, concerned, deeply fond face of the only female friend she had in the world, the only woman besides Elizabeth, the cook, who'd ever treated her with affection and real interest, the only person besides Andy and Barney who cared about her.

She wiped her eyes and huddled in the corner of the sofa. "My so-called mother's husband died and left me money, that's what the document has to be about," she told Polly in a shaking voice.

"He wasn't your father?"

"No. And I don't want his money."

"Wait a minute. What's wrong with inheriting money? He was your stepfather, why shouldn't he leave you money? That doesn't make sense, Maggie. And you've never spoken of a mother, much less a 'so-called mother,' whatever that means. You never mentioned a family, you never go home for holidays . . . ?"

"Polly! If I tell you the whole story, will you promise me never to mention it again, ever, as long as you live? Nobody in the world knows it except me and the woman who gave birth to me."

"I'll promise, and you can count on me to keep my promise, but I want you to be sure you truly want to tell me," Polly said, more serious than Maggie had ever seen her. "There's nothing worse than telling a secret to a friend and then hating yourself afterward because you wish you hadn't. It's ruined many friendships and no secret's worth that. I'd much rather not know than have you regret that you told me."

"Polly, I *have* to tell someone and I trust you entirely. It's eating away at me, I try not to let myself think about it, I *forbid* myself to think about it, but it keeps coming into my mind anyway, all the time, and I dream about it, so many nights . . . such sad, sad dreams. If I can share it with you, I'll feel better. I certainly won't feel worse. I think I need some sympathy and there's nobody more sympathetic than you."

"Tea-and-Sympathy Guildenstern," Polly laughed.

"An unbeatable combination."

"Well, then, go ahead and tell me."

Maggie took a deep breath and, in as few words as possible, told Polly her whole story, leaving out any identification of the people involved. She kept her eyes fixed in her lap as she spoke, as unemotionally as possible. As the story unfolded, Polly grew more and more outraged, although she kept her feelings to herself until

Maggie's silence indicated that there was nothing more to tell.

"What kind of inhuman bitch could do that to her own child?" Polly finally burst out after Maggie stopped talking.

"Tessa Kent could do that, Tessa Kent, who was born Teresa Horvath, she could do that to me, she *did* do that to me."

"You're . . . you're Tessa Kent's daughter."

"Biologically, yes. In any other way, no."

"My God. Tessa Kent! Tessa Kent . . . I . . . it's . . . my God, how could she? *How could she!*"

"That's exactly what I keep asking myself."

"It's what anybody sane would ask."

"Oh, Polly, it is, isn't it? There's no *excuse*, is there? I've tried and tried to think of one, but I can't."

"You can't because it doesn't exist! What she did is beyond inexcusable! When you think of all those movie stars having babies without being married and showing them off in the magazines . . . it's not as if there's a stigma attached to it anymore, not in Hollywood. And she's young, she's not of the older generation, she can't be more than . . ."

"Thirty-three."

"Look, Maggie, you've been treated so badly I don't know what to say, there are no words to express how I feel. It's been a tragedy for you and all the sympathy I have won't help, not if I talked all night, which I'm afraid I just might do. But right now you've got to be practical, you don't want an angry lawyer showing up looking for you at S and S and causing a lot of talk. Now that they know where you live, you're going to have to open the letter and see what it is and deal with it."

"I know, I've known all along that it wouldn't just go away. You're right, damn it." Maggie ripped open the envelope and read the pages it contained. "Well, it's what I guessed it would be. They're finally finishing the settlement of Luke's estate—the husband who died—

and they need me to sign as one of the people he left money to. If I sign, I get the money when I'm thirty-five, meanwhile it'll be in trust and I'll get the income."

"Are you absolutely sure you don't want it, Maggie?"

"Absolutely, a hundred percent. I'm going to write out a strong statement to that effect and send it back with this letter. A person has a right to refuse a bequest, don't they?"

"I don't really know, legally, but realistically, how can they force you to take something you don't want?"

"They can't," Maggie said grimly. "I intend to stay independent, no matter what."

"I'd take it myself, in a wink, no matter what. It would be something, anyway, that you'd get out of all of this. A private income never did anyone any harm."

"It's not what I needed all of my life, it's not what I want, now, or ever wanted."

"Too little, too late, you mean?"

"No, Polly, too much, much too much, and much too late."

26

W here's a temp? I have to have one desperately! Somebody, find me a temp!" Maggie looked up from the Xerox machine to see a woman she knew only as Lee Maine, the head of the press office, standing in front of the elevator doors with a wild look on her distinguished, lovely face.

"I'm a temp," she said, leaving her machine. "What can I do for you?"

"Man the battle stations! This is ridiculous! I have to go to Philadelphia in ten minutes to work on the blasted American Primitives sale and there's nobody, not one solitary soul, in my blasted department! My second-in-command had a premature baby over the weekend, I still haven't replaced the little traitor who defected to Sotheby's last week, and my last remaining assistant just called in sick with flu! Damn all three of them! Now listen closely. I want you to sit in my office and answer phones, take messages, tell one and all I'll be back tomorrow. If anybody in this place tries to get you to do something else, anything at all, tell them Lee Maine said she'd strangle you with her bare hands if you so much as left the desk except to pee."

Maggie grinned down at the beautiful, dark-eyed woman with a long curve of straight silver hair that fit her elegant head perfectly. She had small bones and was probably four inches shorter than Maggie.

"I warn you, I'd probably put up a fight," she heard herself say.

"I don't have a sense of humor, whoever you are, but I insist on a minimum, a bare minimum of competence."

"I won't even pee," Maggie said hastily.

"That's better. And while you're at it, take a look at the piles of work on the other desks. Maybe you'll find some little thing you can try to do between calls, but don't leave the office, on pain of death. That phone must be answered! We live by the phone!"

"Got it, don't worry. Do you want me to call you with messages during the day?"

"Good God, no, don't tie up the phone lines. I'll be back tomorrow. And you'd damn well better be there," she warned. Lee Maine belted herself into a long red coat, jammed a Cossack's black astrakhan hat on her head, and, pulling on her long gloves, took off without another word, leaving Maggie to find the press office for herself.

Within five minutes she'd settled herself at one of the three assistants' desks and started eagerly going through the various auction catalogs she found lying there. She soon realized that many of the sales coming up, according to the dates on the catalogs, were unaccompanied by any sort of press release. Memos, all begging for releases, were tucked into many of the catalogs, along with the forms for such releases.

Perhaps they'd already been written, Maggie thought, and the memos were out of date, but an interoffice phone check of the departments involved revealed only that they were waiting impatiently for the press releases to arrive so that they could send them to their usual media sources.

Did Lee Maine have any idea what an unholy mess

her department was? Maggie wondered, as she bent over a computer. She'd said that she insisted on a bare minimum of competence, but it didn't look to her as if she'd been getting even that from her staff. If some of these releases weren't written at once, they risked appearing only a week or so before the sales involved, and it was self-evident that the longer people knew about a sale in advance, the more popular it would be.

In her days running the school paper at Elm Country Day, Maggie had been accustomed to putting out the paper almost single-handedly, writing everything from humorous columns to thoughtful editorials. She found a file of old press releases and quickly realized that there was no mystery to them. The process obviously should start with studying each sale's catalog to pick out the most newsworthy items, and translating that into a lively press release, short enough to be read quickly but long enough to tantalize the imagination of possible collectors. She could write as well as or better than the sample releases, she thought, grinning to herself. Most of them were too long and didn't grab her attention.

In spite of frequent phone interruptions, by lunchtime she'd finished the work on one desk and started on the second, finding a floater to bring her a sandwich and a secretary to sit by the phone while she made a hurried visit to the ladies' room. It was one thing to promise not to pee, another to carry it out. By nine at night, Maggie, working as if the devil were riding behind her, had finished every press release that had been left undone on all three assistants' desks, printed them out on the laser printer, and stacked them in a neat pile on Lee Maine's desk, each attached to the relevant catalog. Next to them she put the neatly written pile of dozens of phone messages that had arrived during the day.

The next morning she was sitting primly at one of the desks outside of Lee Maine's office when the press office head arrived, in a flurry of questions. "Who called? Any emergencies? Did you find anything you could manage to do?"

"Everything's on your desk," Maggie said, biting her lip in nervousness. Had she presumed? Was her method the right one for writing press releases? Lee Maine disappeared into her office, closed the door behind, and stayed there for at least a half hour without buzzing. Suddenly she rushed out.

"What's your name?"

"Maggie Horvath."

"Do you insist on being a temp?"

"Good God, no! My ambition is to be a galley slave."

"Perfect. You're hired. Only don't work this hard or they'll cut my staff down to just you and you'll burn out at this pace. Also, you'd better write the next batch of releases quite a bit longer to give the editor something to cut, editors always have to find a reason to cut, remember that, or they'd be out of their own jobs."

"What—what do I call myself if anybody asks?" Maggie ventured, electrified with excitement.

"Press officer for Scott and Scott."

"Press officer? Oh, Miss Maine, thank you!"

"Thank me? I'm the lucky one. And call me Lee, everyone else does, unless they really know me and then they call me Lee, darling. When did you get here? At S and S I mean, not this morning, because you must have slept in the office last night."

"I started last fall, in September."

"Good grief! It's almost March—you've been a temp for more than five months. What's wrong with the people here?"

"Nobody ever asked me to see what else I could do. Xeroxing has been my chief mode of self-expression. Sending a fax made my day."

"Madness, sheer madness," Lee Maine said in wonder. "All right, Maggie, take these around to where they're needed and report back here. I have a bunch of notes from Philadelphia for you to start working on with Fred Cashmere in the catalog department, he'll explain what to do. I've got to rush down to the sales rooms. There's a Contemporary Print sale on exhibition and I have to do some serious media hand-kissing. Wait a sec, that still leaves nobody to answer the phones . . . well, find a temp somewhere, grab her, and make sure she stays here till one of us gets back."

"Will do. What should I tell the personnel department?"

"That you've been promoted—no, make that hijacked, full time—that you're working for me now, exclusively, and they'd better find another temp to take your place."

"Miss Maine . . . salary?"

"Whatever you've been making, plus twenty-five dollars a week and lots of free lunches. PR is about free lunches, among other things, including keeping this auction house going almost single-handedly." Lee Maine disappeared with a wave.

Press officer, Maggie said to herself, PRESS OFFICER! Oh, yes! Polly would be thrilled for her, "press officer" sounded so wonderfully butch. And Andy . . . Maggie, in her daze of delight, suddenly remembered Andy, still a floater. How would he feel?

She probably wasn't going to have a terrible problem with Andy's reaction to her new eminence, she decided, on reflection. He seemed quite content with his humble position, showing a lack of ambition that puzzled Maggie.

On the other hand, she had to admit that his job, which so lacked any status, was ten times more interesting than that of a temp. Since she'd known him, he'd floated to Toronto to help out at an important sale of English furniture; he'd floated to Mexico City with a group of experts who were cataloging the entire contents of a Mexican collector's huge estate; and he'd floated to L.A. with the chief of the Department of Impressionist Paintings, because the widow of a studio head had decided to divest herself of her husband's world-renowned collection so that she could find a renewed social life in buying the work of contemporary artists. "They always need somebody to go out for pizza," was Andy's standard comment when Maggie enviously asked him the details of his travels.

During the past few months, he'd been floating in the loftiest of departments, doing his vague, many-faceted, unimportant thing, whatever it was, in the executive offices of S & S, which she'd never yet entered. She'd seen Mr. Scott and Mrs. Sinclair from a distance and plagued Andy with questions about them, to which he only replied that they were "just plain pizza lovers only with more money."

Perhaps the reason he gave the impression of aimlessness, the reason he didn't take floating more seriously, Maggie thought, was that his true destiny was to work as an expert, and floating was only a matter of being able to call himself employed until he moved into a position in Porcelain and Ceramics. But how long would he have to wait? Now that she came to think about it, she didn't know Andy's timetable for success any better than when she'd first met him.

Tonight, since they hadn't seen each other for several days, Andy had been so ravenously intent on making love that she hadn't had a minute to tell him about her new job, Maggie realized, as she sat up in bed and watched him nap. If he didn't wake up soon she'd have to get up and scramble eggs or perish of hunger. He'd been so anxious to fuck her that he hadn't taken the time to feed her after work, or even to stop for a drink in their favorite bar. It was, she supposed, flattering, in its own way, but most certainly not her idea of a well-choreographed evening. Flattering, perhaps, polite, no. Lusty, yes, thoughtful no. She'd be damned if it would happen again.

The depth of Andy's sleep began to irritate her seriously. Why were men so exhausted by sex that they had to restore themselves with a trip to unconsciousness? She'd never felt more alive! But how could she generalize about men when Andy was the only man she'd ever known intimately?

Maggie heaved a little sigh as she thought of the variety of love affairs she'd once planned for herself at college. Oh, how naive and innocent and full of herself she'd been, not even a year ago. Just look at her now, lying here quietly starving to death with one man; one man with whom she'd had an exclusive relationship for many months; at the moment a slightly snoring man. Yet Andy's lovemaking was so inventive and ardent that, Maggie thought philosophically, she should not, in all fairness, feel deprived.

But it was too damn domestic! And yet not domestic enough in certain ways. At Thanksgiving Andy had gone home for the weekend, explaining that if he took a girl with him his absurdly conventional and conservative parents would consider him engaged, and over the Christmas weekend he'd wangled a week off that included the New Year's weekend, ten days in all, to go skiing with a bunch of pals from Harvard, an annual blast that he told her never included women.

Andy'd never actually said he was in love with her, but then she'd never told him she was in love either, Maggie brooded. The truth was that she didn't know if she was or not, her only yardstick for love was still Barney, and that was such a complicated, tormented, tangled web of emotion, that she couldn't compare it to anything but itself. Andy was charming, funny, and whimsical, wonderful to look at, but . . . but . . . was she ready to really fall in love, whatever that meant? If you were ready, would you have to ask?

Maggie lay back on the pillow, wondering if her black clothes were the right gear for a press officer. Twenty-five dollars extra wasn't enough to branch out into anything but one more piece of black, she decided, poking Andy gently. He turned over, seeming to fall more deeply asleep. She buried herself under the covers and pulled his ears and blew on his eyes until she was satisfied that he was rising up out of the depth of sleep.

She wasn't going to wait another minute to tell him her news.

"Andy, Andy, darling?"

"Yeah, yeah," he mumbled, aggrieved. "What time is it?"

"Dinner time. Listen, Andy, do you know who Lee Maine is?"

"Lee . . . great gal . . . think Uncle Hamilton . . . always . . . had sorta letch for her," he yawned, still three-quarters asleep, trying to bury his head between her breasts and plunge back into oblivion.

Maggie pushed him away, recoiling almost before the words made sense to her.

" 'Uncle Hamilton'!"

"Oh, Jesus!" Shocked fully awake, Andy blinked at her. "Did I say that?"

"You said that. Uncle Hamilton *who*, Andy?"

"Well, obviously . . . oh, shit!"

"If Hamilton Scott's your uncle, Mrs. Sinclair's your aunt! You're some sort of Scott! How the hell could you not have told me?"

"I didn't want it to influence you," he replied, looking badly caught out.

"In what way?" Maggie demanded, hopping out of bed, pulling a robe around her and standing wrathfully against a wall as far as she could get from him.

"It was damn stupid but I thought it could have made you like me more, or less, depending—you could have thought I had unfair pull or . . . well . . ."

"I could have played up to you because of your connections? Don't you know me better than that?"

"Of course I do! Shit, Maggie, that's the last thing you'd do, you're the most emotionally honest person I know, but by the time I got to know you, I'd let it go so long I didn't know how to tell you, there never seemed to be an exactly right time." He struggled out of bed with as much dignity as he could muster, wrapping a blanket around his waist.

"Thanksgiving, tell me about that, Andy. Tell me

about your conventional parents and why you couldn't invite me."

"I felt like a bastard about that, Maggie, oh, darling, really, you've got to believe me, I hated leaving you alone in the city, but my mom, Minnie, is Uncle Hamilton's and Aunt Liz's younger sister. Years ago she appointed herself the family Thanksgiving dinner giver, so most of the family was there, the McClouds, the Scotts, and the Sinclairs. I've never brought a girl home for Thanksgiving, they'd have been buzzing and wondering . . . you can see the problem, can't you?"

"I'm very good at seeing exactly that sort of problem."

"There are only a few people at S and S who know who I am: Lee and some of the department heads, and the head of the International Office . . . people I've known practically all my life. My floater job has been a way of training me . . ."

"Going out for pizza is your way of working your way up the company ladder?"

"Well, pizza was just a euphemism. I've actually been working my ass off learning the ropes. I need the practical experience of seeing how everything runs, from top to bottom, from the day a consignment arrives until it's sold and paid for. Eventually, unless I screw up big-time, I'll become head of S and S. It won't happen for many years, of course, but none of the other kids in the family wants to go into the business. Aunt Liz has two married daughters in California, with their own busy lives; both of Uncle Hamilton's sons are doctors; and my sister doesn't care about anything but the ballet; so that leaves me."

"The Porcelain and Ceramic Expert," Maggie said flatly.

"That's perfectly true. There's no reason why an executive can't be an expert too. That's why I went to business school, so I'd have both kinds of training. Oh, come back over here, sweet, beautiful Maggie, don't look at me as if I were a monster."

"Is this apartment really rent-stabilized?" she asked, not moving.

"Yes, thank God. But I don't live on a floater's salary, I have what is known as a small but adequate private income."

"Is there anything else I should know?"

"Well . . . yes."

"Don't you think you'd better tell me?"

"Hellfire and damnation! Next month I'm going to Geneva."

"For a sale?"

"No . . . for a year. Oh, Maggie, I can't help it, Uncle Hamilton made the decision. I'm going to be working directly under the head of the Geneva office, for upper-level training, and then I'm going to the London office for more of the same, another year or so, maybe more."

"That's two things," Maggie said. "Maybe even three."

"You can see that I intended to tell you everything, how could I leave for all that time without explaining why?"

"No, that would have been too much to lie about, even for you," Maggie said, from behind the closet door where she was quickly getting dressed.

"I wasn't lying, Maggie! I just wasn't being straight with you, there's a difference!"

"You're playing with words." She emerged, ready to leave, her sulfur-yellow muffler wrapped tightly around her neck, her eyes narrowed in disgust. "You've lied every night we've spent together since you knew me enough to trust me; you would have kept on lying tonight if you'd been even half-awake. A lie of omission, steady omission of the truth, is as much a lie as any other kind, Andy, didn't you ever learn that at Harvard?"

"But Maggie, you can't leave, I'm crazy about you!"

"Were you planning on taking me to Geneva?"

"How could I? But I thought—"

"That it would be much easier to wait till the last minute and then just drop the bomb."

Andy fell into a silence of admission while Maggie studied his face. No, she'd never been in love with him, how could she have ever wondered if she was? There was a strong physical attraction between them, nothing more. The hurt was in being lied to, but that particular hurt would always be the most painful, the most unforgivable one for her because of her past. Andy had behaved the way many men would when they want to keep a girl without making a commitment to her, and, in all fairness, she'd never asked for more, not so much as hinted. She'd been as content with the status quo as he'd been.

"Andy, don't do this again to another girl. It stinks, it's beneath you, it isn't fair," she said gently. "But I owe you, so I forgive you."

"Owe me? What are you talking about?"

"I owe you for a glorious, five-star, incredibly thorough and imaginative erotic education. It's going to be marvelously useful in the future. After all, Andy, remember, you were my first. I certainly never planned for you to be my one and only."

"Oh, Maggie! Don't go!"

"Good-bye, Andy. I have to go out for pizza."

27

When she reached thirty-six, in August 1991, Tessa formed her own production company. There had been no noticeable lessening in the number of scripts offered to Aaron for her attention, but she'd seen too many major actresses suddenly wake up one day and discover that there were fewer and fewer roles for them as they approached forty, to assume that the same thing wouldn't happen to her.

It was as sure to happen as the effects of gravity on the human face, she thought, and although Tessa, in the most demanding, thorough, and severely professional inspection of her looks, still couldn't find any damage to her skin, her features, her hair, or her body, she knew that through some change behind her eyes, through some difference in her expression, she had changed vastly from the girl who'd started playing Jo March to someone who could and should be playing nothing but a woman. A young woman, of course, but one who had done her full share of living and loving and maturing. She'd been in front of the cameras for twenty years, she'd grown up in front of those cameras, and it showed in a million ways that no moviegoer could pin down but each one would recognize.

Fiona Bridges had been willing to join Tessa in the new production company in exchange for Tessa's commitment to do one film a year for the entity, leaving her free to make pictures elsewhere. To have this call on the services of a star as internationally adored as Tessa, was vitally important to Fiona. As partner in Kent-Bridges Productions, she had taken two or three giant steps. Aaron Zucker had been retained to be business manager for the company, as well as continuing to serve as Tessa's agent.

"No full-frontal nudity," Tessa stipulated, as they celebrated the formation of the new company.

"That the only no-no?" Aaron asked. "How about hookers, addicts, abused women, serial murderers—that sort of thing?"

"That's Oscar nomination material for any actress of my age," Tessa giggled. "If you can find a script in which, at some point or another, I'm committed to an institution, preferably maximum-security, where I don't wear makeup, have no costume changes, and never get my hair washed, it's almost a sure thing. However, there's got to be a white phone in my cell."

"And Fred Astaire takes you out dancing once a week," Fiona murmured, "and they let you wear your jewelry."

"Fiona, darling, you've always understood me," Tessa remarked lightly, wondering what Fiona would say if she knew that since Luke's death she'd continued to buy herself extraordinary jewels on many of the special occasions he had observed, spending princely amounts of her enormous wealth on what had become a necessary part of the content, the very rhythm of her life. She owned so many treasures that there wasn't an important jeweler who didn't notify her when a truly exceptional gem came into their hands. In the small, tight world of important gemstones, she had progressed from a woman who merely wore the jewelry a man gave her, to the status of a major, serious private collector.

"Understand you? That's more than I can say," Aaron muttered into his champagne.

Kent-Bridges's first success had been a film in which Tessa played a lawyer defending a character played by Bruce Willis on murder charges. The picture owed fully as much credit to Willis's splendid performance and the chemistry between them as it did to her own perform-ance, but his monster salary had chewed deeply into their profits.

Now, a year later, in the fall of 1992, not long after Tessa turned thirty-seven, she had set her heart on making a film in which the meatiest part belonged to her.

"Aaron, have you finished the biography of Lady Cassandra Lennox?" she asked impatiently.

"Considering that it's nine hundred and ninety-seven pages long, I'm proud to say I finished it last night. That's over three hundred pages a day and my wife's ready to leave me. Again. I've been reading till two in the morning."

"Well?"

"Hey, I didn't think women could get away with that sort of stuff back in Queen Victoria's time. No wonder she was considered the most scandalous woman of her era. All those lovers, all those little bastards she popped out so easily, all that travel from one court of Europe to another, all that stealing other women's husbands—who wouldn't admire a dame like that?"

"But did you find out about the rights?" Tessa asked impatiently.

"I sent you a memo on it this morning. The guy who wrote it, Dr. Elliott S. Conway, flatly refuses to sell. To anybody. He's had a heap of offers. Warner Brothers and Lorimar wanted it for Michelle Pfeiffer, Jaffe/Lansing for Glenn Close, Paula Weinstein for

Susan Sarandon—only Woody Allen and Streisand haven't been heard from, to hear his agent talk. Dr. Conway maintains that Hollywood would only sensationalize Lady Cassandra, turn her into something she wasn't, leave out the important things she stood for. He spent seven years researching her life and he says there's no way he'll allow anyone to turn it into a two-hour movie. He wants people to read every page of the entire book and nothing less."

"That's ridiculous. How could Cassandra be shown as more sensational than she really was? And how can he refuse a movie deal? Nobody refuses a movie deal," Tessa said, more amazed than irritated.

"He doesn't appear to be aware of that. The guy's a history professor at Columbia, with a major ivory-tower attitude."

"I bet he has a trust fund as big as his ego," Fiona said, "or a very rich wife, probably both."

"I've got to meet him," Tessa said resolutely. "I have to play Cassandra, it's my part, not Susan's or Glenn's or Michelle's or anyone else's and that's all there is to it. Aaron, can you arrange it through his agent? I'll fly to New York any time and meet with this absurd professor."

"What if he won't take a meeting?" Aaron asked.

"Tell his agent I'm a devout fan and all I want to do is buy him a drink, tell him how brilliant and wonderful his book is, and get my very own copy autographed."

"What if he doesn't fall for that line of sickening bullshit?"

"Oh, Aaron, you've been around me so long you take me for granted," Tessa sighed. "I tell you that if he's any kind of man he'll want to meet me, and if he's gay he'll want to meet me, and if he's an alien he'll definitely want to meet me and take me back to his planet for breeding purposes, good luck to him."

"Yeah, Aaron, she's Tessa Kent, remember?" Fiona weighed in, wishing, as usual, that Aaron could be less pessimistic. Didn't he realize how lucky he was to have kept Tessa's loyalty? Every last nominee for an Oscar performance last year had been a CAA client, and Ovitz would grab Tessa in a Beverly Hills microsecond if he got the chance.

"I'll give it my best shot," Aaron said, repressing a groan.

Two weeks later Tessa waited in a unreconstructed neighborhood bar far uptown on the West Side near Columbia for Dr. Elliott S. Conway, who was, at this point, a half hour late. He'd declined to come downtown to have a drink at the Carlyle Bar, or in her suite, because, as he put it, he had severe limitations on his time. He could at least have the courtesy to be prompt, Tessa fumed, tired of pretending to be engrossed in a copy of *The Life of Lady Cassandra Lennox* while avoiding making any eye contact in a bar jammed with men who were staring openly at her.

She couldn't remember the last time she'd been in a bar by herself, Tessa thought. Had she ever done so? Hadn't she, all her life, met strangers or friends on her own territory or in protected, privileged spaces, rather than this kind of down-at-the-heels, seedy hangout, which reeked of a hundred years of beer? As she'd left the shelter of her limo, parked discreetly around the corner, she'd twisted her wedding ring so that the huge green diamond lay on the palm of her hand, an automatic action whenever she walked on the streets of any city.

She'd prepared herself for this meeting as carefully as possible. She'd had a burgundy suit designed which, without being in any way a costume, possessed a subliminal Victorian influence in its silhouette: a tightly laced waist, a full skirt, a wide-lapeled jacket that outlined her breasts and opened, at her throat, on a blouse of precious white lace. Around her neck she wore a dog collar of small pearls that clasped at the front with a cameo; delicate cameo earrings hung from her ears; and her dark hair was brushed into a highly modified version of a Victorian hairstyle, up off her neck and into a careful array of curls. She'd stopped well short of looking over-the-top, Tessa was certain as she left her hotel, but she hadn't reckoned on the uniform of blue jeans and baseball jackets that the local barflies wore.

She realized too late that she looked as if she'd wandered in from a costume party, but there was nothing she could do about it now. After all, what would Dr. Conway expect Tessa Kent to wear? she asked herself. Anything at all from her ordinary wardrobe would have looked equally out of place in this joint full of bums. But she'd shown her hand by wearing something evocative, no matter how cleverly, of the Victorian era. She should have worn the most cutting edge outfit she owned, something futuristic by one of the new Japanese designers. Bloody hell! If she didn't get to play Cassandra Lennox she'd never forgive herself!

Calm down, Tessa told herself. A man who habitually drank in a sinister gin mill like this wouldn't even notice clothes, wouldn't have the subtlety to realize that her eagerness to buy the rights to his book was emblazoned on her back. And what difference would it make if he did? He had to know she was eager anyway, or else what would she be doing waiting alone in a rough part of town for a rude, self-important, pompous professor of history?

"Let me see the book," a man said, sitting down next to her, wearing a bulky leather jacket and corduroy trousers. As Tessa yelped in surprise, he took it away from her and laid it flat on the bar table, open to the halfway point. Then he flipped through the following chapters, quickly opening the book to certain pages, until he came to the end.

"Either you've really read it or somebody else has," he said, extending his hand. "I'm Sam Conway, which was it? You or somebody else?"

"Me, of course," Tessa answered, bewildered. "What were you doing to it?"

"Checking. You can tell if a book really has been read. You open it in the middle and if it falls flat, the back's been cracked. Then you look for the signatures, folds of printed paper stacked on top of each other and glued to the backing, each one the same length, and you can see if they've been skipped or not."

He was young and burly, a huge man, and he didn't fit her expectations of a dour, arrogant, ancient Herr Doktor Professor with his long, tough, battered nose; the quirky, humorous light in his eyes; his capable big hands; and his badly cut, untidy thatch of curly blond hair, shades lighter than his heavy eyebrows. He looked like a longshoreman. He looked as if he needed to be on a horse, or on a small boat in a stiff breeze, Tessa thought, as she studied him.

"Why would I be here if I hadn't read the book?" Tessa asked.

"Someone could have read it for you and given you coverage, that's what they call a reader's report."

Tessa laughed. She'd known what coverage was since she was sixteen. "Aren't you going to give me a pop quiz? Cassie has no secrets from me that she didn't keep from you, Professor. And how come it's Sam and not Elliott?"

"Elliott's not my style. Samuel's my middle name. How come you call her Cassie?"

"That's my own private name for her," Tessa answered. "Lady Cassandra Lennox seemed too long after the first twenty pages. I hope you don't mind."

"I think of her as Cassie too. A pisser, wasn't she?"

"A first-class pisser."

"What are you drinking? Oh, by the way, sorry I'm late, a student tried to talk me into a passing grade and it took a long time to say no, and explain exactly why."

"Why didn't you say yes and get here on time?"

"Can't do that," he said, shocked. "Where are your morals? So what'll it be?"

"Vodka straight up," Tessa ordered, hoping that the alcohol might sterilize the bar glass, that notorious conveyor of germs.

"Jim, two Stolis straight up, very cold, bring the lady a straw."

"How—?"

"I read minds." He grinned at her, with a flash of whimsical complicity Tessa was not accustomed to inspire in strangers. "You don't exactly look at ease. This place may be humble but they do use a dishwasher. Still, you'll be happier with a straw."

"Well, I admit, I didn't feel comfortable before you showed up," Tessa said, opting for the charmingly frank approach. "I've just realized that I've never been in a bar alone in my life, much less one where a mob of guys are staring straight at me. Most people are too cool to do that, they just give a peek out of the corners of their eyes, the instant celebrity once-over that says they're not impressed."

"That, I guess, would be out in Hollywood and in your better neighborhoods, like the Carlyle."

"Exactly."

"But by showing up here, you just made me at least four hundred bucks."

"What?"

"I said I'd bring Tessa Kent in for a drink and everybody bet me five bucks apiece I couldn't do it. That's why they're all checking you out, making absolutely sure I'm not pulling a fast one, as if a Tessa Kent lookalike could possibly exist. I guess they want their money's worth."

"My God, how *old* are you!" Tessa exclaimed.

"Thirty-eight."

"And still playing fraternity house tricks?"

"Why not?"

"But you're a full professor, you have a doctorate in some deeply meaningful subspecies of Victorian history, you've written a great, great book, aren't you too old to—"

"Soul of a teenager. That's what my wife said." He shook his head ruefully at the memory.

"Wife?"

"Ex-wife. I couldn't get rid of the soul."

"How many wives?"

"Only one, long gone. I was much worse in my twenties."

"Children?"

"Nope. You?"

"No one." Her fingers fluttered all complications away. "Fancy free."

"Soul of a teenager?"

"I grew up fast, at fourteen. I never had time for one."

"That's too bad," Sam Conway said seriously. "You missed something wonderful. But it's never too late. Hang around me, you'll see, it's catching."

"I'd like to hang around you," Tessa said, taking the plunge resolutely. "I'd like to play Cassie."

"Well of course you would. That's why you're doing a most wonderfully subtle impression of that ravishing creature in her prime. But I don't want to sell the rights to the book."

"Sam, look, you may be immune to money but don't you realize how many people will be exposed to the story of Lady Cassandra Lennox if a film's made? You're not being fair to her."

"Book's hit the top of the *Times* nonfiction list right now," he said with a hastily smothered look of satisfaction, "and my publisher says it should stay at number one for another six weeks minimum, according to his calculations and the reorders. Even a couple of months, until the next big book comes along."

"Which means about three, maybe four hundred thousand copies will be sold in hard cover, maximum, because most people don't buy books they can't read in bed in comfort, and say two, two and a half million plus in paperback over the years, although, again, thousand-page paperbacks are a hard sell, because they're too heavy to carry around. Oh, and college bookstores. Make it three million copies all together, plus foreign rights, and that's way on the high side," Tessa snapped, remembering all of Fiona's publishing lore. "And I'm being generous and it will take years."

"That's a lot of books from where I sit. I can't even begin to imagine three million people."

"A movie, on the other hand," Tessa continued, with every ounce of fire she could command, "would make Cassie a household word, all over the world, with millions and millions of people seeing the film when it's released two years from now at a time when they've practically stopped buying the book. That means a major return trip to the paperback bestseller lists. Then, every time the movie is run or rerun on television, more multiples of millions of people will watch it. And a percentage of them will go right out and buy the book and read it for the first time. Why do you think *Gone with the Wind* is still in print?"

"*Gone with the Wind* is the perfect illustration of what I don't like," Sam said, turning so that he could look at her closely. Intensity darkened his dark blue eyes. Jesus, Tessa thought, the man filled the room! He was off the wall, yes, but what presence he possessed! She could imagine him lecturing to a mesmerized classroom, she couldn't look away from the open neck of his work shirt where the springy blond hair—stop it Tessa! You want something, this is business! She made herself listen intently.

"Now, *Gone with the Wind*, there was a book full of history, slanted toward the Southern point of view, I grant you, but still history, crammed with vivid research, and what did they end up with? A movie about Vivien Leigh's costumes and four people with fucked-up love lives. The script included five percent or less of the book. The Civil War was treated as a plot device, just enough to hold the romantic narrative together."

"But there's no war in your book," Tessa retorted

passionately. "It's not a true historical tome, it's the story of one real woman's amazing life, she's front and center the whole time. She is the narrative, the spine of the story, the Civil War, Scarlett, Rhett, Ashley, and even poor Melanie all rolled into one. Every page lives and breathes Cassandra Lennox. You wrote biography like a novel and now you're thinking like a historian."

"And you're talking like an agent."

"I am not!" Tessa glared at him in fury.

"Just kidding, take it back, wanted to see what you'd say," he said, stumbling over his words at her rage. "You're talking like an actress who's fallen in love with a part, aren't you?"

She sat in sullen silence.

"Well, aren't you?" he persisted. "Yes or no?"

"True," she snapped. "Did any of the others talk to you like me?"

"No, it's all been agent-to-agent talk, I haven't gotten into it at all. I just keep saying no."

"Shouldn't you be less rigidly academic, more flexible and most of all more thoughtful about the future of your work," she prodded him.

"I played football to get through college, never had much of an academic attitude till I discovered history. Shouldn't you be more show biz, more snotty, more Hollywood?" His grin told her that he wasn't to be influenced easily.

"Do you see Susan Sarandon as Cassie?" Tessa demanded. Maybe a change of pace, even if she had to mention a rival for the rights, would at least make him think about the possibility of a film, and nudge him off his prejudices.

"Nope, too much of a wholesome American redhead, too mature for the early scenes."

"Michelle Pfeiffer?"

"Too fragile. Essentially tragic. Cassie had more blood and guts."

"Glenn Close?"

"Too tall, beautiful in her own austere way, but she doesn't drip sex and Cassie did. Now Meryl Streep—"

"Streep?" Tessa stopped just short of screeching.

"Just kidding."

"I hope you're having fun," she said coldly.

"I am," he said, looking pleased with himself. "Another drink?"

"It must be ego-gratifying to have every major star in Hollywood wanting to play Cassie," Tessa said, tapping her empty glass. This wasn't going to work, the man was some kind of tin-pot despot, more interested in protecting his precious rights than giving Cassandra Lennox to the world. She might as well have another drink.

"Not particularly," Sam Conway replied slowly, suddenly sounding uncharacteristically bashful. "What is ego-gratifying is that you, Tessa Kent, want to play Cassie. I kept seeing you as I researched and wrote the book. I know this sounds totally corny, but you've always been my favorite movie star. I cried at *Little Women*, disgracing myself completely with my high-school buddies, not at Beth but as Jo—you broke my heart, you were so beautiful . . . almost as beautiful as you are now. And *Gemini Summer* was the only sex-ed class I ever needed. I wouldn't sell my book because I was saving it for you. But I wanted to see if you'd read it. *I wanted you to come to me.* My adolescent soul again, and my adolescent crush on you, and I guess, shit!, my adolescent insecurity."

"Oh." She could only look at him, her lips parted in astonishment. He was blushing violently, but he held her gaze until she dropped her eyes.

"You know what?" he mumbled. "Let's go ice skating at Rockefeller Center, this minute. You're dressed just right. And we can tell our agents to make a deal tomorrow. Sound good to you?"

"I haven't ice skated since I was sixteen," Tessa stammered.

"Don't worry, I'm a whiz. I'll hold you up, won't let

you go, can't have Tessa Kent flat on her ass in front of her public."

"Sam, I'll be a great Cassie, I promise you."

"I knew that years and years before you did. Jim, put this on my tab and collect my winnings. So long, guys, well worth losing five bucks, wasn't it?"

As they left the bar in a storm of applause, whistles, and catcalls, Tessa thought that she knew what it felt like to have the soul of a teenager after all.

28

Maggie settled herself, as comfortably as she ever could in a plane, and reflected thankfully that there was no one on the flight to present her with a birthday cake and wait for her to blow out twenty-three candles. No one who knew, as she returned to New York from Hong Kong, that this June day in 1993 it was her twenty-third birthday.

The previous year the ladies of the press office, led by Lee Maine, had made a big deal out of her turning twenty-two, just as they'd done for everyone's birthday since she'd been one of them, but something in her hated the thought of having to face "Happy Birthday" again. Was it a reflex of inhabitual shyness when confronted with that perfectly awful song, an ordeal that required everyone to put on a happy face and pretend delight and surprise? It should be banned for grownups. Or was she merely reacting to the incredible stress that went hand in hand with the utter exhaustion that came from supervising the press on the largest sale in her career?

In any case, Maggie was relieved that her birthday would be well over by the time this plane landed. She'd been gone two weeks, working the publicity mill for all it was worth. For a month preceding the trip she'd worked in New York with the Chinese wire services and the two English-language Hong Kong newspapers as well as with journalists from the most important of the dozens of magazines that crowded the Hong Kong newsstands. Once there she'd held a press conference attended by more than a hundred journalists, and worked without respite with writers for the score of Chinese newspapers, trying to give each one a different story angle. She'd organized every detail of the catering and flowers for the weeklong exhibition and the actual sale, held in the Regent's largest ballroom. During the sale she'd dashed between journalists and the bank of phone bidders, finding out which purchasers were willing to let their names be used. She'd kept herself going on room-service scrambled eggs, tuna fish sandwiches, and long dawn and late-night swims with which she religiously released her tension in the Regent pool.

Although Maggie wasn't, like Caesar, actually bringing back the spoils of war to parade them in front of the Romans, she felt as if she were leading a train of elephants loaded with booty. In addition to the commissions on the hammer price on the many millions achieved by porcelain, Chinese furniture, Chinese paintings, and the results of the jewelry sale—largely jade, watches, and the fancy colored diamonds so admired by the Chinese—she was returning with the ten percent commission on 1.7 million dollars that had been paid for a rare and extraordinarily fine jade necklace composed of 107 of the precious beads, a world record for S & S or any other auction house.

She was still in shock, she realized. If you calculated in Hong Kong currency, in which it had been sold, the price fetched was more than HK13 million. Thirteen million, two . . . the price of that necklace, in addition to the great success of the entire sale, had finally established S & S as a major player in Hong Kong.

Was it possible that only five years ago she'd been the

most temporary and inexperienced of temps and that now she was Lee's chief staff officer, with three assistants to supervise and entire auctions to publicize on her own? Was it possible that as soon as she returned to the office she'd start working on her next auction, a sale of Postimpressionists for which she'd go to Geneva?

Well, why not? Maggie thought. She sipped another glass of the champagne the flight attendant kept bringing her. Five years in the auction business, she was convinced, counted for more than fifteen years in any other job. Any press officer has to be prepared to be pushed, not just to the edge, but over the edge, totally and utterly consumed by the business at hand, and auction followed auction relentlessly. Lee had warned Maggie not only that she would frequently find herself truly homicidal, for which she recommended strenuous exercise, but that she would have very little time for a personal life. Lee had been right; in fact she'd underestimated. But, Maggie thought smugly, *but* what little private time there was she used well.

She was as direct as any man when it came to sex. If there was a real attraction she not only didn't expect courtship, she didn't want it. Courtship took up precious time. She came to the table to play, not to look around, and she made it a rule not to accept an invitation from anyone, not even for a drink, if she didn't have a strong suspicion that there was a good chance that she'd want to go to bed with him.

Sometimes, Maggie thought, the rapid development of her many affairs, and the unsentimental way she dropped lovers in whom she'd lost interest, even managed to shock Polly, and that took some doing.

"You're so *frisky*," Polly had commented recently. "Meaning what?" she'd asked. "You're like a puppy, chasing its tail. Why don't you settle down with one guy for six months and see how it feels?"

"Like you and Miss Jane Robinson?" Maggie had asked, laughing. "Remember, that snowstorm brought you together, so I was the inadvertent matchmaker."

"Laugh, laugh, I don't care, I'm a happy woman," Polly had replied. Well, "happy" for Polly now meant steady domesticity, and that was the last thing Maggie wanted. She was simply having too much fun. She had no intention of getting married to anyone, and when men got serious about her, as, unfortunately, so often seemed to happen, she let them down firmly. It was kinder that way than to keep them dangling with false hope. She hadn't missed all the pleasures of a college education after all, now that she came to think about it.

Of course, even with her mild disapproval of Maggie's frenetic sex life, Polly was no longer fully privy to the details of Maggie's private life since she'd stopped being a boarder. As she'd advanced in the press department, she'd earned more money. It still wasn't much, public relations never paid well, but she managed to make her salary cover her brutal haircuts that were never in or out but were essential to her look, expensive Wolford panty hose that wore like iron and were a true economy, shoes she tended so carefully that they lasted forever, and a very occasional replacement to her consistently all-black wardrobe. By being fanatically careful about expenses, Maggie'd managed to rent an amazingly cheap two-room apartment one flight down from Polly. It gave her the advantage of the increased privacy she now wanted for her busy love life, and the reason to start slowly buying at auction for herself.

Maggie had never realized that she had a deep need to own her own things, always living in other people's houses as she had, but once she learned enough about furniture, art, and objects from the friendly experts at S & S, all of them eager to educate her on the chance that she'd shine extra publicity on their departments, she'd been able to pick up a few true bargains at various sales. There were invariably days when, by sheer luck, there was little interest in a piece on which she had her eye. She'd been able to snatch up some wonderful antique textiles for Polly as well, by way of repayment for the amounts of Polly's food she'd consumed.

Nothing could repay the permanent, deeply affectionate welcome she always found at her friend's studio.

Her own tiny apartment was, Maggie thought dotingly, as eclectic as you could get. It was still fairly empty, but everything in it mattered to her. No matter how many shelter magazines she pored over or how many decorating editors she huddled with for her work, she'd never chosen to make a single "design statement," which, as Polly said, was damn lucky, considering what an incredible mishmash she was creating with her magpie eye. But it was the home she'd never had and always longed for.

She didn't entertain there and probably never would. Lunch almost always took place at a fashionable restaurant as, sometimes with Lee and sometimes alone, Maggie became friends with the many journalists a press officer needed to know: the ladies and gents of the art and antiques magazines, the fashion magazines, the general-interest magazines, and the specialized magazines for collectors. There were two magazines for teddy bear collectors alone, Maggie thought, still surprised after all these years, and small fortunes were spent on old Steiff bears in good condition. *Life* had done a big piece on their last teddy bear auction and was waiting eagerly for the antique doll sale that was coming up.

"May I offer you a little more champagne?" the flight attendant asked.

"Please," Maggie said, holding out her glass. This stuff wasn't getting to her, she was still too high on the last two weeks to be touched by wine.

What a fantastically international business she was in, Maggie reflected. No matter where an auction was held—New York, Munich, Lugano, London, or Kuala Lumpur or anywhere else—the bidders came from every country where people had money. If they weren't there in person, they'd bid by mail or by phone.

You could put all the auction houses in the world on an island—something the size of Bermuda, for instance—

and as long as there were good hotels, enough sales rooms, and plenty of free meals for journalists, you could declare it the auction capital of the world. No force known to man, not even a legion of furious golfers, could keep the collectors and dealers away.

You'd need marvelous mail service for the catalogs, and an international airport, but in the end the results would be the same. Some people wanted to sell and others wanted to buy; if you had a fine enough silver service you could march off into the middle of the Sahara and knock it down for eight million dollars. You could slip a Fabergé Imperial Easter egg into your pocket, climb a mountain, and pull in three million in change.

God but she loved doing something really well, and she was getting better at it all the time. She loved her two crazy little rooms; she liked each of her lovers; she loved her friends: Polly, Lee, Jane, Hamilton, Liz. . . . And then there was her oldest friend, Barney, who was always there for her, Barney about whom she could never think without a deep pang in her heart, a muddled turmoil in her brain, and a peculiar longing that seemed to come from her wrists and radiate up her arms to . . . Never mind Barney, she was the luckiest girl in the world, Maggie decided.

An empress of China had once collected apple-green jade and tucked it away in 3,000 ivory cabinets. Where had it all disappeared to? How much per bead were 107 jade beads—or jadeite, to give it its proper name—into 1.7 million dollars? she wondered. The human desire to own was a marvel. How much per round, green, carved little rock? Maggie tried to figure it out in her head, but the amounts she arrived at kept changing as she drifted off to sleep.

On the first Saturday night in September 1993, just as business hours were ending, Maggie met Barney at Chopper Dude's, the custom motorcycle shop he'd opened with a well-financed partner several years earlier. Soon after his arrival in New York his alliance to his Harley had melted into total immersion in the world of handmade swingarms, skyscraper sissy bars, stretched headlights, and hand-hewn fenders; a world in which one company alone made 250 different kinds of motorcycle seats, a world in which a seventy-year-old CEO might spend four years working on his Springer, gold-plating the chrome on the shoulders, the front fork, the brake and clutch levers, the screen behind the carburetor faceplate, and the band behind the nitrous bottle.

Maggie and Barney had reached an agreement never to talk shop. Even the brand names of the bikes competing in the Daytona 500 remained as foreign to her as the very existence of a Philadelphia Chippendale tea table remained to him.

"Take me out of this testosterone-as-a-lifestyle pit," she demanded. "I have something to talk over with you."

"Where the hell have you been? I haven't seen you for it seems like months," Barney complained as they walked down Ninth Avenue.

"Working," Maggie said briefly, mindful of their agreement.

"Working too hard to give me a quick call?" he asked, hurt.

"In Hong Kong," she said tersely. It wasn't true, but how could she tell him that something about the light of summer evenings in the city made her long for him too much to permit her to see him safely? She'd rationed herself to this casual drink tonight.

"Okay, I understand, enough said. Don't tell me why."

"I wasn't going to, you hard-core, real-deal chopper dude, darling."

"Want that drink, beautiful?"

"Need that drink," Maggie replied, turning off the noisy street into a little bar with pretensions to Barcelona chic. They sat silently, waiting for their drinks, happy just to be together. Barney looked so much older than he was, Maggie thought, scanning his beautifully muscled body, his perpetual squint that came from working on pieces of evil machines, his perpetual tan that came from test-driving the grotesque monsters. There was something pagan about him, something barbaric, monolithic, almost . . . regal . . . with the confidence of a young prince. A man now, a man to be reckoned with.

But it didn't matter one whit how safe he said his beloved bikes were, she distrusted them all, not for anyone else, but only for him. How many women felt the same way? she wondered. And what good did it do them once the bike virus bit? She'd never understand the relationship of men and speed, she'd realized long ago. It must be some sort of useless extra gene. But oh, he still smelled so powerfully good; clean sweat, motor oil, and that special Barney smell she'd always known, like a perfect apple hanging on a branch on a sunny afternoon.

"So what's your problem?" Barney asked, finally. "It can't be about your job so it's got to be about a guy."

"It's not about a guy," Maggie said slowly.

Relief washed over him. He'd dreaded the day she'd meet the right guy, dreaded it for years. No matter how good it might be for her and how inevitable he knew it was, how bound it was to happen in the course of her life, he honestly didn't know how he'd live through it.

He'd tried fruitlessly not to worry about it, but he'd never managed to forget the possibility every time he thought about Maggie, and that was often. Christ, much, much too often, for all the good it did him! How did she dare to get more luscious? It infuriated him! She'd slimmed way down, not that he thought she needed to, without losing her fabulous tits, and she'd accomplished some evolving and mysterious alteration of her black uniform, so that she resembled every other chic, unmistakably New York woman from the neck down. But Maggie's skin looked as if she spent her days in a rose garden near Connemara, wearing a sun bonnet. No woman in Ireland had eyes as blue, he was convinced, and certainly no one had ever managed to make hair so short into hair so sexy. Or have a laugh that gave every man in earshot a hard-on.

"If it's not about your job and it's not about a guy, you must want to buy a bike," he said.

"Great guess, but just off the mark. No, Barney, believe it or not, it's about my future. I've had a job offer from another auction house, a much bigger house, at more money, with more opportunity."

"Which one, Sotheby's or Christie's?"

"How'd you know their names?" Maggie was startled.

"Classic car and bike auctions."

"And that's dumb of me, because of course we have them, too, so I should have realized."

"Well, which?"

"Sotheby's."

"Why don't you want to take it?"

"I don't?"

"If you did, you wouldn't be asking me, you'd have done it already."

"Hmmm, you're smarter than you used to be."

"Yeah, I think I escaped Dad's share of the gene pool when it came to brains."

"And you're certainly not like your lovable mother in any way that I've ever noticed."

"Aren't you full of compliments today?" He smiled down at her. "Either they adopted me, or else I was switched at birth. There's no other explanation."

"Do you see them?"

"You know I do, from time to time, now that they almost approve of me. Success has had a way of tempering their parental horror at my wicked ways. Stop changing the subject. Why don't you want a better job? Especially at the best place?"

"I've thought and thought about it, and it keeps coming back to loyalty. Lee and Hamilton and Liz have just been so damn good to me. They've trained me, they've molded me, patiently and with kindness. I love all of them. And there isn't one of the other assistants who could begin to do the job I do, and where would that leave Lee? Especially now that she's getting married."

"Married? Isn't she in her fifties?"

"Barney, really! What's wrong with you? Lee was working on a major Old Master sale—sorry, sorry!—and the chief consignor and she fell head over heels. She's going to keep on working, but he's a very rich man who takes frequent vacations and she'll want to go with him."

"More work for you, then."

"Unquestionably."

"More money?"

"Probably, but not as much as I was offered."

"I don't think you should consider moving," he said with complete conviction.

"Why not?"

"Because you said you loved all of them. That's the best reason I've ever heard for staying put."

"Hmm . . . I thought it was loyalty . . . but no, it is love . . . everyday love, basic love, just about the most important thing in the world. . . . I knew I should ask you—Barney, what's that on your arm?"

"Nothing," he said, hastily rolling down his sleeve.

"Show me," Maggie demanded.

Sheepishly, he rolled his sleeve back, revealing the edge of a tattoo.

"Oh, for Pete's sake, not you too! Let me see that awful thing."

"*No.*"

"Yes," Maggie insisted, using both hands to yank the fabric almost up to his shoulder. A good-size heart, pierced by an arrow, appeared on his bicep, adorned with an M on one side and a B on the other.

"Oh," she said and lapsed into silence. After a minute she asked, "How many others do you have?"

"That's the only one. You can search my body if you don't believe me."

"I believe you."

"Happy Valentine's Day, retroactively."

"Thank you, Barney," Maggie said gravely, more touched than she was willing to admit.

"I'll never have another, you know that, don't you? And I wasn't drunk when I had it done . . . well, maybe just a little, but I'd wanted one for years."

"I do know, I do, sweet Barney. You're such a romantic, aren't you? You'd ride off to war for me, you'd fight dragons for me, you'd jump into a pit full of snakes and cut their heads off for me, wouldn't you?"

"Damn it, Maggie, you know I would," he said passionately, fussing with frustration. "I'd do anything in the whole wide world for you, I'd go into outer space for you, with or without a spacesuit, but unfortunately, that doesn't seem necessary right now. You're riding high."

"So are you," she replied absently, thinking hard. She had to deal with this . . . thing . . . about Barney sooner or later. It had been going on for five years, it stood in the way of her ever caring about another man, or even, if it came to that, wanting to care. The basically heartless, bitchy way she treated men, the way she flittered and fled from one to another, was directly related to this schoolgirl obsession she'd never been able to let go because she'd nourished it by not living it out. And it wasn't sensible or healthy for Barney, either. That new tattoo proved that he hadn't forgotten, that he still cherished what he mistakenly thought were romantic feelings for her. Without them he'd have found other girls, available girls, and many of them, long ago. They'd both be happy if they weren't stuck in their shared past. But were they both condemned to remain so attached to an idealized concept of each other, a myth of their teenage years, that they could never grow beyond it? Were they that helpless?

They'd never know, Maggie realized, her hair rising on her closely shorn nape, unless they did something about it. It was the only remedy, the hair of the dog as it were. As long as they remained inaccessible to each other, they'd remain slaves to their old fantasies. But a fantasy realized, a fantasy acted on, would be a fantasy no longer, just mundane reality that could be easily judged for its true value, and discarded, leaving them free.

"Maggie, you're a million miles away. Not still thinking about that job offer?"

"No, just . . . relaxing. It's Saturday night, remember? Date night."

"Except that this isn't a real date, it's just the two of us," Barney drawled wryly. "Two old buddies, comrades in arms, pals for life, like a couple of leathery cowboys sharing a bottle for old times' sake, just as if you didn't know that I'm in love with you, more than ever. Fuck! I shouldn't have said that. It slipped out, a bad habit. It won't happen again."

"Barney . . . ?"

"What?"

"Oh, Barney, I don't know . . ." she sighed.

"Maggie, you? You always know. You're the one with all the answers about us. Right from the beginning. Not that I'm bitter, I just sound bitter, oh, hell, so maybe I am a little bitter, what the hell, I can live with it."

"What if you didn't have to?"

"I'd be a happy man, but don't kid yourself, it's not gonna happen just because it makes you feel more comfortable to think it might. It's not your problem, Maggie," he said brusquely, "it's strictly mine, don't worry about it."

"But what if? . . . Barney, what if you could stop feeling bitter?" she persisted.

"You talking lobotomy? I don't think they do that anymore."

"No." Maggie sat up straight and looked him directly in the eye. She knew she was blushing, but she didn't care. This had to be said and said clearly. "I'm talking about making love, you and me, the way we never did, and getting it out of our systems, once and for all."

"Is that . . . is that," he asked carefully, "what you really think would happen?"

"I'm sure of it," Maggie answered, overcome by the rightness of her thought process. "It's logical and it makes perfect sense."

"Hmmm. What if you got me out of your system but I didn't get you out of my system? What then?"

"Barney, remember how right I was before, that day when you left home? Even you had to admit that we couldn't make love then. Well, I'm right again. Now we can, now we're old enough," Maggie insisted, made more stubborn and impetuous by his unexpected resistance. "We both have fantasies about each other that have to be exposed to daylight, or they'll persist, or even get worse."

"Let me get this absolutely straight, so I don't take advantage of your theory. You propose that we make love, in cold blood, so we won't moon around about each other anymore?"

"Exactly," she answered, her eyes shining with conviction. "No more mooning, it's childish."

"When and where?" he asked quickly.

"Tonight. The sooner the better. We could go to my place or your place, it won't matter."

"You know you're nuts, don't you? Completely, absolutely nuts."

"I've never been saner in my life," she said urgently.

"Let's go to your place. Then I'll be the one who has to get up and go home afterward, not you."

"Fine."

"Now?"

"Now," Maggie said, with resolution, even though her mouth was dry and her feet were cold and she longed for him with her palms and her fingertips and she ached for him in the pit of her stomach and the back of her neck, it must be now because once it was over, once it was real, she wouldn't feel this unendurable need again.

Maggie woke up in the middle of the night, woke up completely, as if it were broad daylight, and knew, without a single doubt, that she had never had a happier minute since she'd been born. Everything in her life had led to the harbor of this bed in which Barney lay quietly sleeping on his back, an arm flung across one of her breasts. She felt as open and fertile as a field in spring, ravished, teeming with possibility, lying, rich and receptive, under the light of noon. She eased herself away cautiously so that she could turn around, lean on her elbow, and gaze at him in the dim beam of the street-lamp that filtered through her curtains.

He was the stuff of dreams, this man of hers, he was the pink-silver of a spring dawn, the honey of a summer afternoon, the moth-dreaming indigo of twilight, oh, he was the cat's pajamas, all right. And if she hadn't been brilliant enough to prove that to herself, once and for-ever, she might have missed understanding that he was the love of her life, and always had been, Maggie thought, suddenly terrified at her close call.

Admittedly, she'd followed a roundabout path to find out the truth, and her logic had been faulty, but oh, so beautifully faulty, a full 180 degrees faulty, so perfectly wrong that in the end, wasn't she all but forced to understand that she'd been right? What was her insanity but a higher form of sanity? What was being so certain of her own thought process but a subtle form of readiness to be convinced that she was wrong? And wasn't she the wickedly clever one, Maggie admitted, in a sudden giggle of honesty, to find a highfalutin way to get Barney into bed without even letting *herself* know what she was doing? Much less him?

The whole of the crowded island of Manhattan centered on this one rumpled bed, on this trance of adoration with which she contemplated Barney's profile. She felt as if she'd never had anything to do with another man, and in fact, she never had . . . well, that was, as it were, to be specific, not really, not truly, because she'd never experienced emotional fulfillment before, never felt a part of someone else, never allowed herself to let go of her borders and be bound to another, in bonds of unquestioning love.

How many women had Barney conquered to make him into such a magnificent lover? she wondered. She suppressed a pang of jealousy. Neither of them should ever ask each other any questions about what they'd done while they were waiting for each other. The past no longer existed.

"Have we reached the part where we stop mooning about each other yet?" Barney asked sleepily, his eyes still closed.

"Oh, no, no, no, not yet."

"Not ever? Promise?"

"Never, my love, *never*."

29

It had been a year, Tessa realized, one whole year since she'd met Sam Conway. Her thirty-eighth birthday had come a few weeks ago with the end of the summer of 1993, but in her happiness she hadn't given a thought to something as unimportant as a birthday. Sam and she had been inseparable since that night they'd gone ice skating. No one could slide a piece of paper between them, Tessa told herself, hugging the thought, no one could break into their universe.

She'd fallen in love twice in her life, both times at first sight. How many women had ever been that fortunate? Apparently that kind of sudden, certain, all-consuming emotion wasn't reserved only for the very young.

The girl who'd known instantly that Luke Blake was the man for her had become a woman of thirty-seven, a woman who lived alone, a woman who'd learned to get through each day, forcing herself to act courageous until she became truly courageous. She had spent five years without Luke, years in which no other man had entered her consciousness.

And then Sam. Such a different man from Luke, this new love of hers. And yet, in certain ways, so much the same. Bold, inwardly directed, used to authority, heedless of opinion—they had all those qualities in common.

But Sam was not a restless rover over the face of the earth, absorbed by making things happen, commanding hundreds of men, forever seeking new ventures, new areas to conquer. His strong sense of self had nothing to do with money or possessions or the ability to make other men follow him.

Sam, Tessa had discovered, was a contemplative man who found his deepest satisfaction in teaching and writing. His antic sense of humor, his essential boyishness, and his love of mischief masked the fact that he measured success by his own sure standards: delivering a good lecture, inspiring his students to ask thoughtful questions, finishing a chapter of his new book. Even one good page was enough to bring him deep pleasure.

They lived life at a slower, quieter pace than she'd been used to since she'd made her first film, more than twenty years ago. Sam's work at Columbia had kept them in New York during the academic year. Over the summer they'd gone to seminars at Aspen and Berkeley, where he'd been a guest speaker, and she'd managed to get him to Los Angeles for a few weeks, long enough for Sam to get to know Fiona and Aaron as well as the brilliant scriptwriter, Eli Bernstein, who was working ten hours a day turning *The Life of Lady Cassandra Lennox* into a film.

"I'd rather not meet him," Sam had said. "Who wants to meet the man who's chopping up your beloved child into little bits and pieces and relishing every minute of it?"

But when the two men had met they'd liked each other immediately and plunged into a conversation about the psychology of Cassie that continued for days. Afterward, Sam felt that he and Eli agreed entirely on what made Cassie tick. Even if he was going to have to use only the highlights of the book to make the script short enough to work for a movie, it would still be an epic film.

That script should be finished soon, Tessa realized, as

she returned to her apartment in the Carlyle after a day of lazy shopping while Sam worked in his office at Columbia. She bought only casual clothes now for her new understated world.

Sam's friends, of whom there were a bewildering quantity, had been guarded when he first introduced her to them, and they'd taken their time to look her over. She had used all her art to underdress without looking as if she'd worked at it. Yes, she was a movie star, she couldn't pretend she'd wasn't, fame clung to her as naturally as her fingernails, but she never once made other women feel dowdy—that had been her aim. And she treated everyone with the same warmth and friendliness. Sam's friends were important enough in their own fields to slowly grow to accept Tessa as a human being, not an incomprehensible creature from an alien world.

Tessa's jewels, except for a few basic pieces, like her triple strand of pearls and the engagement ring she always wore, were put away in their bank vaults. She'd bought no new jewels. She'd gone to no auctions, looked at no catalogs; she'd utterly lost interest in more acquisition of gemstones.

Nevertheless, Tessa clung to the existence of her own jewels in memory of Luke's love and that major portion of her own existence that was embodied in them. Her jewels were the twelve years of her life with Luke, they were the personal collection she'd amassed to try to comfort herself after his death. In ways too complicated and symbolic for her to put into words, her jewels were an absolute extension of herself, Tessa recognized. Whether she wore them or not, whether she left them in the vault, a secret treasure, or sported them every night, their existence was an intrinsic part of her own sense of identity, they were an indispensible layer of her selfhood.

Frequently, when Sam was teaching a late class and she found herself alone, she thought about them, visualizing each piece safe in the shelter of its velvet box, and wondered how it would feel to wear them again in public. Had there really been a day when, wearing lilac satin and illuminated by a historic web of Fabergé diamonds, she'd presented an Oscar in front of the world? Many, many times Tessa went to the vaults she rented and visited her jewels, played with them in a private room lined in beige velvet, tried them on, one marvel after another, and gazed at herself in the mirror that stood on a large table. In those hours she became another Tessa Kent, Tessa Kent who had existed in a triumphant whirl she'd thought would last forever, a Tessa Kent she knew too well not to miss keenly in spite of Sam. Oh, yes, she loved all her jewels deeply, still, and forever, every last one of them. *Her jewels were her autobiography.*

Yet since she'd met Sam, Tessa had automatically refused all film offers, even those that would be shot in Manhattan, because she hadn't wanted to alter the rhythm of her new life with him.

However, once Eli completed the script, and that shouldn't take more than a few months, she'd have to go to the Coast for the casting process—Lady Cassandra's lovers demanded a full roster of strong leading men—and inevitably, a start date would be set. The locations of the film were all English and European. How many of them would require her to travel and how many interiors could be reproduced in Hollywood? she wondered. She was torn already between the prospects of a role she'd been born to play and a man she didn't want to leave, not for a day.

Resolving not to worry about something that hadn't happened yet, Tessa kicked off her shoes, stretched till her bones cracked, and rang for tea. The room-service waiter who brought it also brought a dinner menu.

"I thought I'd leave this for you and Dr. Conway," he said, "unless you're going out tonight."

"Thanks, Joseph. We'll order later." One of the joys of the hotel was twenty-four-hour room service, Tessa thought, and one of the joys of Sam Conway was that he was sure enough of himself to allow her to corrupt him in unimportant ways, to live there with her and not ask her to move into his bachelor apartment on Riverside Drive, because of some stiff-necked principle. But she would have, if it had been important to him. She'd do anything for Sam Conway, Tessa told herself, with the shy, secret, brimming emotion of a girl thinking about a lover. She would have cleaned for him, she would even have cooked. Well . . . she would have given it a try, at least. Who knows, she might have turned out to be a natural.

"Do you know anything better than Midol for cramps?" Tessa asked Fiona, a few days later toward the end of one of their frequent, coast-to-coast phone conversations about the progress of the script.

"Midol and gin," Fiona answered. "Why?"

"I've got them bad, really worse than ever," Tessa said miserably, her brow wrinkled in pain.

"Haven't you seen your doctor?" Fiona questioned.

"A year ago to get another prescription for the Pill, right after I met Sam. I figured I didn't want to get pregnant and have another miscarriage. I had my annual checkup then, Pap smear, and a mammogram too. You know I've always been a bit paranoid about my health. But my cramps weren't bothering me all that much at the time."

"This is what my mother did," Fiona advised. "She'd take three Midol, fix a glass of room-temperature gin and plenty of it, put it on her bedside table, wrap herself around a hot-water bottle, and tell the family to leave her alone. She was usually all right by the next day. As I remember, she had three periods a month, just for a little peace and quiet."

"Room-temperature gin? Ugh. I can't even stand the smell of it in a cold martini," Tessa responded.

"That was her absolute prescription, just the way it comes out of the bottle. It has to be gin, Tessa, sorry, but it's a well-known home remedy."

"I can order some in a minute, from room service."

"Well, take a good slug, just remember to hold your nose when you swallow," Fiona advised, "and you should feel better soon. What about a hot-water bottle? As I remember, you don't have one."

"I'll have them send to the nearest drugstore. Sam would go, but he's at Yale for a week, giving a seminar. I knew I'd get my period now so I didn't go with him."

The next day Tessa, haggard and weak, answered Fiona's phone call.

"Well?" Fiona asked, anxiously.

"Now I have a truly hideous hangover on top of the cramps," Tessa said. "and I don't want anything but a Bloody Mary. I refuse to drink gin again, ever. It's poison. Your mother should be ashamed of herself."

"Tessa, you've simply got to see your gynecologist."

"If she says warm gin, I'll be surprised. Home remedy, indeed!"

Dr. Helen Lawrence, whom Tessa saw the next day, was a small, middle-aged woman with a pleasant manner, and she had the reputation for doing the most gentle pelvic exams in town. After Tessa dressed, Dr. Lawrence invited her into her office.

"I'd like you to have an abdominal and pelvic ultrasound, Tessa. It's possible that you might have endometriosis. In any case, that's the first thing to rule out."

"Endrometriosis? What's that?"

"One of the most common causes of painful periods. Some of the uterine lining gets outside the uterus and develops implants, which bleed into the abdominal cavity."

"Does the test hurt?"

"Ultrasound? Not in the slightest," Dr. Lawrence said, handing Tessa a card for an outpatient radiology facility where the test could be performed.

"Does it take long?"

"No. I'll go ahead and make an appointment for you. There's a very good radiologist there, Doctor Henry Wing."

"Please, Helen, just let me know when. I want to get this over with before my guy comes back."

"Miss Kent? It's Doctor Wing."

"Yes," Tessa said anxiously. "I've been waiting for your call. Do I have endometriosis?"

"No, there's no sign of it."

"But there's got to be something!" Tessa exploded, as much in anger at not getting a quick answer as in fear at what no answer might mean.

"I do see some evidence of an enlarged pancreas, Miss Kent."

"Is that the problem? Cramps from the pancreas? I've never heard of that."

"No, there's no connection."

"Oh, for the love of God, what the devil do I do now? Why did I ever start this nonsense anyway?"

"Miss Kent, I'd like you to go for a test called Computerized Tomography, a CT for short. While the doctor is at it, he'll do a CT-guided needle biopsy."

"A . . . biopsy . . . ?" Tessa asked. What the hell did this doctor know, suggesting a biopsy. "A biopsy of what?" she asked, keeping her voice as level as she could make it. A flutter of confused apprehension began to rise in her stomach, like a bad smell she couldn't avoid.

"Of your pancreas."

"Why?" she demanded, fear of her fear making her sound bold.

"The pancreas is, as I said, enlarged. We have to find out why."

"Oh, this is so typical! You go to a doctor for a pimple and the next thing you know he sends you to a leper colony! What if I don't choose to go, Doctor Wing?"

"I think you should talk it over with Doctor Lawrence, before you make any decision. I can only tell you what the ultrasound showed."

"I certainly will! Good-bye, Doctor Wing," Tessa said, narrowly preventing herself from slamming down the receiver. It was natural and normal to feel apprehension about another of their damn tests, Tessa told herself, who wouldn't? One test always led to another, nothing ever had a simple answer. But mostly, she told herself, she was furious at the medical profession, every last one of them. Christ, she hated doctors!

"Well, Fiona, the good news is the lining of my uterus is staying right where it should be and not creeping around my belly. The bad news is I have to have something called a CT and a fucking CT-guided needle biopsy, whatever the hell that is," Tessa reported as soon as she'd talked to Helen Lawrence, who had insisted on the necessity of additional tests.

"What's a CT?" Fiona asked, her lips white. She refused to say the word "biopsy," phone or no phone.

"It's short for Computerized Tomography. Naturally that doesn't leave me any smarter and frankly, I didn't want to ask for too many details. For all their future-world terminology, wouldn't you know that they still have to use needles? Doctors! Damn them all to everlasting hell. But Helen won't take no for an answer and I have to admit that she's the best gynecologist in New York. She says it's only slightly uncomfortable, they use a local anesthetic before they stick you with the needle. I'm going tomorrow. I want to get this nonsense all over with before Sam gets back."

"Tessa, I want you to see one more doctor," Helen Lawrence said calmly, after she'd learned the results of the CT and the biopsy. "Her name is Susan Hill."

"Not another doctor! I don't believe it! My God, Helen, all I came in for was cramps! I should have stuck with the gin and the hot-water bottle!"

"Well, that's been known to work, but you really need to see Doctor Hill."

"What kind of doctor is she?"

"A medical oncologist," Helen Lawrence said quietly.

"An oncologist?" Tessa said, so stunned that she could feel her heart turn over in her chest. "But . . . but Helen, an oncologist's a cancer doctor! Is that what you're suggesting? You know perfectly well I couldn't possibly have cancer. *That's out of the question.* How could I possibly need to go to a cancer doctor for cramps? This whole thing has gone beyond ridiculous!"

"Your cramps are complicated. You need a doctor who knows more than I do," Helen Lawrence replied, her voice firm.

"But a cancer doctor! That's insane! Why can't you handle my problem, Helen, why do you think I came to you? I don't want to see anyone else. Why are you handing me over to every damn doctor in this damn city?"

"Tessa, I know how you feel, but like it or not, you really need to see someone who knows more than I do," Helen Lawrence insisted. "I've made an appointment for you. Doctor Hill will see you this afternoon. Fortunately she had an opening in her schedule, she's a very busy doctor."

"But . . . but . . . look, Helen, what's the big rush? I feel doctored up to the hilt right now. And my cramps are gone, as usual. Nothing's different, I just have to learn to live with them."

"Tessa, the sooner you see Susan Hill the better. There's never going to be a perfect time and I want her to get into this, she's the best I know. Is your gentleman friend still out of town?"

"Yes, but Helen, this afternoon? Really this afternoon? It usually takes an eternity to get a doctor's appointment in New York. This sounds suspiciously like your typical Beverly Hills celebrity service to me. Why do I have to go now?" Tessa asked, her voice childish with reluctance.

"You'll like her, Tessa."

"Oh, no doubt about that. I'll be crazy about her. I've always wanted to meet a medical oncologist."

How could a cancer doctor be so wholesomely pretty, have such flaming red curls, and look no more than thirty-eight or -nine? Tessa wondered, trying to distract herself as she sat in front of Dr. Susan Hill's desk. What kind of person could possibly choose to be an oncologist when there were so many other specialties in the world of medicine?

"Doctor Hill, how long have you been an oncologist?" Tessa asked, nervously, feeling as if she should be seeing a wise old man instead of this young woman, who could only be a few years older than she.

"I've been in practice for twelve years, Miss Kent," she said, smiling.

"May I call you Susan?" Tessa asked impulsively. She'd feel more comfortable if she didn't have to say "doctor" every five seconds.

"Of course, in fact I'd prefer it. And I'll try to call you Tessa, even though that seems a bit like name-dropping."

"Good. Is that your own hair color?" Tessa asked, nervous enough to ask any question she could think of that had nothing to do with her visit here. Susan Hill laughed.

"It used to be, until five years ago, but now I have to give it a little help. Still, I wouldn't feel like me without it."

"Where did you go to medical school?"

"Out in L.A., where I grew up. I graduated from UCLA Med School, and then I did my internship and residency at New York Hospital, when my husband and I moved here. I always wonder why doctors' diplomas are hung on the wall too far away for anybody to read them, but where else could you put them?"

Tessa Kent would run out of questions soon, Susan Hill thought, but she was right to ask as many as she wanted to. If you're going to an oncologist, you need to know something personal about him or her. It still didn't level the playing field: In time she'd end up knowing a great deal more about this strikingly vivid personality, this woman she'd seen on screen more than a dozen times, this actress who was so much more beautiful than she looked on film, than Tessa Kent could ever know about her.

"Why did you pick this particular specialty, Susan? How come you didn't want to be in something more agreeable, dermatology, for instance, or plastic surgery?"

"Because there's such immense progress being made in the field of cancer," the doctor answered, a smile of genuine enthusiasm flashing across her face. "It's the single most fascinating area of medicine today. This is where I can do the most interesting work and see real results."

"So, tell me, what's wrong with me?" Tessa asked abruptly, disgusted at her postponement of the questions she knew she should really be asking, instead of playing for time.

"I've studied the radiology and biopsy reports carefully." The doctor's smile faded. She'd rather have answered more questions. "They indicate a tumor of the pancreas."

"A tumor—you mean a cancer?"

"Yes."

Tessa felt death inhabit her body. Death, unmistakable. She closed her eyes and dropped her head, raking her hair back from her face with all the strength of her hands. She was going to faint, she thought dimly, through an icy mist.

"Put your head between your knees, yes, that's it, way down. Stay like that and breath deeply, long, deep breaths. Take your time, don't lift your head until you feel ready."

Eventually Tessa fought through the mist and faintness. She fought the word "death." Cancer *wasn't* death, cancer was cancer and she could be cured of it. She felt the doctor's hands on her shoulders, steadying her.

"Sorry," she said, lifting her head. "I didn't know people still almost fainted in this day and age."

"That's the least of it," Susan Hill said, pouring her a glass of water.

"Where exactly is the pancreas?" Tessa asked. Chemotherapy, she thought, draining the glass of water. Ten to one that's what she'd have to have, but her hair grew amazingly fast. If it all actually fell out, she could always wear wigs while her hair was growing back in. She was accustomed to wigs. No one need ever know.

"Look at this chart, Tessa. Here's the pancreas, that transverse organ, that looks like a longish, horizontal piece of liver, thick at one end, thin at the other. It's surrounded by the duodenum here, the liver here, the spleen, and the stomach. Your particular tumor is right here, at the thin end, where I'm pointing."

"It's a nasty-looking organ," Tessa said with as much bravado as she could. "What's the purpose of it?"

"It's a gland that secretes pancreatic juice, a fluid made of different enzymes that help in digestion, and it also secretes insulin."

"How important is it? Is it indispensable, Susan, like a heart or a liver?"

She was asking the right questions, Susan Hill thought, and going straight to the point. Tessa Kent was a smart, direct woman, making that serious effort certain patients were capable of to be thoroughly informed about something they've never before, under any circumstances, wanted to understand or even think about.

"No, it's not actually indispensable. There are some patients in whom the pancreas can be removed surgically. Then they can be maintained on artificial pancreatic fluid and insulin injections for the rest of their lives."

" 'Some patients'—do I need that operation, Susan?"

"No, Tessa, you don't. The only time to operate, what we call the 'resectable' time, is when the tumor is confined to the pancreas. Yours is not. You see, one of the problems with this particular tumor is that it doesn't cause any symptoms, such as pain, in its early stages, so it's rarely discovered at a time when an operation is possible. You wouldn't have known you had it at this point if you hadn't gone to a doctor for other reasons."

"So if Helen Lawrence hadn't sent me to Doctor Wing . . ."

"Exactly, you couldn't have known yet."

She only answered the questions a patient wanted to ask, Susan Hill thought. It was vital to let them set the pace of their tolerance for knowledge. No two patients were alike. They all had different points at which they turned off the spigot of understanding, a different comfort level at which they could accept or permit themselves to learn things. Tessa Kent looked, from the brilliant determination in her extraordinary green eyes, as if she were going to keep on going right to the end. If that was her choice, she had every right to know as much as it was possible to tell her.

"You said the tumor isn't confined to the pancreas?"

"No."

"Where did it spread to?" Tessa persisted.

"Certain lymph nodes close to the pancreas, the celiac nodes. Yours are enlarged, a sign that an operation isn't possible."

"Well, you can't get rid of my pancreas. So that's one option I don't have," Tessa said, squaring her shoulders. "What *will* you want to do next, what treatments are available? Is it going to be chemo or radiation or a combination of both?"

"You know a lot of medical terms."

Tessa had said "chemo" and "radiation" with such fine, careless courage, as if they were just two words without resonance, Susan Hill thought, yet she hadn't been able to hide the slight trembling of her lips. Her age, her age. Only thirty-eight. My God, but she was young. Much too young for this.

"I read a lot of magazines," Tessa explained, "and you can't get away from seeing articles about cancer, can you? And you can't always make yourself skip them, much as you'd like to. So what exactly are you planning to do to me?"

"I can't be 'exactly' sure, until we talk it over. We have treatments for pancreatic cancer that will prolong life," Susan Hill said carefully.

" *'Prolong'?*"

"Yes."

"*Prolong* . . . what the hell kind of word is that? It could mean anything! Look, Susan," Tessa demanded, suddenly ferocious, "say I take every single treatment you can throw at me, how long can I expect to be okay, after that?"

"That—that differs in each case."

"Damn it, give me an average!"

"Even if the treatments are successful, the tumor will eventually return—"

"How soon?" Tessa interrupted savagely.

"In a year and a half, perhaps two, perhaps a little bit longer."

This was where they'd been heading, but most people would never come this far, most people would not ask such precise questions. Susan Hill felt sick. Nothing, no amount of experience, had ever hardened her to this moment.

"So soon? So soon?" Tessa whispered. Her features were stone, her eyes almost black with shock.

"Tessa, in medicine there aren't any hundred-percent guarantees, I can only give you my best opinion, but I could be wrong, nothing is an absolute . . ."

"Susan," Tessa said desperately, "wait a minute, Susan, you said, perhaps longer than two years. Tell me what's the longest I can expect to be okay if everything goes well, the treatments work out perfectly and I get very lucky."

"It's an inexact projection. A little longer, a few months, perhaps even a little more . . ."

"And then? *What then?*"

"Tessa, there isn't a permanent cure for pancreatic cancer."

"You mean that I have an *incurable* cancer? You're telling me that even all the treatment in the world won't make it go away?"

She'd understood this sooner, Susan Hill thought, she'd heard in several different ways that the tumor would inevitably return, she'd grasped that perfectly, but she still insisted on making it crystal clear, in boiling it down to "incurable," a word she would not have used herself with a patient. Why, oh why was Tessa Kent so strong, so stubborn, a flagellant, determined to do herself the greatest damage she could? She was adamantly pronouncing the ultimate sentence on herself. Yet who had a greater right?

"Yes. Yes. Tessa, I wish I could say you were wrong but you're not. There are no miracles in this kind of cancer. I'm as sorry as it's possible to be. The most important thing I can offer you, Tessa, is a minimum of pain. The tail of the pancreas is where a tumor gives the least possible pain and most of that can be handled with narcotics. I believe in the most aggressive pain management possible."

Tessa was silent, trying to think through the iron casque of shock that enveloped her and invaded her brain with utter numbness. Wasn't there something else she could ask, something else that would give her some hope?

"Does everybody have treatment?" she asked, finally, barely able to offer the question.

"No, they don't. They decide that they don't want treatment, they don't want the side effects, since, well, since it's not going to fix the problem permanently."

"I see. If there's no 'fix,' Susan, the people who do choose to have treatment—why do they pick it?"

"Usually to try as hard as possible to be around for some special event, a child's graduation from college, for instance, or a grandchild's wedding or a golden wedding anniversary."

"So . . . so. That means I must be . . . very young . . . for this."

"You are. Exceptionally young."

"Is there anything I don't know? I don't want to go home and remember some question I forgot to ask."

"Tessa, I've almost never had a patient walk out of this office who asked every possible major question, but you have. You know all the options."

"You mean the lack of options, don't you?"

"This isn't one of the days I'm glad I went into oncology. I'm here for you, Tessa, for everything. Any other questions no matter how small, any fears, any medication, anything at all, at any time of day or night. That's my job. That's what I do. Will you let me know as soon as you've decided how you intend to handle matters?"

"Besides die, you mean."

"I mean I'm here for you . . ."

"Thank you for being so honest with me." Tessa got up carefully, so that she wouldn't stagger. She pulled herself up as tall as she could and forced a small smile.

"See you around, Susan."

"Yes, Tessa. Whenever you want, remember that."

30

Three hours after she had left Susan Hill's office, Tessa snapped out of a time period she would never rediscover in detail again, and found herself sitting in the Madison Avenue office of an unknown travel agent, about to sign an agreement to take one of the four Crystal Penthouses on the *Crystal Harmony* for a ninety-six-day world cruise that started in January in Los Angeles and crossed the Pacific going toward Hawaii and points west, following the sun.

"I'm sorry," she babbled to the travel agent, trying to hide her confusion. "I've just realized that I really can't take off ninety-six days. Oh my God, I must have been quite mad to think I could. I'm so terribly, terribly sorry to have wasted your time, please forgive me, I'm so very sorry."

"But Miss Kent, you insisted . . . I pulled every string to get the accommodations . . ."

"I'm so sorry, I'd really love to go, but it just isn't possible. Do forgive me, I'm sorry," she blurted and fled, carrying with her a full burden of shopping bags. She'd raided Bergdorf's, Tessa noticed as she dumped the contents of the bags on her bed back at the Carlyle.

She'd bought cruise clothes of every sort: a dozen pairs of fashionably flimsy high-heeled sandals, five bikinis, each with its own robe, a heap of imported lace underwear, seven tubes of designer lipstick, and a pile of sparkly, frilly summer dresses with little wraps to pull on over her shoulders.

Everything could be sent back to the store tomorrow, Tessa realized, and with that, she began to weep, slowly at first and then more and more violently, howling without words, wailing, high and shrill without any thoughts, lamenting ruinously without any end but the sheer brute need to weep her heart out. She was shaken by hugely mounting sobs, wrenching, painful sobs, wave upon wave of them, until she slowly stopped only because she had wept as much as her raw, aching eyes and throat could endure.

When she was able to look at her watch, Tessa realized that she must have been lying on her bed, her pillow over her head, pounding the mattress, for hours. If Sam had been home he'd have asked questions, and insisted on answers, she thought, and that was the one thing she was determined not to have happen. Her eyes were burning and felt enormous, stretched like the skin of some rotten fruit about to burst; she had a murderous headache and a hungry pain at the pit of her stomach.

How could she possibly be hungry? Tessa thought as she phoned room service for a double order of scrambled eggs and toast. She stood under a hot shower for a long time, and then, wrapped in her toweling bathrobe, took off the metal covers that had kept the eggs and toast warm, spread the toast with the entire contents of a pot of jam, and wolfed down everything, just to fill her stomach. She went to the bar and made a compress of ice wrapped in a napkin. She locked the door to the apartment, lay down on her sofa, put a big tumbler filled with iced vodka within reach, and adjusted a heap of pillows under her, intending to move the compress from place to place to try to make her eyes feel better.

She was exhausted, she told herself, she needed to rest, she needed, in the comfy English phrase, to put her feet up.

In a few seconds Tessa was shaken by a rage so destructive that it made it impossible for her to remain motionless on the sofa. Gulping the vodka, and pouring more, she paced back and forth, muttering to herself in an incoherent monologue composed of the vilest words she'd ever heard. She'd like to kill somebody, yes, more than anything, she'd like to hit and hit and hurt and hurt until somebody died. If she had the power she'd order a hundred executions, she'd hurl thunderbolts, she'd wipe out cities, she would, she meant it, she yearned to do it, she thought in a concentrated passion of fury that lasted for hours until, weak and drunk, she fell on her bed and slept dreamlessly, without moving.

She woke up at three A.M., disoriented at finding herself in her robe, lying on top of her quilt, her feet freezing. For a minute she remembered nothing of the previous day, and then it all came rushing back in a blast of realization so horrifying that she didn't think she could survive. Finally, forcing herself to think, she painfully began to reconstruct the entire conversation with Susan Hill, detail by detail.

It could not, it could not *possibly* be as bad as all that, she thought, with sudden, clear conviction, pulling on heavy socks. It couldn't be a death sentence, not because she had bad cramps. Helen Lawrence, Dr. Wing, Dr. Susan Hill, what did they know? Tomorrow she'd go to see some good doctors, better doctors, doctors who would tell her that the needle biopsy had been a mistake, that she had fallen into a nest of the worst, most unprofessional medical frauds you could find in the City of New York. Look how they all knew each other and passed her from one to another. She shook with hatred as she thought of them, people who hung a dozen diplomas on their walls and then lied and lied and lied for no reason at all except to frighten her.

Lied for no reason at all.

Fuck! If she could only manage to believe that. If *she could only prove it.* But they were all first-class physicians, each one of them, and she knew it, Tessa admitted, any other idea was absurd. She stared in utter confusion at her image in her mirror. She didn't look like a woman with no more than two years to live. If she was lucky, two years and a few months. If she wasn't, a year and a half. She'd only just turned thirty-eight. In two years she'd just reach forty. *Forty was nothing!* She looked like someone who'd spent a night with some brutal stranger she should never have gone home with, badly bruised around the eyelids, nostrils raw, cheeks mashed, her whole face disheveled and glazed but unquestionably very alive.

But she'd never reach forty. She'd never celebrate the birthday that foolish, lucky women complained about in make-believe misery, even lied about. Why did people lie about their age? Why wasn't every birthday a brilliant triumph to be toasted and celebrated, another year you could boast about because you'd survived? Were people utterly crazy, not to realize that survival was a gift of the gods, to take it for granted, to actually feel bad about getting older? *About having lived more life?* What were wrinkles, what were forty extra pounds or weakened muscles or gray hair, except signs of the best of good luck?

It was too much to bear. It was too unfair. It was the most unfair thing she'd ever heard of happening to anybody, nothing that had ever happened was unfair compared to this, not even Luke's death. It was the ultimate unfairness and no one to blame but some cells gone mad. She felt knocked to her knees by the unfairness, yanked and punished and dragged like a wet mop across the floor, skinned alive, gashed all over her body, gutted like a fish, yes, even nailed to a cross—*that* unfair, *exactly* that unfair, not a bit less, and not for any reason, any deed, any thing she'd ever done or said or thought. At least Christ had convictions He knew were worth dying for.

She wished, for the first time, that she hadn't lost her faith after Luke had died. Maybe then someone could try to convince her that this unfairness was for a purpose, but she knew it was random, she knew it was impersonal. Yet Tessa felt as if she'd been targeted, as if it were focused, as if some malevolent force loathed her, specifically her, with a direct, evil calculation that had already measured out the dose of poison that would kill her twice over. Random and targeted at the same time . . . that shouldn't make sense but it did.

She'd go back to the church and never miss an early morning mass or a Holy Day of Obligation or a single weekly confession if she could reach forty-five. All she asked was to be middle-aged . . . that unattainable heaven that other actresses dreaded. She'd never make love to Sam again if she could reach forty-five, or eat another good thing or drink another drink or buy another flower, if she could reach forty-five: she'd give up her work and give up Sam and slave in a homeless shelter eighty hours—a hundred and twenty hours—a week, she'd do anything . . . become a nun . . . if she could reach forty-five. Become a nun? As if they'd take her. Tessa had to smile bitterly at her own craziness. A nun indeed.

Tessa realized suddenly that she must have been steadily ripping apart a gauzy, sequined white dancing dress she'd bought earlier. It lay all around her in shreds and strips. She hadn't known she was doing it, she hadn't known she had that much strength in her hands. Was that what people meant when they talked about a frenzy of grief? Had she been rending her fucking garments? Well, she damn well wasn't going to do any more of that, she thought, angrily throwing the entire heap of clothes onto the floor of the nearest closet.

She knew only one thing with any certainty. She wasn't going to have any treatment. No chemo, no radiation. She wasn't interested in spending one second in a hospital or a doctor's office to see her nonexistent granddaughter get married. She'd never have another wedding anniversary or see anyone she loved graduate or celebrate a new decade of life. There would be no future of simple, daily joys with Sam, no more major markers in her life's history, no "remember-whens" to be talked about with Fiona when they were both wise enough to get out of the industry. She'd never face the need to think about a face-lift, she'd never know the regret of being over the hill, she'd never decide to take character roles—oh, she'd give anything to be too old to play another romantic part, *too old* to play a character part, the right age to play a crone, *a withered crone*, without makeup and have it believable!

She felt a blanket of the blackest depression, bleak, dismal, and hopeless, start to sneak over her, smothering and all-but-irresistible, and Tessa knew that if she didn't think of something else quickly, the two years she still had left could be spent, would be spent, in a hell of self-pity. She had used up years of her life mourning Luke. After he'd died, she'd actually believed she had no reason to live. How stupid she'd been! How wasteful! All those priceless days thrown away on grief. There was no time left, not a day, not a minute, to mourn for herself. It was a luxury she couldn't afford.

What did she have left? she asked herself, trying to focus. Sam? But how long could she keep this from him . . . how long could they love each other without the shadow of the future spoiling every minute? Her work? She couldn't play Cassie, she couldn't count on having the time to finish the film; they'd never get insurance on her now anyway. So, at best, she could assist Fiona in some way, and watch Streep play Cassandra Lennox, or if not Streep, another actress. All her friends in California and New York? Friends, Sam, work. Wasn't that more than a lot of people ever had? It was, she tried to tell herself, it really was. She'd had decades of stardom to look back on . . . Luke, she'd had her life with Luke. She'd had her year with Sam. How many women could say as much? Wasn't that enough? No, it wasn't. It was *not* enough.

She was going to be denied most of the experiences of a mature woman, there was no getting away from that. She would have no forties, no fifties, no sixties, no three score and ten. She would never accept it, she could never forgive it, but she knew it was a fact she had to bite into with all the power left to her.

Tessa saw her life stretching forward, a narrow ribbon, a short strip, with a sharp snip cutting it off not far from her feet, the ribbon curling back on itself. But narrow ribbon or not, she vowed, she would make it so full of reality that it would count as much as a longer stretch of time. For a moment she let herself make believe that nothing had happened, that she could release herself into the casual, unthinking dailiness of life, but she couldn't sustain the idea. The ribbon kept snapping and curling backward.

But . . . but . . . there existed one *essential* transaction she must make, a way to control her short future, one single thing she could do, one thing she still had time for, one experience no one could refuse her, one way to still create, to leave something behind that would show that she had lived a life outside of her films, some bit of her that would survive and make a difference.

She could make her peace with Maggie. She could know her daughter again. She could try to heal the rift between them.

There was time, Tessa thought, plenty of time for that. Her life had been cut short, but it hadn't been abruptly terminated, like her parents' lives, like Luke's life. There was still time, time for Maggie.

Maggie. She had a daughter and her daughter would have a daughter or a son some day. No cancer could take that chance away from her. A daughter who had inherited half of whatever she was would eventually, inevitably, have children of her own, descendants . . . her descendants, who would know that Tessa Kent had lived. . . .

Her excited thoughts slowed down. It had been

roughly five years since Maggie had refused to accept the millions Luke had left her. Maggie would have had a yearly income of hundreds of thousands of dollars. Had she even stopped to think of what she was turning down in her haste to have nothing to do with anything that linked her to her mother? Probably not in such detail. She was too young to understand the financial consequences of what she had done, but the gesture said clearly that she was not too young to have made up her mind, once and for all, that her mother was cast out of her life.

But that could not be allowed to stand. She would not permit it! She had her rights, damn it, cancer or not, and Maggie would have to admit them, whether she wanted to or not.

In five years, Tessa calculated, on fire with her idea, Maggie must have changed, must have mellowed. Five years were forever, she knew that now. Maggie was an adult, she'd passed her twenty-third birthday months ago. Tomorrow, yes tomorrow, she'd go to see her, go straight up to that apartment she was living in, that apartment Tessa had never ceased to have quietly checked out by a private investigator every six months, and confront Maggie, yes, have that confrontation she'd never dared to risk before because she believed that Maggie would shut the door in her face and that had seemed too much to endure. What a vile coward she'd been, to let so much time go by. She'd tell Maggie that she only had a short time to live, force her, *force her*, to listen, just to *listen*. That's all she asked.

No one could turn down a dying woman.

31

When Tessa woke up, after a few hours of fitful sleep, later that morning she knew, even before she opened her eyes, that the confrontation with Maggie she had been so convinced about in the middle of the night was a lousy idea.

If she presented herself as a dying woman, as a case for pity, no real relationship could be established between them, much less any honesty. It was hard enough, if an incurable disease struck one loving partner and not the other, to maintain the former balance between them. And she and Maggie were not, had never been, partners. Sisters, unequal sisters, but adults together, never. There must be another way to reach Maggie, a way that didn't involve anything to do with her health.

Maggie's work at S & S—that was the only path left to her, Tessa realized as she ate breakfast. She'd known Liz Sinclair socially and casually for years. They had many of the same acquaintances from the days when Luke was alive, and there wasn't anyone important in the auction business she didn't know.

Why? How? What reason could she give Liz Sinclair

to explain that she had to talk to Maggie Horvath, had to see Maggie Horvath?

Suddenly Tessa knew what to do. She had Liz Sinclair on the phone in minutes.

"Tessa Kent, what a lovely surprise! I couldn't imagine how you'd managed to disappear from sight in the last year, although I did hear something about a devastating professor, hmm? How are you, Tessa? It's been so long, Hamilton was just saying—"

"Liz, I haven't time to be polite. Just assume we've had ten minutes of charming small talk. I intend to auction my jewels, everything but my green diamond and a few strings of pearls."

"Tessa!"

"For charity, of course. That goes without saying. S and S has the auction . . . no Liz, don't interrupt, there's no need to compete with another auction house, no need to give me a guarantee, it's yours on one single condition. I don't want to work with Lee Maine on the publicity. She's tremendously good, I know, but I want to work exclusively with Maggie Horvath. Why? Liz, I know that Maggie's made it a point of pride never to trade on it, but she's my younger sister. I was born Teresa Horvath."

"What! Good grief, Tessa, I had no idea . . ."

"I know you didn't. Maggie and I have actually been, well, I suppose one could call it, at arm's length, for the past few years. Actually an estrangement. We haven't spoken, can you imagine? Silly family stuff. I want to end that. Now. Quickly."

"But, but . . . sell *all* your jewels! Tessa, are you sure? You could never duplicate . . ."

"Liz, what a tender-hearted woman you turn out to be," Tessa said, impatiently. "Hamilton would be shocked if he heard you. Of course I'm sure. They're only . . . things. Very lovely things, but they don't have hearts."

"Well, no, of course not, Tessa—" Liz said, still almost dumbstruck by this turn of fortune.

"I expect you to make it the biggest single-owner auction since the Duchess of Windsor's," Tessa continued. "My jewels are easily equal in quality to anything she had, and there are a great many more of them. *And I'm alive, Liz.* Not a dead duchess. I can publicize the sale from here to Saudi Arabia and I will. But it all depends on your delivering Maggie to work on the publicity with me. She won't want to do it, I'm pretty sure of that. And if she refuses, I won't sell the jewels, not anywhere. It's either S and S or no one. And it has to be quick, within six months, no more. I know that's short notice, less than you need for your usual preparation, but that's the way it has to be," Tessa said firmly. If she allowed more time, how much would she have left in which to be with Maggie, be with her as a proper mother! S & S could do it in six months if they pulled out all the stops.

"Good God Almighty, Tessa, I'm stunned. I may faint."

"I tend to doubt that, Liz. As soon as you've set up a meeting with the director of your jewelry department, you and Hamilton and I can get started. But Maggie has to be there, right from the start."

"I understand. I'll call you as soon as I've talked to Maggie."

"Thank you, Liz. Use all your powers of persuasion. It's vitally important."

"Never fear. I'll make it happen or die trying."

"We'll both do that, Liz."

"Maggie, Mrs. Sinclair wants you to go up and see her right away," one of the assistants said, after she'd answered the interoffice phone.

"She say why?"

"No, just get moving."

"Miz Liz," Maggie said cheerfully upon entering Liz's office. "You wanted to see me?"

"Yes, sit down, Maggie, and have some tea."

"No tea, thanks. What's going on?"

"It's complicated, Maggie. It concerns the future of the house."

"How's that?"

"You know we're not the top dogs and never will be."

"S and S is still a mighty big business."

"How come you didn't take that offer from Sotheby's?"

"You knew about that?"

"In the auction world everybody gets to know everything, sooner or later."

"I simply decided I liked it better here than I could anywhere else. I'm happy as a lark. I truly love working with Lee and you and Hamilton—you've all been wonderful to me since my days as a temp, so why should I change all that, even for more money? Although, Liz, if you've called me up here to offer me a raise, I accept."

"I'm offering you a chance to help me with a great opportunity, one I never dreamed we'd have."

"An opportunity? What kind?" Maggie asked eagerly.

"Something's come up, something that would do more for S and S than anything else that could happen, ever. We've been offered a historic sale, a fantastic sale of one of the finest, most famous private collections in the world, almost certainly the finest in this country."

"Oh Liz, great news! What's the sale?"

"It's a single-owner sale that will get us more publicity than either you or I can imagine. It's a sale, Maggie, that will make S and S a true worldwide household word for the first time since it was founded. There's no question that it will put us on a par, as far as status goes, with Sotheby's and Christie's. Smaller, yes, but *just as good*. That would mean everything to Hamilton, and to all of us. This sale will open the door to dozens, hundreds of other great sales in the future. People will think of us who've never even considered consigning their property to S and S. It's not an exaggeration to say that this sale will change our future forever."

"But you still haven't told me what it is—are you trying to make me beg? And what about Lee? Why are you telling me first?"

"Because you have it in your power to make sure that this sale takes place. You also have it in your power to prevent the sale, to keep it from ever happening."

"Oh, Liz! For heaven's sake! How could that ever be?"

"Maggie, the sale . . . it's . . . the jewels of Tessa Kent."

"You . . . you . . ." Maggie stopped and looked away, shaking her head in total negation.

"Maggie, I know she's your sister. She called this morning and told me. I know the two of you have problems, but Maggie, dear Maggie, you see the only reason she's willing to auction her jewels is to get a chance to be reconciled with you. She wants you, not Lee, to handle the press. How terrible can that be, Maggie? It's a job you're thoroughly capable of doing. Tessa said she'd never sell her jewels unless you were in charge of the publicity."

"No, Liz, no, she can't get at me through you."

"Maggie, the older I get the more I realize that happiness depends on people, not things. You can't get through life without family and a few good friends. Much as I adore my husband, my life has been deeply enriched by my daughters and Hamilton and Minnie more than I can tell you."

"No, Liz."

"Whatever the problem is with you and Tessa, believe me, as the two of you get older, you'll *need* each other. The ancient hurts and hostilities will come to seem unimportant, even absurd. In time you'll forget the details. But the two of you—sisters—will have something priceless together in the years to come, someone to talk to who remembers the same family things you do, who came from the same parents and grandparents, who understands you from the earliest days, who speaks your language the way no friend ever can . . ."

"Liz, I do realize what family sentiment means," Maggie said, forcing herself to sound patient and reasonable. "But what went wrong between us isn't something any auction can change."

"You don't know, you can't be sure of that! Tessa's willing to help with the publicity on this in every way, travel with the jewels to previews and exhibitions, pose for any pictures, do any television—Tessa Kent, one of the rare, truly great stars, Tessa Kent who so rarely gives an interview, the very famously private Tessa Kent. Oh, Maggie, just think what that would mean to us! Her only stipulation is that the auction has to take place no later than six months from now. Of course we really need a year to do it right, but what could I say? She intends to give the proceeds to charity, maybe that has something to do with it. I didn't find out what the rush was, I was too excited, but it will mean a mountain of immediate work, a triple-time rush, I'll get you all the extra help you need—"

"She said six months? Exactly that and no more?"

"Yes."

"Then you can't expect me to give you an answer in six minutes," Maggie said, red-faced with suppressed words, as she took her leave.

"Polly, I have to talk to you," Maggie yelled through the door. She'd left the office right after she'd talked to Liz and hurried home to take counsel with Polly. This wasn't something Barney and she could discuss. He didn't know anything about Tessa and her.

"Keep your hair on. I'm coming." Polly unlatched her door and watched calmly as Maggie dashed in like a furious ball of dark tumbleweed, turning around and around for a place to light.

"Oh, do sit down, for mercy's sake. What's the matter? Had a fight with your very own Barney? Already?"

"Of course not. It's Tessa, can you believe it, after all these years?"

"Did she try to get in touch with you again?"

" 'In touch'? Oh yes, you could say that. She's blackmailing me the strongest way she knows how. She's offered S and S an auction of her jewels—but only on condition that I run the press on it, meaning we'd be in constant daily contact for six months. Liz has just been at me, singing siren songs, playing hearts and flowers, telling me that the future of the house depends on me, and me alone. Pure blackmail. That, Miss Polly, is why I'm in a state."

"Mercy."

"How well expressed, how finely spoken. Mercy, indeed. Tessa's probably got the greatest collection in the world except for a few Saudi ladies who can't wear them in public, the several wives of the Sultan of Brunei, and Queen Elizabeth."

"She must really be desperate to make up with you, Maggie," Polly said, in her most serious, thoughtful voice.

"Guilt, pure guilt. Although why it struck her now I can't imagine."

"I can't either. But something's better than nothing. At least she feels bad enough to sacrifice her jewels."

"And I'm supposed to make her feel better about all those years of rejection by helping her make a terrific success of the auction? Hah—at least it's for charity."

"Something tells me that she wants to feel better by getting closer to you. I'm sure she can't be eager to part with her jewels. She could just give the money to charity if that were all it was, she has enough. People don't usually sell their jewels unless they need money or they're dead, do they?"

"They're absurdly important to her, she's fixated on them, that's something I'm sure of. We used to play with them, dress up in them . . . talk about them end-lessly . . ."

"Why are you still so opposed to trying for some sort of, oh, I don't know, I hate to say 'relationship' but I can't think of another word to replace it."

"Oh, not now Polly, not when I'm so happy," Maggie cried fervently. "I've put her out of my mind, forgotten about her. Why reopen old wounds?"

"Is that fair?"

"I don't give a flying fuck if it's fair or not. That woman has no right to expect *me* to be *fair*. How can you even ask me that sickeningly sanctimonious question, Miss Priss? 'Fair' my ass!"

"So you still want to punish her? The way you do when you regularly send her letters back without reading them? Nothing's changed in five years. You haven't let it. Talk about carrying a grudge, you're the champ."

"You do say what's on your mind, don't you?"

"That's what it is, isn't it? Pure punishment?"

"Right. And it's the least I can do."

"First you turn down money, then you send back letters, now you won't work on a big exciting auction—wouldn't that be good for your career?"

"Damn right it would. Of course what motivates Liz is the world-beating, slam-bang auction that's going to make such a difference for S and S."

"Will it?"

"Of course it will. It'll dwarf anything else this year."

"And you said no?"

"Several times, Polly, trust me."

"So now you're punishing Liz and Hamilton and the entire house of S and S too, not just Tessa Kent? Can't you let it go? Can't you stop being so desperately something or other—immovable, proud, stiff-necked, hard, stubborn, impossible? That's certainly not the Maggie Horvath I know and love."

"When were you elected to become the voice of my conscience?"

"The day you moved in, a sad, lonely case, really

needing a place to live, and I fed you for months, or rather years to be exact, and let you rent my beautiful room, and became your best friend and still am."

"*Low blow.*"

"Well?"

"I'll think about it. Bitch!"

32

"Want to eat here tonight, sweetheart, or go out for Chinese food?" Sam asked Tessa soon after he arrived back at the apartment, three days after she'd spoken to Liz Sinclair.

"How hungry are you?" Tessa asked, holding him as tightly as she could.

"I'm not, really. I had an enormous lunch with the head of my department, he's a two-fisted eater and if you don't match him bite for bite he broods and sulks. Rumor has it that a young professor was once fired for ordering nothing but a salad."

"Could we just sit here for a while? I have something I have to tell you."

"That sounds ominous. You haven't stopped loving me? You don't want me to pack my bag and go? Because, you'd have to physically remove me and you're half my size."

"Nothing like that. This is all about me."

"Now that'll be a treat—you talk about yourself less than any female I've ever known. If you weren't so famous, you'd be my wonderful little secret, my very own private woman of mystery."

Sam's love for her showed so openly, so happily, and with such a lack of complication, that Tessa could scarcely endure it.

"Sam, sit down, drink your drink, and listen to me. Don't interrupt. I have to get this out all at once."

"Tessa, what the hell—"

"Just listen. *Please*. When I was fourteen I had a baby. Maggie. Mary Margaret Horvath. My parents brought her up as my sister, to hide the disgrace. By the time Maggie was three I'd already made *Little Women*. I'd become Tessa Kent. I neglected her shamefully, I was too wrapped up in my own future, too full of ambition, too high on my own totally wonderful self, to even *think* of getting to know her. I had plenty of opportunities because I lived at home for the next three years, but I allowed my mother to take over Maggie completely, I never even put up a fight. I was . . . grateful; it meant one less distraction in my exciting, brilliant, self-important life."

"Oh, come on Tessa, that's not you at all, that's—"

"Then I met Luke and married him," Tessa continued without giving Sam a chance to say more. "I was twenty, Maggie was five. I never told Luke about her, although now there's no question in my mind that if I had, right at the start, he would have accepted the fact that Maggie existed. Hell, he was forty-five, a grown-up, a kind man, and I knew he was crazy about me. There was a window of opportunity, and I blew it. He wanted to think I was a virgin, right from our first date, and I let him believe I was. That was the worst of my lies. Afterward, I couldn't admit I wasn't—not that I was remotely tempted to—I lied and lied, even on our wedding night. I could never be honest—no, I *could* have been, Sam—I could have but I chose not to."

"Tessa, you're so hard on yourself, you were a kid—"

"You weren't there, Sam, I was. I'm merely being accurate. The week Luke and I were married, my parents died in an accident and Maggie was left all alone. *I let her go, Sam,* I let her go to Luke's stepbrother's family, the Websters, and grow up there. My daughter could have grown up with Luke and me, with a mother and a stepfather, instead of being stashed away with strangers, but I never had the courage to admit she wasn't my sister. I was an utter coward, a shameful coward."

"Tessa—"

"Don't, Sam, let me finish. I visited Maggie from time to time, and she visited me, not nearly as often as it should have been. I never truly knew if she was happy or not. I could have found out, so quickly, if I'd only had the guts to ask her the right questions, but I kept our relationship bright and easy and utterly superficial. The truth must be that I didn't really *want* to know, not in my heart of hearts. That was easier for me. So much less complicated. My life with Luke came first. Before my own daughter, Sam. I wasn't even a good sister to her. All the real family Maggie ever had was this remote movie-star creature who threw glamour dust at her every once in a while instead of steady, daily love and caring. Barney, the Websters' son, adored her. That's all the real love she got, Sam, from the time she was five until she was eighteen. That was most of her life—she's twenty-three now. Even after Luke died I didn't tell her."

"Then why now—?"

"Wait! Maggie found out I was her mother when she was eighteen, five years ago. I'd finally decided the time had come to tell her, but she found out first. She's never spoken to me since, or opened a single letter I've sent her. There's one chance left, but I'm afraid Maggie won't let it happen."

"One chance for what?"

"To somehow get closer to Maggie."

"Are you looking for forgiveness?"

"I guess . . . oh, shit, of course I am!"

"I don't blame you."

"If there's the slightest chance, it's worth trying. Maggie works in publicity for S and S, the auction house. I called a friend there, one of the owners, and told her I'd sell all my jewels at auction, but only on the condition that Maggie would work on the sale. That way we'd be thrown together all the time and she'll have to talk to me, and maybe . . . but I don't know yet if she will or won't."

"Do you have a lot of jewels?" he asked, in surprise. "All I've ever noticed is this unbelievable green rock and some pearls. Oh, and those cameos you were wearing the day we met."

"Oh, Sam, darling Sam, Cleopatra had more jewels than I do, I'm sure, but yes, I have jewels. I just don't wear them with you or your friends. They're a . . . distraction."

"You mean something like a million bucks' worth of jewelry?" he asked incredulously.

"Tens of millions."

"That just might have made the wrong impression at faculty parties." Sam gave a snort of laughter. "When will you know?"

"When Liz Sinclair calls me. I have very little hope."

"If there is an auction, when will it be?"

"I told them it had to be held within six months, I don't want this situation to drag on and on."

"Will it take up a lot of your time?"

"Almost all, and I'll have to travel a lot to publicize it."

"Tessa, we've been together for a year and you've never said a thing about Maggie. You never so much as told me that you had a sister. Is it because of the auction that you told me the whole story tonight?"

"No, Sam, no! There probably won't be an auction and I certainly could have waited to find out if it was going to happen. But I couldn't stand lying to you anymore, lying by not saying anything, even though chances are you would never have known." She couldn't tell him everything at once, Tessa thought with a twinge of guilt.

"And even though you thought I might stop loving you. Admit it, you did think that. I know you so well now, I could tell."

"But how *can* you keep loving me, Sam?"

"You made one hell of a lot of mistakes, rotten judgment calls, you were a thoroughly lousy mother and not even a decent sister. But that was then and this is now, and there's hope for you, Tessa Kent. So you thought I would change, you actually believed that was possible?"

"Yes."

"I guess you don't really know me yet," Sam said, grabbing her and pulling her tight. Tessa sobbed into his shirt for long, unutterably relieved minutes while he kissed her hair and patted her back as if she were a baby. Finally, she looked up at him, her mascara running down her cheeks, and said, "You haven't even asked what this will do to the movie schedule, how long we'll have to postpone starting production."

"What movie?"

The next day Maggie, grim-faced but bowing to the arguments of wily, irrefutable Polly Guildenstern and to her own intensely rooted loyalty to S & S, agreed to handle the publicity for the auction of the jewels of Tessa Kent.

A preliminary meeting was immediately scheduled for the following morning, a meeting that would include only Liz and Hamilton; Tessa; Maggie; Monty Foy, the director of S & S's jewelry department; and Juliet Tree, the director of marketing. As within every auction house, the big sale, or the prospect of one, was a tightly held secret known only to the few top people who would work on it from the very beginning.

Everyone but Maggie had arrived and taken their places around a table by the appointed time. Earlier that morning Liz had gathered Monty Foy and Juliet Tree together and told them that the only reason S & S had the prospect of Tessa Kent's auction was that Maggie Horvath was Tessa's younger sister. Unless Maggie ran the press, there would be no sale, but they must not make any reference to that fact during the meeting.

They had to be informed, she realized, so that they wouldn't make a gaffe about the absence of Lee Maine, who normally would have been there.

Tessa had refused to sign the Master Consignment Agreement even after she'd telephoned her with the news that Maggie would participate, Liz thought, tapping her foot. Tessa was waiting to see if Maggie was actually going to show up, in spite of Liz's assurances, and by now, Maggie, who was usually so punctual, was ten minutes late.

"Who'll have more tea or coffee?" Liz asked, presiding as she always did at staff meetings, behind a Georgian silver service.

"I'd love another cup of coffee, Liz," the normally collected Monty Foy said nervously, rubbing his bald head in an automatic gesture.

If that man has more coffee he'll explode from nerves, Liz thought, glad that she'd substituted decaf without telling anyone. She knew she couldn't take another drop of caffeine herself, without risk, to say nothing of Hamilton, who looked as taut as she'd ever seen him.

The presence of Tessa Kent certainly did nothing to lower the level of tension in the room, Liz noted, trying not to look at her watch. In most cases, the owner of a collection is dead. Everyone in the room was accustomed to dealing with heirs, using tact, discretion, and tacit sympathy. The auction business, Liz reflected, is a profoundly people business, a service business that has to please everyone, sellers and buyers, yet an infernally delicate business because you can never forget that you're coping with people who are in varying degrees of pain about selling their personal property, so often things they care about but can't afford to keep.

However, the presence of one of the most radiant film stars in history sitting at their conference table changed everything. To all of them, even to her, Liz realized, Tessa Kent was the sum of many things, the unforgettable roles she'd played, the Oscars she'd won, the sheer mythology of her Hollywood glamour, the cloak of inaccessibility she'd drawn around herself for twenty years, her position as Luke Blake's widow, and, of course, her jewels, that incredible collection of jewels that was not, until the contract had been signed, theirs to sell. And it was impossible to keep your eyes off her beauty, which made them all look as if they belonged to another species.

"Miss Kent," asked Juliet Tree, breaking the silence, "have you seen the Sotheby's catalog of the Thurn und Taxis Collection belonging to Princess Gloria that's being sold in Geneva in November?"

"I glanced at it the other day," Tessa replied.

Just what had given the otherwise clever Juliet the idea of mentioning Sotheby's at this particular moment? She must stop grinding her teeth, Liz told herself. The dentist had warned her about that. Let him go into the auction business, that fussy little man, he wouldn't last a week.

"I guessed it would interest you," Juliet continued, "since it's a single-owner catalog, and those, you know, are exceedingly rare. Did you happen to notice the three-page genealogy of the House of Thurn und Taxis in the front?"

"How could I miss it?" Tessa answered. "All those princes and princesses, with an archduke or an infanta or a king thrown in now and then, related to half the aristocracy of Europe, and the whole thing based on running a better postal service. Just imagine what I might have accumulated if, like Princess Gloria, I'd married a man whose family had started transporting mail for the Holy Roman Empire five hundred years ago? But alas, my genealogy is shorter, simpler, and vastly more humble. There seemed to be an abundance of tiaras in the sale. I wonder how many people are in the market for tiaras? Of all the jewelry, I preferred the green beryl and diamond brooch in the form of the neck badge of the Order of the Golden Fleece . . . it was fantastic enough to have been designed by Verdura."

Why was she chatting on and on like this? Tessa wondered, feeling her hands cold with sweat. She'd never been one to chat, especially with perfect strangers.

"You mean . . . Miss Kent, you're going to keep on buying jewels after your own auction?" Monty Foy asked, agog, putting out his cigarette.

I'd kill him, Liz thought, but death would be too good for that fool.

"Well, who knows if this auction is even going to happen," Tessa said lightly. "Maggie doesn't seem to be showing up, does she? But no, Mr. Foy, I'm not selling my jewels in order to start buying more. I was interested in the extraordinary light green of the beryl. After all, what is an emerald but a beryl with traces of chromium in it? I love green jewels more than any others. Give me a peridot rather than a diamond any day. On the other hand, I've never said no to an emerald. In fact, I've always gone rather seriously overboard about them. No one is aware of it, but after my husband's death, I started collecting. Collecting seriously, as a connoisseur, not just to wear. It seemed to comfort me. But, of course, you'll see everything for yourself, depending on Maggie, that is. I'm almost ashamed to confess it but many of the great jewels that were bought at auction by phone, anonymously, during the past four or five years were sent straight home to me."

Good God, Liz thought, she has even more than all the jewels we've seen her wearing in photographs. I can't stand this. *Maggie, where the bloody hell are you?*

"In fact," Tessa continued, "I've just remembered something I noticed last night—about the color photos in the Thurn und Taxis catalog. They were better than any I've ever seen for any auction, but not good enough to satisfy me. Who works on the catalogs?"

"I do, Miss Kent," Juliet Tree answered. "That falls into the marketing department."

"I want Irving Penn to take the photographs, all of them. It would make the catalog a permanent artistic treasure, like his flower books."

"Penn! But . . . but . . . he's—he's the most expensive—"

"I'm aware of that. Even Estée Lauder pales at his prices. I'll pay for them myself, of course. Always assuming that there is an auction."

"Tessa," Liz asked, clutching at anything to keep her staff from returning to the magnificent Thurn und Taxis catalog, "have you decided which charities you plan to give the proceeds to?"

"Cancer research, Liz, curable cancer. First breast cancer and then others. I'll have to educate myself about where the greatest progress is being made, if, that is, the auction actually takes place."

"Lung cancer?" Monty Foy asked curiously.

"No, that's incurable, didn't you know?" Tessa said. "You may live with it for quite a while, but you can never cure it."

The urbane Mr. Foy paled. He'd smoked a cigarette just before the meeting. It would, he vowed, be the last he'd ever smoke. He wished he'd known, he might have enjoyed it more. Or less.

Hamilton Scott couldn't keep silent any longer. "*If* the auction takes place, as you put it, Miss Kent, we'd be well advised to make sure that no other big jewelry sales are scheduled at Sotheby's or Christie's for the same time period. And we'd have to light a fire under Mr. Penn, today if possible."

"But I've already established a firm time frame, Mr. Scott," Tessa answered, irritated. "Didn't Liz tell you that any sale has to take place no later than six months from now?"

"We will, naturally, respect your desires, but I still don't quite understand the reason for such haste," he persisted, undeterred. Tessa Kent might be the most important consignor they'd ever had, but his family had been running auctions for almost two hundred years.

"That's the way it is," Tessa snapped. She wasn't about to explain her reasons to anyone, she thought wrathfully. And if Penn couldn't take the pictures quickly enough, she'd find another great still-life photographer who could, not that there was anyone who came close. It could be made to happen quickly in Hollywood. What was wrong with these plodding, cautious auction people? She felt herself beginning to get warm with growing rage. She didn't like pompous Hamilton Scott. She should have gone to Sotheby's . . . but Maggie didn't work there, worse luck.

"More tea? More coffee?" I'm starting to squeak, Liz Sinclair thought. If only she'd thought of getting Danish pastries or bagels, the wait might seem shorter. Maggie was well over a half hour late as it was. She must have changed her mind and be too embarrassed to admit it, damn the girl! Why hadn't she had the gumption to phone?

"Give me some tea, Liz," Hamilton Scott grumbled. "Whoever made this coffee should be fired."

"I'll get a floater to brew a fresh pot," Liz said, wishing her look were a death ray and she could make her brother disappear in a puff of smoke.

"Sorry! Sorry everybody, the bus broke down, we all had to get out, the next three buses were so full that they didn't even stop, so I had to walk the rest of the way," Maggie said breathlessly as she slid into the vacant chair between Juliet Tree and Monty Foy. She busied herself with opening her handbag and taking out a notebook and pencils, not looking at anyone in the room, a neutral expression fixed firmly on her face.

Tessa's heart was cleft by a burst of thanksgiving at the sound of Maggie's voice. She could find no armor to protect herself from her emotions. She felt as bare, as stripped, as she'd ever felt in her life.

"I believe we can get started now," said Liz Sinclair, managing to remain majestic as she slid the Master Consignment Agreement across to Tessa, who was seated next to her, and indicating the place for Tessa's signature. As soon as Tessa scrawled her name, Liz continued. "From now on, Maggie, you're to travel with a car and driver. Your time's too valuable to be wasted."

"Great," Maggie responded, opening her notebook and arranging her pencils according to some unknown order.

She won't look at me, Tessa thought, but oh, she's here, she's here. Tears started into her eyes as she stared hungrily at Maggie, all but a stranger after five years, a self-assured, consummate New Yorker, transformed, God knows how, into one of the bright-eyed, swift, strong, stunningly self-possessed young women who strode the streets of the city as if they owned them. Maggie, her flamboyant, downright voluptuous daughter, who owed her nothing, whose difficult path through childhood and adolescence had been traversed without her, Maggie who'd created herself triumphantly, with the only cards she'd been dealt. Maggie, almost unbelievably, was here today, ready to go to work. Maggie, her daughter.

"Maggie," Tessa managed to say, "you look wonderful."

"Feelin' fine," Maggie replied briefly, with a nod at the room in general.

She won't say my name, Tessa thought. She won't look at me. But she's here. We've made a start. Thank you, God.

33

I t could be called "unseemly haste," Tessa reflected, as she sat and watched the transfer of her jewels to the possession of the house of Scott & Scott, or it could be called an intelligent use of time. Each day for the next six months had suddenly become vital once she'd signed the Master Consignment Agreement and made the auction a reality.

It was only hours since this morning's meeting and yet Monty Foy and two of his assistants had begun an inventory of every piece of jewelry she owned, in a room two stories underground that the bank had put at their disposal.

Tessa sat next to the table where they worked, watching them carefully open each jewel box and take out and triple-check each item in low, colorless voices, each man scrutinizing the piece in question and repeating its description. They wrote a preliminary account of each item on a separate sheet of paper, which Monty Foy gave her to sign, and then replaced the contents, closed each box, and added a special seal. Outside the room a large team of couriers and armed guards waited.

In the room, at their feet, lay a heap of heavy canvas

bags, worn and battered briefcases, and sturdy paper shopping bags in which, as each day's inventory was completed, the jewels would be distributed and hand-carried from the bank to S & S in specially rented taxis and ordinary cars. Foy estimated that they'd be finished in three days.

They undoubtedly knew what they were doing, Tessa thought. Harry Winston usually employed the U.S. Postal Service to deliver his precious pieces; Van Cleef had always given her unmarked, plain manila envelopes to slip her purchases into. Did any jeweler but Tiffany's advertise with those unmistakable turquoise bags, which so often, after a trinket had been taken home, were used to hold brown-bag lunches until they fell apart?

The velvet mountain of unopened boxes that had been assembled from her various vaults seemed to diminish slowly, yet the pile of sealed boxes on a four-wheeled metal carrier, which looked like a miniature airport baggage truck, grew steadily as the highly trained men worked in deep concentration.

It was vital, Tessa had been told, to make the transfer as quickly as possible so that S & S's experts could begin to examine each jewel for an estimate of its value. Their resident experts in the Geneva, Zurich, and London offices had all been notified to come to New York immediately to help Monty Foy and his juniors, who couldn't possibly cope with the volume of work required.

The catalog would require a highly detailed description of the size, condition, and number of specific jewels contained in each and every piece, as well as all the details available of provenance. The appraisers would examine every piece and send them through the S & S jewelry laboratories for a thorough check of the quality of each jewel before they set the high and low estimates of what the piece was likely to sell for on the open market, its "fair market value."

All jewelry bought at retail, rather than at auction, is routinely marked up to include the retailer's profit, his insurance, the reputation of his establishment, his advertising, and his cost of doing business. Prices at an auction are less than retail prices by a high of fifty to sixty percent, and a low of twenty-five percent, of the retail price. Tessa knew this, particularly since she'd started collecting.

Going into a great jeweler's, selecting a jewel, and taking it home was a luxury for which one paid dearly. But Luke, like the majority of jewelry customers, had been willing to pay that huge markup for the pleasure of dealing with the top jewelers of the world, for their individual design styles, for the knowledge that they stood behind their wares and vouched for their quality, and most particularly for the human desire to buy exactly what you wanted when you wanted it, especially when it was intended as a gift.

As each box was opened, Tessa felt herself getting more and more irrationally disturbed at the sight of three strange men handling her property. They were as dignified, respectful, and ceremonial as priests serving mass, as they went about their task. But how did they dare so much as touch her jewels, she raged, feeling her heart beat faster and faster as each box was opened and its contents were gently taken out and thoroughly inspected.

When she'd signed the Consignment Agreement, the "contract" as everyone called it, she hadn't realized that she would actually witness this scene, this hideous desecration, this rape! So far, everything they'd inventoried had been given to her by Luke. Monty Foy had put his nicotine-stained paws all over the same jewels Luke covered her with before they made love. Now the odious man was holding up the emerald necklace Luke had given her in Èze, on their honeymoon, and intoning, in his detestably monotonous and oily voice, "One emerald and diamond necklace, five pear-shaped emeralds, one pear-shaped emerald pendant, detachable, all six emeralds set in diamonds."

His mere contact with the necklace violated one of

her most precious memories, made it vanish into a crass transaction, drained it of its magic, turned to ashes the memory of her innocent bliss on that thrilling evening. She'd had no idea how violently it would hurt.

Tessa turned her head away from the table, concentrating on her engagement ring, trying to escape the sight and sound of the three men, until the moment she had to quickly turn back to sign each description. She was filled with a feeling of astonished wrath at herself. Had she been pig-stupid enough to decide to sell her jewels at auction without ever truly comprehending, in her heart, that an auction meant that she would have to strip herself of these beloved symbols of her past? Was she so slow-witted that she'd believed she could avoid the outrage of strangers treating her most personal belongings as mere objects? Hadn't she understood that many other women would soon be wearing, at their ears, their wrists, their throats, the only tangible remains of her most private moments? "Oh, yes, you're absolutely right, it did come from Tessa Kent's sale," said with a self-satisfied laugh! Couldn't she accept the fact that this surprisingly painful defilement was the price she had chosen to pay? Had she somehow had the notion, baroque in its elaborate flourishes, that she could sell her jewels and keep them at the same time? Hadn't she known that finding a way to have access to Maggie would come at a severe price?

Shut the fuck up and stop complaining, you ridiculous little twit, she told herself savagely. Just because Maggie never once looked at you today, just because she rushed off halfway through the meeting in order to huddle with Juliet Tree and Penn's rep, is no reason to whimper. There are almost six months to go. Anything can happen. Something *must* happen. Nothing was guaranteed except that Maggie and she would be working together on the auction.

"One triple-strand ruby necklace, set in diamonds . . ." Monty Foy had reached the boxes and boxes of rubies, carefully set aside in their own vault, not one of which Tessa had touched since Luke's death. She would have gotten rid of them long ago, but even the idea of coping with their existence had been too much to face. She couldn't stand the sight of them.

"I'm going out to get a cup of coffee," she said, rising abruptly.

"But we can't continue without you," Monty Foy said. "I can't touch these boxes unless you're here to verify the inventory."

"For Christ's sake, Mr. Foy, I trust you. You're not going to stuff them in your pockets! Or smoke them! Finish the inventory of every last ruby without me and I'll initial each sheet of paper," she ordered him.

"I'm afraid I can't do that, unless you appoint someone, a lawyer or an accountant, to do it in your place."

"Send in one of those security people."

One of Foy's assistants opened the door and motioned to the first man standing against the door.

"What's your name?" Tessa asked him.

"Bernie Allen, ma'am."

"Mr. Allen, please witness the inventory of my rubies, sign each paper Mr. Foy gives you, and I'll sign them again when you're finished."

"Yes, ma'am." He raised an eyebrow at Monty Foy, who shrugged his shoulders and waved him forward.

Tessa left the room and headed for the ladies' room at the end of the corridor. Suddenly, walking toward her, dark against the glare of the fluorescent light, was the tall, slender shape of a girl wearing the black outfit Maggie had had on this morning. Tessa's hand flew to her throat. Maggie! Oh, Maggie! The girl approached, and quickly she realized that it wasn't Maggie but a stranger, with dark red hair worn in close-cropped curls, dressed in that black quasi-uniform they all wore.

"Miss Kent, I'm Janet Covitz, Maggie's assistant press officer. She sent me over to see if there was anything you needed. Can I get you a cup of tea or a Coke or some Perrier? Have they made you comfortable in there? Are there any personal errands you'd like me to run for you while you witness the inventory? Any phone calls you'd like me to make? Maggie told me to tell you that from now on I'll be totally at your disposal."

"No, thank you, Janet, nothing. I'm just taking a breather. What do you mean, 'totally at my disposal'?"

"Maggie's going to be super busy for every minute of the next six months, Miss Kent. She's formed a team with one of the other press officers and two floaters to work directly with her, and she's delegated me to do everything she'd normally be doing for you herself if she had the time."

"I see. I could use a cup of coffee. I'm just going to stand out here in the corridor for the moment. It's claustrophobic in there."

Her mind a blank, searching helplessly for a way around Janet Covitz, Tessa paced the hall, oblivious to the security team, until Bernie Allen reappeared.

"Mr. Foy's finished with the rubies, Miss Kent."

"Thank you, Mr. Allen. When a young lady shows up with coffee, please tell her I've changed my mind about it. She can go on back to her office."

Tessa returned to her chair, just as Monty Foy lifted her Tiffany pearls from their box. "I'm keeping these," she said, snatching them from his hands.

"Quite right," he said understandingly. "They're hardly in the same ballpark as the rest of the collection, are they? Some sentimental value, I assume."

"No more value than your lungs, Mr. Foy."

34

How'd the meeting go?" Sam asked eagerly even before he'd kissed Tessa. All of yesterday evening, he thought, she'd been negotiating her way across a tightrope of nerves in a way that was completely foreign to his experience of her. She had been so wound up that she could talk of little other than the fact that today, this very afternoon, since all the jewels were now in the possession of S & S, she'd find herself in the same room with Maggie for the first time since the day when she'd signed the auction contract.

"I'm not sure," Tessa answered in a white, muted voice, her vitality and conviction lost. "I'm just not sure at all. I may have blown it."

"What are you talking about?" he asked, tipping her lips up for a kiss. "You said this was just a preliminary strategy meeting. How could even you, with all your amazing ability to screw up your life, possibly blow a six-month effort right at the beginning, darling?"

Tessa gave him a smile that was no more than a faint attempt at smiling, so miserable that he felt genuine alarm. "Tell me everything that happened," Sam ordered, "from the beginning, so I can explain it to you, because you don't make sense."

"There were seven of us, sitting around a conference table—Lee Maine has lent the room to Maggie for the duration, and—"

"Who were they? Pretend you're a historian, baby. I want details."

"Besides Maggie and Juliet Tree and me, there was that girl Janet Covitz I told you about, and another I hadn't met before, Dune Maddox by name, a rakish, very social blond with more brains than you'd think to look at her. Also there were two floaters Maggie recruited, kids, Sam, probably no more than twenty, and adorable, a matched pair of brunettes, both obviously bright and eager, named Aviva Beach and Joanne Corday."

"Were you the only grown-up there?"

"No, Juliet Tree's in her forties, a true professional who's been at S and S for years, an elegant woman, the chignon and tailored suit type, who seems a bit square, especially compared to the others. Obviously Maggie's a cult figure; the others are all Maggie clones, like Janet, even down to that haircut, and except for Juliet, they treat her word as writ."

"So you're sitting there with a bunch of females, and you're looking . . . how?"

"Semi–movie-star. Oh, Sam, I was up half the night obsessing on what to wear, and I decided it would be affected to dress down the way I do for your department head, that I should look more or less the way they'd expect me to look, but not anything over the top, so I wore the same thing I had on the day I met you. I hoped it would bring me luck."

"But remember, you had me in thrall from adolescence on. Then what happened?"

"Oh, I behaved myself. I pushed my chair just far enough away from the table so I wouldn't seem to be intruding on Maggie's turf, since she was running the meeting, and I shut up and listened. She explained how they announce an important auction, keeping it totally secret until the actual morning of the press conference, so it makes headlines all over the world. She said Hamilton Scott would make the announcement of the sale and then I'd speak, explaining why I'd decided to auction my jewels and telling the press that the proceeds would go to cancer research and answering questions . . . the usual stuff. Dune Maddox seemed surprised that I was going to be doing that, as if somehow a movie star wouldn't be able to open her mouth without a script, and I told her public speaking didn't bother me."

"So far, so good."

"Oh, Sam, you said to start at the beginning, damn it! So don't keep giving me progress reports on what I tell you."

"Don't you think you want a drink?"

"Not particularly. It'll just make me more depressed and worse tempered than ever."

"Don't you think you need a drink?"

"Probably. Thank you, darling. Why do you take such good care of me?" Tessa asked plaintively.

"Why shouldn't I? You're my designated lifetime sweetheart, and on top of that, you're a good provider. Now drink this and tell me more."

"Juliet wanted to know if I had any scrapbooks and I told her that Fiona had made them of every picture ever published of me since my first film and I'd let her know to send them here right away. They need the pictures for the catalog and to distribute to magazines."

"But there must be thousands upon thousands of photographs."

"There are. The idea is that every magazine that does a story on me will get entirely different photos from different movies and different occasions when I was photographed in real life wearing my jewels. Maggie's trying for cover stories in most of the magazines I read—like *Vogue, Town and Country,* and *Vanity Fair*—and in some I don't, like *People* and *Hello!* and

Life and even in some of the decorating magazines like *Architectural Digest* or *House and Garden*—she says they rarely do celebrity covers but if they can come here to photograph me at home they almost certainly will. And she's hoping for *Newsweek* and maybe even *Time* the actual week of the auction."

"Isn't that publicity overkill? Almost the only ones she's left out are *Spy* and *Rolling Stone.*"

"Apparently she doesn't think overkill exists. She's going after the big television interview shows too. I didn't question it, just said I'd be available for anything except lying in my tub with bubbles up to my armpits."

"Will you mind if anyone gets wise to us? You've kept it so quiet all year."

"Mind? I'd take out an ad in *Publishers Weekly* if you'd let me. Will you mind is more the question."

"I wish everybody knew," Sam answered. He understood Tessa's discretion intellectually. He realized that she didn't want them to be the focus of worldwide gossip and speculation, but he yearned for an official romance. Hard to have with a public figure, he told himself impatiently. If only she'd marry him! She'd been on the verge, before the auction came up, but now all her emotional focus was turned toward Maggie.

"Your study'll be off-limits anyway," Tessa continued. "Photographers won't want me in front of a desk."

"You can do this stuff in your sleep, can't you?"

"Just about. I publicized every picture I made, but I never did an interview just for the sake of keeping my name in front of the public. That's probably why I'm supposed to be something of a recluse. Anyway, I gave all the press department an open invitation to come on and take a good look at this place so they'll have an idea of how it could photograph. Janet and Dune jumped at it, the two floaters didn't quite dare speak up yet, though they'll get here sooner or later."

"What about Maggie, doesn't she want to see it too?"

"Clearly no. She told them she was delegating all questions photographic to Dune and Janet. She gave Juliet Tree first choice of pictures for the catalog. They think there's a good chance they can sell it in the hundreds of thousands, what with the serious buyers, the merely curious, the Irving Penn fans and my own fans. It can sell as a gift book since it'll be out in time for Christmas. I told them that S and S was donating all their profits on the catalog to cancer research too."

"When did that happen?"

"When I called Liz Sinclair this morning and suggested it."

"Do they know it's your idea?"

"Of course not; it's got to be perceived as Liz and Hamilton's gesture."

"So far, strictly as a historian, I don't see where you blew it."

"The next thing that happened was I took a really good look around the table and I decided that whatever I said, no matter how informal or available I was, and believe me, I was giving my all, they were still looking at me—all but Maggie, that is—with a stifling mixture of awe and curiosity and disbelief and oh-me-oh-my-she's-*really*-Tessa-Kent stuff. They all called me 'Miss Kent,' of course, even Juliet Tree, and they couldn't stop darting tiny sideways glances at me, checking me out over and over, all of them except for Maggie."

"But she knows what you look like," he said reasonably.

"No, Sam, that's not the point. She made absolutely no eye contact with me, *none*, Sam, even though we had been in that meeting for at least two hours. She looked at all the others whenever she talked to them, but I could have been completely invisible. When she looked around the table she'd skim way above the top of my head, moving her eyes so quickly that no one could tell. She never once, *not once*, used my name, Sam, she referred to me as 'the consignor' as if I weren't right there in the room, and managed to make it sound as if she were just being terribly correct and polite. She was actually *ceremonial,* as if I were the hundred-year-old hereditary ruler of some feudal country."

"So then you blew up?"

"No, nothing that sensible. Then I suggested that since we were all going to be working together for a long time, we should be like people on film sets, at least my sets, and use first names. I asked everybody to call me Tessa, because that way Maggie would have to go along with the rest of them."

"Well, what's wrong with that?"

"They all looked at Maggie, as if for permission, and she raised her eyebrows slightly as if I'd said something embarrassingly over-friendly, like a puppy dog wagging my tail, and that's when—oh, shit, Sam, I was so frustrated by the icy, determined way she was giving me the invisible treatment, I was so desperately anxious for her to *acknowledge* me in some way, yes, Sam, *just* like a puppy jumping up and down for attention, and planting his muddy paws all over a white skirt, that I explained, in an entirely natural, casual way, that Maggie had been leaning over backward to be proper because she didn't want to trade on or presume on the fact that we were sisters."

"Hmm."

"What's that supposed to mean?"

"Not much, I wasn't there. How did Maggie react?"

"She didn't. They did. They were rocked by the news. You could literally feel their astonishment hit as they took in the word 'sisters.' They were incredulous and shocked and fascinated and salivating at the gossip value, but, to their credit, they held it down pretty well. A couple of them blurted out 'Sisters?' and Juliet looked as if she'd just solved some large puzzle, and Maggie didn't say anything at all, just kept on consulting her everlasting notes, so I blundered right on, doing a Miss Innocence number, and I said that I'd assumed they must all have heard by now, that Liz Sinclair and Hamilton Scott and Lee Maine knew and I simply imagined that everyone in the publicity department would know . . . Christ, I really blathered all over the place, fool that I am."

"How can you be so sure if she didn't react?"

"Because the entire rest of the meeting, which lasted another endless hour, Maggie *still* didn't look at me or use my name, and I could tell that she'd become ten times colder than before, and now she was deeply resentful, because I'd pushed too hard and confronted her. And I had! Oh, Sam, I had, damn it to hell! I pushed her into being in charge of the publicity for the auction and then I pushed her again, the very next time I saw her! I didn't *need* to bring that up, Sam. I should have let it come out if and when Maggie chose for it to come out, or never be mentioned at all, if that's what she wanted. Instead of walking lightly and carrying no stick at all, I stomped on her toes and bashed her over the head with a baseball bat."

"Okay, so you've had a setback, I won't try to tell you otherwise, but you haven't 'blown it,' darling." Sam said after a moment's thought, "You've gotten a modified version of the truth out in the open, so at least you don't have to go around acting as if you two had never met before, which would be pretty hard to keep up for six months, especially since other people at S and S already knew. And it's good that everyone will be calling you by your first name and feeling more comfortable with you. You're not just Tessa Kent anymore, you're Maggie's big sister, so that makes you human."

"Do you really think that or are you just saying it?"

"I really think it. You know I don't soft-pedal things to you. When you get right down to it, it's not the sister stuff that's the big deal. It's the mother–daughter connection that's making her act the way she does, and that's been going on for so long that it won't go away until . . . it goes away. Somehow. Or other."

"Oh, Sam, I was so awful!"

"You were natural, you weren't on guard, you were too happy to see her, you wanted to shout from the rooftops. You weren't very smart. Even you, darling, have moments like that. But, remember, you've still got six months. Anything can happen. Six months is a long time."

"Oh, Sam. Six months? Six months! They'll go by so quickly!"

"You can accomplish miracles in six months . . . we've only been together a little more than a year and I can't even imagine how time passed before I knew you."

"I guess . . . time . . . is always relative," Tessa said in a small voice, drifting to the window and looking out blindly. Six months, not even two full seasons of one year. One day Sam would be a fine old man, a famous old man, still teaching, still writing, happily married, the father of a family, one day, twenty or thirty unimaginable years from now. Oh, Sam, when you look back, will you still think six months was a long time? Will you have any idea how much I would have given to grow older, year by year, with you? How often will you remember me, my darling? How long before a day will pass without your thinking of me? How long until you meet another woman? Please, be happy, Sam, but don't forget me—not too soon . . .

35

"You look so tired," Polly told Maggie, inspecting her friend's face. "Is it the same reason I've been hearing about for the past few endless months so I can keep on feeling guilty, or is it something else?"

"Keep feeling guilty," Maggie said grimly. "You have no reason to hope for anything better."

"Tessa Kent is still the trooper of troopers?"

"Honestly, Polly, if you could just see her. Today, in a long list of other appointments, we had an interview lunch with a particularly difficult stringer from the London *Times* who obviously considers movie stars deeply beneath him, particularly those with spare jewelry to hawk—an old-line Labour Party supporter who made it clear that he'd confiscate the Crown Jewels if he could and abolish, if not behead, the entire Royal Family—and by the time she'd finished charming him, the guy'd have agreed to increase the Prince of Wales's revenues and chipped in his own money to help buy the House of Windsor a new yacht. Talk about manipulative! Thy name is Tessa Kent."

"Isn't that her job?"

"Sure it is, I'll give her that. But she's such an *opera-*

tor. It's sickening to see the way she gets people to eat out of her hand."

"How'd she do it?" Polly asked, always avid for details.

"Damned if I know. She used the familiar wit and the familiar warmth and smiled at his attempts at jokes and pretended she didn't hear his snide remarks, and finally, God knows how, got him to tell her about his wife and how he had been suckered into buying her an engagement ring from Asprey, who are three times 'by appointment' to members of the Royal Family, because that's what his wife had been dreaming about all her life, and after that it was off to the races about the psychological reasons for women's inner attachments to jewels until finally she led him down the garden path with historical stuff like Mary Stuart's famous black pearls that Queen Elizabeth got her hands on even before she ordered Mary's head chopped off—"

"Aha, the old black pearl ploy."

"Exactly. Now this Brit has decided to do a two-piece story on the whole subject, concentrating on her collection of a particular kind of rare and valuable Tahitian black pearl—their color is called 'peacock' because it ranges from deepest purple to dark green—a large, perfectly matched string could bring close to a million dollars . . . please, Polly, it's sickening. This reporter is well on his way to becoming a black pearl expert and there are some seventy different shades of them. She hooked him good, with the help of poor Queen Mary . . . she played Mary years ago, that's how she knew about Mary's pearls. Aviva was sitting there looking as fascinated as he was, but then of course she can do no wrong with her little cheering section."

"It's not so little," Polly murmured.

"Only Juliet, Aviva, Janet, Joanne, and Dune. Every last person in the press department," Maggie admitted grimly. "Lee can't get over her either, the way she's cooperating. I always bring at least one of the others along for an interview and they're all getting a version of the treatment I got when I was a kid—the stories she tells the press are simply more adult, more detailed, and cleverly tailored versions of the way we used to play with her jewels when I went to visit her. She had ways of making these stones into more than they really are, and somehow adding their luster to her own. Oh, I'm so confused, Polly! She's doing a dream job, no one of us could ever come close to working the press the way she does—after all the jewels don't belong to us, we don't know anything about them, we're not the person who's auctioning them for a good cause—but it still makes me furious! I'm disgusted with myself, but I can't help it."

"You're not, by any chance, just a little jealous of her admirers?"

"Polly, that's sick! The reason she's collected this little band of worshipers is that she's trying to get at *me*, and who knows it better than you, who talked me into it in the first place? And if I don't bring one of them along, I'll end up being alone with her in the limo on the way to the restaurant and back."

"God, I honestly don't know what made me say that! Sorry! I must have forgotten, for a minute, why all this is happening."

"I wish I could forget," Maggie said limply.

"She must be totally determined to 'get at you,' as you put it, or she couldn't possibly be going to all this trouble," Polly said thoughtfully. "I imagine that Tessa Kent has better things to do with her life than win over some journalist who came into the lunch with a hostile attitude . . . she can't be used to having to do that."

"Of course not. When the studios arranged her press interviews it was always a major coup for whoever got to meet her."

"So look," Polly said hopefully, "don't jump down my throat, but if she's putting herself through all these hoops, with months more of the same to come, with every day an exhausting one, which you've admitted yourself, to say nothing of the travel still to come to those foreign cities where you're taking the highlights of the collection and where she'll be doing mobbed press conferences—not to mention that she might even be attached to some of these jewels she's selling—why couldn't you—"

"*Don't start with me!*"

"Why couldn't you be . . . a little less . . . *unbending,* I guess is the word I'm searching for."

"Polly, you promised!"

"I know, I know, but these complaints of yours have been going on and on for months. You know what my opinion was of Tessa Kent when you told me your story, but now I'm beginning to think no matter how bad a mother she was to you for eighteen years, she's trying her hardest to get to know you *now*, and that *now* should maybe . . . be given some, just a little bit of . . . credence, allowed to have some truth of its own. It's real enough, God knows. You can't dismiss it when you live with it all day, when you see the effort she's making— and all of it to try to get through to you."

"A few months effort? Eighteen *years* of neglect. Do you think that's a fair balance, Polly?"

"Of course not. There's never going to be any fair balance. Forget you ever heard the word 'fair'; leave it out of your vocabulary. Tessa Kent can never make up to you the vital things that she didn't do while you were growing up. Not ever. But do you have to hold so tightly onto the crime, Maggie? Isn't there ever going to be any forgiveness? Not the slightest bit, no matter what she does to try to earn it?"

"Hell, I can't deal with you, Polly. You're almost as manipulative as she is. I feel totally awful. My energy level is down to my shoes."

"PMS?"

"God no. I don't even believe there is such a thing . . . I've never had it anyway, not so I've noticed, maybe because I've been so irregular all my life. I haven't even had a period in ages. I had a dry spell like this when I first came here and was working as a temp. It's stress that's getting to me. Seriously getting to me. She's driving me crazy and so are you, Ms.-life-isn't-fair-Guildenstern. Did you think up that idea all by yourself? I'm going downstairs to see if Barney's home yet. He was going to work a little late tonight."

"How's my bright-eyed boy?"

"Bliss. Pure bliss." Maggie brightened and stood up, ready to leave, all thoughts of Tessa driven from her head. "If it weren't for this auction I'd say that my life is so utterly glorious it's frightening. I never guessed I could love anyone like this. We were born for each other, and don't give me that theory of yours that you knew it all along, from the first day you saw us together."

"But I did," Polly said serenely. "I should have written it down and mailed it in a sealed letter to myself and waited till now to give it to you—then you'd believe me."

"But you would have been wrong because if it had happened then it wouldn't have worked out. Now is the perfect timing, and the rest of our lives will be the perfect time."

"I know this is a ludicrously old-fashioned idea, but has the thought of getting married crossed your mind?" Polly asked casually as they walked toward her door.

"Oh, we have eons to think about *that*," Maggie said with fine disregard. "We're together and we'll never be apart—but marriage?—all those deadly formalities? Having to see Madison and Tyler again? We'll simply have to elope, but all in good time. What's the rush? Living in sin is so much fun—as you ought to know."

"Jane and I would get married if we could," Polly said wistfully. "I'd just like to have the legal opportunity. If you decide to go the traditional route, will you let me give the wedding?"

"Oh, you mistreated, generous creature, of course!" Maggie cried, remorsefully, hugging her friend with such enthusiasm that she all but lifted her feet off the floor. "I'd even let you pick out my dress, or else I'd end up in slinky black velvet or something equally unbridal."

"Go find Barney. Just thinking about weddings makes me cry," Polly said, pushing Maggie out the door.

Tessa carefully checked the laden tables that room service had just brought up to her apartment. Almost from the start of the auction planning she'd invited the press department to an early breakfast every Friday morning so they could sit around in comfort, assess the work done in the past week, and get a jump on the next week's plans.

It was the only way to keep herself firmly focused on the progress of the complications of the publicity schedule, Tessa had decided, after a few meetings at S & S had been interrupted by unrelated phone calls or questions from the members of the press office who were handling the publicity on S & S's other auctions.

With Liz Sinclair, Juliet Tree, Penn's rep, and occasionally Monty Foy, who was composing the part of the text that related to the history and quality of the jewels themselves, Tessa had weekly meetings at S & S to work on the layout of the catalog, which was almost ready to be printed and mailed. Never, everyone agreed, had jewels been photographed so imaginatively and alluringly, never would there be better shots of an owner wearing the jewels in the company of intensely famous people at seriously glamorous parties, and certainly never had there been an auction catalog that contained, in the owner's own words, her thoughts about the occasions on which she had bought or been given the jewels, and her memories about the times she best remembered wearing them.

When Tessa studied the photographs, culled from Fiona's scrapbooks, she found herself at a strange distance from them. Yes, there she indisputably *was,* not more than eight years ago, in a pale-blue satin strapless Givenchy gown, dancing with the king of Spain at a ball in Venice, wearing yards of cornflower-blue Kashmir sapphires as lightly as if they were bubbles; there she *was* laughing with Tom Hanks, Tom Cruise, and Kevin Costner at an opening night party of some Imagine Entertainment comedy, only three years ago, in a short, unadorned black satin shift and a throwaway pair of oval diamond earrings of fifteen carats each that Graf of London had found for her. They could easily look, to the untutored eye, as if they were costume jewelry, because the diamonds were that startlingly pure bright, flawless Fancy Vivid Yellow that only the Sultan of Brunei also possessed. They were set in a nine-million-dollar pair of earrings, each carat costing three hundred thousand dollars . . . *but there she wasn't.* Not really. Another world, another life, another woman. Her emotional removal was a blessing, Tessa thought, or else she might well have felt regret at the way she had chosen to use these six priceless months of her life, as it became more and more certain that Maggie wasn't going to soften one whit toward her, no matter how much time they spent in the same room.

The concierge announced the first of the troops from S & S, and soon they were all gathered around the tables, helping themselves to heaping platefuls of the enormous breakfast Tessa had provided—everything from croissants for the delicate eaters, to scrambled eggs and smoked salmon, or baked ham and sausages with pancakes, for those in the majority who jumped at the prospect of a hearty breakfast, instead of their usual fare.

What great girls they were, Tessa thought, as they took time to enjoy their food before they started on the business at hand. Now that she'd gotten to know them, or rather now that they'd gotten to know her, a genuine relationship of easy warmth and camaraderie had come about. She felt as young as they were; the sixteen or seventeen years that separated her from Aviva and Joanne seemed nonexistent. This is what it would have been like to have a big family of daughters, Tessa thought, except that love, maternal love, would have been allowed to enter the way she looked at all of them . . . there would be love in the way they looked at her. She'd be able to casually smooth Dune's hair, or kiss Janet's cheek. They'd be bound together, even if they disagreed, bound for life. She'd be there when they met the men they were going to marry, she'd hold their children, she'd go to the birthday parties . . . oh, the path not taken! And if she hadn't had children other than Maggie, this might have been a breakfast party she was giving for her daughter, this group of girls might be Maggie's bridesmaids, and she'd be the mother of the bride, Tessa thought dreamily, the mother hen, deep into the fascinating details of invitations and menus . . . no wonder people had big weddings.

The atmosphere at this morning's breakfast was especially exciting, Tessa realized, coming back to the present moment, because tomorrow, on Saturday morning, she, Maggie, and Dune were leaving on a nonstop United Airlines flight to São Paulo, where the first foreign exhibition of the highlights from the collection would take place the following Monday night. S & S was giving a gala reception in the ballroom of the luxurious Maksoud Plaza Hotel, where they were all staying, to which every potential bidder in South America had been invited. On Tuesday and Wednesday there would be wall-to-wall private appointments for those women who wanted to try on the jewels and inspect them carefully, since they couldn't be taken out of their cases during the exhibition. Dealers would have to travel to New York before the auction for the same privilege. São Paulo, the South American equivalent of New York, was not just a center of vast wealth and big business but a hub of journalism, and a press conference had been called for Monday afternoon, which hundreds of reporters from all over South America were expected to attend.

Security was as important as publicity in any foreign exhibition and Tessa, Maggie, and Dune would be traveling on one plane and the jewels on another. The jewels would be accompanied to the airport in New York by one large group of inconspicuous security men and would be met by another such group hired by S & S's São Paulo office. A heavy force of Brazilian police would keep the jewels under armed surveillance during every second of their stay in Brazil.

While the others were in the middle of breakfast, Maggie, who was seated close to the door of the living room, put down her plate and slipped quickly out, unnoticed by anyone but Tessa. After a few minutes of hesitation, Tessa followed her. Did Maggie even know that the guest bathroom was around the corner and down the hall?

The door to the guest bathroom was open and the room was empty. Where had she disappeared to? Tessa wondered. Had Maggie simply left the meeting for some reason? Worried, she looked next in the empty bathroom off the library and finally went to her own bathroom, where a large, mirrored dressing room and closet were separated by an inside door from the toilet.

The door to the dressing room from the hallway wasn't entirely closed, and as Tessa stood outside, unwilling to disturb Maggie, she heard the unmistakable noises of vomiting, violent and uncontrollable, relieved for seconds as Maggie gasped for breath. Finally, after a long period of dry heaves, she heard Maggie flush the toilet twice, let herself out of the locked toilet, and cross the marble floor toward the sink.

Holy Mary, Mother of God, Tessa thought, morning sickness. There was nothing else it could be. She'd never forgotten that sound. She'd bet all she owned that what Maggie had wasn't stomach flu, the excuse she'd invented for her own mother. Tessa found herself clasping her arms across her breasts with her hands at her throat, as she closed her eyes and automatically whispered a prayer.

Don't go in, she told herself, fiercely trembling with

the desire to rush to Maggie; don't you dare to go in. Remember what happened the last time you intruded on her right to privacy. She's pregnant but you may not, *you must not*, discuss it with her. She's pregnant with your grandchild, but you must seem not to know. She's pregnant and you don't know who the father is, she's pregnant and you don't know when she'll have the baby, or if she'll have the baby, and you may not, dare not, must not ask! All you can do is thank the God you no longer worship and pray the prayers you no longer think do any good.

Hastily, Tessa blotted tears of excitement and joy from her eyes and fled down the corridor to rejoin the others.

Maggie gazed wide-eyed at herself in the mirror over the sink. She spit out the mouthwash she was gargling because she was grinning so widely that she'd almost swallowed a mouthful. Good God Almighty, so *this* was why she hadn't had a period in so long! PMS, stress . . . no, a baby, Barney's baby. Contraception didn't always work, she'd always known that, but she hadn't guessed how marvelous it would be when it didn't. What would Barney say, what would Polly say, what would Liz Sinclair say? What difference did it make what anyone said, Maggie thought, her heart jumping with wild happiness. What would Tessa say when she found out she was going to be a grandmother? She frowned at herself in the mirror. Tricky, all this, especially leaving for Brazil tomorrow. She'd just sit on the delicious knowledge, hug it to herself, until she'd had a chance to tell Barney. She gargled one more time, splashed her face with cold water, reapplied her lipstick, and set off sedately for the living room. There had better still be some croissants left . . . she was starving!

36

Maggie frowned and consulted her watch once again as she and Tessa waited in the VIP lounge for their eight A.M. flight to São Paulo. Dune should have joined them at least a half hour ago. How could she, the most obsessively reliable of all her assistants, have failed to realize how vitally important it was for her to be on time this morning? The plane would be ready to load in twenty minutes.

"Miss Horvath? There's a phone call for you," an attendant said, "you can pick up right here." Maggie grabbed the phone and listened grimly as Dune, sobbing with anger at herself, informed her in disbelieving outrage that she'd broken her ankle running for a taxi and was calling from a pay phone in a hospital emergency room, where she was waiting to have it set.

"Damn it, Dune, why'd you wait till the last minute to call?"

"I've been trying to get someone to replace me first. I've tied up the phone here for an hour. I tried Janet four times, the last time just a minute ago, but all I get is her goddamned machine. I'm sure she's at her boyfriend's place till Monday. Then I tried Lee but she and her guy are out of town. I called Aviva and Joanne and those two both, can you believe it, both, left for hot weekends last night, according to their roommates. They didn't leave numbers where they can be reached and they're not expected back till late Sunday night. While the cat's away . . . I thought checking on their availability was more important than calling you with bad news."

"You did right. So nobody's available. Even if Janet calls her machine, the next plane doesn't leave till tomorrow."

"Why would she call her machine if she's with her boyfriend?"

"Good question. Maybe they'll go to her place, probably not. I'm sorry about your ankle, Dune."

"Oh, Maggie!" Dune wailed. "How could I have done this to you?"

"We should have sent a limo for you too. Don't worry, no big deal. I can handle it alone. Feel better, take care."

Maggie walked over to Tessa and told her the news.

"Oh, that poor girl! She must be miserable," Tessa said, even as she reproached herself for being thrilled by Dune's accident, which left them inescapably alone for the first time.

"She is," Maggie said, tight-lipped, as a United Airlines official arrived to escort them to the gate where they'd be boarded before anyone else.

Tessa and Maggie, lacking the hapless Dune, each took a window seat in the two first rows of first class, one behind the other. They spent the uneventful nine-hour trip with only the most perfunctory communication, Maggie properly concerned with Tessa's comfort while she remained entirely aloof on a personal level. In the São Paulo airport, at six in the evening local time, they were met by the capable, energetic, and very elegant Señora Marta Pereira, the director of the local S & S office, bearing a huge bunch of flowers for Tessa and accompanied by her two senior employees. They were driven through the immense metropolis of sixteen million people in an air-conditioned Bentley that had been rented for the occasion, and soon they were settled in their magnificent suites on the top floor of the Maksoud Plaza Hotel, built around an enormous atrium. It was spring in Brazil, although except for the temperature and the masses of spring flowers in their suites, there was no way to glimpse any countryside, even from their elevation, so sprawling was the city itself.

Before she unpacked, Tessa phoned Sam in New York and told him about Dune's accident.

"Until the press conference on Monday afternoon I'm totally at loose ends here, darling. I've finally got Maggie to myself and it's obvious that she's going to keep herself so busy that I'll never be alone with her," she said sadly, almost with resignation. What else had she expected, anyway?

"Tomorrow she's planned a whole day around Marta Pereira, inspecting everything from the placement of the exhibition cases and the mike to checking on the local security staff and meeting everyone who's going to actually handle the jewels when they're finally put into the cases. Then she's checking personally on all the arrangements made by the hotel catering staff and the florists even though that's all been planned locally for weeks. Maggie's already adopted Marta Pereira in the place of Dune, so we'll never be alone, but there's nothing I can do about it, I can't tag along when I'm unnecessary." Tessa paused while Sam spoke.

"What will I do? I'm going to order something light to eat and go to bed early. Nine hours on any plane trip leaves me feeling as if I have jet lag, even though we've gone through only one time zone. Do you miss me yet? Oh, sweetheart, say that again. And again . . . please. Thank you, Sam, that helps so much. It's lucky that I brought three books with me; Sunday promises to be a long, lonely day. I'll call often and early . . . if you're out, call me back, all right? Oh, I do love you!"

*   *   *

In the middle of the night Tessa was awakened by a faint but persistent knocking on her door, coming from the circular entrance hall that led to her bedroom.

"Who is it?" she called, startled.

"Maggie."

Tessa switched on a light, jumped out of bed, and ran to open the door. Maggie stood there in her bathrobe, her face totally blank of any emotion but panic, her eyes huge.

"I didn't want to bother you . . ." she faltered, standing unsteadily in the doorway.

"Maggie, what's wrong?" Tessa cried, pulling her into the room.

"I—oh, hell—I'm bleeding."

"Oh, no! The baby! Lie down on the bed right away, yes, flat, feet up on this pillow."

"How did you know—?"

"I heard you throwing up yesterday. How long have you been bleeding?"

"I can't be sure. Fifteen minutes ago I woke up and went to the bathroom and noticed . . . it was brownish, at first, and then there was some bright red blood . . . so I just came here . . . I didn't know what else to do . . ."

"Any cramps?"

"No, just the bleeding."

"I think it's a false alarm, just spotting, but I'll get a doctor immediately." Tessa sounded more reassuring and knowledgeable than she felt. If ever, this was the time to convey calm and self-possession.

"Why a false alarm?" Maggie gasped.

"I've lost two pregnancies. I could never have made it down a hotel corridor on my own. I had terrible cramps and I lost blood like mad. Now keep quiet, take deep breaths, and try to relax."

Tessa picked up the phone and spoke to the night operator.

"Operator, this is Tessa Kent. What's your name?

Dolores? Excellent. Now, Dolores, connect me to the manager of the hotel, no, Dolores, not the night manager, the general manager, *at his home*, immediately, and tell him to call me at once. This is an *emergency*. It's very serious, Dolores. *I am Tessa Kent and I'm counting on you*. After you've reached the general manager, call the night manager and tell him to come up immediately to Tessa Kent's suite with an empty hot-water bottle and two buckets of ice cubes. Immediately. It's an emergency! Thank you, Dolores. I'll hang up so the general manager can phone me directly, at once, you understand? At once, *immediately*. Don't try to inform the night manager until *after* you've reached the general manager, and remember, Dolores, ice and a hot-water bottle, for Tessa Kent. Yes, of course I'll sign an autograph, if you hurry. But only if you hurry."

She turned to Maggie, whose face was twisted with apprehension. "I'm going to get some towels, it won't take a second," Tessa said. She hurried to the bathroom and returned with an armful of towels.

"Here, I'll pull your pajama pants off over your feet, and you put one of these between your legs. No cramping? Good girl."

She turned to answer the phone. "This is Tessa Kent. Thank you, Señor. As you know, I am staying in your hotel. Thank you, Señor. Yes, it's an emergency, a *major* emergency. I need the best gynecologist in São Paulo here in my suite *immediately*. What's the best hospital in the city? Good. Now, please call the Albert Einstein, immediately, you understand, and tell them it's for Tessa Kent, I'm in an emergency situation. Ask for the Department of Gynecology and write down the names and home phone numbers of their top doctors. Explain that it's for me, Tessa Kent. If anyone doesn't want to give out home numbers, call the director of the hospital at home. *Immediately*. If one of the doctors is available right now, at the hospital, go get him and bring him to my suite at once. Otherwise, call them at home, ask the first one who answers to come here for me, Tessa Kent, at once. *Immediately*. Tell him to speed, it's an emergency, Señor, in your hotel. No, not the hotel doctor. Never a hotel doctor! Would you send your wife to a hotel doctor, Señor? I thought so. I'm counting on you, Señor."

Tessa turned back to Maggie. "Would you mind if I took a look at that towel? Good, there's not too much blood, but you're still bleeding. Here's a fresh one. Just relax and lie still."

"I never thought I'd hear those words so often in two phone calls," Maggie said in a weak voice.

"Which words? 'Immediately' or 'emergency'?"

" 'Tessa Kent.' "

"They work best. Oh, that must be the ice," Tessa said, relieved, scrambling to open the door to the night manager. She took a tray from him and told him to go downstairs to wait for the general manager. Quickly, she filled the hot-water bottle with ice cubes, wrapped it in a hand towel, and placed it low on Maggie's abdomen. "The ice would drip too much without a hot-water bottle," she explained.

"Where'd you learn all this?" Maggie asked to distract herself.

"I've put in my time with gynecologists."

The phone rang again as the general manager reported that he was driving a top gynecologist to the hotel, leaving that minute, for Miss Tessa Kent.

"Won't they be surprised when they see you're up and about?" Maggie whispered, unsmiling but visibly relieved that a doctor was coming. "And in that nightie?"

"Good Lord, I'd better put on a robe. Would you like a wet towel on your forehead?"

"Yes, please."

"Would you like a piece of ice to suck? No, better not. Who knows about the water anywhere? A sip, but only a sip, of mineral water?"

"Yes, please."

Maggie lay on the bed and Tessa brought a wrung-out, cool, wet hand towel and the water and pulled up a little chair to sit beside her. She gave Maggie a little water and quietly ordered, "Now just close your eyes, it won't be long."

Maggie sighed and obeyed. Tessa looked at Maggie's hand lying protectively over the hot-water bottle and willed herself not to touch it or to speak. Perhaps Maggie could fall asleep for a minute or two, Tessa thought, breathing as quietly as she could. Soon, very soon, even in this gigantic city, the doctor would arrive, but until then she gave herself up to imagining that she was spending a whole night alone with her daughter, waiting and watching and keeping her from harm, in the circle of pale yellow illumination made by the lamp on the bedside table.

Soon a knocking on the door announced the arrival of the night manager, the general manager, and a short, powerfully muscled, handsome, middle-aged man who announced that he was Doctor Roberto Goldenberg.

"Thank you gentlemen, thank you so much," Tessa said, shutting the door on the hotel men and admitting only the doctor.

"Miss Kent, what seems to be your problem?" he asked in a deep voice that resonated with self-assurance.

"It's not me, it's my daughter. She may be having a miscarriage. I've got her flat in bed with an ice pack on her belly."

"How long ago did it start?" he asked, as he hurried across the entrance to the bedroom.

"I'm not sure. Maggie woke me up about a half hour ago."

"You work quickly, Miss Kent. From the hotel manager I imagined you must be having triplets this very minute."

"Where were you in medical school, Doctor?" Tessa demanded.

"Harvard, and later Johns Hopkins. Hello Maggie. I'm Doctor Roberto," he said, smiling with very white teeth. "Now, let's take a look at you. *Mamãe*, wait in the sitting room, please," the doctor said, bending over Maggie.

Vanquished by a superior force, Tessa retreated, reassured by the doctor's manner, and huddled in a chair in the sitting room, watching, without seeing, the spinning, spilling field of lights of the vast city.

After some time she was joined by the doctor, who sat down next to her.

"In my opinion, Maggie's not having a miscarriage," he said, patting her hand kindly. "The chances are very low, although you realize that they're never zero, that she will lose this pregnancy. This kind of spotting is frequent, and it has almost stopped. However, it's best to be on the super-cautious side for the next three days. Don't let her get up except to go to the bathroom, and before I leave I'll give her a stool softener so she won't get constipated. She can eat whatever she wants, and if she doesn't want to eat until some time tomorrow, don't force it. She can live on soup. Your little girl is very far from delicate, *Mamãe*. The most important thing is rest, rest, rest, and plenty of fluids."

"Did you give her all those instructions?"

"I'm telling you, isn't that enough?"

"You're going to have to repeat the rest part to Maggie. She's down here to work and she won't listen to what I say."

"She'll obey me," Dr. Goldenberg promised, with a chuckle.

"How pregnant is she?" Tessa asked.

"That's what Maggie wanted to know. Astonishing! My own patients pay very close attention to such questions. They come in and say, 'Doctor Roberto, I'm two weeks and five days *gravida*. In Maggie's case, I'd say close to three months, but without the date of her last period I can't tell exactly, and she seems to have no idea when that was. Extraordinary, you North Americans."

"Could you possibly come back tomorrow, Doctor?"

"Certainly, Mamãe. Every day. Every evening if necessary, but I don't think it will be. And on Tuesday, I'd like to see her in my office for an ultrasound, so we'll be able to see what's going on in there."

"Oh, Doctor Goldenberg—isn't there any way you could bring the ultrasound machine here, to the hotel? I don't want to risk the drive through this city, the traffic, the elevators, the crowds—" Tessa looked at him imploringly.

"It's . . . unusual, but . . . yes, of course, Mamãe. The machine is portable, after all. Now come with me while I put the fear of Doctor Roberto into Maggie."

The doctor looked at Maggie severely, as Tessa stood by his side. "Listen, Maggie, I've told your mamãe and I'm telling you, the only way to be sure you don't lose this baby is to stay exactly where you are, with your feet up, and rest for three days. Drink lots of fluids, eat what you want, *but stay in bed.* You don't need the ice pack now. You can get up carefully and slowly walk to the bathroom. But you absolutely cannot go downstairs and run around that exhibition you were fretting about. You may not! Under *any* circumstances. Doctor Roberto completely forbids it. Let your mamãe wait on you hand and foot. Understood?"

"Oh, Doctor Roberto, I have so much responsibility," Maggie protested weakly. "This couldn't happen at a worse time."

"Someone else will take care of everything, count on it. Your mamãe will manage that as well as she managed to get me here in the middle of the night. Now, Maggie, it's time for you to sleep. I'll come back and check on you late in the afternoon tomorrow."

Tessa accompanied the doctor to the door to her suite. "Oh, Doctor Goldenberg, you're an absolute angel! I can't possibly thank you enough!"

"Not at all. You must understand, I'd do as much for anyone . . . well, perhaps not the ultrasound, but everything else. However, in your case . . ." he looked suddenly shy. "Would you mind?" He handed Tessa his prescription pad and a pen. "I won't pretend the autograph is for my wife, it's for me. I'm a shameless fan, I've seen all of your movies. How, and I ask you this strictly as a man of medicine, you understand, can you possibly be old enough to have a grown-up daughter?"

"It's a long story," Tessa laughed, "and one that probably only a gynecologist would believe."

37

Tessa closed the door behind Dr. Goldenberg and marched into the bedroom armed with a feeling of complete authority. Maggie was sitting up in bed, with the beginning of a potentially rebellious expression on her face.

"But Tessa—"

"You heard what the doctor said, Maggie. You're not going anywhere." Oh, the simple joy of saying those words, Tessa thought, words every mother must have said a million times.

"Wow, talk about a Brazilian Alpha Male! Calling you 'mommy' and referring to himself in the third person! He's devastating, isn't he, that Doctor Roberto?"

"I worked in Brazil once, years ago. Their word *mamãe* is pronounced 'mommy,' but as I understand, it's just a way of saying 'mother.' "

"If I have to stay here, you take my suite."

"Nonsense. There's plenty of room for both of us. Doctor Goldenberg was horrified enough that I didn't know how many months pregnant you are. Can you imagine what he'd say if I left you alone? Consider me your personal Florence Nightingale. I'm in thrall to Doctor Devastating."

"Why did he expect you to know all the details?"

"I guess in Brazil the *mamãe* is the first to find out."

"Well, you *were*. I didn't know until a few seconds before you did. Yesterday was the first time I had morning sickness. I didn't have any today. Oh, God, do you think I'll have it again tomorrow?"

"Probably not," Tessa said with more conviction than she felt, but she didn't want to eliminate the power of suggestion. "There was all that eating going on, all those food smells, added to the stress of knowing we were leaving the next day. It could easily have been a onetime thing. Doctor Roberto said you were about three months pregnant and that's almost always when morning sickness stops. After all, you were fine this morning."

"It could just have been a fluke," Maggie said dismissively, looking concerned. "The worst of it, besides being out of commission, is I can't reach Barney to tell him. He took that gorgeous Ducati he's in love with and went off with her for the weekend. Damn!"

Tessa waited a few well-timed seconds before she murmured, without any inflection at all, "Ducati." Oh, God, let Maggie not be involved with a man who didn't adore her.

"His new motorcycle. Very special, I gather. Barney owns a custom bike-building shop. Don't even ask, but he does well, very well."

"Barney," Tessa all but hummed in a way that kept any element of question out of her voice. Tensely she waited for Maggie to reply.

"You remember Barney! For heaven's sake, Tessa, you can't have forgotten Barney?" Maggie asked with as much indignation as she could summon lying down.

"The only Barney I remember actually seeing with my own eyes wasn't quite five years old." Barney, she thought, with a leap of her heart, remembering the little sunburnt boy who had taken care of Maggie from the moment he met her, Barney, protective Tarzan to Maggie's timid Jane.

"But we've talked and talked about him! Don't you remember how he'd never leave me alone? Always pestering me?"

"Barney Webster? . . . Your old faithful Sancho Panza?" She started to breath again in relief.

"Tessa, really! There's *never* been another Barney in my life."

"He certainly never gave up, did he? Making you *gravida* seems an ultimate form of pestering, if you ask me."

Maggie giggled, sleepily. "Neither one of us ever gave up, not really."

"Will he be happy?"

"Beyond happy . . . way, way beyond happy," Maggie said faintly, as she closed her eyes and fell silent.

Tessa watched her intently until she was satisfied from the changed sound of Maggie's breathing that she was fast asleep. Now that Maggie wouldn't be disturbed, Tessa began the slow, stealthy labor of tugging, inch by inch, two deep, heavy armchairs until they came together near the bed. She positioned them so that they faced each other and formed a short, downy couch on which she planned to curl up for the night. She found a pillow and an extra blanket in a closet and snuggled down, her knees bent, in what seemed to be a fairly comfortable position, but sleep eluded her. She couldn't make herself close her eyes and waste this opportunity to look directly at her daughter as much as she liked.

Even in sleep Maggie had a theatrical quality, Tessa thought. Even without the play of her eyes she was vibrant, vivid; her parted lips looked as if she were waiting for a kiss. A curtain could rise and show her sleeping and an audience would immediately be caught by her, would wait patiently to see what was going to happen to this vital, young creature with her eloquent coloring and laughter-promising features.

What would it have been like, Tessa asked herself, as she contemplated Maggie's face, if she'd never met Luke, if he'd never come to Edinburgh Castle and instantly transformed her entire life just by existing? After her parents died, Maggie naturally would have come to live with her, that serious, roly-poly, staunch little five-year-old, and all Maggie's problems and hurts would have been brought to her for comfort. Her career and Maggie's life would have been intertwined. When she came home from the studio, Maggie would have been there, working earnestly on her home work, waiting to read her a composition or asking to be drilled on a spelling test. If Maggie had fallen, she would have been the one who gently washed her knee and applied iodine and a Band-Aid. She would have planned Maggie's birthday parties and gone shopping with her for party dresses and her first pair of high heels; she would have sent Maggie to summer camp and seen her off, protesting that she didn't want to go, and two months later, welcomed home a surprisingly taller girl, tanned and laden with prizes, a girl who missed her friends from camp and temporarily hated everything about her home life.

Tessa gave a great sigh as she thought of all the things she'd missed, of all the potential of their history, lost forever. She would have told Maggie about sex and love, and the many shades of difference between them; she would never have married a man who hadn't passed Maggie's inspection and didn't know that she was Maggie's mother. As soon as Maggie had been old enough to understand, by six or seven, she would have told her what they truly were to each other and by now the idea that she had once claimed Maggie as a sister would have faded into a dim memory, not a painful lie that had been temporarily suspended, in order to simplify matters for a doctor summoned in the middle of the night. Everything would have been very different . . . so difficult to imagine . . . so many other things could have happened . . . too complicated . . . Tessa thought as she finally drifted into sleep.

Many hours later, Maggie woke to find Tessa sleeping alongside the bed. Soundlessly she slid out of bed on her way to the bathroom.

"Where do you think you're going?" Tessa asked, one eye flying open.

"The john. I thought you were sleeping."

"I was." Tessa sat up, threw off the blanket, and yawned. "And then I dreamed you were trying to escape, so I woke up."

"I'll be back one of these days," Maggie said, putting one foot down in front of the other in slow motion, with a show of caution.

Tessa scampered to the second bathroom of the suite to splash icy water on her face and run her fingers through her wild hair to try to smooth it down. Every limb ached because of her awkward sleeping position, but she welcomed the evidence that they'd both managed to get some rest. She quickly rejoined Maggie, who'd dutifully returned to bed.

"Any bleeding?" she asked, trying to sound casual.

"Nope. Not a sign. And I feel terrific. In fact I'm starving."

"Oh, Maggie, that's the best sign of all! What would you like to eat?"

"A gallon of orange juice, bacon and eggs, piles of toast, strawberry jam, tea, oh, my God, what time is it?"

"Two in the afternoon. I'll open the drapes and order for both of us."

"If I had morning sickness, I must have slept through it. You can't get it after lunch, can you?"

"All I'm certain of is that it's not something you can sleep through," Tessa said, as the springtime sunlight of Brazil flooded the room, "and I've never heard of anything called afternoon sickness, although I have heard of rare women who have all-day sickness from day one through the delivery."

"They must be passionate to have a baby, to put up with feeling hideously queasy and throwing up for nine whole months."

"Umm."

"That means you're wondering how passionate I am about it, aren't you? Do you think I don't know what that noncommittal sound means?"

"Umm."

Tessa threw up her hands and indicated that there was no more she was going to ask.

"Oh, Tessa, I'm dying to have a baby! I didn't know it until I thought I was going to have a miscarriage, but I want a baby with Barney more than I want anything else in the world. I honestly can't imagine how I got pregnant—it certainly wasn't on purpose—but, now that it's happened, I'm blissed out! I never expected to feel this way. It wasn't in my plans, at all. Of course, now we'll have to get married, which will make Polly's day."

"Polly Guildenstern?"

"You ought to know, you and your private eyes, you know perfectly well who Polly is, you probably have her Social Security number and her psychological profile. Just the other day she hinted at a wedding because she knows all about Barney, and I promised Polly she could give it if we ever had one. Oh Lord, do you think we *have* to invite Tyler and Madison?"

"There's no way out of it," Tessa said, her heart jumping in jubilation at this question. It was the first time Maggie had asked her advice in many years.

"Well, they probably won't stay long, if they even show up. I'd give a lot to see Madison's face when she finds out I'm going to be her daughter-in-law. Mrs. Barnaby Alcott Webster. I love it! I'll order calling cards and leave her one someday, when I'm sure she's not at home. Oh, here's breakfast, or is it lunch? Doesn't it look good?"

Maggie was half-finished with her eggs when her hand flew to her mouth.

"Sick?" Tessa jumped up, alarmed, immediately ready to help Maggie to the bathroom.

"I just remembered! Marta Pereira! I'm supposed to meet her at three."

"She'll call up from the lobby. I'll explain that I'm taking your place. Trust me, I'm good at making up convincing excuses, as well as a demon at checking arrangements. I'll pretend I'm you and I won't be satisfied with anything but pure perfection."

"That's all very well for today," Maggie admitted, glad to be vanquished, "but Tessa, tomorrow! The press conference and the gala reception at night. Every single potential important bidder from all over South America! What am I going to do?"

"Guess?" Tessa asked, repressing a smile.

"I'm going to stay here in bed, flat on my back," Maggie muttered, "and let you handle everything, which you're perfectly capable of doing, as I'm aware, without anyone's help. After all, you're Tessa Kent and, more than the jewels, Tessa Kent is what they're coming to see, like that day at Elm Country Day."

"I have three books you can read, and I can get you magazines from the newsstand in the lobby."

"Maybe later. Aren't you going to finish your breakfast? Look, you left half of it. Because if not . . . thanks. You know, if you'd let me get up very, very carefully, just to brush my teeth, I think I could go back to sleep for a while."

"I'll get the maids to change the bed while you're in the bathroom. Just don't try to get fancy. No baths, whatever you do," Tessa said warningly. "You're allowed to give yourself a sponge bath, but, Maggie," she said, feeling the most delicious sense of matronly power, "you have to promise me to be careful, to do everything very, very slowly. Here's a fresh nightgown."

"And a very sexy one too. Thank you. I promise,

cross my heart, to make no sudden moves. After all, Tessa, I'm almost as involved in this baby business as you are. I wonder what the divine Doctor Roberto will think when he sees me in this . . . he'll know it couldn't be mine. Had you noticed that he has the hots for you?"

"Maggie!"

"Mamãe!" Maggie retorted, laughing, as she drifted as slowly as a turtle toward the bathroom.

38

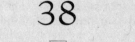

Taking great care to make no noise, Tessa opened the door of her suite, late on Monday night, only to find Maggie lying in bed, still reading.

"I couldn't possibly sleep," Maggie explained, putting down her book, "until you came back and told me how it went."

"It was a fantastic success, a brilliant, glorious gala!" Tessa exclaimed, excitedly flinging down the cape of silver lamé that swirled in pleated folds around a bare, slender column of silver satin. "Oh, Maggie, I was riding so high I could have personally auctioned off every last piece in the exhibition for twelve times its high estimate, but Marta wouldn't let me. She's still down there making appointments for women to come and try on the jewels—they're keeping the pieces here two extra days because they can't handle the requests in less time than that."

"But—"

"No, don't worry, she called New York and cleared it. We'll go back as we planned. Oh, I wish you could have been there! Such glorious people, such superb clothes. They really know how to dress up . . . it was the way I imagine Hollywood must have been in the fifties. I felt a bit of a country mouse."

"Poor thing," Maggie mocked, "you should have borrowed some jewelry, instead of having nothing to wear but your skin, since you can't count that dress. Did Doctor Macho take you up on your personal invitation?"

"Of course. We tangoed—divinely, of course—and then he bent over and whispered in my ear, 'Tell Maggie that she's been a very good girl and Doctor Roberto is pleased with her.' "

"You get to tango and I get to stay in bed and be a good girl. What's wrong with that picture, I ask you?" Maggie complained wickedly. "I supposed he kissed your hand too?"

"Possibly, possibly. It's only fair, considering the process that landed you in bed. You can't get *gravida* from the tango, at least not immediately," Tessa replied, pulling out the pins that kept her hair swept up high and letting it tumble down around her flushed face. "Since I don't believe Sam knows how to tango, I made the most of it."

She'd made the most of the entire evening, Tessa thought. She'd never flirted before, not really. Luke and Sam weren't flirtations but headlong, mutual flights into love, and there had been no one before Luke or after him until Sam. She could have, should have, made a career out of flirting, Tessa thought, if she'd had time, if she hadn't met Luke, if she'd had a few free years she would have flirted with an army. Now her entire knowledge of her amazing power to flirt would be forever compressed into illuminating a ballroom of willing South American men. Better late than never, she told herself, smiling at Maggie.

"So Sam isn't perfect?" Maggie asked.

"He is, with that one exception. Does Barney tango?"

"Not unless they taught it in dancing school, along with the box step."

"Oh, Maggie, I'm so glad it's over," Tessa said, sitting down on the edge of the bed. "The press conference, the gala—everything a triumph—now all that's left is the ultrasound and the flight back home. Won't you go to sleep now? There's nothing left to worry about, and with this first trip under your belt, speaking loosely, you know the others will simply be more of the same. You can finally relax."

"But you must be exhausted. You've been on your feet for two days."

"Oh, maybe just a little, but it doesn't matter . . . you only live once." Tessa yawned and stretched, and unzipped her dress, letting it slither to the floor. Maggie lay back with her eyes half-closed until she heard Tessa return from the bathroom in her bathrobe and sit at the dressing table to take off her makeup. Maggie pulled herself up on her pillows with quiet determination, while Tessa, her back turned, concentrated on silently turning the lid of a jar of cleansing cream.

"Who was my father?"

"Oh! Good God! You scared me! I thought you were sleeping."

"Who was he?" Maggie demanded firmly. "I want to know all about him, every last detail. Don't leave out a thing. I would have asked sooner but I didn't want to get into it and probably upset you before the big night."

"Your father's name was Mark O'Malley and you look very much like him. He was tall and beautiful and as Irish as they come, and he had your curly dark hair and your marvelous big blue eyes, and he was seductive and confident and had a charm no one could resist. Like you. He was a local hero, Maggie, the captain of the high school football team. I was besotted with him for two years. I promise you, I was violently in love and I know how that feels."

"Two years? You had a two-year romance with him?"

"Hardly that," Tessa answered soberly, remembering. "He didn't know I existed . . . my love was a mad, completely one-sided passion. I adored him from a distance, I dreamed of him night and day. It was first love, and there's nothing like it. All-consuming. You ought to know, you and your Barney. Finally, when I had just turned fourteen, a friend and I crashed a party at his house and I met him. I told him I was eighteen and he believed me. I looked much older than I was and I dressed the part. He took me upstairs and he . . . more or less . . . seduced me. He never knew my name, he never knew I'd gotten pregnant, he never saw me again."

"You mean . . . he could be alive?"

"Well, of course." Tessa laughed. "He's probably a perfectly nice forty-one-year-old guy with a wife and four football-playing kids somewhere."

"That son of a bitch!"

"No, no Maggie, don't say that! I had on a lot of makeup, he thought I knew what I was doing; I led him on, actually, he certainly didn't have to force me, so you can't blame him. Blame me, I'd had too much to drink and I wanted to."

"Is that what you mean by he 'more or less' seduced you?"

"Well . . . no."

"Then you mean you seduced him?"

"Not that either."

"So how in the name of God did you get knocked up?" Maggie asked impatiently.

"Do you absolutely insist on knowing?"

"I do."

"I warn you, it's quite improbable."

"I have a right to know," Maggie insisted sturdily.

"He was . . . overly . . . aroused . . . and when he . . . ah, when he . . . penetrated me, he only managed . . . about an inch . . . before he had an orgasm, and that was that."

"An inch! That's how you had me? An inch! You were still a virgin, for Christ's sake!"

"I was, but who would believe me? Your grandparents didn't want to know a single detail; they knew I was a sinner and that was enough."

"So I owe my existence to a horny high school hero with super sperm who suffered from premature ejaculation and a horny high school girl who let *him put it in*! Where were you when they taught sex ed?"

"In deepest Catholic school."

"Great. Just great." Maggie shook her head at the ways of yesteryear.

"Well, think of it this way, if it hadn't happened, you wouldn't be alive."

"Oh, God," said Maggie, "an inch, an inch, one lucky inch . . ." and she began to giggle so hard that the mattress started shaking. Soon she began to howl with laughter. "An inch, an inch, I owe my life to just one inch . . ."

"Stop it, you're getting hysterical," Tessa begged, beginning to laugh herself. "Please, please stop it, Maggie, honestly it wasn't funny at the time, but you made me tell you all the details . . . oh, oh, I admit it's really . . . too ridiculous . . . when it doesn't happen . . . to you, oh, an inch, that's all it was, an inch . . . not . . . not that he didn't have . . . much more . . . oh, oh . . ."

"I assumed . . . he did . . . dear old Dad . . . oh, oh, poor *Mamãe* . . . what a rotten break, what lousy luck, I always knew I was special but I never guessed I was the product of a virgin birth. Oh, you're right, it is improbable . . . but I believe you, even if nobody else ever did."

Maggie and Tessa gave full rein to their fill of mirth until they both fell silent with the realization that this discussion wasn't over.

"When I got that letter from my grandfather," Maggie said, solemnly, "what just about killed me was not the whole teenage mom story, because anyone would understand that, but the fact that when you could have acknowledged me, you didn't. I totally get it that when you became famous at sixteen you couldn't be allowed to have a kid, but what about when you married Luke and my grandparents died? That's where the whole thing sucks! Since I was supposed to be your sister *anyway*, not some stranger, why didn't you and Luke just take me instead of sending me to the Websters?"

"There are a dozen answers to that, none of them any good."

"Yeah? Well, tell me a few, just for my information."

"Luke never knew you were my child, that was the beginning of it."

"You never told him?"

"I . . . he wanted to marry a virgin. It was terribly important to him, a real obsession."

"What right did he have to want a virgin!" Maggie sputtered with rage. "Luke was a hundred years older than you, he'd had a million women, what gave him the goddamned right to *have the fucking nerve*, to want a virgin? Was he some kind of god who demanded a virgin sacrifice?"

"Oh, Maggie, if only I'd dared to ask him that! I was too stupid, too much in love, too young, I wanted him too much, I believed he could keep me safe. Oh, how I needed to feel safe! It was like suddenly being able to breathe fresh air after being underground for years. I was desperate. I'd never felt safe in my life, especially after I got pregnant . . . I don't expect you to understand or forgive me, I'm just telling you exactly the way it was. I was afraid to lose Luke, so I *lied* by letting him believe it, and then, afterward, I couldn't even consider telling him the truth because it was such an enormous and *fundamental lie,* Maggie, I believed our life together was founded on his believing me. Depended on it. Even on our wedding night—I played up to it."

"But you'd had a child, couldn't he tell?"

"The doctor who delivered you assured me that he'd done me a favor and stitched me up so that I was 'as good as new.' I found out what that meant the first time Luke and I made love."

"Okay, so you got away with passing as a virgin. But

the man totally, absolutely *adored* you, I know that, so why couldn't you admit it *sooner or later*, once he couldn't live without you? All those years, Tessa! Why couldn't you face up to telling a lie? Tell him to take his belief in you, and stuff it? That's what I would have done!"

"I was a criminal coward, Maggie. Luke was a very selfish man. I always knew it, even when he was alive. He had a terribly jealous temperament and he hated my career, but he let me have it anyway. I didn't want to disturb that delicate balance we'd created. Luke was demanding, and controlling, but even though his world revolved completely around him, I had become the most important element in it. He was incredibly generous in so many ways, to so many people."

"He bought people," Maggie said in a low voice.

"Yes, he did, one way or another, Maggie, but he didn't buy me. I allowed him to set the terms of our life because I *liked* it that way. I didn't have to do it, don't you understand, I wanted to! Deep down, I wanted to be dominated, to be all the things Luke wanted me to be. I told you, it made me feel *safe*, and I thought I couldn't live without that. I wasn't as brave as you would have been. I took the easy way. The lying way. The protected way. The longer I did it, the more it became the *only* way."

"But after Luke died, why couldn't you have told me then?"

"That's the one thing I got right, Maggie, the one action I'm proud of. I was a basket case, nothing would have helped but time and getting through the grieving and loss by myself. I knew I had to just set my teeth, keep busy, and do my mourning alone. If I'd let you sacrifice your last year in school to be with me, it would have been thoroughly wrong and horribly unfair to you. *I'm certain about that*. As soon as I discovered that I was able to make plans again, my first thought was to claim you. But you'd received that letter . . . and it was too late."

"More than five years ago . . . I can't believe it," Maggie murmured.

"Maggie," Tessa said, "you do believe, don't you, that I never understood how you felt about the Websters? I thought you were happy with them."

"I never wanted you to know."

"But I should have guessed!"

"You couldn't have, not possibly. I'm a pretty good liar myself, and I can keep it up for years, like you. Maybe it's a talent that runs in the family . . . your mother, then you . . . and me."

"You don't have to let me off the hook."

"Maybe I want to," Maggie said impetuously, "maybe I'd rather have a mother I can love, than a sister I won't look at and don't speak to."

"Maggie, oh, Maggie, do you mean that?"

"Isn't it time?" Maggie asked, with a sob, opening her arms and pulling Tessa close, so that she could lay her head on Tessa's shoulder and feel the sweet, necessary, longed-for comfort of her mother's embrace.

39

When?" Dr. Helen Lawrence echoed Maggie's question. "I'd guess in about six months, more or less, but I wish you had some clue as to when you got pregnant. It would take a lot of the guesswork out of this."

"I always used my diaphragm," Maggie laughed, pocketing the ultrasound photographs Doctor Roberto had given her to take to her own gynecologist in New York for comparison.

"Always?"

"Well . . . maybe," Maggie said thoughtfully, remembering the frenzied, incredulous, magnificent haste of the first night with Barney, "maybe there's the possibility that I forgot, once, in the spirit of the moment as it were, but what's once, Doctor Lawrence?"

"Even if you *always* used it, there's a failure rate, even if you used a diaphragm and a condom, there's still a failure rate. Almost none, I grant you, Maggie, but never discount the power of a sperm. But since you're so thrilled to be pregnant, it doesn't matter."

"Well," Maggie defended herself, her eyes rolling with mischief, "at least my diaphragm worked for five years, with replacements of course. Don't you remember when I first came to you to be fitted? I didn't know any doctor's name but Tessa's."

"Of course. You were just eighteen and so upset that you couldn't get contraception for free from the college you couldn't afford to go to, that I didn't charge you. It was the very least I could do. After all, Tessa'd sent me plenty of patients in the course of years. How could I charge her little sister? Whatever happened to that ceramic-porcelain person you were so involved with way back then?"

"Andy? He married a bookish, beautiful, and, so I hear, slightly daffy daughter of an earl—very appropriate, young, rich, noble. Just his style—and in about six months, when Hamilton Scott retires, he'll be coming back here to help run the business."

"And the father of this baby of yours? Or is that too personal?"

"Oh, Doctor Lawrence, you'll be invited to the wedding! His name is Barney Webster and I've known him all my life."

"How refreshingly unconventional."

"Don't you mean conventional?"

"These days? When a girl gets married to someone she's known all her life? It makes a doctor's hair stand on end with surprise. It's unique. Congratulations, Maggie, my dear. I'm thrilled!"

"Thank you, Doctor."

"You're sure you don't want to know the sex of the baby? I can tell by now."

"No, I want to be surprised!"

"You're wonderfully old-fashioned, Maggie. Now tell me, how's Tessa doing?"

"She's simply marvelous. She totally wowed them down in São Paulo. She did her job and my job and everything went better than it would have if I'd been on my feet."

"What about her appetite?"

"Her appetite? I honestly didn't notice."

"It's so vitally important for her to keep eating," Helen Lawrence fretted, sitting forward and fixing Maggie with earnest eyes. "I was very upset when Susan Hill told me Tessa had decided against any chemotherapy or radiation, but obviously," she sighed, "treatment would have made it impossible to make all these public appearances for the auction that you've been telling me about."

Maggie, too stunned to seize the deeper meaning of the doctor's words, felt brute instinct telling her to maintain her calm at any price.

"Obviously," she agreed in a voice that revealed nothing.

"Maggie, are you able to notice if she's feeling any pain yet? Doctor Hill has all sorts of methods of keeping it under control, but of course, knowing Tessa, if she had a job to do, she wouldn't use anything as strong as Roxanol, which really does the trick. She'd probably just pop a Percocet or a Dilaudid and get on with the show."

"Roxanol?" Maggie asked casually, her nails biting into her palms.

"Morphine in an elixir, a liquid, form. It tends to slow you down and numb you, you're not as alert or sharp as usual and you won't be as willing to make the effort to eat. Food aversion is such a difficult thing to do anything about. Whatever you can do to get her to increase her fat intake is important, Maggie, since you're traveling with her and seeing her every day. Most people with her kind of cancer lose a shocking amount of weight, and the last time I saw Tessa she didn't have an extra pound on her to lose."

"Fat intake?" Maggie parroted, sitting straight in her chair by using all her willpower.

"She's never carried any extra weight, Maggie, you know that as well as I do."

"True, but how about . . . about her kind of cancer?" Maggie said carefully, keeping her face as immobile as possible and her voice utterly level. If she didn't find out as much as she could from Doctor Lawrence, Tessa was entirely capable of not saying anything to anyone until she absolutely had to. "I don't quite understand it."

"That's not surprising. Most people don't. Pancreatic cancer is so rarely diagnosed before it's spread. There usually aren't any symptoms until it's too late. If Tessa hadn't come to me for something else she wouldn't have known for months. Quite possibly not even now. Often it's other people who notice when they see someone after a period of time and realize how thin they've grown."

" 'Too late,' too late to cure it, you mean?"

"Too late to treat it. Maybe someday there will be a cure, but not yet, Maggie, that's the terrible pity of it. Thank goodness you're having a baby—that's going to be a great happiness and distraction for her. She'll have lots of time to enjoy your baby, months and months with any luck."

"Only . . . months? Not . . . a year?"

"Oh, yes, maybe a year, even a little more, God willing. We just don't know."

"Do you think . . . would it be a good idea . . . if I suggested that she stop making these trips?"

"No, absolutely not. Obviously South America agreed with her. She'll know when she feels too tired to travel. With Tessa's willpower, all this hoopla probably helps to keep her going, now that I think about it, and serves to distract her at the very least. The worst thing would be having too much time to think. Anyway, it's her choice how she spends the time she has left."

"How much . . . morphine is it safe to take?"

"As much as she wants, Maggie. I hate doctors who dole out pain relief to the dying. It's not as if there's a danger of long-term addiction, is there?"

"No, of course not, I never considered that."

"No reason why you should," Helen Lawrence replied briskly as she got up to show Maggie to the door. "Now be sure to take those vitamins I prescribed for you and make an appointment for a month from now with my nurse. I'll call you as soon as I have the results of all your blood work, but from everything I've checked, you couldn't be healthier and you're perfectly all right to travel. You're very pale, but that's what the winter in New York will do to a girl. I guess I should start calling you a 'woman' now, shouldn't I?"

"I don't care," Maggie said, "it doesn't make any difference."

Maggie walked up Lexington Avenue as purposefully and quickly as she always did, although she was absolutely aimless. She wasn't expected anywhere. Once she'd been able to get a doctor's appointment, she'd told the office that she was taking the rest of the day off, since she and Tessa had arrived home so late the previous night.

Everything she passed, every store window, every traffic light, every man and woman on the street looked unnaturally bright and clearly outlined, as strangely and flatly illuminated as if she were walking through a comic strip. She crossed the street when other people crossed the street, she avoided the taxis that made their turns too close to the curbs, she kept from being jostled with her habitual agility, she put one foot quickly in front of the other to keep up with everyone else, but she wasn't conscious of anything except Helen Lawrence's words.

She didn't feel shock, she didn't feel sad, she didn't feel surprise, she didn't feel pity, she didn't feel anything, Maggie realized. She felt blank, as blank as a sheet of white paper covered by fresh snow. She felt cold and blank and white. The only thing to do was to keep moving.

Maggie reached the Carlyle. Without bothering to have herself announced, she took an elevator directly up to Tessa's floor. She rang, and when the maid opened the door she pushed by her and walked into the living room, where Tessa was arranging a vase of flowers.

"I saw Helen Lawrence this afternoon. She told me.

About you. About your cancer." Her voice was hard and furious.

Tessa carefully adjusted a rose and straightened up as slowly as possible, putting off the minute when she'd have to look at Maggie's face.

"Helen must have thought you knew," she said calmly. "I was going to tell you in my own way, Maggie darling, but not yet, not until I had any real symptoms. I feel perfectly fine. I wouldn't believe there was anything wrong if I didn't know."

"Don't 'Maggie darling' me! *How could you, Tessa?* How could you be so cruel to me? Why didn't you just leave things the way they were? Everything was great before you came along and dangled an irresistible auction in front of Liz—all she had to do was turn me over to you. You said Luke bought people—what about you? God damn you, Tessa, I didn't need you, I didn't miss you, I had my own life and you weren't remotely part of it. I never gave you a thought. I didn't hate you, I was indifferent. But now! You trapped me. How could you plan a way to *get* at me, how could you arrange it so that I'd find out what it was like to have a mother? You knew before you started that I'm going to lose you, but no, you weren't satisfied to let me live my own life, you had to make me love you—"

"But that wasn't—"

"Don't tell me that! It was! You know you hoped I'd love you when I got to know you. Deny that!" Maggie challenged Tessa, her anger as unstoppable as breaking surf.

"I can't deny that I wanted us to mean something to each other," Tessa said in a voice that was all but demolished by Maggie's rage. "I wanted to try to repair the things I'd done, I didn't want to die without your forgiving me for the way I neglected you. I had to try to explain why it happened, no matter how ashamed I was of myself."

"*Yourself.*" Maggie shouted. "Always yourself! That's all you thought about, *your* needs and *your* reasons and *your* feelings and *your* lies and why you did this and why you did that for endless whole lousy years! Did you ever put yourself in my place? Even for a minute? Just look at the way you acted in São Paulo, knocking yourself out, showboating, taking care of me as if the world depended on it. So what if I'd had a miscarriage? You knew I wasn't married, what made you assume I even wanted to have a baby? It was an excuse, that's all, you saw a chance to mother me and you grabbed it. Nothing was too much for you. Why didn't you take care of yourself? You knew and you slept on those chairs! You knew and you spent your precious energy running around a hotel doing my job. How the fuck do you think that makes me feel? Guilty, that's how, guilty as sin."

"There's not one single thing I did on the trip that will shorten my life and a rest cure wouldn't make me better, didn't Helen explain that? But seeing your baby . . . that's going to make a big difference to me. I was just being selfish again."

"I understand that, damn it, but it doesn't help, don't you understand anything? I still feel so terribly guilty and it's all my fault. Why couldn't I have opened at least one of those letters you kept sending, why was I so stubborn, why was I so devoted to collecting the injustice of it all, why did I never even try to find out your side of it? Oh, Tessa, *I can't bear it* . . . I literally can't bear it. . . . I don't know what's right and what's wrong anymore . . . I don't know what to do . . ." Maggie faltered, as her storm of emotion swept her suddenly into the tumult of tears she hadn't been able to shed before.

"Come sit down here." Tessa tugged Maggie down onto a sofa and pulled her close. She wiped away the tears that streamed unceasingly down Maggie's hot face, smoothing her cap of curls and giving her little kisses all over the cheek she could reach.

"Don't blame yourself! If there's only one thing I can tell you, it's to not blame yourself. I've done enough of it for both of us. Please, Maggie, I'd have sent those letters back just the way you did, honestly, truly, cross my heart. You had your pride and you were right to turn away from me. It was the least you could do. You were right to resent me. If I hadn't found out how little time I had left, who knows what I would have done? Left you alone, in all probability. I never thought of it from your point of view, only from mine."

"Oh, Tessa, what are we going to do now?" Maggie asked in a tone of uncomprehending anguish.

"We can't walk out of the theater and ask for our money back," Tessa said, with a note of genuine self-mockery in her voice, although tears were running down her cheeks and mingling with Maggie's. "We're stuck in our seats, we've got to make the most of the rest of the performance. At least we can sit next to each other and hold hands for as long as it lasts."

"A pretty pair," Maggie sobbed. "But what are we going to do?"

"Stop crying, I guess, and start living again."

"I love you, Tessa. I've always loved you, even when I thought I didn't, but now I love you so much more. You know that, don't you?"

"Yes, my own darling, my daughter, my little girl, I do. That's what we're going to do now, love each other, very hard and very much. That's the only answer I can think of."

"You're going to tell me something you think I don't want to hear," Sam whispered to Tessa as she lay naked in his arms that evening. "Eli's finished the script, hasn't he, and they want you out on the coast tomorrow."

"Why do you say that?" Tessa asked, her voice muffled in his chest.

"Because I've never been seduced the way you seduced me tonight . . . I felt like an innocent, young, untutored broth of a lad in the arms of a magnificent female who had decided to make a real man out of me. Is this what actors mean by 'getting into the part'?"

"You thought I was being Cassie? Passionate Cassie?" Tessa asked, lifting her head.

"Passionate Tessa with something . . . astonishingly new, something I'd never even dreamed of before."

If only it were that, Tessa thought, burrowing again into his arms. If only her frenzy had been Method acting, instead of a driving need to make love one last time before she had to tell him about her sickness, a last celebration of pure sexual playfulness during which he wouldn't know about her cancer, in which such awareness couldn't cross his mind while they were together.

"But what you don't know, and couldn't guess," Sam continued, "is that I've made arrangements to begin my sabbatical year early so I'll be able to spend it with you, while the picture's being made. I realized I couldn't let you go away on location without me, or rather, to be honest, I couldn't stand to stay here while you were gone. I know it's boredom squared to watch a picture being made so I'll do research during the day and be there when you get back at night, or whenever you have a free minute. How does that sound to you?"

"Like a dream of impossible bliss."

"Nothing impossible about it—it's already arranged with the dean of my department."

"But it can't be, Sam." Tessa sat up in bed, leaned against the headboard, and pulled a robe over her naked body. She took a shuddering breath and reminded herself that if she didn't tell him now, she'd have to do it tomorrow because she couldn't let him find out the way Maggie had. "It can't be because I can't make the film and I can't make the film because I have cancer," she said, forcing her voice to be as ruthlessly direct as a well-thrust dagger.

Sam swung his feet to the floor, his body reacting against the blow before his mind.

"I don't believe it."

"Yes, you do. You know I wouldn't say it if it weren't true."

He looked at her sitting with her arms folded defensively over her breasts, her hands balled into fists, and moved quickly toward her, until he could hold her fiercely close. "Tessa, we'll fight it together, darling, you're going to be all right, I promise you."

"No, I'm not going to be all right, Sam."

"*Don't say that.* Whatever it takes, you have to do it, I'll be with you every second."

"There's nothing to do."

"Who told you that nonsense?"

"The doctor."

"For God's sake, Tessa, what kind of quack told you a thing like that? Tomorrow we'll find the best doctor in New York—"

"Sam, Sam darling, listen to me. I've been to one of the best doctors in New York. I have pancreatic—"

"God! No!" He let her go abruptly, stood up, and punched the wall so hard that she could hear a bone in his hand break.

"Sam?" Tessa asked in the sudden silence.

"My father died of it."

"So you understand."

"Yes."

"How old was he?"

"Almost eighty. Tessa, did you get a second opinion? You're much too young, there's something wrong . . . it's simply not possible . . ."

"I'd get a second opinion, if it would make you feel better, but I've had ultrasound and computerized tomography and a biopsy and a consultation with a top oncologist and there's no doubt. It's inoperable and I refuse to have treatment that would eat up whatever good time is left. It's very early, Sam, I have at least a year and maybe more, maybe even two . . . yes, just hold me, keep holding me, don't ever let me go."

"I won't, my beautiful girl, I won't."

40

Fiona Bridges, who had been in New York for two days of the last week in March, leading up to tonight's auction, perched on the seat Tessa had reserved for her, one of the best in the house, in the middle of the main auction room where she could see all the action. As she waited, Fiona clutched her bidder's paddle, on which she was relieved to note that the numbers were a good eight inches high. She was free to tug her ears, pull her nose, and make any facial or body movement she pleased. Only the paddle, raised above her head, would be considered a bid.

Roddy Fensterwald, sitting in another reserved seat next to Fiona, had repeatedly reassured her of this very fact, but until she had actually received her paddle from one of the dozen young women sitting behind the long tables in the entrance, where hundreds of carefully selected people brandished their invitations and lined up to identify themselves and register as bidders, she hadn't been quiet in her mind about it. Unlike Roddy, who collected antiques and frequented auctions, this was her first such event.

At the Oscars, Fiona was so accustomed by now to

the status of the placement of her seat, just a few rows behind the nominated stars and far forward of the nominated technical people, that she took it for granted. Her last five independent productions had all been solid box-office hits, and for a woman in Hollywood that was powerful medicine. But the mob on Oscar night, black-tie though it was, seemed pitifully small-town and inbred, she observed, compared to this luxurious and fevered assembly of the chirping, squealing, waving, kissing, and preening international ultra-rich who were now crowding excitedly into the high, wood-paneled auction rooms. Fiona craned her neck in every direction, grateful to Tessa for inviting them and producing these seats.

"I feel like an utter hick," she whispered to Roddy.

"Me too," he responded. "I don't think there's ever been anything like this . . . of course I wasn't at the Duchess of Windsor's sale, but that was held in Geneva, out-of-town is out-of-town, darling, no matter what. This auction's electrified New York. That's all people were talking about wherever I went today, even the taxi drivers."

"I didn't dare tell anybody I had a reserved seat, I knew they would have torn me apart in sheer envy."

"Especially since you're not in the market for any of the jewels."

"And you *are*, Roddy?"

"At these prices? But I couldn't resist getting a paddle anymore than you could. It looks as if I'm here to pick up a little something for you, love. How many of these women do you think are going to be bidding for themselves? Almost none, I bet. It'll be the men who'll actually bid, egged on by the women, and it's the men who'll pay."

"Have you realized that it's eleven whole years since that night when Tessa, looking like Titania in *A Midsummer Night's Dream* presented the Best Picture award?"

"Eleven years! Jesus, Fiona, you're right. It was

eighty-two. Missing won, didn't it, or was it *E.T.?* I never can remember."

"*Gandhi*, and how you can forget is beyond me."

"My inner feminist says it should have been *Tootsie*. Were movies better then or were we younger?"

"Both," Fiona responded fervently, "both."

"I still don't understand at all why Tessa's having this auction," Roddy mused. "It isn't as if she couldn't afford to keep her jewels in their vaults, quietly letting them appreciate in value. No matter how dowdy and academic her life's going to be with Sam, she's still going to have years and years of major movie star appearances at which to wear them."

"I think the real reason is no more mysterious than what she wrote in the 'Owner's Note' in the beginning of the catalog, where she said that she felt the resources tied up in the jewels would be better spent now in creating a foundation for cancer research. As simple as that."

"Is our Tessa bucking for sainthood? That's never been her style," Roddy said thoughtfully. "Her jewels are so much a part of her that selling them is as if she's saying good-bye to her past. And that doesn't make sense. It makes me feel sad—and old. . . . I suppose I simply don't like to think of them belonging to other women."

"Maybe this is some sort of sign that the eighties are really over."

"What a terrible thought! Fiona, never, ever say that again! Don't even think it!" Roddy said, aghast.

"Sorry, darling. The eighties will last till the year three thousand, never fear."

"You're sure?"

"Positive," Fiona said wryly. She'd just had alterations made on all the shoulder pads in her large and expensive wardrobe of power suits, yet not one of the jackets looked quite right anymore. There was no way out, she'd have to spring for totally new Armani, the whole nine yards, or forget about the industry lunch.

There was no such thing as investment dressing, and the people who edited fashion magazines were touts. Whatever was changing, and *something* damn well was, she didn't have the handle on it yet. Nevertheless, with her job, she needed to stay well ahead of the curve.

"Where's the private box Tessa's sitting in?" Roddy asked.

"Up there, behind you," Fiona said, turning and pointing to the upper level of the huge room. "See those windows that are almost hidden by the paneling? There's a viewing room up there from which the owners or heirs can witness the auction without being stared at."

"What if . . ."

"What if what?"

"Well, suppose Tessa suddenly changed her mind about a certain piece, couldn't she just bid on it, like everybody else? Maybe through a special telephone?"

"It seems that's illegal, once it's been consigned."

"How do you know so much, when this is your first auction?" Roddy asked suspiciously.

"Tessa told me when we had lunch yesterday."

"And how come I wasn't invited?"

"Girl talk, Tootsie."

Andy McCloud, who had returned home early to be present at the auction of the jewels of Tessa Kent, stood at his privileged place under the raised podium at which his uncle was about to begin the auction, and marveled at the scene. Every seat they had been able to cram into both auction rooms was filled with bidders from all over the world, many of them people who had never come to S & S before, reserving their custom for Sotheby's or Christie's.

Throughout the Western Hemisphere, in Beverly Hills, Chicago, Boston, Dallas, Miami, San Francisco, and Palm Beach, as well as in Toronto, Montreal, Mexico City, São Paulo, Rio, and Buenos Aires, S & S offices had rented hotel ballrooms that had a direct audio feed to Hamilton Scott's podium, so that the people sitting in those cities could hear the auction as it took place. In each of those ballrooms, as here at S & S, the individual jewel being auctioned was shown, in a vastly enlarged photograph, on a giant screen that hung several feet above the auctioneer's head, while an electronic board, just under the photograph of each jewel, would display the current bid in all major currencies.

There was a bank of twenty-five telephones, both here and in the other rooms, each one of which had its own line and its specially trained operator, who would take phone bids from people who either found it inconvenient to travel to the auction or, in many cases, choose to remain at home, in order to maintain their privacy.

Right now, Andy thought, his excitement mounting, there were people everywhere, in every time zone, in both hemispheres, up all night, sitting by their phones, eyes trained on their catalogs, waiting for the call from their particular operator that would notify them when the lots on which they had requested telephone bids were about to come up. The operator would repeat the latest price as quickly as the auctioneer said it, allowing this global network of invisible bidders to participate fully in each sale. The hammer would not fall on a single jewel as long as somewhere in the world there was someone still willing to raise the bid, one anonymous phone bidder prepared to duel with another anonymous phone bidder until one of them carried the day.

And no one in the world, Andy told himself, would know who had won, except for the three people who would go over the auction in detail tomorrow: Uncle Hamilton, Aunt Liz, and finally, after all these years, himself. Even then, many of the most important purchases would be made by someone bidding for someone else, whose identity even they would never know. Jewels were, as they had always been, the most reliable form of international currency, a traditional hedge for the very rich against everything but total destruction of the earth and its population.

What a fabulous business! As much as he was captivated by his porcelains and his ceramics, he had to admit that nothing except a great painting auction could equal the fascination and violent excitement of a great jewel auction. He could positively feel the ebb and flow of the financial structure of the world, as if it were an underground river that tonight had chosen to flow just below the floorboards of S & S.

He had no official job here, unlike anyone else who worked for S & S. "Just observe closely," Aunt Liz had said, "and remember everything." Did she mean to include the sight of Maggie Horvath Webster, Andy wondered, Maggie who looked—and it seemed impossible—even more sexy, even more irresistible pregnant than she had as a virgin? It was, Andy found to his surprise, rather more bitter than sweet to realize that he was the only person in the room who was entitled to make that precise judgment. After all, his wife, Lady Clarissa, had her own much-appreciated charms, all of them delicately blond, delicately boned, delicately bosomed, delicately smiling, delicately—just plain delicate, damn it. How could Maggie, who was all boldness and blossom, all belly laughs and noticeable belly, seem somehow, bewitchingly . . . more . . . feminine? Absurd.

He watched her closely as she was busy greeting and seating the dozens of journalists of every description who were important enough to be invited tonight, so that tomorrow the auction would live a vast second life in the press. Cameras weren't allowed inside the auction rooms; no one wanted to risk being photographed in the act of buying millions of dollars worth of jewels, but certain journalists were welcome, and those rare bidders who didn't object to publicity could discreetly arrange for their names to be released through Maggie or one of her corps of press officers, all of whom had adopted Maggie's maternity uniform of a long, widely flaring black turtleneck tunic over very slim black pants and ballet slippers. Or *were* they all pregnant, Andy asked himself. Perhaps she'd started a new fad?

God knows, it would be understandable after the job she'd done on this auction. She and Tessa Kent. Odd, decidedly odd that Maggie had never seen fit to mention that she was Tessa Kent's sister, back when they were together. Could it be that she hadn't trusted him? Hardly likely, he reflected, all things considered. There must have been another reason. After all, a woman tells her first lover everything—at least she should. Clarissa had, revealing all of her delicate, innocent, girlish little secrets, like a scattering of tiny, unopened buds.

However, be that as it may, he had to admit that there had never been such a formidable team in the history of preauction publicity as Tessa and Maggie, airlifted in the past months from one center of wealth to another. How, he wondered, did that fellow, Webster, feel about having his wife jaunting about, from Tokyo to Lugano, in her present condition? And who was the guy, anyway? A devastating biker chap, according to Aunt Liz, who'd been at the wedding. Rode a Ducati, apparently. Must be some sort of playboy. Well, whoever he was, he hadn't waited long to get his wife pregnant, had he? Not even until the nuptials. Face it, old chap, Andy told himself, as he forced himself to turn his yearning eyes away from Maggie, she'd been a pushover.

Polly Guildenstern, dressed in her one concession to the 1990s, a dark green, high-necked velvet dress that was starkly modern in cut, sat breathlessly attentive, waiting for the auction to start, one row in front of Fiona and Roddy.

She was in a fluster, Polly realized. She hated the East Side of Manhattan, garish, loud, and horribly nouveau. She chose to spend her time alone in her high, peaceful studio, cooking and working on the few commissions for miniatures that came her way, just enough to provide a frugal but decent living. In her free time, hand in hand with Jane, she enjoyed occasionally dipping into the predictable confines of their own, discerningly chosen, bars and discos. But this place! She hardly knew what to make of this overwhelming mass of exuberantly perfumed, gossiping, kiss-blowing, overdressed femaleness, punctuated by the dark blue and dark gray suits of their escorts.

Was it like a harem or opening night at La Scala or a gypsy encampment or the Carnival in Rio without music? All of them put together, she decided, since the thought of any one of those particular events made her feel nervous. The only thing that calmed her was her paddle, which gave her an entitlement she felt she otherwise lacked.

On the other hand, Polly thought, sitting up straighter, her capricious, spicy smile brightening her face, just who here *knew* as much as she? Who here could put the entire picture together, who here knew *why* this auction was happening, who here had *made* this auction happen? Unknown to anyone in this crowd, tonight, *she was the Auction Goddess.*

Tessa and Maggie knew, of course, but they were only two parts of a whole that she had been inspired to create. Sam Conway? She didn't know if he knew, nor did she know if Barney knew. It wasn't the kind of thing you could ask somebody, Polly told herself, with the complacent delight of a confirmed secret keeper. Either you knew and didn't say anything, or you simply didn't know there was anything *to* know. A tiny, self-satisfied expression settled on her face, and her charming face was illuminated as she looked benevolently over the room.

"Excuse me, may I ask you a question?" Polly's neighbor in the row, an older woman with gray hair, wearing a noble amount of rubies with her silver brocade suit, turned toward her.

"Oh!" Polly said, startled out of her reverie. "Certainly."

"That miniature you're wearing fascinates me. I wonder if I could possibly look at it more closely?"

"Here, I'll take it off so you can get a really good look," Polly said, unknotting the velvet ribbon from around her neck. She was particularly proud of the tiny object, which had been fit into an oval of old gold. It was a portrait of Jane against a dramatic, solid blue background, wearing an old-fashioned man's white linen shirt trimmed with lace, under a soft black leather vest, of which just one silver button was undone.

"Oh, how extraordinary! My goodness gracious, I don't think I've ever seen anything so utterly lovely. The details, my dear, the details! I feel as if he must have been exactly like that, down to the last hair on his head."

"Yes, she is. It's rather a good likeness," Polly said demurely.

"You mean, the model's alive? A woman? I thought it was a man because of the clothes. But you can't mean this is contemporary?"

"I finished painting it last week," Polly purred.

"Good grief! I thought it must be seventeenth century! Isaac Oliver probably."

"Thank you. I executed it in Oliver's style; in fact the background is the same blue he used in the portrait of John Donne in Queen Elizabeth's collection."

"Oh, I'm all chills! I can't believe it! I saw that collection just last year. The Donne was dated sixteen sixteen. Uncanny! Uncanny. My dear, you don't, by any chance, accept commissions?"

"I only work on commission," Polly answered, her nose quivering with the pride of craftsmanship.

"How perfect! I've been thinking about next year's Christmas presents, such a problem when you have four daughters and they all have little ones, so I start early. Now, do you think you could possibly find the time to squeeze in miniatures of each of their children? That would take care of all the girls and be *such* a load off my mind. I always give them very special gifts, but obviously the prices here tonight are going to be ridiculous. Miniatures of my grandchildren would be much more sentimental and meaningful than anything of Tessa Kent's, mad as my girls are about her."

"It all depends," Polly said, her brain working madly. "How many children are there?"

"Eleven, so far, counting the babies, and I couldn't leave them out, could I?"

"Eleven. Hmm. That's a lot of children."

"Oh, dear, are there too many? You'd have until next December. That's almost nine months. You could leave out the babies if it were absolutely necessary."

"Well, I suppose I might, just, be able to manage, if I put all my other commissions on hold, and worked like a demon," Polly said with a thoughtful frown. "But the problem is that it would mean disappointing a lot of people. However . . . since children are only young once . . . yes, I could certainly *consider* it, but only because of the sentimental value."

"Oh, my dear, if only you'd agree, I'd be the happiest woman in the world! How much are they, by the way?"

"They're not inexpensive," Polly warned.

"I should think not," her neighbor said indignantly.

"I ask five thousand dollars each, no matter the age of the sitter. Babies are particularly difficult. They haven't developed the optimum amount of facial detail, so it's a triumph to do them justice."

"How exceedingly well put. Indeed, I'd never realized that. Oh, could you please say yes and book your dance card solid for the rest of the year? You can work from photos, can't you? Otherwise it wouldn't be a surprise."

"I've often done that, particularly with children. They do wriggle."

"Perfect. Now, here's my card. If you'll write down your name and address, I'll have my accountant make all the necessary financial arrangements tomorrow. You tell him what you want. A certified check, or whatever you require to give up your other commissions. Oh, but you haven't agreed yet. Do say yes! Yes? Oh, what a relief! Now I can sit back and enjoy this auction without even thinking if I should bid or not."

"I'm not going to worry about it either," Polly agreed heartily.

"There's only one thing . . ."

" Yes . . . ?"

"Well, you see, many of my friends will want to come to you too, once they see the miniatures. Not just for children, either. It'll become a rage, I'm afraid, so I'd appreciate it deeply if you called me before accepting their commissions . . . I don't want to be copied left and right by just anybody until my girls have had at least a year to be original."

"A whole year?" Polly shook her head dubiously.

"Oh, well, if you insist, make it six months. Would that be too much to ask?"

"I suppose it's only fair," Polly nodded slowly. She'd just multiplied her price ten times and ensured work for years to come. Yes, it seemed fair enough. There was a reason for the Auction Goddess to ride forth from her West Side dominions once in a great while, after all, she told herself, in high good humor, as she tied the portrait of Jane back around her neck. You met a richer class of people.

41

S am sat next to Tessa in the comfortable chairs
that were arranged in the upstairs owners' lounge.
Tonight they were alone with the panoramic view
of the heads of everyone in the room, and binoculars
were provided so that Hamilton Scott, at the podium,
seemed only feet away. Although they couldn't see the
numbers on the bidders' paddles, they could hear perfectly through the loudspeaker in the lounge. It was,
thought Sam, something like those special skyboxes at
sports events whose distant, elite placement took a lot
of the sweat and reality out of the game.

People were still being seated as Sam restlessly read-
justed his pair of binoculars. He and Tessa had been sitting here for almost an hour, with floaters popping in
every now and then to ask if they wanted anything to eat
or drink. They'd been smuggled in early through the
employees' entrance so that Tessa wouldn't have to run
the gamut of the huge crowd outside of S & S, attracted
by the arriving parade of the invited society figures and
celebrities. The mob outside was further enlarged by the
presence of mobile television trucks from all three net-
works and CNN, who would be reporting on the auction

as soon as it was over, when they could finally interview executives from S & S as well as the departing bidders.

Would this hellish auction ever start? Christ, he couldn't wait for it to be over, couldn't wait until Tessa could finally put an end to the infernal round of travel interviews, photographs, and more travel. He knew that if she had said, at any point in the past month, "enough," she could have returned to private life and let the auction take place under its own steam. No one at S & S would have complained or thought that she was giving less than she should have.

But somehow, once she'd started on the publicity, Tessa hadn't been able to cut it short by one minute. It used up a merciless, profligate, reckless amount of time, time Tessa didn't have, although that wasn't his judgment to make.

But what would he have done if he'd had the same diagnosis? Sam asked himself. Wouldn't he have continued to teach and write, no matter that his new book would never be finished, even if his courses didn't make any lasting mark on the world?

Did some people who were faced with Tessa's knowledge suddenly embark on an entirely different way of life? he wondered. Were there people who sailed a small boat from one tropical island to another, spent every penny they had left on drink and drugs, moved to Paris, bought an island off the coast of Maine and took up lobster fishing, divorced their spouses and ran off with someone else's wife, embarked on a cruise ship and never got off? Pulled a Paul Gauguin?

No, damn it, there probably weren't. People didn't, as a rule, start something new without an initial period of difficulty and resistance. It took training to sail small boats; a certain aptitude and an indifference to hangovers to go to hell with yourself; and as for divorce, who would want to spend the end of a life in a wrangle with lawyers? Lobster fishing was cold, hard, backbreaking work; living in Paris was dank under any circumstances and lonely if you didn't speak French. The essence of a cruise was that it ended. Even becoming a ski bum took the ability to ski or fake it. Gauguin was all very well, but he'd run away to exercise his already formed genius, with most of his life ahead of him.

Tessa had accomplished the one great single shining thing she had set out to do: become a mother to Maggie. It had meant spending more time than he had imagined possible when she first told him about her plans, but every minute that she worked and traveled with Maggie was a minute of motherhood reclaimed from all the years that had been lost.

Even if he had known about her cancer, when she'd first told him about the auction, he wouldn't have said a word to influence her against the idea. He didn't have the right, nor did anyone else, Sam thought, watching Tessa scanning the room, exclaiming excitedly when she caught sight of someone she knew, laughing at the sight of Fiona and Roddy deep in conversation, her binoculars constantly returning to Maggie, unable to repress her pride as she watched her most noticeably pregnant daughter move slowly through the ranks of journalists, stopping here and there to distribute chosen morsels of information.

"Darling," Tessa said, turning to Sam. "Immediately after the auction, Maggie's going to join us here and lead us out the way we came in. She's coming back to the Carlyle with us. There's something special I want to ask her. Would you mind if she and I had a drink at the bar and talked while you go on upstairs?"

"Of course not. I'll be knocked out. That's what watching people spend tons of money in public does to me. The only time I went to Las Vegas I fell asleep under the blackjack table."

"Ah, but tonight it's in a good cause." Tessa smiled at him, a strangely mysterious smile on her passionately formed lips, with such a loving look glowing in her eyes that he had to clench his fists not to cry out. Had she ever looked so vividly alive? Had her face ever been so deeply expressive? She looked as if she were waiting, with gentle patience, for a deep-throated bell to sound.

Sam knew that today, for the first time, she'd used a pain patch on her torso. He'd felt it under her blouse when he'd held her in his arms before leaving for class. She'd told him that it was called Narto-Duragesic and that it lasted for three days.

"It's pain relief for someone who isn't watching the clock," she'd explained, almost gleeful at the advances of medicine. "Beats anything you can get over the counter."

"What does the pain feel like?" he'd asked, his need to know outweighing any other consideration.

"It's so hard to describe . . . it's not sharp, not something that comes in waves, it's sort of like a stomachache that goes through to my backbone, but just a mild stomachache, sweetheart, nothing to get alarmed about, I promise."

"How long have you had it?"

"Only for a few days. Funny, I felt a real need to live with it for a while, to get to know it, to recognize it, before I used the patch. I'm not sure why. Now that I've put the patch on, I feel it going away."

"Will you promise me to eat a good lunch?"

"I won't have a choice, I'm eating with Maggie and she watches me consume every bite. Yesterday she invented the most caloric, most expensive lunch in the city, two avocado halves, slightly hollowed out and piled high with Beluga."

"Don't tell me she ordered that too?"

"Of course not, way too much salt and too much fat for her. She ordered broiled fish and cheered me on. I couldn't finish it all, nobody could have, so she polished it off. I guess you can only gorge when you shouldn't—when you should, you don't want to. That seems to be some sort of universal law . . . I loathe every bloody universal law. I've never heard of a single one I liked. Don't you agree?"

"You know I do." That oblique remark was as far as she'd ventured, Sam reflected, in discussing her condition, since that first night when she'd told him. She'd never gone for that second opinion and he'd never mentioned it again, he thought, rubbing the bone he'd broken in his hand that was still not completely healed. Mutely they'd reached an understanding that they had time, plenty of time, for whatever Tessa wanted to talk about, whenever she felt like it. Or if not, not. It was up to her.

All Sam knew was that he was on board for the whole trip, he'd be there for her, unequivocally, every step of the way. He loved her more extravagantly each day and they both knew that. All he could do was to hide, as well as he could, the bleak, blank intuition of a future without her that drilled him through and through by day and by night.

The loud crack of Hamilton Scott's hammer brought the buzz below to an abrupt halt. "Good evening, ladies and gentlemen," he announced in his rich, extravagance-inspiring voice. "Welcome to the Scott and Scott Building, and to our historic sale of magnificent jewelry from the collection of Miss Tessa Kent."

As Tessa and Maggie entered the Café Carlyle, to the sound of Bobby Short singing "A Foggy Day in London Town," a burst of cheering and applause broke out as Tessa was recognized. The news of the results of the auction had traveled all over the world the instant it finished, and in Manhattan, radio, television, and word of mouth had spread the story in less time than it had taken them to drive back from S & S to the hotel.

One hundred sixty-two million dollars had been attained, more than three times as much as the largest single-owner sale of all time, that of the Duchess of Windsor in 1987. Not a single jewel had gone for less than five or six times its high estimate, and every record ever made for every catagory of gem had been broken.

Tessa waved and smiled to the startled, congratulatory crowd as the headwaiter led them to the secluded table she'd reserved earlier in the day. The champagne she'd ordered was poured immediately and she relaxed against the banquette, sighing with relief and trying not to hum along.

"Let's not try that auction caper again," Tessa said, laughing, after the set was finished, Bobby Short had left the room, and conversation resumed all around them, creating an intimate place in which they could talk.

"Not unless you've been holding out on me and that was only some of what you've got stashed away."

"The only things left are the pearls and my ring, and a few cameos I keep upstairs. I don't care if I never see another jewel again. Enough! It feels as good as cleaning out your closets and getting rid of everything you haven't worn in two years."

"I've heard that theory," Maggie said. "But I wear everything I have until it falls apart and if I threw out one of Barney's four shirts, he'd have a fit. But you know, there actually is one of them he never wears."

"Don't touch it, take it from me. He needs it. I know more about men than you ever will, little girl."

"Oh, I don't know about that, but never mind the gory details," Maggie replied. "Why do I have the feeling that I'm here for a reason known only to you? Why am I suspicious because Sam insisted that he was too sleepy to join us? He looked deeply thirsty to me, and wide awake."

"He developed a bad case of auction fever." Tessa laughed. "I've never heard a man get so excited, it was ten times worse than when he watched the Super Bowl. What he needs is to take a tranquilizer and go to bed."

"Was he surprised that you had so many jewels?"

"He'd seen the catalog, just flipped through it once or twice to admire the Penn photos and whistle at the pictures of me, but he never bothered to read any of the descriptions, so I don't think it sank in until tonight. Then, when the action began and he actually saw and heard an emerald necklace being sold in a few brisk minutes for eleven million dollars . . . he was knocked for a loop. Even I was stunned."

That was the only time during the auction that she'd

had to fight back tears, Tessa thought. The memory of that magical night in Èze with Luke, the perfume of the lavender, the warm wind of Provence, that marvelous white Dior dress she'd worn for the first time . . . oh, had it really happened a million years ago and was it possible that there'd never be another night like that again for her? Never, ever? No, never. Never. Nevermore. But then would she ever be twenty again or on her honeymoon, even if she were guaranteed to live to be a hundred? What's more, there wasn't a woman in the room who didn't have some similiar memory, she'd told herself, and she'd stopped the silly tears before they spilled from her eyes.

"So was I, and I'm used to auctions," Maggie admitted. "I'd worked myself into a state where all the publicity we did was a self-sustaining fantasy, publicity for the sake of publicity, but tonight the fantasy turned into a huge, very real sum of money. Those people went crazy! They just had to have a piece of you at any price. You or your legend; I guess they're indivisible. It's hard to wrap my mind around it."

"I bet Liz and Hamilton aren't having any trouble getting their minds around their ten percent commission."

"It's an easier sum to swallow. Almost bite-size. Now, Tessa, tell me why I'm here and you're not upstairs with Sam."

"You don't miss much."

"I try not to."

"Actually, darling, I'd like to offer you a job."

"What?" Maggie exclaimed, almost choking on the Sprite she'd ordered instead of champagne. "I've just finished the biggest piece of work in my life and you want to offer me a job? What exquisite timing. Ma, don't you think I need a vacation? Don't you think I deserve one?"

" 'Ma'?"

"Yes, I've decided that suits you. Only when we're alone, of course."

"I love it. I feel like a Ma. Now, Maggie, pay attention. The new foundation will start out funded by the hammer price of everything sold tonight and the profits on a half-million catalogs. That's a lot of money. I started to make my will today and I left most of Luke's money to the foundation as well."

And more than enough to Maggie, Tessa thought, so that she and her children would never be dependent on any man, no matter how much she loved him; but she'd find that out later, when she couldn't protest. And her Tiffany cultured pearls and earrings, which Maggie would actually wear; as well as the glorious three-strand necklace of perfectly matched natural pearls, which she'd probably only wear when she'd grown into them; and the heart-shaped diamond and any amount of odds and ends, including the farmhouse outside of Èze-Village she'd never been able to bring herself to sell. What's more, Maggie would even rediscover a large Irish family, all the great aunts and uncles and cousins Agnes Horvath had fled from, for each of them had been tracked down and left bequests. There was time enough for her to know all about that. Later. Much, much later.

"Holy Mother!"

"Exactly. There will be, eventually, a great deal more . . . several billion dollars for the foundation to work with, with additional funds coming in every year. This foundation needs someone I trust to run it. I don't want to have to count on strangers. I'd like you to consider becoming the head of the foundation."

"Billions! My God, Tessa, I don't know *anything* about running a billion-dollar foundation!"

"Of course you don't. But you're a quick study, you're smart, you're enormously well organized, Maggie mine, and accustomed to working with all sorts of people, and getting them to work with each other. That's the uniquely important thing. For the rest, you'd be able to hire professionals to teach you how a foundation works and pay consulting fees to the best oncologists in the world to guide you in the right directions.

It boils down to the basic question of whether you'd rather be doing that or something else."

"But what about the baby, Ma, your grandchild-to-be?"

"That's the chief thing on my mind. Were you planning to go back to S and S after the baby was born?"

"No, I don't want a full-time job and they expect time-and-a-half minimum from their wage slaves. I want to stay home for two or three years and find something I can do part-time. Barney's doing amazingly well—there're ten bikers born every minute—we can easily afford a housekeeper and I can take care of the baby and do other work besides."

"You could run the foundation from home," Tessa said quietly.

"How could I possibly? A foundation that size?"

"It's not like running a billion-dollar business. Of course someone could turn it into a full-time job, with a large office at a fancy address, a top-heavy board of big-name directors and staff all over the place. That would be a serious temptation to almost anybody I could hire, and who would fire that person? Foundations tend to dig in and spend a lot of money on themselves. I'm wary of the kind of person who'd want to run it just for the prestige it would necessarily bring."

"*No* staff?" Maggie asked with a sniff.

"Of course staff. As much staff as you need. And very good salaries, for you and for them. And an office, to put the staff in, to have a place to meet with the professionals you hire and consult with. But you don't actually have to *go* to an office to learn and think and ask questions and gradually arrive at the point of making decisions, these days, do you? As far as the money is concerned, it would be administered by the same people who administer Luke's estate for me now, so you wouldn't have to worry about that. And it's not as if you'd have to snap right into it. That money wouldn't go anywhere until you felt sure of what you were doing. You'd take little steps and then bigger steps, you probably wouldn't be ready to take giant steps until the baby was in kindergarten—"

"Would I be pregnant again by then?"

"How would I know?" Tessa asked, astonished.

"You know I'm going to run the foundation, I thought you might know that too."

"Oh, Maggie! *Really? Truly?* You'll really do it? You can't have any idea how marvelously happy that makes me. Oh, darling!"

"How could I resist? The more you talked about it, the more I realized I'd resent having anybody else do it. It's your foundation, Ma, the Tessa Kent Foundation, and who else has a better right to make sure it's run on a shipshape basis than your daughter?"

"That's the other thing . . ."

"Tessa? What other thing! Do you have more plans for me that I don't know about?"

"Not plans exactly . . . a question. Now, when I go back to my lawyer to finish drawing my will, do you want me to say that the foundation is going to be run by my daughter—or my sister?"

"Oh, hell, hell, *hell.* That's a big one and I never thought of it. Hell!" Maggie sat absolutely still for minutes, chewing her lip. Finally, she started to speak.

"You can't set up such a huge foundation without making news. It's literally impossible to keep the details out of the press. If you say your 'daughter,' it becomes a major news story and it will never die. Even when the regular press is finished with it, the tabloids will be bringing it up for years . . . remember, they're still convinced that Elvis lives. If you say your 'sister,' that's just a truth that's been around for a long time . . . every girl who went to school with me knows it, all your Hollywood friends, anyone who goes back to when I was born. It's not news, it's normal."

"I want it to be your decision entirely," Tessa said. "You're the one who'll have to live with it."

"Oh, God, I don't know what to say," Maggie cried. "I want people to know I'm your daughter! But I desperately *don't* want to spend the rest of my life having to explain—"

"—why I didn't say so sooner."

"Yes."

"Do you want time to think about it? I'll change my lawyer's appointment. You can talk to Barney, mull it over . . ."

"Or talk to Polly . . ."

"Polly knows!" Tessa exclaimed.

"Oh, she knew first. She's deep, is Polly."

"Polly, Barney, Sam, you, and I . . . we all know," Tessa said reflectively, "and nobody's said anything to anyone." And Mimi, she thought, Mimi could really keep a secret.

"You told Sam?"

"Of course. I couldn't lie to him, too."

"Well, outside of the five of us, when you get right down to it, there's nobody else I care about so much that I feel a burning need to tell them. Since *we* all know, that's enough for me. Tell the lawyer to write 'sister'—oh, my God, Doctor Roberto!" Maggie clapped her hand over her mouth.

"He was convinced that I was too young to be your mother," Tessa said with a wicked laugh. "If he ever reads about it, he'll think I pretended to be your mother to get his full attention. He thought that anyway."

"As if you needed to try. That tango . . . was that all it was?"

"Maggie! You know how I feel about Sam."

"But it was in Brazil . . . people make exceptions in Brazil."

"I don't know where I ever got a daughter with a mind like yours."

"Don't forget my father, whatever his name was."

"I don't remember," Tessa said with dignity.

"Neither do I."

42

The first week in June 1994, not long before Maggie's twenty-fourth birthday, her baby was born, a daughter she and Barney named Teresa Marguerite. They called her Daisy from the minute she was placed in Maggie's arms.

Now, on a honeyed Sunday in early September, glazed with topaz light that unmistakably trembled on the verge of autumn, Daisy was a little more than three months old. All of her short life had been spent in a restored farmhouse in Fairfield County, Connecticut, surrounded by her court of Maggie, Tessa, and Sam. Only Barney went to the city each day, riding his bike back and forth, and even he took three-day weekends.

After the March auction, Tessa had kept herself busy house-hunting in the countryside for weeks, until she'd discovered this old farmhouse with its forty overgrown but flourishing acres, its wealth of noble trees surrounded by low stone walls. She'd known at once that it was destined to be hers, and then Maggie and Barney's. She bought it overnight and quickly made it totally habitable by giving Mark Hampton carte blanche if he guaranteed to finish in two months.

Barney and Maggie hadn't found a larger apartment yet, and Tessa wanted to give them the house so that they could move into it as soon as the baby was born.

It was a home place; it had been a home place for more than two hundred years, and its last owner had been careful to restore the plumbing and add a new kitchen without disturbing its old-fashioned charm, a charm of nooks and corners and dormers and wide porches and cool, low-ceilinged rooms with wide floorboards and huge fireplaces. It was both a rambling and an embracing house, easily large enough for a big family, an unplanned masterpiece of sheltering calm, casually done in an informal style that offered deep comfort and gaiety, and an abiding sense of repose.

It was, Tessa knew, more than a bit of a grand gesture, to give a young couple a newly done-up country house, but she had made a pact with herself to do absolutely everything she wanted most to do, and not ask permission of anyone.

Once the auction was over, Tessa felt recklessly free and rambunctious, as if she'd been let out of school after a long, difficult day of detention. She arranged for the bills for the future upkeep of the house to be paid by her estate, and made no apology for the sheer amount of pleasure it gave her to be able to think of her family spending summers and weekends and long Christmas and Easter vacations here for decades—even generations—to come. After all, who could question the right of a grandmother to celebrate the birth of her first grandchild?

Every morning and afternoon, for three-quarters of an hour, at what had been identified as Prime Daisy Time, after her need for sleep had been satisfied and before she grew hungry again, Tessa and Daisy were left alone together, communing with each other on a wide porch swing heaped with pillows. Daisy alternated between lying on a baby seat that supported her back and held up her head so she could recline at ease and look out regally at the world, and a place in the curve of

Tessa's arm, where she snuggled, nuzzled, chuckled, slavered, and cuddled contentedly, until she felt the need to exercise her limbs and grab anything of interest— Tessa's hair, Tessa's pearls, Tessa's fingers, Tessa's eyelashes, Tessa's clothes, and, lately, Tessa's green diamond ring, which she had taken to sucking avidly.

"Don't you wish it weren't September, Daisy?" Tessa inquired in the low, intimate voice she always used with the baby. "Don't you have the feeling that the summer has come and gone in a flash, that swift, splendid July, that basking, brilliant August—over already? I can hardly believe it. I wish I could tell what's going on in your mind, you preserve a fascinating mystery by not speaking, Daisy; it's the old Garbo ploy, isn't it? I realize you're not old enough yet to measure time in any conventional way. Perhaps a month is but an hour to you, perhaps a lifetime, but I'm convinced that you know more than anybody gives you credit for. If you keep this up the boys are going to say that Daisy Webster's wise beyond her years, are you prepared for that?"

Daisy, in her chariot, held out her arms to Tessa with a little cry. Carefully Tessa undid her tiny seat belt, lifted her up, and tucked her into the cradle of her arm. The baby immediately snatched Tessa's finger and put the ring in her mouth.

"I do believe you must be teething, Daisy," Tessa told her in admiration. "So young to start, or are you right on schedule? And just why do you look at me like that? Why is there an ever-so-faint indication of indignation in your gaze? No one has questioned your immense dignity . . . no one would dare. I don't know anything about infant development, my blue-eyed girl, but I wish I understood why you have so many questions in your unblinking eyes. Is it because there's so much to learn, or could it be that I interest you? If you're about to have a tooth, shouldn't your hair be longer? Not that I'm complaining, but the women of this family rather pride themselves on their fine heads of hair. Aha, so that's what you wanted to hear, so that's what inspires your smile? A compliment in advance of performance—I can't say I'm surprised."

She'd see Daisy sit up, Tessa thought, as she returned the baby's smile and let her play tug-of-war with her finger. She was a strong child. At the rate at which Daisy was growing, she'd certainly be sitting up on her own sometime in the next few months.

She'd see Daisy crawl. But would she see her struggle to her feet holding onto a piece of furniture? Or take her first step? Or totter from one piece of furniture to another? Tessa willfully blinded herself to all but one conviction: *It was not impossible.*

She'd recently graduated, if you could use such a word, Tessa mused, from the simple pain patch to M.S. Contin, a form of time-release morphine sulfate that lasted from eight to twelve hours. Between the two she kept herself pain-free and she'd adapted her schedule so that she felt most alert between Prime Daisy Time and that precise moment in the afternoon when the infant started to fret and it was time to let Maggie whisk her away.

Baby time suited her as well as Daisy, Tessa reflected. Naps had become a frequent refuge for her, even if they didn't have the effect they had on the tiny girl, for whom a nap meant a total transformation. Daisy had two distinct personalities, divided by sleep: divine and horrible. She was privileged to enjoy only the divine.

If only she were one-tenth as hungry as this baby! Maggie was breast-feeding Daisy six times a day, and her appetite was a never-ending astonishment. Sometimes Tessa stretched out in an old wicker chair and watched companionably as Maggie nursed Daisy on the porch, but at other times, when it was more convenient for Maggie to nurse her in the big, cozy kitchen, she drifted away, unobtrusively.

Kitchen smells, even those that had once been most delicious, had grown intolerable. She kept a supply of vanilla ice cream loaded with butterfat in the freezer, and if she allowed small spoonfuls to melt on her tongue, one after another, until she could hold no more, it was the easiest way to absorb nourishment. Carlie, the cook who did for them all, along with a local woman who came in to clean four days a week, had a way of making a chicken sandwich that was almost as easy to eat as ice cream, concocted of poached chicken breasts sliced thin, on triangles of delicate white bread without crusts, thickly layered with mayonnaise. She'd also developed a flawless vichyssoise, rich with heavy cream. White food, almost odorless food, that Tessa made herself eat in spite of a powerful disinclination.

Although she refused to climb on a scale, or look at herself naked in a mirror, Tessa knew by the way her clothes fit that she'd lost an enormous amount of weight. Months ago she'd taken to wearing her full linen shirts outside of trousers, tightly belted so that they wouldn't fall off her hips. Her clothes floated around her, hiding her outline. Every day she made sure to get enough sun to maintain a glowing tan. She used the brightest red lipstick she could find, and she let her dark hair float in its deep, shining waves without restraint.

A girl of summer, she mocked herself, as she looked quickly in the mirror and then looked away. She had the same lack of interest in the still-undiminished beauty of her face as she had in the pile of scripts that lay, growing daily, on the porch near her swing. She hadn't told Fiona the truth, hadn't told Roddy, hadn't told Aaron, hadn't told Mimi, with whom she'd never lost touch. They all thought it was her refusal to be separated from Sam, by a year of location filming, that had made her decide not to play Cassie. Better that than their shock, their solicitude, their pity, and their inevitable phone calls, Tessa thought, jealously hoarding her energy for the people she loved the most.

As July and August had passed, a general agreement had been reached, almost without discussion, that they wouldn't move back to New York this year. Sam worked on his new book for hours every day. Maggie spent some of her time, while Daisy napped, communicating by fax with Dune Maddox, whom she had easily lured away from S & S to work as her primary assistant on the start-up of the foundation. Only Barney commuted to New York to attend to business.

What bliss it was, Tessa realized, to look at the old trees that surrounded the house, already showering a lazy leaf from minute to minute, and know that she didn't have to leave this place just because the wheel of the year was about to turn. They'd settle into the seasons, Tessa thought dreamily as she delicately smoothed the wisps of dark hair on Daisy's head. Soon they'd be in the middle of the slowly exploding fireworks of a New England autumn . . . then the snug, snowy, easeful, firelit winter . . . the delights of spring lay ahead . . . too far ahead to bother to anticipate . . . today was enough; each second was enough.

Sam, who had grown up in the country, had already ordered a vast supply of firewood and a snowblower for the driveway. Maggie had bought extra blankets and a wardrobe of larger, warm baby clothes, even a tiny snowsuit. Carlie, who had so recently finished with their Labor Day celebration, was already looking forward to Thanksgiving. Barney had become an instant captive to the big vegetable garden he'd created on a whim from well-grown seedlings a few months earlier. Now he'd sent for a dozen seed catalogs and commandeered Sam's services for the harvest, and he checked his pumpkin patch for signs of growth every morning.

Daisy's head moved restlessly and Tessa looked down to see the baby's vivid blue eyes with their long dark lashes fixed on her with extraordinary concentration.

"If you were a man, Daisy, I'd say you must be in love with me, but that seems unlikely, given your gender and your tender age." Daisy reached for her finger and began to gnaw vigorously again on the diamond.

"But when you're older, and you ask your mother about her mother—and you will—Maggie can show you the auction catalog instead of some faded photo album . . . it's all in there, Daisy, at least the part I wanted the public to know. Your mother can tell you the rest, the part I wanted her to know. Then there are the things a woman never tells, but if you're so smart, you'll figure that out for yourself. Will my life be something you can't imagine leading, Daisy? There are so many moments now when it seems like that to me. Strange . . . it didn't truly begin, you know, until one afternoon in 1971, when I danced a polka with Roddy and everything changed in an instant. It was twenty-three years ago . . . that wasn't so terribly far away, was it, Daisy? And yet . . . and yet . . . it was forever . . . forever . . ."

Daisy looked up suddenly, turning her head alertly, and Tessa wiped a little drool from her chin. "What a sense of timing you have," Tessa said admiringly, as she watched the small figures of Maggie, Sam, and Barney hurry across the bright lawn, each of them carrying a basket of newly picked vegetables.

"Yes, Daisy, yes, they're all coming, just as fast as they can."

ABOUT THE AUTHOR

Since the publication of her first novel, *Scruples*,
JUDITH KRANTZ has been one of the world's best-
selling novelists. Born and raised in New York
City and a graduate of Wellesley College, she and
her husband, Steve Krantz, live in Bel Air and
Newport Beach, California. They have two sons
and two grandchildren.

Judith Krantz

SCRUPLES
___28465-7 $7.50/$9.99 in Canada

I'LL TAKE MANHATTAN
___26407-9 $7.50/$9.99

MISTRAL'S DAUGHTER
___25917-2 $7.50/$9.99

PRINCESS DAISY
___25609-2 $7.50/$9.99

TILL WE MEET AGAIN
___28014-7 $7.50/$9.99

DAZZLE
___29376-1 $7.50/$9.99

SCRUPLES TWO
___56111-1 $7.50/$9.99

LOVERS
___56135-9 $7.50/$9.99

Ask for these books at your local bookstore or use this page to order.

Please send me the books I have checked above. I am enclosing $_____ (add $2.50 to cover postage and handling). Send check or money order, no cash or C.O.D.'s, please.

Name _____

Address _____

City/State/Zip _____

Send order to: Bantam Books, Dept. FB 4, 2451 S. Wolf Rd., Des Plaines, IL 60018
Allow four to six weeks for delivery.
Prices and availability subject to change without notice.   FB 4 3/99